REDEMPTION 2
ALLISON'S REVENGE
THE MIKE PARSONS TRILOGY

MALCOLM
TANNER

Publishing Coordinator – Sharon Kizziah-Holmes
Cover Design – Jaycee DeLorenzo

Paperback-Press
an imprint of A & S Publishing
A & S Holmes, Inc.

ISBN -13: 978-1-951772-12-3

ACKNOWLEDGMENTS

Thanks to Gail Mewes for help in the production of this work.

Thanks to Linda Knight, my editor. Linda worked tirelessly to make sure that I wrote exactly what I was trying to say. Her hours of dedication and purpose are greatly appreciated

Thanks to all the events in my life that changed both for good and bad that helped me and inspired me to write. All events in the book are purely fictional.

Thanks to Sharon Kizziah-Holmes, at Paperback Press, for the great interior design and formatting of this edition.

Thanks to Jaycee DeLorenzo, at Sweet-n-Spicy Design, for the beautifully done cover for this edition.

When I look back and wonder about all the times that I did not write, it makes me sad. I have felt a book or two, many times in my life and have failed to begin. I thank my wife Sandy for giving me the courage to go forward and just do it. She referred to our favorite slogan as a couple; **"If not now, then when?"**

CHAPTER 1

I was running fast. I could not let them catch me as it would be most assuredly fatal. This craziness was about to finally consume me and take my life. I had endured kidnapping, brutal beatings, drugging and addiction. I had endured my own wickedness that could have killed me at any time. I had endured my ex-wife's suicide and the pain that followed. Now, I was facing the one thing I had feared every day.

Their pace was quickening and I was losing ground to them. I could almost hear their footsteps and heavy breathing. My lungs were about to explode. In a strange city where I didn't know anyone or any place to go, I was going to meet my end. I prayed to God that HE had to know I was trying and I was getting better. I was just starting to find me, the guy I was really wanting to be and I was starting to live my life again. *Please do not let me die this way, I pleaded with Him. I really want to live, I want to know what life is about, to care and to love like I have learned to do again. Please, oh please, not like this.*

For the second time in my life, I began to see flashes of my life flying by in my mind. I saw Sheila and her bloated face in the casket. I saw Jerry with his head exploding on my boat on the lake. I saw Katy and me, kidnapped and suffering in the storm shelter. I saw Andy Marx, a friend and good cop, fighting for his life in a pool of blood, and of course, I saw HER.

Yes, HER again! That one with the silvery, blue steel eyes that hold you. I would never win this game. It was hers to win and she just wasn't going to lose. Driven by her anger over many, many years, SHE had the upper hand once again. Of all the times I thought of how she would have her revenge, this way never came to my mind. Yes, I thought it would be silent, in my sleep or maybe cyanide in my drink. But not like this. Then I made a grave mistake. I was tired and spent and I could not run any longer. I just stopped and turned around, prepared to fight.

Then I saw them, those eyes. Those angry eyes that held you...

CHAPTER 2

I am home, sipping my scotch and water and looking out from my deck in suburbia, USA. The sun is just about down. I could see its orange blaze beginning to light up the early evening sky reflecting an image that could easily be a painting. I have been through a lot in the last year. My days are getting to be more normal than before. I still wonder about Allison Branch. Those eyes that hold you and haunt you. Her courtroom eyes of anger and hate were terrifying. I am looking ahead though, to better days and tomorrow will be just another work day. She is a demon that I have to put behind me.

It was good to go to the lake and try to make it a safe haven again, as it always used to be. It is a sanctuary and I am going to take it back. It had always been the place that could calm me. It cleansed my soul. That is, until all hell broke loose there. There is so much to do and so many people I need to attend to, including myself in the aftermath of all the

3

destruction. I, Mike Parsons, am going to make that happen. I am going to find the redemption I seek in this life. I will get better!

My thoughts are interrupted by my cell ringing. I see that Andy Marx is on the phone.

"Hello, Marx, great to hear from you. What's up?"

"Hey Mike. Just checking in on you and seeing if you might have changed your mind. I've got a rough cold case here and wonder if you would be interested in helping me solve this?"

"I don't know, Andy. I am still trying to reconcile what happened and what everything was all about."

"Well if you do change your mind you know my number."

"I'll give it some thought. By the way, how are you anyway?" I said trying to change the subject.

"I'm pretty good," Marx said. "I am healthier now and have started to work out again. I've got a new partner too. Good cop. His name is Morris Reynolds, but I call him Mo. He's not a rookie. He's been around a while."

"Great, well your world is getting back to normal too, I see."

"Pretty much it is. I still can't find a woman. I think I'm being too picky," he said laughing.

"Good-looking guy like you should have no trouble. Me, I just stink at relationships. I'm not looking for one."

"You make me laugh, Parsons. Listen, I've got to run, but if you need some excitement in your boring life, professor, then give me a call. I could use your thoughts on this case."

"Okay, Andy, I'll think about it. Have a good evening."

I hung up and the thought crossed my mind. *Andy Marx and I, heroes and solving the case together...no, that couldn't happen could it? Anyway, I would probably get knocked out a couple of times again and those concussions were rough. I don't need any more of that again. But, curiosity about the case started to nag at me. Who were the victims and why? Are there any suspects in the case? Is it local? I needed to stop this. I'm not cut out for that kind of job. I have a good, safe job and a place on the lake. My safe haven is here. I don't need that much excitement. Or do I?...*

I got up and switched off the lights and set the alarm. I always set the alarm now. Tonight, I hope to sleep peacefully without the recurring nightmares that come every so often. There are ghosts and demons from my past life in these dreams. My nights are sometimes interrupted with waking from a horrible dream about the one demon that haunts me to this day. The one with the eyes that hold you...

Sleep didn't come and I had to get up for a few minutes. I went to the living room with a bottled water I grabbed from the fridge. I sat down in my recliner and thought back to the days of captivity. I began to think of dear Katy, and what she was going through. Would she always be haunted by the nightmare of that kidnapping and the fact that I could not return her love? I thought of James and how he would always remember pulling the trigger and would live with this for the rest of his days. Once again, he may feel that way, mostly because of me. What about Andy Marx? Does he really want me to help? I pondered it for another few minutes and talked myself out of getting involved one more time. Though these thoughts still haunted me, I gave in finally to sleep and remained in my recliner until dawn.

I woke up and got ready to head home to my condo. When I got home I unpacked and turned on the coffee, trudged to the bathroom to shave, shower and get ready for the day. I just had to start sleeping better. For months my sleep patterns had been erratic. After I shaved and showered, I stood in front of the mirror, inspecting the drawn lines on my face. My eyes had circles below them. I could not take my gaze from the face I saw, worn with worry for my condition and that of others. I never did care that much for others before, but my way of thinking had been changing over time. *Was I getting better? Would redemption of my soul be a possibility?* I wanted that to be true, but there is still that part of me that thinks it is not what I deserve. That I am not worthy of redemption. I think that I may be improving, but there will still be a price to pay and not everyone is willing to pay that price. Was I?

CHAPTER 3

Another dawn, another cup of coffee and the prospects of my life starting to slow down is appealing to me. Thoughts of being able to see myself better through a lot less clutter were in my head. I sit on my deck at the condo, still thinking of all the characters in that episode in my life. I felt it necessary to be awake at sun up and sun down. I did this many mornings and evenings. They were the most enchanting times each day where my thoughts were separated and compartmentalized. I didn't necessarily drown in those thoughts but I swam in that pool more than occasionally. Those times of the day were the best for those thoughts.

I still thought of Marx's offer and had those grandiose thoughts of heroic deeds by the law professor and his buddy Andy Marx. I really did try to shrug off these thoughts. I wanted to make myself believe that I was so much better off with this simple life of mine. Yet, there was something intriguing to believing you could actually do something completely different and maybe make a positive difference in other people's lives. Playing this crazy ping pong match in my mind, I decided to just derail this thought process and get ready to inspire the young and restless minds that I taught.

I was ready in about a half hour and left my apartment and got in my car. On the way I heard the piano version of "It Had to be You" on the easy listening channel. It brought back the memories of what I thought almost happened with Allison Branch. It was now embarrassing. It was a black spot in my past dingy life. She was something I just had to forget...

_____▲_____

Allison Branch could make friends. Many people found her to be completely engaging and mysterious, just like the many prison guards and other workers in the prison. They often labeled her as one of the nicest people in the place. She was planning an event. She had made these plans with her new best friend, Henry Hannah. Henry was working as a guard and transported prisoners to medical facilities for their medical appointments. Allison worked Henry very well. She would tease him and rub his back for him. He knew where to hide from view where he even stole a kiss or two. Henry was in love you could say. Allison, on the other hand, was a charmer who could use him and dispose of him when she got out of prison. She was a user, a black widow type. She wasn't in love, but she could make any man think she was. Henry would help her, of course. He had grand ideas of where they could go. He had his share of drug money stashed away from his dealings with other inmates. Escaping together to some foreign land was only something of which he could dream. A woman like Allison Branch was also just a dream for most men like Henry. But, through his imagined great fortune, his dream was becoming a reality.

Henry was walking to her cell area on his way to supervise the walk to the exercise yard today. Allison caught his eye and froze him as she had with so many others. She motioned for him to come closer. Henry moved closer and she whispered, just audible enough to be heard.

"Henry, I think I have an idea," she whispered in a soft, cooing voice. "When I'm out exercising in the yard, come by and we can talk. You're going to get me out of here."

"Then we can make the mad dash out of the country and live happily ever after," he replied.

"You got it, lover boy."

Ah, that smile, those eyes, the ones that hold you. Henry was filled with a sense of something he had never before experienced. Sure, he had girlfriends in the past, but this one was different. She was definitely the prettiest of any of them. She was also quite crooked, just like him. His relationships always ended badly because he just didn't understand that women did not want to be abused like his own father abused his mother. Actually, Henry thought it to be normal behavior in which all men took part. But, this woman did something to him. That something made him softer on the inside and for Henry that was not normal. Henry's dad always told him, 'Don't be a damn sissy. When you let your guard down they all take advantage of you.' Henry usually went by that rule. That is, until he met Allison Branch.

Henry walked around the exercise yard watching and supervising. He did his job and did it well. But the undoing of Henry Hannah would be letting his guard down. He walked closer to Allison where he could talk to her without anyone being within earshot.

"Henry, I've got a plan to get me out of prison. When I was a cop, they use to have drivers for the medical trips for prisoners. On Wednesday, I know that you are driving, right? Well I'm going to fake an illness for a few days and get them to take me to the hospital. I can convince them, don't worry about that."

Henry looked over her head towards other prisoners as he was digesting what she was saying. His ears were intent on her, but his eyes were somewhere else. He could not show that they were having this conversation.

"OK, but how do we ditch the vehicle and the other guard? You know they don't send me on that detail alone, and you will be cuffed," he said, not quite understanding the plan yet.

He turned and walked a distance away not wanting to be on camera while having this long conversation with a prisoner. That would raise suspicion. He returned a minute later.

"You leave that to me. I have some friends that will help us but you need to get them the message. I will give you the number. You tell the woman who answers, that you and I are planning my break out and to meet us at the medical center, give her the address. She'll have a couple guys there with guns and I will pretend to choke, they will be behind you. You pull over in the parking lot, they will knock your partner out and you just act it out and go along with it. I will go with them, and then you go back to the prison and act like a victim. I'll send a car for you later at some location away from your house. Then we get help from my friends leaving the country." She never turned to face him as she spoke.

Henry pondered this for a minute as he walked away and checked other prisoners. He walked near her again. "Okay, next week," he said as he slowly turned his back to her. "Shoot for next Wednesday. The ride can meet me wherever they decide is best. It's needs to be far enough away from my house to not cause a problem."

Allison turned to him and cocked her head to the side. She smiled that smile and her steel-blue eyes grabbed Henry. He had no idea what was in store for him. He had no earthly idea. All he knew for sure was that she was the most beautiful prisoner in the yard.

___▲___

Andy Marx and Morris "Mo" Reynolds were at the precinct. They were trying hard to uncover the clues on the most recent kidnapping case. Mo was imposing with his six- foot -four- inch frame and solid two-hundred-forty pounds. He had a short haircut and was beginning to gray a bit at the temples. He was a bad dresser and Marx had tried to school him in the art of dressing for success. Unfortunately, Mo was really not interested. He had divorced several years back and never really got into the marriage market again. He loved football, hockey and hunting. Mo was a great shot and had a few mounts in his home that suggested a wide range of prey that he hunted. Since he had taken the detective upgrade, he had little time for hunting. Mo was from Saginaw, Michigan and was a huge Wolverine fan. Marx was from Wisconsin, so he rooted for the Badgers. Every year they made a case of beer wager on the winner. Lately, Marx had the upper hand.

They became close friends when Mo was transferred from Michigan to Milwaukee. Mo's Aunt lived in Milwaukee. She had no one else so Mo thought he needed to be close by to look in on her. She resided in the senior living complex downtown. He made trips at least twice a week and usually brought her something special to eat as he was a pretty good cook. Mo knew the story of Allison Branch and all the mayhem that had taken place at Mike Parson's lake place.

"You know, Marx, this kidnapping that went so cold is not leaving us any clues. The guy was just driving and his car is empty. No note, no prints but his own, and no clues whatsoever. Limited family life and the family he did have, disowned him," Mo said as he thumbed through the report.

"Yeah, I just know there is something that we are missing," Marx said, as he was tapping his pen on his desk. "There has to be just one tiny clue that we are missing."

"Hey let's drive to the scene and take more photos. Different angles and maybe a different perspective sometimes make the light go on," Mo suggested.

Marx was still focused on something. He was staring out the window and still tapping his pen. He had pondered the idea about having Mike Parsons help with the case. He had become friends with Parsons and thought the ordeal Parsons had been through had given him a little background on the 'why' part of these types of cases. That could certainly lead to solving kidnappings. He knew the answer he would get if he asked, but he was going to ask just one more time. What else did they have? Marx picked up the phone and dialed.

My phone rang that afternoon as I was leaving school. I saw it was Marx and laughed to myself, recalling our earlier conversation on whether I would do what Marx was going to ask. I still had not decided yes or no, but I had to admit that I could not just put the idea to bed.

"Hello, Andy, and I know what you're going to ask," I said standing in the parking lot near my car. "So, go ahead and ask."

"Okay, do you want to help on the case?" he asked so bluntly that it surprised me.

"Not even going to beat around the bush?"

"Look, I know it's sort of a long shot. This case has spun me around in circles and we are at a dead end. Why don't you just try for a few weeks? I won't put you in harm's way," Marx said.

"I pondered for a while last night, Marx. I went back and forth and certainly wouldn't want to get physically punished like that again. I had enough hospital visits," I said still cringing at the thought. "But I think I will say yes as it's starting to feel like a challenge I can't turn down."

"Great! Come by my place at 6:00."

I hung up and got ready to go home. I didn't know what I was going to say about it all and once again, I began to feel that I was biting off more than I could chew. But for me, this was a change, a challenge. I loved challenges. I had to admit how unqualified I felt for this job, or consultant's position, or whatever it was. I truly felt that my experience may help though. I was ready to shave and shower, and once again, I had no idea what would be in store for me for the next year...no idea.

CHAPTER 4

Andy Marx lived in an upscale complex in Milwaukee. His apartment complex was one of the newer ones in the area. Go figure. But, like I said before, I thought him to be quite arrogant. I got to like Andy over time and was excited that we would be able to work on something together. I think I always envisioned doing that in my mind, but my practical side put it away quickly. I told myself that life was just kind of chugging along and that this would give me a boost that I desperately needed.

Driving towards Marx's apartment, I reflected back to the time that I was held captive with Katy. How close had we come to dying in those days? This would bring back those memories and I questioned myself once more on whether I wanted those memories to keep flooding back. On the other hand, if it helped someone find a loved one or kept someone alive as it had with Katy O'Neal and I, then it would be worth it.

I was about five minutes late. I walked up the long

sidewalk leading to the steps in front of Marx's door. I got to the door and rang the bell. Marx answered the door and let me in. We walked down the long hall to the living area. Wow! The big screen was huge with a nice sound system to boot. Furnishings were very modern and well kept. Marx kept his house spotless, very well-manicured and not a strand of hair or stick of furniture out of place.

"Hey Mike, this is my partner, Mo Reynolds. Mo, this is Mike Parsons."

"Thanks for coming," Marx said as he passed around a few paper plates for the two pizzas laid out on the coffee table. "First to let you know a bit about Mo here. He has been in the department with us for quite some time and is newly promoted, good man and great cop. We've been working with each other for a while now and are getting along great. Mo is from Michigan, but I try not to hold it against him. But when he transferred here, he made his mark right away."

"Congratulations on your promotion, "I said. "I hope Wisconsin is suiting you," I said and then took a large bite of pizza and washed it down with a swig of cold beer.

"Thanks," the big man said. "I have worked with a lot of good cops that made me look good."

Marx broke in getting right to the point. I hardly got my first piece of pizza down and a couple of swallows of beer before he started to explain the case.

"Here is what we have, Mike. We have a cold one, seems to have vanished in thin air. Not many clues and concrete evidence to go on. The man's name is Oscar Stephenson. He is the CEO of a large corporation here in the Milwaukee area. The company handles large financial accounts and makes international investments. He came up missing some three years back. The date was February 1, on a Monday, when he didn't show up for work. He's worth a lot of cash and the first thought was, of course, a ransom demand. When that never happened, we had to go with the idea it was either personal or having to do with shady activity outside of the business. There have been several tips on the tip line, but most are just people trying to insert themselves into the case. The calls we get are sometimes decent leads but all have led to dead ends. Most of those calls were "sightings" but none of them checked out and they were too sketchy to have any good follow-up."

"I'm sure you checked family and friends," I said looking at both of them. "I know, in my case, it was family and friends that got me involved."

"Yeah, we looked, but could only find one relative," Mo said looking intently at his notes as he spoke. "We found he had a sister, Andrea Stephenson Raines, who lived in the area. She resided about 10 miles from his house. We questioned her and searched her house but got nothing from it. She said she was just as stumped as we were and really didn't know many of his acquaintances. Their parents died over the past decade and they were all they had left of family. Andrea was a nice-looking lady, about 50 years old, divorced five years ago, and had not seen her ex for several years."

"We checked him out too," Marx said and then swallowed the last of his bottle of beer. "His name is Chris Raines. He was in California. Raines had no contact with the family for the past five years, which matched her story. We had nothing, but we wanted to keep an eye on him and his whereabouts. He said he had read of the case but didn't know any of the details except for what was in the news."

"What about the empty car?" I began. "Are there

any prints? Are there any footprints around where the car was abandoned?" I was sure they had checked that out but I had to ask that.

"No, none," Marx said. "The only thing we are thinking here is someone drove that car to that destination, gloves on and covers over their shoes. It is possible not to leave prints that way. There just wasn't anything there that suggested that he walked away from that car. No footprints, just his own prints in the car. It is baffling, but I think we know that the kidnapping took place somewhere else, not where we found the car."

"We've also checked out all the contractors and cleaning services who made any trips to his house," Mo said as he frowned and looked at me raising his hands to the sky. "Nothing. We tried to establish a time line for his disappearance and we come up with the fact that his sister Andrea, was the last person to see him. That makes her a person of interest, of course. She last saw him at 6:00 pm on Monday. She said he had stopped by her house to check on her."

Marx broke in, "She said she got a call from his office at noon on Tuesday and his secretary was wondering if she had seen him. Andrea told her not since the evening before around 6:00. That was a matching story, too."

"Disappearing into thin air happens more often than you think," Mo added. "There are many cases each year, where no witnesses, no clues, nothing. Some of the people disappear and don't want to be found, some are found, most are found dead."

"I know I am the rookie here," I said looking back and forth between the two detectives, "but I am having the feeling that the guy may still be alive and is one of the few that may be alive and doesn't want to be found. Something stinks here and I think the guy may have had a reason to disappear. I suspect something, either he staged it along with Andrea, or he's mixed up with some bad people, similar to my own case. I'm not saying I'm absolutely sure, but it is just a feeling. Maybe something at work, but you probably checked with all of his colleagues I am guessing."

"Guessed right on that one, Parsons," Andy said. "No one at his work had any idea of any dealings with employees or any outsiders that had gone bad. Everyone we talked to said they really didn't see any signs of any friction with anyone in the company."

"Well, it's interesting to say the least and very puzzling. Not much to go on, but I am sticking with my feeling that Mr. Stephenson doesn't want to be found and his sister is in on that plan," I said trying to be hopeful that I just might be right.

Marx and Mo put their papers back in folders and we began to notice time was slipping away. I was just getting up and putting on my jacket and about to shake hands with Mo and Andy when Andy's cell rang. He raised his eyebrows and said, "Hey, I think we got a tip. Let's go for a ride."

CHAPTER 5

H enry Hannah was making plans. He had lived all forty-three years of his life in a miserable fashion. Now, he was about to turn everything around. The ghosts that were haunting his past would become extinct. He had enough visions of the old man verbally and physically abusing him. He was going to put those to rest. Every weekend he was in high school, Henry tried to be like the rest of his small circle of friends and be out and about on Friday nights. That came to an end, when he found his mother crying at the kitchen table every time he came home. The older he got, he realized that his old man was nothing more than an alcoholic bully and he despised him more and more. He would one day find a cure for all of this and get his mother out of that situation.

He had gone over his own plan to rid his mother of this clown many times in his head. The old man would never be found. Ten years later, terminating his father had never taken place. His mother died of cancer on his 28th birthday, and since that day, Henry could think of nothing else but plans to end the life of his father, Jedd Hannah. He was sure he wanted to do it, but something always stopped him, some weakness in his personality.

Each time Henry thought he had the perfect plan, he would balk. He still feared his father, even up to this very day. The plan was never put into action. Henry actually thought himself to be helpless because in each scenario, he always feared that some way his father would spoil the plan and kill him. Henry was gutless and void of the courage it would take to dispose of the old man. The giant shadow cast over him by his father would not allow him to overcome his fear. Fear, fear...Henry's life was dominated by it, but not this time. Henry had a new girlfriend. She would be the one to show him the light. She would give him the confidence he needed. He would not be scared this time. He wanted Allison Branch and no one, not even his bullying old man, would keep him from having her. He had two main goals in his immediate life. One was to run away with this woman with the eyes that lured him and haunted him. The other was to rid his world of the one last shadow hanging over him. The old man had to go down.

Henry went back to packing clothes and making lists, trying to figure out all angles of this escape plan he hatched with the beautiful prisoner. *It all seems so possible that I, Henry Hannah, can pull this thing off. You can't back out now Henry. She just cannot see you as weak. It's time for your life to change and for you to become everything you always thought you could be if it hadn't been for your miserable wretch of a father. It's time and you know that somehow, things were all going to be better. All because of that woman that just entered your life, the one with the mysterious eyes that hold you...*

Henry snapped out of his thoughts and back to reality. He went to get the two pistols out of his closet and placed them neatly in his travel bag. Henry Hannah was going places. To get there, he thought he would need them.

Two days until Wednesday and Henry was looking forward to kissing the job and the world he once knew goodbye. One more day and Henry would be free, as would Allison Branch if everything went as planned. It just had to. Henry picked up the phone...

Allison was staring out of her cell and had hardly touched the food they brought as she said she was too sick to go to the dining room. She had a lot on her mind this Monday. Her escape was two days away and tomorrow, she would need to find some floor cleaner that she could put in with her water. Just a bit to make her sick enough to be taken on Wednesday. She had Henry look it up for her and figured the right amount that would do the job. Henry was wrapped around her finger and when she had a guy on the hook, Allison could do her best work. Henry was not that attractive, but it was her way out of here and she would do what needed to be done to make that happen. She had done it before, right? She would not be stopped in her effort to gain freedom. The plan would work and she knew she could depend on the one best friend that she had left. He would come through for her.

Henry was also a key player in this escape. She had to keep him close and focused for this to work. Just follow the plan and she could be long gone in a couple of days.

Allison's thoughts drifted...

It's that Parsons and Marx. Those two are the ones responsible for me being here. I'm not staying here long. I'm getting out and then I will get back at every one of those people. They will pay! It was that damn Marx. He should have been dead. No way in hell anyone survives those gun shots. Parsons was just a helpless dope. If it wasn't for his brother and dumb luck, he wouldn't be walking this earth right now. I'll get him, too! James, Katy, Marx and anyone else that stood in my way including that selfish Mike Parsons. He could have had me long ago. He just had no idea how much I could have loved him. It's his fault I am the way I am and his fault I am here in this hole. I got a few friends left, and those friends will get me out. He will pay......HE WILL PAY! Mikey!!

Allison could feel the warm tears begin to flow down her cheeks. These tears always came with the anger that consumed her every day. It was her demon, her one fault that made her dangerous not only to others, but to herself. Her mother knew it, her teachers knew it, her friends knew it. Marx knew it and for sure Mike Parsons knew it. Soon she would be on the hunt...very soon.

Katy O'Brien was closing the bar at O'Shea's. As she put away the last of the bottles and glasses left on the bar and had everything wiped down, she thought of her favorite customer that never came in anymore. Katy had not seen Mike Parsons since the day he walked away from her house. She missed Mike, but she had learned to cope without his presence.

Katy still feared Allison Branch, even though she was still in prison. She kept believing in the back of her mind that Branch would escape. She feared that Branch would stalk her, trail her, find her and eventually kill her. She had dreams of Branch, dreams that made her wake up in a cold sweat. Of course, her therapist had told her time and again that she had nothing to fear. Branch was in a high security prison, and her escape would be impossible. Katy believed it was possible and each night before she went to sleep, she looked out her window to see if she could find a moving shadow. She believed that Branch would escape and she checked for her every night.

Katy wrapped up the register tape and copies of credit card receipts and put them in the back office. She checked her purse for her hand gun and then slipped it into her coat pocket. She wasn't taking any chances. She waved goodbye to Nick, and then headed through the lit parking lot to her car. Katy looked in all directions as she moved to the car and even peered underneath before unlocking the door. She did this every time she headed to her car, whether it was night or day. She got in and turned on the key, holding her breath and fearing an explosion. When there was none, she put the car in gear and headed to her new home. She was not taking chances. Her new-found paranoia was taking up residence in her mind. It took fifteen minutes to get home and by the time she had reached her front door of her apartment, she was breathing heavy and small beads of sweat had formed on her upper lip. She opened her door, walked in and checked every room and closet in the apartment and the locks on every window and door. This was her routine every night she came home from anywhere. She even put a chair against the inside of the bathroom door when she showered and kept her gun near the tub. Sometimes Katy felt that she would really never get any better. Her life would always include the ghost of this woman from her past, the specter that dominated her extremely lonely and frightening nights. When would she be free?

—▲—

Morris "Mo" Reynolds was driving at a decent clip with Andy Marx in the passenger side and me, in my new role as crime solving savant, in the back. MO and Andy were discussing the tip and the meeting place was to be at a sports bar just outside the city limits of Milwaukee called *Triple Play*. We arrived around 8:00 PM and entered the bar seeking out a person with a red ball cap who was to be sitting alone. There seemed to be no one of that description, but there was an empty booth with wings and a half full beer. Just then, the guy in the red ball cap appeared from the restroom, I assumed, and sat at the booth to continue eating the wings and sipping his beer. Andy left Mo and I at the bar and walked over to the booth and sat down. Mo and I ordered a beer. The televisions had the Monday Night Football game on with the Packers and Giants dueling in a close one. Marx sat down in the booth and flashed his badge at the informant as to not cause any alarm.

"Andy Marx, Milwaukee Police," Marx said as he looked at the informant to assess his physical appearance. The man was approximately six feet about 180 pounds and appeared to be in good shape, probably about thirty something years old. He wore a pair of glasses that oddly didn't seem to fit his face. He appeared to be Hispanic or maybe South American. Marx noticed that his demeanor was a bit nervous and, as if on cue, Mo left me at the bar and cruised around the room a bit to survey the crowd, as if he thought someone else was watching this.

"Jake Benson. Look, I'll make this quick, as I don't really want to be seen, but I wanted this meeting to be public. It's about that missing guy, the cold case. I remember seeing it on the news years back but something happened today that made me think there is a chance that this guy might have wanted to disappear." Jake sipped his beer and looked around casually as if he was looking for a particular person.

"Okay, Jake, what do you know?" Marx asked as he studied Benson in more depth.

"My girlfriend, Carrianne Martinez, worked late cleaning the offices of that Stephenson guy. She usually went in there around seven in the evenings to clean the offices. Most of the time he was not there but occasionally he would work late and ask her to skip his office and get it the next night. She never really thought much of it. Neither did I until the guy went missing and I had asked Carrianne if she had seen anything. She told me she could not recall, so I just forgot about it." Benson looked to Marx for some sort of reassurance but got none.

"But you're telling me now that something flipped on a switch for your friend, and she later said something to you about going to the cops?" Marx asked. "We interviewed the cleaning company before and had nothing."

"Well, yeah. A few years later she brought up the fact she remembered about one odd night when she was cleaning and he was working late. She remembered three men and a woman who were buzzed in by security. She remembered them walking past and distinctly remembered they spoke in Portuguese. She was sure of that as she is Brazilian as well and bilingual. She could not really recall what they said as she was not close enough to make it out. But she was positive it was in Portuguese." Benson looked around once more, with a bit of a paranoid expression that Marx caught.

"So, you think these people are bad guys?" Marx asked. "Certainly, there would have been footage on the surveillance cameras that would have got them coming into the building. If you pinpoint the date and let Carrianne know I'd like to talk to her, maybe we can put some things together. Just wish I had known this sooner."

"I know, but it didn't hit her until after the news story came out about how long he had been missing on Channel 7 the other night."

"I get it, but to keep this confidential, I need you and Carrianne to come to the station and get this story down. We will need to check for video surveillance history and get some descriptions of the characters." Marx slid his card across the table and said "Try to be at my office tomorrow around 9:00 am."

With that Marx got up and started to walk out of the bar. Mo and I followed when Mo said it was okay to do so. Outside both Marx and Mo were quiet until we got in the car.

"Guy says he has a girlfriend who may have seen some characters enter the business when she was cleaning that evening. I have his name and address in case they decide not to show. This may or may not be something, but it's much better than what we had to go on."

"Marx and I will work on this tomorrow and get back to you," Mo said as he put the car into gear and headed back to Marx's place. "We can discuss it maybe tomorrow night after we chase it down."

And with that, I was now committed. Now I can do something that really interests me. Hmm, **Mike Parsons, Crime Solver**. I think I might like this.

CHAPTER 6

It was Wednesday morning and Allison Branch was feeling a little more nauseated by the minute. Her escort was to arrive soon to take her to the hospital to diagnose her vomiting spells. Henry Hannah had made sure that she was attended to and got the ride she was looking for. The sweat on her forehead and neck were real and she felt that she may pass out. Contacts were being made thanks to Henry and the boys from Brazil would be sure to take care of business.

Complex de Coreia was one of the toughest drug infested slums in Rio. Drug trafficking began to take root there in the 1980's. As the US drug policies began to force drug traffic from the North to the South, this slum began to become one of the most dangerous in South America. Being connected to these men had its good points but it had its dangerous ones. The men were violent and unforgiving, but would do anything to protect their women traffickers. Allison felt confident that Henry would not blow this and was sure that when contact was made, they would let him know there was no room for mistakes. She began to look into the future and plan.

Recover in Santa Teresa and then I can go back on the hunt, and I WILL go back on the hunt. Henry is one of those disposable people, use them and dispose of them, and then he will need to disappear. Hunting Parsons and his friends down would be so satisfying. It would be the moment that I will look forward to with great lust. My thirst to kill had become greater during the time I spent in prison. The only way to make it right, the only way I live on, is to carry this plan out, just as I had others. I will end up being number one in the class and that stupid Mike Parsons...l will end him for good.

Snapping back to reality, Allison began to sweat more profusely. She needed Henry to hurry up and get here. She needed out of here and today was the day.

Just then she heard the footsteps that seemed to be like music to her ears. Henry Hannah was walking down the hall. As soon as they opened her cell door, it would be the last time they found her in confinement.

"Okay up and at 'em lady," Henry barked as he had them open the cell. He and his partner, Sam Jost, put the leg shackles and cuffs on her. They made the long walk clearing all the security points and made it to the van that would take her to the hospital for medical treatment. The walk had been quiet and no one spoke. Allison was placed in the back, behind the steel divider between her and the guards. Henry got into the driver's seat and cleared the last checkpoint at the gate. His partner, Sam, got in the passenger side. He headed down the street and made his way to the interstate, headed to the hospital. The drive was slow as traffic was heavy this November morning. The air was cold with the temperatures in the 20's. They made their way to the parking area on the north side of the hospital and at the stoplight just one block away from the entrance to the ER, Sam noticed a black van at the stoplight on the left. The windows were dark and he did not see the occupants inside. Henry pulled the white correctional facility van into the parking lot as Allison was appearing to be choking. Henry asked Sam to check her as he put the van into park. Sam jumped out and opened the back door to the van. He did not see the black van pull in behind him. Four men jumped out of the black van. Two of them grabbed Allison and quickly put Allison in the back of the van. The two other men disarmed Henry and Sam of their weapons and communications equipment and finished them off with a knockout rabbit punch to the back of the head. The deed was done and Allison was on her way to freedom. The black van sped away and Henry looked sideways underneath the white van to see if Sam was still out cold. He was and Henry then got slowly to his feet, taking his good old time. The guy that hit him on the head made the blow hard enough to hurt him but not put him out. He took his time and waited at least five minutes before getting up and trying the radio in the van and sure enough, just as planned, the men had pulled and cut the wires of the unit. Perfect. Planned to perfection. His prints would be on it but he had the excuse of needing to call but the radio was shot.

Henry waited about five more minutes and then went to the ER in a panic to call 911. It was just enough time for the black van to execute part two of the plan. Henry would be busy for a while explaining all this to the cops but he had done all the right things. He got the emergency people to come and get Sam and take him in for treatment, called 911 and had also called the prison. The APB was out on the black van with the prisoner and four suspects. That would be hard to identify. They would not find the black van when they went looking for it, in fact, they would be in three separate vehicles all going in different directions. Allison in the grey Impala with her drug dealing contact was heading south. A green Jeep was heading north, and a red Firebird was heading west. Poof, they were gone.

On the inside Henry was proud of himself. He had pulled it off. He knew he had a long day ahead but at the end of this day, when he was allowed to go home, he was done with that crazy job. He was heading south to meet his new love, where they would jet off to South America and live the life he had always dreamed of living. On the outside, Henry remained calm yet wanted to appear flustered. He had to act before in front of the old man, and he could do a good acting job now. He had acted for his survival and this would be no different. He didn't figure on a guy like Andy Marx pressuring him and he was about to meet Mr. Marx.

Andy Marx and Mo Reynolds arrived at the hospital about 11:30 that morning. They were quickly trying to investigate this escape as they had a vested interest in the escapee. They entered the emergency waiting area and wanted to see Henry Hannah as soon as they possibly could. Henry was done with being checked out by the medical staff and was heading to the waiting area. Marx and Reynolds spied a man they hoped was one of the guards. They approached him.

"Andy Marx and this is my partner, Morris Reynolds," Marx said as they both pulled badges and flashed them at Henry. "We want to ask a few questions about the incident this morning and the escape of Allison Branch. Why don't we move to a quieter place to do this interview?" They walked outside to Marx's vehicle where Henry was instructed to get into the front seat and Mo got in the back.

"Alright, no problem, detectives. How can I help?" Henry noticed the intense look on the face of Andy Marx. He knew it was coming as Branch had given him the inside scoop. She had told Henry not to be too fast to answer Marx. She had told him to think through his questions and then give him the answers she had told him to give.

"Why did you pull into the parking area before getting to the emergency room?" Marx asked as he stared intently into Henry's face looking for a weakness.

"The prisoner appeared to be choking," Henry began as he waited just a few seconds to answer. "I pulled over and told Sam to check her. As I was getting out, I had a gun in my back and Sam did, too. Two other guys with masks on grabbed the girl and then they cold-cocked both of us. When I came to, I noticed my shoulder communication radio was taken from me and my gun was gone. I immediately went over to Sam and was trying to get him to come to. I checked the van radio and the wires had all been cut. When I realized Sam was hurt worse than I was, I ran inside to get him help. I quickly then called 911 and let them know what was going on."

" What about these men, did you get any description?"

"They had masks, but they were average height, saying I guess, not taller than me. But I only saw them for a short time. But the van that pulled up to the light behind us was black. I am sure of that. That may or may not have been them, but it was the only vehicle near us that I could see."

"Did they say anything, did they speak English?" Mo asked.

"One of them said, 'get the girl'. I remember that and his English was plain."

"Anything else you can remember?" Marx asked. "Anything at all that would be helpful?"

"I can't think of anything right now," Henry replied.

"Okay, give the rest of your information to Mo here. I am going to radio this information to officers in pursuit. We may need to speak with you again. Are you available later this evening?"

"Sure, sure. uh, yeah sure."

That hesitation, that small hesitation was caught by Marx. Although he said nothing about it right away, he thought it funny to hesitate for that answer. He would make a note of that and check his story with the 911 operator later. Marx had a funny feeling about this Henry Hannah, a funny feeling that would bear out.

Henry walked back to the van and phoned the prison for directions on what to do with the van if Sam had to stay overnight. Since the cops wanted to keep the van and dust for prints, he would need a ride. Sam's wife needed a call, and he needed to get out of town. The head guard at the prison arranged for someone to pick up Henry and bring him back. He had a lot of explaining to do. He needed to be there and he needed to perform just one more time. Then he would be on his way to Florida to meet his new girlfriend and this would all be a brief hiccup in his world. The life he had dreamed of was just hours away. Just a few more days and he and Allison would be somewhere they would never be found.

On the gravel road in rural Wisconsin, Allison

Branch and her driver, Andres Montoya, were on the way to his farm. There the medical treatment she needed to feel better would be available. Andres owned the farm under the name of John Middleton. He told people in that area that he was Native American, and that he originally had made a living being a crop duster before he bought the farm. He flew planes alright, but he flew for drug runners who used Venezuelan air space to get to Brazil. Andres Montoya, aka John Middleton, ran drugs. In reality, he had grown up in the tough Rio de Janeiro slum of Complexo de Coreia. He had money, lots of it. He also had planes, and they all weren't just for the crop dusting he did for local farmers. He was going to take Ms. Branch somewhere that she could disappear for a while. She had helped Mr. Montoya run his drugs through the fine state of Wisconsin and she was needing just this one favor and then she would help again. Allison Branch was going to change. She would change just enough to not be recognized. Brazil, was where it was going to take place. Andres would make sure she would get there. Allison Branch would then go hunt again, and she knew the prey.

CHAPTER 7

Henry Hannah had a lot of explaining to do. He had thought this through with the help of his new beautiful partner in crime. She had given him every detail and also almost entirely every word he would need to get through the line of questioning.

He was approaching the warden's office and he knew he could not let them see him sweat. He entered the office and was prepared to be grilled. The warden had been there for fifteen years and was showing his age now at fifty-five. He was a gruff, round man with old-fashioned spectacles by the name of Bobby Vinson. When a person saw him, the first impression would have been that he was easy going and maybe even jolly. That was deceiving. He was a hard man that was molded by growing up with five brothers all younger, whom he raised alone after their mother died from cancer. His dad drank himself to death and that left him at the age of twenty-one to care for his siblings. He worked three jobs and when the boys were old enough to be on their own, he went back to community college. Then at thirty, he graduated from Wisconsin Stevens Point and worked his way from prison guard to warden over time. Bobby never married. His work had been his life and his life had been nothing but work.

"Have a seat, Hannah," he said looking directly at Henry. "I have the report here and allowing this very dangerous prisoner to escape creates a lot of problems. You do know how dangerous Branch is and this is certainly a mark against us for not doing our job."

"I realize that, Warden, but it was hardly something I could have prevented," Henry replied as he looked straight at Vinson. "

"Well, why don't you try to explain to me how this happened? We don't just allow prisoners out. In fact, in fifteen years this is only the second escapee we have had," he said pounding his fist on his desk.

Henry began to fidget, just as he had many times when his father would begin to yell at him. "I realize that, Warden, but they must have had quite the plan, because they were on us before we could move."

"Why did you pull into that parking lot? You were close enough to get to the hospital emergency entrance."

"The prisoner was choking and I pulled over and let Sam check her. He did and then we were ambushed. Sam and I had done this before many times without incident. The plan was just too good. It happened so fast," Henry said recovering from his initial fidgeting.

"You need to go fill out this report and then bring it back in," Vinson said still appearing to be seething. "We will talk some more about this when you are done."

Hannah moved to the outer waiting room as

Vinson's phone began to ring.

"Hello," Vinson said. "This is Warden Vinson, how can I help you?"

"Detective Andy Marx here, I was wondering if I could have a few minutes to ask you a few questions about today's escape? I worked the Branch case and have a high interest in capturing this fugitive."

"Oh yes, I remember reading about you and how rough that case was. Sure, come by as soon as you can. I have a guard filling out the incident report. How soon can you be here?"

"Can be there in about 20 minutes," Marx said with urgency. "See you shortly."

Henry brought his report back in and laid it on the warden's desk. Vinson began reading the report and took off his glasses. He looked at Henry and then back down at the report again. Vinson was still steamed and Henry knew it. *Be calm boy, just be calm here. Don't let them trip you.*

"You know that this is so sketchy and there is a detective coming to see me in a few minutes. Guy by the name of Marx from Milwaukee. So, I'm going to send you down to your area break room. He may have a couple of questions for you."

"Warden, he questioned me already at the hospital," Henry said as he now felt sweat begin to roll down his back. He didn't know if he could handle Marx twice in one day. He was getting nervous about Marx being there.

"He may want to see the report and get back with you."

"Alright, anything else Warden?"

"Not at the moment. Look I know this is a rough deal, but this sort of thing brings tremendous heat to the place, and, I don't like the heat."

Henry walked out and was hoping not to see Marx

before he got out of there. He grabbed the handle of the door that exited the waiting room and opened it and Marx was standing in his way.

"Mr. Hannah, excuse me, I was just going to see the warden," Andy said staring at the eyes of Henry Hannah intently.

"Yes, I think he's waiting in there for you," Henry replied trying hard to hold eye contact with Marx.

That moment was strange. It seemed like an eternity to Henry but it must have been very short. Henry felt himself going weak. *Not now, NO! Don't go weak just like you had always done with the old man. This Marx, this warden, I just got to get out of here. I can't until Marx is gone, but I am running out of performances and somehow, Marx knows it. I can see why Branch let that cocky bastard have it. I just can't fold to him now. I have to come through one more time and make her proud of me. Then I am free.* He continued to walk to his area break room. Marx was in his head. Just where Henry didn't want him to be. Henry was sure Marx made his head drop. *Damn it!*

―――▲―――

Marx sat down across from Vinson, eyeing him carefully. He wondered if he could trust him or would he protect Hannah. He would soon find out.

"Detective Marx, please ask away. I have already interviewed Mr. Hannah and to be honest, I am not quite sure what to make of his answers."

"First off, I'd like to note what your standard procedure is for transporting the prisoners to health care," Marx asked.

"Well, we always send two officers with the prisoners. They are armed and equipped with communications equipment. The van also has a radio for direct communications with us here at the prison. It would be hard to derail the van unless they were heavily armed and could ambush them. Hannah said he pulled over in the parking lot and that was puzzling to me. Their directions are to not stop until they reach the hospital entrance unless there is a major emergency. Hannah knows that and for him not to follow that is disturbing."

"Did he say he had an emergency?" Marx asked tapping his pen on the desk.

"He did say the prisoner appeared to be choking and he instructed Sam to check on her when he pulled into the parking lot," Vinson replied looking down at his notes. "I am thinking that part is fishy."

Marx studied Vinson. He was feeling that Vinson was giving him the truth. "Did he see anything? Could he give a description of the assailants?"

"He said it happened so fast and the only thing he could remember is that they had masks on."

"Warden Vinson, there are three things that bother me here. One, when I asked Hannah if he was available for questioning later, he hesitated. He acted as if I wouldn't need to question him later. Two, he really dropped his gaze when I met him at the door of the waiting room. That made me think he was in on this thing. Third, you and I both know that even if she was choking, they were close enough to the hospital to complete the trip. She could have gotten medical assistance at the entrance. Two and two are not adding up to four here."

"I agree with what you are saying. I can call him back up here and you can question him further if you like."

"I won't need to do that yet, but I think if you have an employment file, I'd like to see that. If he could sign off on me looking at his file, it would save me a trip to the court."

"Okay, I'll call him back up here."

With that, Vinson telephoned back down to the break room and had Hannah come back. Marx sat patiently and within five minutes Henry was back in the room. Henry appeared slightly nervous, something that Marx had noted and jotted down in his notes.

"Henry, Detective Marx has a few more questions for you if you don't mind."

"Sure, no problem," as Henry talked to himself and told himself to remain calm.

"I just asked Warden Vincent about protocol for the trip. Why would you pull over in the parking lot when you did as you were only a block from the hospital entrance?" Marx asked looking hard at Hannah.

"Well, it had started earlier and by the time we hit the light, she had turned bright red. Her face looked like it could explode. I felt it best to get it pulled over right there," Henry said wringing his hands just a bit.

"I see," Marx replied. "How is it that you were not treated for the severity of your injury like Sam?"

Henry wasn't prepared to answer this one. He stumbled through it saying that the bump on his head was there, he just didn't get cut.

"You sure you don't have something going with the prisoner?" Marx was zeroing in with what he thought. "You know these kinds of things have happened before. You and Branch got something going?"

Henry felt the sweat begin to form on the back of his neck. *I just can't blow this. I've invested too much. Be calm here. She told me what to say to this. Tell him how much you despised her, that I could hardly look at the bitch. That if I could right now, I could rid the earth of her.*

But he couldn't. "Well, of course not. I am surprised that you even asked that," Henry said clenching his fists.

Marx saw it and he knew he needed this guy's file. He would go by later to really put the heat on Henry Hannah.

"I need to see your employee file. Do you have a problem signing off on that for me?" Marx asked looking intently at Henry who did not return his stare.

"Uh, no. Sure, I'll sign off on it."

Vinson produced the signature form for the employee file and Henry signed it.

"Don't leave town," Marx said. "I would like to talk with you later. Right now, I have to meet my partner for another interview. Leave a working number for me to call and we will set a time to meet at the station."

Henry was starting to panic on the inside. He would need to leave sooner than he expected. He knew Marx had him cornered and now he needed to run.

"Okay, fine," Henry said.

"Here is the file," Vinson said as he handed it across to Marx. "Henry, you can go on home now. I will have the rest of your shift covered for the day."

Henry got up and left the room quite hastily. It gave Marx the impression that he should go right after him, but he knew he couldn't, not yet. He thought of him as a flight risk and he would be right. Henry was in on it and Marx's instincts were right on target.

Marx got up to leave and shook hands with Vinson. "Thanks for the help, Warden. This one is serious and we need to capture this fugitive. I really think Henry will lead us in the right direction. Here's my card. If you need anything or hear anything, give me a call."

Marx left and had already planned in his mind what to do next. He was on the trail of two cases which would prove to be his most dangerous work in his career. He had more than a full plate. But Marx was a pretty damn good cop. Marx was thinking to himself, *this guy is running and I know he had something to do with helping her escape. I just have to prove it. The clenched fists and nervous behavior, the dropping of his gaze when his eyes met mine, all those things indicate that he's suckered in by Branch to help her. Where in the hell is she? Where is Allison Branch?*

He decided to call Mo at the hospital and have him stake out Henry Hannah's place. He knew he was going to run. Mo had to get on this before Henry took off. He dialed Mo who answered on the first ring.

"Mo, I got a bad feeling about our prison guard here. I think he's in on this and he's going to run. Get over to 5500 Magnolia here in Oxford as fast as you can. I don't like hanging around Oxford, Wisconsin, any more than you, but I think he's going to run."

"Alright Marx, I'm on it. We've got a lot of loose ends to tie up. I will call Milwaukee and have them hold the interview with Martinez and the boyfriend until we get back. It will be a long ride from here. By the way, there isn't much here in Oxford, just one main street and a few hundred people. Got it, Mo? Just be there. Should be driving a black 2012 Ford pick-up truck. Let me know his movements while I finish up here," Marx said starting to wonder if Mo would connect with Hannah. "He's our ticket to Branch, we've got to keep him in sight."

Marx hung up and called Milwaukee to let them know to cancel the interview with Martinez and the boyfriend. "Hey, Frank, tell the Martinez woman and her guy that we have to reschedule the interview. I'll get back to them when I get back."

"I would, but they never showed up," the desk

officer said.

"Damn, get someone to call them and if you can't get ahold of them go looking. They were going to nail Hannah first. Then he would get back to finding Branch. He needed this lead. He had to have it. Things were changing very quickly. *Where is the boyfriend and my key witness?*

CHAPTER 8

*Whenever you open a cabinet door and find a rat,
beware, as rats never run in ones.*

Carrianne never had any intention of showing up
at the police station. Jake had done his part by
planting the seed of doubt about people in the
building where Carrianne worked that night.
Carrianne Martinez, aka Maria Santos, grew up poor.
She came to America looking for a better life. Growing
up in the tough streets of Complexo de Coreia in Rio,
she had known poverty and violence well. Her father
had been shot in an argument when she was four. Her
mother, Angelina Santos, tried hard to work and
provide what she could, but it was never enough.
Carrianne grew up most of her life without and she
would do almost anything to get out of the slums and
to America. At sixteen, her brother Julio had
introduced her to a friend of his, that could help get
her and Julio to America. He knew people. He took

care of Julio and Maria by giving them money and protected them. To Maria, he was a hero, much older than her and Julio. Julio's friend had a sister once, but she was gunned down in a cross fire of gang elements in the Complexo. He had taken on Maria and Julio as his to watch over. He had liked her and Julio and he would get them out of this hell hole. He was tough. Anyone that tried to give Julio and Maria trouble paid the price. He never once lost a street fight. Being older than Julio and Maria, they idolized him. Oh, and the part they liked the most about him was that he made them a promise. He had promised them both, he could get them to America and out of Complexo de Coreia, and in time he would, and in time, he did.

—▲—

Marx was nearing his destination and he knew he smelled a rat. He knew that Henry Hannah was that rat, and he wanted to grill him until he gave up the others. He turned sharply onto Magnolia Street and found Mo's car 100 yards ahead of him. He pulled over the side of the street well behind his partner's car and picked up his cell to call Reynolds.

"Any sign of him?" Marx asked.

"No, I expected him to be here already according to the time frame you gave me," Mo replied.

We can't give him much longer. He may already be on the run."

"Could be partner," Mo said as he fidgeted in his seat. "Maybe he and the girl are meeting up somewhere and he's left us behind.

"Could be, just can't put out an APB yet, we need to give it about thirty more minutes. You sit tight and I'm going to radio in to get local info and make contact in case we need to get an APB done."

Henry Hannah was on the road and headed to a town called Friendship, Wisconsin. That's where his beloved Branch had told him to go. He had called as soon as he left the prison and she advised him to high tail it up to Friendship. She would meet him there. He had to drive fast, but not draw too much attention to his Ford pick-up. He was putting distance between him and Marx and he had to keep that distance and ditch the vehicle where she had told him too, down Farm Road 18. He saw the road, exactly where she had told him it was, and made the left turn down the gravel road.

Henry was feeling better and more confident now. He had ditched Marx and his partner and all he had to do was make it to the bridge over the small river that rolled under the road. He was looking for the bridge when suddenly out of the side road came a black SUV ramming into the side of his truck. It stunned Henry as it knocked his vehicle into the ditch on the side. His instincts told him to run and immediately the thought that he had been crossed ran through his mind, and that thought was right. He opened his door and headed down the road. The large man jumped out of the SUV, and with his weapon with silencer attached, dropped Henry with just one shot to the back of the head. The last thought that ran through his mind was his father telling him how weak he was. It was his very last living thought.

The men put the body in the back of the SUV and covered the blood on the road kicking rocks and dust over it and pushing it into the ditch with their feet. The taller of the two men then jumped into the Ford truck and started to drive it to the "Cleaners" to be chopped into pieces where it would never be found. The "Cleaner" was good, very good. The body would be taken to a farm, just outside of Friendship and would be buried deep in the wooded acreage of the farm. One more hour of work and this one would be in the books and no trail whatsoever. This wasn't the first job for these two, and it wouldn't be the last. Life was fast, violent and profitable for these men. They were paid well and had a thirst for this kind of work. Growing up as they had, they had good reason.

CHAPTER 9

Marx and Reynolds waited another half hour. No Hannah. No sign of him at all. Marx radioed in an APB for his Ford Truck and told Reynolds they were packing it in. They would be heading back to Milwaukee and it would take two hours. Marx called Vinson and told him his guy had skipped out. Vinson was upset and pledged everything he could do to help in the matter. Marx then called the state patrol to see if they could locate the truck. They sped quickly back to Milwaukee.

My phone rang. It was Marx.

"Hey, I'm sure you saw the news. She's escaped and the guard I assumed helped her has disappeared. We have an APB out on Hannah and his truck with the state boys," Marx said.

"I don't know what to make of it," I said feeling the hairs on the back of my neck begin to stand up. "I know she's dangerous, but I don't think she's coming back here, not yet."

"You think she's skipping the country?" he asked.

"That would be my bet. When she had me kidnapped, she said I didn't remember her, that she had different hair. I wouldn't have remembered her if she had not stated that. I think she may leave the country and try to disguise her appearance," I replied.

"I'm coming back to Milwaukee. We need to talk. I'm guessing it has to be close like Canada or maybe South America. Remember the drug connections she had? They have to be helping her. Somehow and some way, the drug cartel and the fact that Brazil has the second leading number of plastic surgeries done in the world connect. No way the Feds don't get involved here."

"All that makes sense, call me when you get in. There's a lot to think about including where is Branch now?" I said hoping she wasn't watching me from outside.

"Stay safe and be careful until Mo and I get there."

I hung up the phone and every terrible thought I was trying to rid myself of was coming back.

Where is Allison Branch? What does she and her cronies have in store for me, Marx and anyone else that gets in her way? If she gets out of the country she would do well to stay away. But I know what she wants and her life doesn't matter to her anymore. She's angry and revenge is what she wants. Plain and simple, she's smart enough to have a good plan and will really try to throw us off this time. Every day of my life will be out of kilter. The life that I was slowly putting back together is now entering that place where I never wanted to return. I was better, wasn't I? I was starting to see things in a way that most normal and settled people do. Now HER, back in my life again. Why do I feel so sorry for her? She kidnapped me, tried to kill me, and yet I just can't let that go. I have to let that go. There is this picture in my mind of this beautiful cop that I thought loved me. There is also a picture of this demon, fire coming out in her angry voice and angry tears of hate and frustration. My life once again will be filled with bad karma. I just didn't know how bad...

Marx had notified the Feds and the hunt was on. He and Reynolds were nearly back at the precinct. They entered the building and went directly to Marx's office. He picked up the phone and dialed the phone number of Carrianne Martinez. There was no answer. He next dialed Jake Benson and the result was the same. This was not good, but they had to be found as they were the connection between the two crimes, Marx was sure of it. Reynolds was not so sure. Mo was more worried about the whereabouts and safety of those two and that they had possibly been killed and disposed of.

"Look, these people are into something, that we are certainly aware of," Mo began. "I am not sure they aren't captive to the real villains here or maybe even dead."

"I get it Mo," Marx replied. "I understand why you think that. But I have to think just a bit different. I am thinking that maybe in some way they are involved, yet more like the silent partners in this deal. I think the guy is in on all the drug trafficking and she is just a plant. I really don't think they are boyfriend and girlfriend. The guy is hiding something and trying to set us up. Otherwise, they would have shown up here at the precinct for the interview. They are the distraction."

"Any word from the state or Fed boys?" Mo asked.

"Nothing. Only that they found the black van burnt to a crisp on a gravel road. No sign of Hannah's vehicle and no sign of any other vehicle tracks near the black van. These guys are good. They had a plan and they are leaving no traces. She's going to be long gone before we get off square one," Marx said dialing the phone. "I'm going to call to find out how to track down air traffic. I have a feeling if she's getting out, she's going the fastest way possible."

CHAPTER 10

It was Thursday and my phone rang early. It was Mo calling me. I picked up and greeted him warmly.

"Hello, MO, good morning to you."

"Good morning, Mike. Andy has called about any flights running out of the area and how they are being monitored. Right now, he wants me to ask a favor of you."

"Sure, go ahead."

"You know, he hates to have me ask you to dig up old memories. But, he wants you to follow up on some old acquaintances and possibly trail a person for us that may lead to a few clues."

I thought before saying yes to this. I didn't want to go back and run through the violence of my past adventure. There were some limits to what I was willing to do.

"Okay, but to be honest I am limiting myself on what I am willing to do. I want to help and I am excited to do some things. I hope you understand."

"Sure, I get it, man. Marx just wanted you to trace back to your late father-in-law. Knowing he had the drug connections from the trial, he thought maybe you could somehow connect Branch and her drug trafficking to someone, anyone, that could lead us to finding Branch," Mo replied.

"Okay, I think I can do that, but Margaret is off-limits. I really don't want her to know any of what is going on."

"Thanks, and here's what he wants you to do..."

Andres and Branch were driving along smoothly in the cab of the 18-wheeler headed south. The destination of this trip was Miami, Florida. They would be there in twenty-six hours. It was cold but there was no snow to slow them down. Andres knew exactly where the 18-wheeler was headed and exactly where he was dropping it for his other private plane. The one that would take Branch to Rio. Andres had always known who to talk to and where to go. Organized crime was good with connections. Ever since signing up for the cartel, he had made several connections. Getting to Miami was the hard part, getting to Rio was simple.

The ride was quiet as neither one spoke much. Their relationship had been strictly business over the years, but Andres was good to protect her and give her all the connections she would need. She was only a piece of the organization but yet an important one. She could be used. She was pretty, she was smart, and she had eyes that made people do things they didn't want to do.

The disguises they wore protected them from detection and the paperwork they had for the trip was impeccable. They would make it to Miami, she was sure of it. The man driving the 18-wheeler was proficient and, yes, dangerous. Allison had all the confidence in the world in this man, Andres Montoya, and she knew he would get this job done. He looked over and his coal black eyes met hers. Her deep blue, penetrating eyes held his, longer than he thought was good for him. Yes, John Middleton, aka Andres Montoya, would do just about anything for Allison Branch. Just about anything...

After the rundown from Mo, I felt uneasy. I had worked very hard to get back to "normal". I had to get over to work today as we had a meeting at 10:00 am. At the meeting the faculty was to discuss insurance and retirement benefits. I hated these meetings, but I went because I felt obligated to be a part of the solution if I was bitching about the problem. The meeting started on time and I sat next to my old friend, Ed Weston. Ed was a much more settled person than I was. He had been married for thirty years and at fifty looked about forty. He had thinning dark hair with gray around the temples. He wore wire frame glasses and usually was dressed more casually than most of the faculty members.

"Hello, Ed," I greeted him as I sat down. "Looks like another boring discussion of benefits for the members of the good ole state university."

"Yes, I suppose you may be right," he answered looking at me thoughtfully. "You know, I know I don't say much about a guy and what his social life is like. You and I don't talk much about that. But I was wondering if you might be interested in going to lunch with me and a friend who is also like you, single and in need of some company."

"Wait a second, Ed, I'm not really looking for a date. Sometimes my mind works better when I just think for one and not balance that with what another person is thinking," I said.

"Well, she really is attractive. She's smart, funny, and she even likes sports. How could you go wrong with just one meeting?"

"I know, Ed, but I wasn't actually looking for a date right now," I said almost getting a bit more upset as the conversation moved along.

"I realize that, my old friend, but just lunch. You tell me what you think about her when it's done. If you don't like her or can't get along with her, then there is no harm done right?"

"Okay, just this once Ed, but no more matchmaking. If I want a date, I'll just ask someone. But, I do appreciate you looking out for me. You're a good man, Ed, and a good friend. I'm only doing this because I like Ed Weston."

Ed chuckled and pulled out his phone to text my date and where we intended to have lunch. I sat back and thought to myself, how weird that is for me, my age, to be thinking of having a date. *Hell, I should still be married but I could not make myself understand the discipline and work that marriage took. I sometimes considered myself mostly unworthy of any female companions for life. I almost didn't trust myself. I just can't hurt any more people. Besides, I just like being single. Well, for the most part. It does get lonely. But, loneliness was conquered most of the time by hitting a local pub, having some conversation, and, maybe, even getting lucky occasionally. I really didn't need this date. I was just going for Ed. Right, just for Ed.*

The meeting ended with a few healthy debates and at least some resolution to the problem of health care deductibles and we headed to our cars. I drove myself and we met down at the Roadhouse Steakout. The

Steakout had good food and a group of about twelve of us had a table reserved by Professor Weston. Ed had beat me to the place and had arranged where everyone was sitting. There were a few people from our department and some others I did not know by name but had seen before.

"I want to introduce you to my friend, Joanna Presley, Joanna meet Mike Parsons," Ed said as we faced each other across the table. I extended a hand and we shook lightly. She seemed to be shy and quite uncomfortable with our meeting. As a matter of fact, so was I. Not shy, but somewhat uncomfortable too. "Joanna works in the Arts Department and teaches drama and theater. She is new to the staff and moved in down the street from Ann and me. She has been to our house for dinner and sometimes for drinks." *Okay so Ed and Ann get to watch out the window to see if Mike and Joanna are dating or what? How creepy, Ed.*

"Well, it's my pleasure to meet you and hope that you are enjoying the university," I said studying her face for a few seconds.

"My pleasure as well, Mr. Parsons," she replied. "So far, I am enjoying it just fine. I love the students here."

"I do too, when they apply themselves," I replied. "I hope you find living in Wisconsin not too cold for your liking?" I asked.

"Being from Pennsylvania, it's not much different."

We both smiled and sat across from one another. *That voice. It was smooth yet was covered with an eastern accent. Smooth and educated, she exhibited class with how she talked, how she looked, and how she interacted with others at the table, except for me for some reason. I thought I was doing my best for old Ed here, but she responded much more to other people around her than to me. Okay, so it's not going to work Mike, just enjoy the lunch and listen to all the other conversations. This will end soon, and you can get on with the rest of your day.*

Lunch ended with literally no more conversation. We paid our tabs and headed for the parking lot. Ed stopped me before I could get in the car.

"Well, what do you think of her?" he asked.

"Honestly, not too much. I thought going in that this person, Joanna, would at least be able to carry on a conversation. She didn't talk to me much," I responded, sounding too angry I suppose.

"Hey, it's only the first meeting, Mike. Give her a second chance. Ann and I know her, and she really is a classy person," Ed replied furrowing his brow. "I know I may be getting too involved in this, but she is a good person. Why don't you ask her out one more time?"

"Look, Ed, give me her number and I might, and I do say **might**, ask her out again. If I do, I hope she is better at conversation than this time. I'm also not saying that I will. I've kind of been working this second job and it's keeping me busy."

"Alright, I understand. But, I am still saying this might be a woman with whom you can be more settled. You can't share with yourself forever. It's not good for a man."

"Okay, but don't hold it against me if I don't. I just didn't get good vibes from her."

I drove along heading back to my place. I kept thinking of trying to describe Joanna Presley. *Classy came to mind. Shy and reserved also seemed to describe her, too. Most women I chose to date at least had a passing interest in me. Not this one. She was pretty, well spoken, and thoughtful when she spoke to others. She just didn't speak to me. But face it, Mike, you didn't really initiate much conversation either, did you? You could do better. But she just didn't seem interested. I know I didn't like the idea to begin with, and maybe that's how I came off to her. Ask yourself, just what in the hell makes you think you want to date her? Is there anything there you liked? Ask yourself one more question; has everything that has happened to you in your life now make you gun shy? Are you just afraid to be involved with anyone? Just what in the world are you afraid of Mike?*

Just then my phone rang. I could see it was Mo Reynolds on the line I picked up on the third ring. Looks like I will be working tonight...

CHAPTER 11

Mo filled me in on the details of my
assignment that Marx had explained to me
before. I was ready to go out and be a crime
solver. I think I was. When Mo finished talking and I
hung up, I went by my place to pick up a few things I
needed. I made a thermos of coffee and took along a
pair of binoculars and a note pad. I left and got back
in my car. On the way I reviewed my task as Marx had
explained it.

*Okay, I was going to watch Andrea Stephenson
Raines for a few days. Marx suspected she knew a
hell of a lot more than she was giving him. I
wondered if she knees where Oscar is? Did she ever
see him if he was still alive? How does that happen?
She goes to him or does he come to her? Is he
kidnapped, dead and buried? Marx was thinking he
was still alive. Marx is hoping, by chance that he will
appear if I watch. I am not sure what I believe, but
this may be kind of interesting.*

I parked a distance from the house and tried to be very aware of my surroundings. I poured a cup of steaming coffee into my thermos top. I took out my binoculars and scanned her front yard and then the driveway to see if I saw anything. There were no cars in the driveway. It was possible the car was garaged or that she may be out somewhere. I slumped down in the seat to not be noticed and then looked both ways for a car that may stop there.

An hour had passed by and I was about to doze off when I saw headlights coming down the street. I slumped down farther until the lights were past me and then grabbed the binoculars and watched the car enter the drive of Andrea's home. A woman got out of a Mercedes and retrieved a small suitcase from the back seat and headed for the front door. She was only in there for five minutes. I noted the time on my note pad and then looked through the binoculars to see that she was once again on the move. She backed out of her driveway and the Mercedes went south. I put down the binoculars and followed.

I stayed a good distance back and followed her until she got on the interstate headed to the downtown area. O'Shea's was just two blocks away. The closer we got to O'Shea's, the more I thought it was possible she was headed there. *Surely not, she's not going there. I said I was staying away from there. I was leaving Katy alone to survive and get better. I can't go in there. Katy, who had been through that awful kidnapping with me where we almost bought the farm was my favorite bartender and one of my best friends that I had to keep at a distance.*

I came back to reality as the Mercedes stopped in the parking lot. The woman got out and I could tell from the photo that Marx sent to my phone that it was Andrea Raines. She made her way to the front door of

O'Shea's. I waited for five minutes to see if she would come back out of the bar. There was no sign. *Should I go in there or not? I needed to tell Marx if she was with anyone or was talking to someone. Okay, I was going in. Maybe Katy wasn't working. That way she wouldn't see me. Maybe she's got another guy now and there is no need to even worry about it. I had to trail this lady. It was part of my new job. I just can't upset Katy.*

I walked in about 8:00 by my watch, and looked around the tables to see if I could spot Andrea Raines. It was crowded, and I was not finding her seated at a table. *Maybe she was in the bar? Oh no! Not the bar. I just can't go in there. I missed Katy, I missed our conversations and I missed that great smile. Maybe it wouldn't hurt just this once, but I did have to follow the Raines woman.*

I spotted Andrea Raines as soon as I turned the corner. She was seated with a man, someone I did not know, of course. I wanted to take a photo but that would be too obvious. Just then my strategy was interrupted by a soft voice that I recognized: "Hello there, stranger."

I turned to the voice and there she was, the someone I had cared so much for but had chosen not to love. The pretty brunette that smiled that gentle smile and made you believe that she would always care for you. *Not now, especially not now.*

"Well, hello there yourself. If it isn't my favorite bartender," I replied feeling the hair on my neck stand up. If I didn't know it then, I knew now, she was such a knockout. "I was just passing through and thought I could stop by for a drink."

"Well, I'm glad you did. I have missed our conversations."

I wanted to hold her, hug her, ask her how she was

doing. I couldn't although every bone in my body wanted to. We had been through so much. Each of us was trying to put our lives back together. Each of us was struggling to do just that. We needed each other, not so much as partners, but for support and I wondered if I had failed her by staying away. I knew though, that I had made the right choice.

"I have too." As I took my old seat at the bar, I then proceeded to tell Katy about Branch's escape.

"That's not good. I still have some nightmares and I always carry my gun. Still scared of her and knowing she has escaped, I am even more afraid now."

"I get that." The light behind her put Katy in a semi-glow that shone above her head. It gave her an aura that moved me to an emotion that I couldn't define. *Mike, you can't, you just can't. Not now, not ever!*

"I have to ask, what kept you away so long? she asked. "I have tried not to, but I have missed your presence," Katy said as the glow seemed to increase around her. The light was catching her clear and bronze, beautiful facial features.

"Oh, I just had to give you time. I just didn't want to dredge up old things that you may doing much better with by now," I said, looking over my shoulder to see if the subject of my surveillance was still seated at the table. "I do hope for you that you are at least moving forward for yourself."

"I am, actually for the most part, I am doing very well." Katy was already admonishing herself in her own mind for lying. She wasn't doing well. The inner part of her that would not let go of Mike Parsons was screaming at her to tell the truth. Tell him it had always been him. Tell him she just can't get over him. Tell him she loves him and always will. But, she didn't. She kept the mask on that covered her feelings.

"Do you think you might pour me just one more scotch?" I asked

"Sure, anything for you if you promise to stay just a bit longer to talk." I turned and noticed my subject, Andrea Raines, was getting up from her seat. She was leaving. What now?

"Uh, Katy dear, I have to take a rain check on the drink. I promise I will come back, but I do have an early meeting tomorrow."

"Ok, sure Mike. Do come back though, I have missed you," she said with a pouting look.

"I will, I promise."

With that, I left a generous tip for Katy and headed out of O'Shea's to the parking lot following the subject.

Marx was stumped. It was not often that when working these cases, that they had led him to dead ends and no leads. He often found his leads productive as he was very smart. Right now, he just had too many possibilities. He just couldn't chase each theory because he didn't have the time. He just had to choose the right one and follow it until he hit a snag. He thought much longer, and then he settled on a theory. Was she leaving the country or staying to commit mayhem? He chose leaving the country as the theory and began to work towards that theory. He called the Feds and suggested Florida. He knew in his heart she was headed south and not just in this country. Intuition told him she was headed to drug cartel country. It would be where her connections were. But where? Which country? He had a pretty good idea, just a hunch, but he was going to follow it. The fact that Jake Benson had told him Carrianne thought the people were speaking Portuguese made him think Brazil. He called his high school buddy, a former FBI agent, who would help him. Brian Stowe would respond. He would be working with a former FBI agent, not a kosher deal, but even if he had to quit the department, he was going to find her and bring her back, dead or alive.

CHAPTER 12

J ake Benson and Carrianne Martinez were the fictional American names for Julio and Maria Santos. Julio and Maria had come to this country with John Middleton, aka Andres Montoya. Montoya had made sure they had what they wanted and needed. He was their guardian. In return, they had to do a little work for the cartel. The next assignment for them would be a difficult one. They would have to protect Allison Branch in Rio. The ride in the back of the 18-wheeler was a rough one, but they had been on rougher journeys. They were going back to Rio. The plan was for them to watch over Allison Branch during her recovery from plastic surgery. They would not have to go to Complexo, as she would be staying in artsy hotel in Santa Teresa on the hill overlooking Rio.

They would only have to be around for a week to look after Allison Branch after her scheduled plastic surgery. Then John Middleton would take them back to America. They could continue helping with the distribution of drugs. They would be armed and John Middleton would be close by. This would be an easy job.

Allison Branch had met these two many years back. They had worked with her and Breanne Jackson for years in the drug distribution market under her protection. It made their jobs a whole lot easier and profitable. So, for Jake and Carrianne being used to protect her, Allison was quite comfortable. Just a few weeks in Rio and then Branch would be back in the states. Back in the states, to hunt, and in particular, kill the three people that had caused her so much pain and grief. By 5:00 pm they would be in the air. By end of the week, she would be under the knife and her appearance as she knew it would be changed forever.

Marx had two things on his mind as he doggedly worked his mind into a frenzy over this case and the connection to the other. Those two things were Jake Benson and Carrianne Martinez and their whereabouts, and, of course, Branch. Who were they? Where did they come from? He had the Feds on that one, but they were just coming up with two Americans who had disappeared and all of the papers and green cards were good under those names. So, he had to think they were missing, but were they really? It was mind- boggling. The second thing on his mind was Branch. Mike had told him that she had changed her hair color and was not recognized in the beginning. Was she going to change her appearance again? If she did that and was undetected before that, it would be awfully difficult to find her. But, one thing he knew for sure, she would show herself. He knew that because she was thirsty for revenge. The revenge for being jilted and the revenge for not being tops in her class were all a part of her that she could not let go. It would not be enough to just hide. She would come out and when she did, it could be a very dangerous thing not to be able to see it coming.

Marx dialed Mo and let him know that he and Brian Stowe would be leaving the country for a week and what his idea was. Mo was going to try and find out what had happened to Henry Hannah and, that in itself, was a sticky problem. Marx thought that Jake Benson and Carrianne Martinez knew what happened. He knew that somehow those two were connected to the crime, it was just in his gut. Mo would be tracking anyone who knew these two.

Marx was at the airport waiting for Brian in the airport lounge. He sipped a beer and then saw Brian approaching. They exchanged pleasantries and then Brian ordered himself a beer. Looking around and finally settling in at the table, Brian opened the conversation.

"Great to see you, buddy. I made sure no one was following as you just can't trust anyone," Brian said taking his first sip of beer.

"Good to see you, too. Been a long time. Let me tell you this case has me going bonkers. I'll tell you what I have so far. I have an escaped con who used to be my partner, and a missing business man, Oscar Stephenson, who has been missing for years. My only connection between the two cases is a young couple that are boyfriend and girlfriend, Jake Benson and Carrianne Martinez, that are now missing as well. I think they are the weakest link if we can find them. Jake met with me and drew me into this, but now I think that was on purpose, as they are somehow connected. He stated to me his girlfriend, Carrianne, had information that might have been helpful on the Stephenson case. I told them to meet me at the station and we could question them further. When Branch escaped, they didn't show up for questioning and have been missing since."

"Geez, that complicates things. Think they might just be getting you involved, setting you up?' Brian asked.

"Yeah, I think so. But the escape even complicates it more because the guard who was with Branch when she escaped also slipped us and may be with her or it is even possible he met his demise."

"Sounds tough. What makes you think Brazil is the right place to go?" he asked. "It's too late now but tell me why Brazil? I trusted you when we made the flight arrangements," Brian said.

"I just feel she may need to change her appearance, and after doing some research, I found out that Brazil does the second most plastic surgeries in the world. The United States is first but she wouldn't hang around. Someone is helping her navigate this and going to Brazil is a hunch. But you know my gut."

"Yeah, I do buddy," he said. "I'm going with you on this one and I know how well your instincts speak to you. We won't be able to chase it far. If it doesn't happen there and we get nothing, that will be the end of going out of the country unless there is something solid."

Marx's flight was called and he and Brian were headed to Rio...

I had just gotten home from getting my passport, when there was a knock at my door. I went to answer and carefully looked out of the peep-hole to see who it was. It was Mo. I let him in and told him to make himself at home in the living room.

"Want a beer?" I said as I walked towards the kitchen.

"No, thanks," Mo said looking puzzled. "I just can't

seem to wrap my head around a couple of things in this case. The woman escapes and is helped by the guard. The guard can't be found. How does he disappear into thin air? He couldn't have gotten far, not in this time frame. Branch on the other hand is long gone. What are your thoughts, Mike?"

"Not sure, but I am sure about one thing, I really misread her. I foolishly let her get close to me. I just wanted to solve the case when Sheila committed suicide. I thought she could help me. She's evil in the worst way, but I truly felt she was falling for me. When she had the gun on me, she let it fly. She held nothing back but was accusing me of not remembering her and not "choosing" her over some other girl in a bar one night."

"Super jealous, sounds like. But, it also sounds like she did have feelings for you," Mo replied.

Mo looked at me pondering something. "You know, I remember Marx telling me how confused Branch must have been. Whether she was into men or into women or maybe both, you are still the main target. You took two things from her. One, the love she so desperately wanted and needed from you and, two, the woman she was in love with at the time. Now she has neither and it makes her that much more dangerous."

"I guess that's true. Why do you think she may risk her freedom just to get revenge?" I asked.

"Good question, but I remember a case a while back that a woman, supposedly in love with a married man, poisoned the man's wife and when he wouldn't be with her, she cut his throat. So, you need to be careful. Jealousy is a big, green monster, man."

"You're not making me feel any better, Mo."

"Just want you to be safe, my friend. I just heard from Marx and he and his old buddy, Brian Stowe, are headed to Brazil on a hunch. Marx has it in mind she will try to change her appearance, you know, facelift."

"Could be, as she changed herself before."

"Look, be careful man. If they don't find her, it could be anyone. Anyone on the street if she slips them and comes back. Who knows, she could be running around here looking for you right now. You have my number. Call me if you see anything weird."

"Got it, Mo. And Mo, thanks."

"Now get some rest and keep the doors locked," he said as he headed for the door. "See ya later."

"Yeah, be careful. See you later."

I waved at Mo and he waved back. I had a funny feeling in my gut. I had the feeling that this was the last time I would see him. I don't know why I had that feeling, but I couldn't shake it. I was just being silly, I suppose, and tried to put that thought to bed. I made myself a cup of coffee and sat back in the living room. The longer I sat, the more the feeling about Mo went away. I got to thinking of Joanna and drifted into another conversation with myself.

"Well, what did you think?" Ed said.

"Not much," I replied. There was something about her, I must admit, but I couldn't see us together at this point. Was I not giving it a chance? Was I just that shallow not to have the right conversation with this lady? Was I giving up too soon? She is attractive and that word, classy, just kept coming back to me. I would call her again, wouldn't I? Sure, yes, call her back. But I had to trail Andrea Raines. That would take time, and I may not want to get involved with Joanna or even have her involved in this. Maybe I wouldn't call her back...you know how you got Katy involved in the last episode and this person probably needs to stay away from me. I'm trouble...big trouble. You're hopeless.

Just then my phone rang. I picked up quickly thinking it may be Marx or Mo.

"Hello, Mike," that sweet and completely recognizable voice on the other end said.

Oh God, not now, please not now. I just can't deal with this right now....

CHAPTER 13

*"The hunger for love is much more difficult to
remove than the hunger for bread"*
-Mother Teresa

A t three o'clock, Branch and the others arrived in
one of the most unique neighborhoods in the
world, Santa Teresa, in the heart of Rio de
Janeiro. The city was often referred to as the "artistic
heart" of Rio. It is home to mansions that were once
home to the city's wealthy and elite. The mansions
now are mostly artists' studios or used as rentals to
guests. The area had been re-vitalized by imposing
taxes for gas, energy and water to eliminate the poor
and the growth of the slums. The walling off of Santa
Teresa from the poorer elements of Rio turned the city
into a relaxing mecca for artists, tourist and
politicians seeking a moment to relax.

The breezy hilltop location lends itself to
comfortable strolls through the neighborhood which

would certainly be a pleasure in itself. The pace of life for Allison Branch would be slower here, giving her the time she needed to change herself, transform herself, and to prepare herself for what lay ahead.

Andres pulled the black SUV up to the Santa Teresa Hotel and had Jake and Carrianne help Allison check in to her accommodations. Andres had taken care of this and it was fully paid for by the cartel. He waited outside with a watchful eye to his surroundings. His life was filled with these kinds of moments. He had always prevailed in these situations but something was telling him that this one was different and that he must be more intense in his supervision. He thought this to be true especially for the young adults he had brought over to America. They were still kids. They knew the rules but he was not sure they possessed the discipline necessary to carry out this task. He waited a bit and Jake reappeared to get the bags.

Andre gave Jake strict instructions to only be in Santa Teresa and not to wander too far. "Remember, I will be close by. We can't mess this up. She is a vital player for us and knows the ropes. She has to be watched and not trusted. That's your job, Jake," he said looking as intimidating as ever.

"Got it," Jake said. "I go by Jake Benson. Carrianne is my girlfriend, and we keep a close eye on her until her surgery tomorrow. I won't let you down."

"Be sure that you don't. I have taken care of you and your sister for years. I promised your mother years ago that I would."

"I know and we both appreciate it so much. I will keep my eye on her. Carrianne is sharp, too. She will be a great help."

"And Jake, don't be alone with her. She is evil and I don't know her well enough. Do not look her in the eye. She has eyes that make you do what you don't want to do."

"Yes, Andres. I understand."

Andres knew he did not understand. How could he? Jake is too young and thinks only with his sexual needs. He must have discipline and not be tempted. He needs to be strong. Jake took the bags and Andres climbed back in to the SUV and slowly pulled away. Jake was sure of himself and began the trek up the steps to the hotel lobby. Andres thought to himself; *I can't go far, I want to trust him, he's a good boy, but I know I can't go far. I will go see my brother and will return. I just wish I could trust them.*

He drove on and continued on to meet his brother in Complexo de Correia. Andres was too smart to stay away long. His gut was telling him something bad.

Jake Benson and Carrianne Martinez were back to playing boyfriend and girlfriend for a brief time again. They entered their room after making sure that Allison Branch was comfortably okay in her room. Jake was trying to keep himself from being confused. *Who am I today? Jake or Julio? Boyfriend or brother? Brazilian or American? What name do I answer to and when do I answer? What language to speak and when? Too many questions. I need something different. I need to be loved.*

Carrianne was tired of this act of being boyfriend and girlfriend. *It was creepy to her after living in America. She had a man that she was interested in. This act had gone on for some time and had provided good cover for Andres and the cartel. But she needed something, something different. She needed to be loved. She was young, beautiful and vibrant. Her life could not always be the cartel. But there was no way out. Andres had done so much for her and Jake. They could not disappoint him. He was the only thing they knew as a father figure now. No, they could not disappoint him.*

Allison Branch sat alone in her room. Her thoughts were whirling in her head. She looked out the window, and once again her thoughts turned to Mike, to Andy, to Breanne, but mostly to Mike, because in some strange way she just couldn't get him out of her head. At one point, she had needed him. She wanted him desperately. His unknowing of how much she wanted him caused her some grief and confusion about her own sexuality. She was a confused adult, but she was also always confused. Not only confused but also angry. Anger had consumed her and she was going to make all the people that ruined her self-esteem pay for their transgressions on her ego. It was their fault that she considered herself worthless. She would make them pay. But the one thing she could not deny to herself, no matter how hard she tried, was that what she really needed was to be loved.

I'm at home debating so many things and then this call. "Hello, Katy. I could ask how you are doing, but I think I know the answer to that. You called. So, I am sure you would like to talk."

"Well, yes," Katy replied. "I was hoping I could follow through with the scotch that I didn't get to pour you. Maybe, hopefully, we could have that conversation I was missing?"

I was slow to answer. I really have my misgivings here. I was hoping without me in her life in any way, that Katy could move on without our friendship. But this call was feeling like she wanted more than friendship. My hesitation was duly noted by Katy. I could sense it.

"You know, I was hoping..." she said as I heard her voice beginning to crack. She sniffled and then I knew right at that moment what I would say.

"Okay, okay, listen I can be there in about ten minutes." *I am already starting to hate myself.*

"Oh please, Mike, just for a little while," she said. "I promise that I won't keep you long. I just need to talk to someone and I guess just not anyone would do. I need to talk to you."

"Okay Katy, I'll be there in about ten minutes."

I grabbed my keys and jacket. I started to head out the door when I thought I heard something outside. I froze for a second and then grabbed my Lueger. I turned on the outside lights and saw nothing. I slid the glass door to the back deck open and looked around. I saw nothing. *Hell, this is just my imagination. Nothing to see here.* I closed the door back up and locked it. I headed out remembering I told Katy ten minutes. I can't really keep her waiting that long. I dismissed the noise as me being irrational and headed to my car. As I walked, I kept looking behind me. *Not letting that happen again. No sir, I am much more aware than before.* I started my car and headed towards Katy's place.

Katy met me at the door and her smile was something I wasn't quite prepared for. For some reason, it hit me harder than any other time before. It was showing me that she was better, that she was okay, and it also gave me warmth inside. It let me know that we were really not alone since our awful ordeal and the memory of it. We still had each other to rely on to take away the pain, the fear and the newest fear that others would be soon coming for us again. The paranoia was striking deep within both of us, so maybe this time, just for us, it was going to be okay.

"Well, hello my favorite bartender," I said holding back somewhat from just wanting to hold her.

"Well, hello yourself my favorite customer," she said. "Please come in and sit for a while. I'll get you that scotch you didn't get earlier."

I almost held off and was about to say no, but hey one wouldn't hurt, right? She walked into the kitchen and I couldn't help but notice her graceful walk as she went to make my drink. Katy wasn't tall as she was 5'6", but she had a graceful way of walking and smiling that made me feel comfortable. I guess that's why I liked visiting her so much in the past. If I ever felt down and out, which seemed to be often, she was there to lift me up. She had a way with me that I could not put away. I felt weak about my intentions to come here and leave early.

Katy reappeared with two drinks in hand, a scotch and water for me and a rum and coke for her. I smiled politely and thanked her. I took a deep breath. She sat next to me on the couch. Neither one spoke for a brief moment that seemed longer than it actually was. I spoke first.

"Okay, cutting to the chase, what are your feelings now? What has happened inside you since our ordeal?" I asked. Those were the two questions I guess needed to be answered so I could get some insight into her heart. "I understand," I said as I gulped a large drink of my scotch. "You have the floor, dear Katy."

"As far as to what has happened since those events, I got better. I went to therapy, which you knew, I am sure. My therapist worked me through the violence and the fear that someday she would return. That was completely shattered when I heard about her escape. She was evil and I worry for me and for you, too," she said as she looked me in the eye.

"Look, I have to be up front with you on this. I understand where your mind is right now. This escape has me frazzled too. I can't walk anywhere without looking behind me," I said.

"I know, I can't go anywhere without carrying a gun," she said as I noticed the fear in her eyes. "I keep thinking that I will meet her on the street somewhere and she will kill me on the spot. I think of her and those eyes of hers staring at me, those ugly people in the cellar torturing and drugging us. It is the reoccurring nightmare that I have almost every day, well almost, because somedays I don't think about it. But I keep thinking they are out there, more of them, more of those hateful people. I'm really scared."

She stopped and drank heavily from her glass as if she couldn't kill the pain fast enough. *Mike, you can't tell her what you are doing, she will totally freak out. Not now, she just needs you to reassure her. Tell her things will be okay.*

"Look, I know it was a living hell. I still have mental scars too. They seem to pop up at the worst possible times. I can't forget what happened, but more and more I see her face less and less. I am getting better. I have to admit that since her escape I have been more on edge. I am getting better and you will too." *Why am I lying?*

"What did you see in her?" she asked. "I told you before and you know I thought at one time I had a chance with you. But then she came along and I felt I was out of the picture. Then the kidnapping and violence happened and then I thought, in some crazy way, that it would bring us closer, that you could find a way to actually love me."

Tears began to form in her gorgeous eyes and I reached up and wiped the first one that fell away. *Mistake. Damn it, mistake Mike. You weren't going to touch her, you weren't going to hug her, you weren't trying to give her any false impressions that would make her feel so deeply. But it's too late, you did it.*

She reached up and touched the palm of her hand to my cheek and kissed me. Her arms wrapped around my neck and I put my arms around her and pulled her close. The kiss that lasted longer than most any kiss I have known, breathed a life into me, one I could never have felt before but yet knew was wrong. We stopped and she put her head into my shoulder and began to weep. I felt her sobs and felt her heart slowly begin to beat faster. I held her longer, maybe longer than I have ever held a woman before...

Mike, you can't, you just can't. She's beautiful, she's kind, she wants you, but you know how really vulnerable she is. Just hold her, comfort her as long as she needs. But you know the answer to what she will ask of you, you just can't.

I held her longer into the night, her head resting on my chest. It was two o'clock in the morning when her red and teary eyes looked up at me. I knew what was coming. This woman, so needy and wanting was also very sincere. Her question was simple and direct; "Mike, can you love me? I love you more than you can ever know. Can you at least try?"

"Our lives were connected by me being at a bar, and then with the kidnapping and everything we went through. I know what I am and I would just not be good for Katy O'Neal. I care for you so much, but in the end, I would let you down. I can be your friend, someone you can count on when you need one. But I just can't commit, not now, or maybe not even ever. I am still trying to find out if I can ever love anyone again." *I was hating this answer, I don't like this answer, and in some ways, I don't think it is the answer that I feel. But I also know that it is the right answer. The one that would keep me from ruining a sweet girl like Katy. It would be the one thing I may have done right in many years.*

"But you know, you did feel it, right? I mean, when we kissed?"

There was no way I could honestly say no. I can't lie, that kissed moved me on the inside.

"Yes, it did move me. But, listen, please, please understand that I am too still searching for what I want to be or even what I am capable of being. I could never hurt you, and what I say is not intended to do that. You are an angel. Someone, someday is going to be a very lucky man. But I am not good for anyone until I can find what I am searching for."

I knew I had to leave as what I had just finished saying was my cue. I grabbed both of her hands and pulled her up from the couch. I hugged her once more and she slowly walked with me to her front door. It was then that Katy said something that would ring in my head for many years to come.

"Thanks, for coming over," she said as her eyes sparkled with moist tears. "I will always love you. There is nothing that can change that. But, I want you to know that I understand what you are saying. You can be whatever you want to be. There will be no one who cheers harder for Mike Parsons to be what he would like to be. If you ever have a change of heart, or if you find you can love again, I will always be here. I can never in my mind see me loving someone else."

With that, she kissed me gently on the cheek and once again, I was leaving Katy's house, never to return. Or would I?

CHAPTER 14

I hadn't looked at my phone for hours. I saw a message from Mo Reynolds it was about 11:00 pm. *"Why don't you come by as I think I have something to ask about Andrea Raines."* I dialed his number and called back, he did not answer. I thought he was busy so I would try again later.

Something about Andrea Raines. I was trying to figure out who the guy was. I really had no idea if I had ever seen the guy before. Younger than Andrea, the man was about 40 or so. Dark hair graying at the temples. No facial hair. Handsome gentleman. What was that all about?

I was headed home and was going to call Mo later, but I decided to turn the car around and head to his place. I dialed Marx, just to get the directions to Mo's place again. He answered and I said," Hey, I was needing directions to Mo's place again...I was..."

Marx interrupted me. "Don't go, Mo's dead."

"What the..."

"Look, I called him last night to check up on you guys as I was leaving for South America. He didn't answer. He always answers. But I thought he may be busy or out with you. I called again later and again no answer. I got worried and called a guy at precinct to go check on him. House was broken into and his throat was cut. Mo was careful and had cameras at this house. They're going to have to look at the video to see what they can. I'm on my way home. I have to go tell his aunt. My friend, Brian is in South America hunting Branch. This hurt. Look if anyone questions you, you say nothing but the fact we are friends. Don't say anything about working with me. I could get into trouble for that. I will call you when I get back."

I was stunned. I was out last night. Would they hold me as a suspect? I wasn't sure but they would certainly come and talk to me and I would be honest, I was at Katy's. I turned the car around and headed for my place. This is crazy just flat out crazy. I pulled up to my house and the police were already there. My god, now what? Andy had prepared me but I was just wanted to compose myself. I had gotten to like MO and this news of his death had shaken me. Just what are we into here?

When I got to my door, I let them in and had them sit in my living room. They shot the basic questions at me and I answered as Andy had instructed. I told them where I was and who I was with during last evening. My mind was racing with questions but not theirs. The questions were my own.

They finally finished and left my condo. The questions buzzing through my head. Who killed Mo and why? Just who in the hell was Andrea Stephenson Raines? Where is Oscar Stephenson and how do he and Andrea connect to Jake Benson and Carrianne Martinez? And who are they, really? Who was the man with Andrea? My world was once again upside down. And one more question; just where in the name of God is Allison Branch?

CHAPTER 15

Day three of being the caretaker for Allison Branch was getting boring for Jake Benson, aka Julio Santos. He needed to be out for a while and his lust for life had taken over his decision making. He was going to sneak away for a few hours and hit the town a bit. He knew of a good bar nearby, the *Largo de Guimaraes*. He just had to find some kind of action. If nothing else at least have a few drinks and unwind. He was sure that Andres had gone to the Complexo and thought his little venture out wouldn't hurt anything.

The bar was close so Jake got showered and dressed to head out for the evening. He told Carrianne to keep an eye on Branch and he would not be out too long.

"I don't think that is a very good idea, Julio," she said pressing her lips together in a grimace. "You know Andres. He would not like you leaving your post."

"Andres is at the Complexo. Anyway, what will a few hours hurt?"

"I'll watch her, but don't be gone long. If Andres comes back, I won't lie for you."

"Seriously, I won't be gone long. But I just need the company of a woman just for a while."

Julio left the room and headed for town. Carrianne thought this was a mistake, but she felt she could handle watching Branch. Maybe she would go talk to her. She was more than curious about Branch. But in the meantime, she would be worried about Julio. Not that he couldn't take care of himself, but he was wild and sometimes impetuous. He tended to be careless.

Carrianne went to the room next door and knocked. Branch came to the door, still bandaged and still moving slowly, but was nice enough to let her in. Her room was nice and the furniture better than Carrianne was used to. She sat across from Branch and began the conversation.

"I hope you are feeling much better," she said wondering how much conversation would pick up.

"I am," Branch said slowly through the bandages. "Just hope this recovery picks up the pace."

"You were very pretty before," Carrianne remarked. "Why do you want to change yourself?"

"I have plans. I cannot be who I was before to make my plans work. You see, you and I both work for Andres and this cartel. I did what I was supposed to do until some people got in my way. You know what happens to people who get in the way."

"Yes, I do. I have worked for them for a while. But I'd like to ask you something personal." Carrianne did not know if Branch would answer this question. But she was going to ask it anyway. "Have you ever been in love. I mean really in love?"

"I have, but I'll tell you, I have loved a man who I

hoped would love me. He didn't. I also fell in love with a woman who was very much like me. I didn't know I could even do that. But that cop Marx killed her and he tried to kill me. But I survived and I will have my revenge," Allison said through her clenched teeth. "You see, Carrianne, you can't overcome the need to be loved. It lives through jealousy, it lives through anger. Someday, someone will love me, like I want to be loved. But for now, I am focused on revenge. Revenge against those I hate and against those that have taken away the things from me that I have loved the most. If I can't have him, there is no one who will. I will make sure of that. I can't help but still have feelings for him. Strange as it may sound, I could have loved him forever, but he didn't choose me."

Carrianne froze for a second, thinking deeply about what Branch had said. She too had a deep desire to be loved. Working with Andres and the cartel had made social life almost impossible. "Can I ask you something else? I mean, when you loved the man, how did you feel? How did you feel inside of you?"

"I had so many problems growing up. I was a rebel. I didn't want to conform to rules. I knew everyone was out to get me and I had to win at everything. But when I loved this man, it filled my heart. I could think of nothing but him. He betrayed me, he didn't pick me. I had moved on to a girl that I loved very much. I wanted to kill him and I tried to. I could have done it, but I was going to leave that to his ex-father-in-law, but this time, I will do it myself."

Carrianne was digesting what this dangerous woman was saying. *I have never killed anyone. Why is she is set on doing this when she could stay hidden forever here in Brazil? I need to keep my distance from her, but I am sure Andres knows her story better and has a reason to keep her in the cartel. She is older and I want to ask her how I can find a man, a man that would care for me and love me. But does she even know? Has there ever been a man that loved her? I mean, really loved her. Or was she so confused about who she was that she could never possibly be loved? She is dangerous and I need to keep my distance from her. I am doing this for Andres and I must not disappoint him. But I need try and stay alert with this woman so she doesn't kill me. I can't make her angry.*

"It may be the only way you can move on," Carrianne said smiling at Branch. "My job is to watch over you while you heal. I am going to take care of you and get you back to good health."

"Thank you, Carrianne," Branch said sounding a bit tired. "I would like to get some air, but being seen around here by anyone could be a problem."

"There is a pool just outside the main floor with a tree that grows in the center. It is beautiful. The view of Rio is spectacular. Would you like me to take you there?" Carrianne asked.

"That would be very nice. When I talk of these things in my head, I just have to slow down. I need to relax as I feel my muscles are all tense and tight. I can't get in the water, with these bandages and all, but to sit by the pool would be just what I need."

"Okay, I will get my suit. I may want to get in myself and let the water refresh me," Carrianne said.

Carrianne left and went back to her room to change. Allison kept thinking about this girl, Carrianne. *She seems nice, sweet in fact and working for this cartel? I mean, how did she get hooked up with these people? She would have been better off not getting involved. She's very attractive and could have any man or woman she wanted. She is someone I am attracted to, but I know and feel she is not like me.*

Forget it. She wouldn't be up for it...

Carrianne knocked on Branch's door. Allison opened the door and together they went to the pool. There, they could sit and talk and relax. Julio was gone and wouldn't be back for a few hours, or so he said. Carrianne didn't know how much more she would find out about Branch, but she wanted to know more. She knew to stay her distance, but she was curious about many things concerning Branch. She would find out plenty...

Julio entered the bar and was glad to see the many young ladies his age that populated the bar. He went to a table for two and sat alone. A waitress came by and he ordered a beer. He was in an element he liked. He loved the music, the dancing and the lights. Now, he just needed to find someone to share it with.

His waitress came back and set a beer in front of Julio. She smiled and he returned it and tipped her generously. He had become accustomed to the ways of the American male that thought smiling and tipping well would get you a date. He sipped his beer and looked around hoping to make eye contact with a beautiful Brazilian or even American tourist. His eye caught a young American beauty dancing with her friends out on the floor. His eyes followed her graceful moves that were sexy and very fluid. He caught her eye and flashed his handsome smile at her. She seemed to return it or was he just imagining it? Julio moved from his seat and took his beer with him to a closer seat by the dance floor. The song was over and Julio held up his glass and motioned for her to join him. She turned to her friends and said something to them and turned towards Julio and smiled. She walked over and stood by Julio.

"Please, sit down and join me. Can I buy you a

drink?" he asked.

"Sure, I'm Clarice, and you are?"

"Jake, Jake Benson. Pleased to meet you Clarice. What brings you to Santa Teresa?"

"Fun, of course. Some of my friends and I decided to take this trip to get away. We had heard it is beautiful here and wanted to see Rio from up here in Santa Teresa. My father has a rental here that he rents out to tourists. We are staying there tonight."

"It is a fun and beautiful place. I work for a firm in the states. I had some vacation time built up and decided to hit Rio," Jake said taking a sip of his beer.

Jake studied her face and her eyes. Her eyes were round and wide and highlighted by arched brows. The hazel-green pupils shone brightly as she was alive and engaged in this conversation. Her smile shone through beautiful, glossy red lips. She had enthusiasm, she had style and Jake Benson was feeling that he wanted to know more. He was ready to ask her to dance.

A slow song came on and Jake offered to dance with her. Clarice accepted and they moved slowly to the floor. Jake did not get too close. He didn't want to scare her off. But her hand was warm and her other hand she placed gently on the back of his neck. Jake was feeling her electricity. He could sense that her need may be just as strong as his. The connection between them was warm and the longer they danced, it was getting just plain hot. With his right arm Jake pulled her a bit closer and he could sense that she was interested.

"I was born here in Rio," Jake said as her face was no much closer to his. "I will be here a few more days if you would like for me to show you the sights."

"I really shouldn't leave my friends," Clarice replied. "We had this planned for so long."

"It would only be for three or four hours. Would it really hurt anything for you to get away for a few hours? Anyway, your friends would be sleeping this hangover off tomorrow and we could make a morning out of it."

"Maybe, why don't you call me in the morning?" she said. "I'll give you my number at your table."

"You know, you are beautiful. How is someone like you not married?" Jake asked.

"Never found the right guy."

"Are you looking? Maybe the right guy is right in front of you, dancing with you."

"I hardly know you," she said smiling.

"Maybe you can get to know me."

"I think I would like that."

The song was finished and Clarice looked at Jake, his dark complexion and his brown eyes so intense. Not scary, but full of life and adventure. She could handle this. She had some bad relationships and this guy seemed so nice. Stranger first meetings had taken place she thought. It could just be the right guy. She knew she was blushing and she wanted to be in control of herself. But her better instincts were not taking hold. She would leave with Jake, leaving her girlfriends to fend for themselves. They had keys, right? She wanted to be with this man, this handsome and dark stranger that made her feel alive. She spoke to her friends and grabbed her jacket.

"Let's get out of here," she said.

Jake agreed and he was filled with the ego that had always driven him with women. Jake had once again found a beauty to satisfy his aching need. This night would be a good one. Jake knew he would be back late, but hey, Andres was at the Complexo and Carrianne will watch the Branch woman. Things would be okay. He was out on the town, and by god, he deserved it. Clarice had suggested going back to her father's rental before the girls came back. She had every intention of sleeping with this man. She was, in fact, quite taken by him.

From another table much further from theirs, a man had watched this whole scene taking place. He had kept the pictures Andy had given him and recognized Jake Benson. The Martinez girl could not be far away. All Brian Stowe had to do was follow this guy around for a bit. He would get to the bottom of this story. Marx was probably already back in the states and he had a lot on his plate. Brian was dead set on coming through for Andy. As they got up to leave Brian was careful not to be noticed. He followed them out the door from a proper distance. Brian Stowe was going to follow, not too closely but without his car and on foot, Brian was good at staying concealed. This is a timing thing here and Brian had to be patient. He wanted Jake to reveal Carrianne, and maybe, just maybe, reveal Branch to him on this night. He would follow and when the timing was right, he would find what he was looking for. He was feeling that Andy's hunch was right.

Arm in arm, Clarice and her new love interest Jake Benson, were walking and carrying on a conversation. From behind them, Brian could see her head leaning into Jake's shoulder. They seemingly were getting along really well and they would soon be at the villa. Brian turned around quickly as he thought he had heard something. Not wanting to lose sight of his suspect, he returned his gaze to sight in the couple again. He could see her fumbling around for her key to the front entrance. He froze for a second, thinking that if they went inside, he would be out here waiting a while. He looked for a place out of the way that would provide some cover and spotted a group of hedges that he could be near if someone would walk by. There was a park bench right in front of the hedgerow that he could at least sit down for a while. He thought as he sat down; *this may or may not be the place. The villa would be a good spot to hide Branch but she had the key. Obviously, it can't be right. The Benson kid was just trying to get some action before he went back. He would have to wait for him to come out. I'll call Andy while I am waiting. I really feel bad for him. First, he loses his partner to prison and her replacement is murdered. I'm curious as to what is going on. Is it connected to Benson and these people? His girlfriend, Carrianne, wouldn't like it one bit if she knew what this guy was up to. Should have gotten a picture. I will when they come out, yeah, I'll get a couple pictures of the cheater...*Suddenly Brian was gasping for air as a wire was around his neck. The strength of the man squeezing the wire garrote around his neck felt like two men. Brian reached for his gun but his lack of oxygen made him clumsy and he was losing all sense of balance and coordination. The man squeezed harder and Brian could feel himself losing consciousness and slowly his knees began to buckle and the very last thing former FBI agent Brian Stowe felt in his life on earth was his lungs exploding for lack of air.

Andres Montoya looked down at his prey. He stuck the garrote in his pocket and dragged the agent into the bushes and then hoisted him over his shoulder and carried him to his parked car. He threw him in the back of the SUV. He picked up his phone and called his contact in the Complexo to take care of the car and this body. Andres had taken the keys and phone from the dead agent and said he could meet his contact with the body and get him the keys and let him know where the car was.

"Chop the car and trash it. Make sure it's not found ever. Take the body out in my boat and sink it. I don't think anyone will see you. Mine is the only boat there right now. Call me when it is done."

Andres hung up and went to meet the contact. He would deal with Jake when he got back. He would only be gone an hour and surely Jake's fun evening would not be over yet. Andres sped off with the body in the back...

Jake stood facing Clarice in her room. She was nearly undressed as she smiled ever so seductively at him. Jake could feel his heart pulsating quickly. She was so beautiful and her lips were glossy and just aching to be kissed. He put his arms around her and could feel her own intense heat radiating from her body. He would not resist, he had time and he had this need for so long. Their lips met and Jake Benson felt the fire in Clarice's lips. They had both needed this and they were so into the moment. They made love for an hour and Jake was fully satisfied. Clarice was looking up at the ceiling fan and glowing on the inside. *This man, this Jake Benson, he is so full of life and energy. I know I don't know him, but he is giving and he knows what a woman wants. This is too good to be true!*

Jake knew he needed to get back. He just couldn't leave his sister to all the duty. He began to dress and Clarice said, "Please, can't you stay?"

"I can't, I really want to but I have a text and something with my business came up," Jake lied.

"Will I see you again?" Clarice asked.

"Here is my number, I will be here for a few more days. When we are back in the states, we can meet up again. Tonight, was magic and I really do want to see you again," Jake said, and that was not a lie.

She gave him her number and Jake Benson, was on his way out of the villa. His steps were light and his need had been fulfilled. He was headed back to his car which was not far from the bar. He felt light, filled with a sense that maybe, just maybe he had found someone with whom he could actually have a relationship. His head was empty with no thoughts except her hair, her eyes, and her fragrance. It was impossible that he would find someone that so easily melted into his soul. He turned the last corner and from the dark of the alleyway came the huge hand that grabbed him by the scruff of the neck. The hand quickly pulled him into the darkness and Jake recognized the voice...

CHAPTER 16

I called Katy, which I really didn't want to do for some time, but warned her that she may get a visit from the police. I told her that I couldn't come over just yet, but that I was once again involved in something that could be dangerous.

"You just need to stay clear of me for a while," I said. "This may take some time, but call me if you see or hear anything suspicious. Keep your doors locked, carry your weapon, and don't talk to anyone you don't know."

"Mike, you are really scaring me. Is it her? Is she back?"

"I don't think that right now, but it could happen. Like I said, you see anything, call me."

I hung up the phone and could not help but think of Andy Marx and his next duty of telling Mo's aunt what had happened. *I don't know if I could do that. But I have been through something like it. It brings back the memory of Sheila once more and why, why in the world she would take her life? Then I think of Breanne and Branch and how they were so evil. Did they force her to do it? It was just something I couldn't fathom, but I also could not dismiss it...I have to lay down for just a minute, I'm feeling exhausted and overwhelmed...need sleep...*

My dream was real, vivid and the same cast was playing out the scene. Tied to a post, the three of us, Katy, Marx and myself, heads bent over with our faces unrecognizable. We had been beaten, and dried blood and bruising was all that was there. I tried to speak but nothing came out. I could hear them but, was that Jake, Jake Benson? Andrea Stephenson, surely not her, and that large man, who was he? They began to laugh and they took their guns out and pointed them at us an inch from each of our heads.

"It's the last time they will interfere," they said.

"These are the last three, the hunt will be over and SHE will have been avenged," the large man blurted out.

"HOLD IT RIGHT THERE!" the voice that I knew, the voice that haunted me daily screamed out. "This was my hunt, this was for me. Cut them loose, now! I'll give you twenty seconds, run as fast as you can because one by one I will cut you down."

The large man cut all three of us loose and we staggered a bit not able to gain our balance.

"RUN I SAID!"

With that we ran. We ran and ran over hills and through valleys. The large man and SHE was chasing us. She finally caught Katy and gunned her down. Marx was next. I kept running, I couldn't stop, I had to keep going. My lungs were about to burst in the cold air...

I awoke from the nightmare startled by the phone ringing. Trying to get my bearings I answered.

"Mike, this is Andy. I have been to Mo's aunt to let her know. It was very painful. She cried and was overwhelmed. He was all the poor woman had left. The staff there had to medicate her."

"Uh, yeah. Um..."

"Parsons, are you okay?"

"Yeah, just had a bad dream right before you called," I said.

"Look, come over to my place in an hour," Marx said. "I want to talk to you about all this that has happened. We have so many loose ends to tie up. I need a friend and with Mo, there will be several things I need to get done for him. When the funeral is done, Branch will be back and the hunt will be on for us. We have to get prepared. Some things are coming together in my mind and we have to be prepared. This is one very dangerous situation."

"Alright," I answered. With that I hung up the phone.

What in the hell is going on? Why in the world has my life become such a pressure cooker? The first episode was so frightening that no one could possibly have imagined this all happening again. I could have stayed away. I could have stayed out of this mess. But, I had let my curiosity get the best of me. I always thought I had to know everything. But now I see, that there are some things that one should never know. Am I doing this for the Marx's friendship? Or is Branch the key? I just can't put this away and Katy, Marx and I know how dangerous the people were that we dealt with. I have a feeling in my gut, which talks to me a lot these days, that the people we are about to be dealing with are much more dangerous.

I got to Marx's place and it had been only a short time since Mo's death. He let me in and we both sat across from each other with heads bowed. It seemed to be silent for a few minutes as it was hard for Marx to find his voice. At last, he spoke.

"Well, if you didn't know the obvious, you do now. We are dealing with some very rough people. I am sure this is related to the drug issues we dealt with in the last case. Stripping down the layers and finding the head of the crew is the only way we can solve this," he started.

"I do know and, yes, not actually being in law enforcement, I feel ill-equipped to keep going forward with this," I replied.

"I understand but consider this; you are still one of the only people besides me that know Branch well. We both know how mentally unstable she is, and if you think she's not coming for us at some point, then you are being naïve."

"I get it, but I'm not prepared to help in the physical ways that trained people can. I am not the guy that can shoot, fight or even kill someone when I would have to. I'm not made that way."

"Don't mean to be rude here, my friend, but you better find a way. You better believe that you may face her again, you may not even know who she is which could make it that much more dangerous. You need some training and I will do that."

Marx picked up his phone and dialed his friend Brian again. Again, there was no ring, no nothing.

"Something's up with Brian. I know it's not good. I need to call the FBI, but I can't because I was not supposed to tell anyone I went with him to Brazil. I am afraid he is missing, or maybe worse, dead."

"Look, you can't hide from the FBI on this, they will know soon enough," I said. "They will try contacting him too. He will be considered missing."

"Yeah, okay, I will call them soon. But you, what

about you? Are you willing to let me train you, at least with the gun? I can help you at least feel more confident with that and then teach you some self-defense."

"Alright, I guess so," I said. "But there is one more thing, well...two. One, let's wait until after MO's funeral. Two, I have to see that Katy gets protected too. Somehow I have gotten her into this mess and I don't think Branch and her mob will stop with me and you."

"Okay, it's a deal. You and me get your training done and we protect Katy. We three are in this together. We can't let one another down here."

"No, no, we can't..."

CHAPTER 17

The next few days were a whirlwind. I went to Mo's funeral with Andy. It was a sad occasion and although I barely got to know him, he seemed like a really good guy and dedicated cop. I called Katy once and talked with her, even though I said I wouldn't do that. Marx also took me to the shooting range where I was learning how to handle myself with my hand gun. I improved a little each day, but I often wondered how I would be if I was ever face with the prospect of using it under pressure. Marx told me that the key was to have a steady trigger hand and make sure that I supported it with my left hand to keep it steady and to "squeeze" the trigger and not "pull" it.

Marx was mystified about his friend Brian. He was really worried that Brian had met some ugly death, because there was no sign of him nor was he answering the phone. Marx was sure he needed to go back to Rio to find him.

Marx called at 10 pm on Saturday and I answered on the first ring. "Hey. Andy, what's up?"

"Look, you did get a passport, right?" he asked.

"Yes, got one last week," I replied.

"Good, we need to make a trip together. I just have to check out Brian. I am really worried that asking him into this mess, I might have gotten him hurt. I just can't seem to get a break here. I am up to my ears in both of these cases and now I am becoming obsessed."

My inner voice was wanting to say no. I am not going with some obsessed cop to Brazil to find who knows what and possibly get killed myself. I knew what kind of pressure he was under and after all we had been through, I owed much to Detective Marx.

"Okay, look, I will go, but I am hesitant to get this far into this matter, but I think I owe you."

"You don't have to," Marx said. "I know what I want and I just think that when I am hunting for HER, that you have the instincts and may just know her about as well as I do. I do think we can do this together."

"I will go."

"Good, I booked two tickets for tomorrow, I knew you wouldn't let me down."

"I guess we're partners now," I said.

"Yes, silent partners. We are going rogue."

———▲———

I hung up the phone and began to think and pack at the same time.

I may be in this way over my head. I just want to help but will I really just be a liability? What am I leaving behind? What else should I wrap up before I go? I will need to call Katy, and then there is the

Joanna thing...Joanna Presley. Call her tonight or when I get back? There is still something about her that is intriguing, something about her that makes me still curious.

I called Katy and reminded her to be very careful. I told her I was going with Marx and said we would be out of the country. I reassured her I would be back in a few days and that she should keep her doors locked. Next, I called administration and got a leave of absence with a wild story of how a relative out of the country needed some legal help and advice. My next call was to Joanna Presley. I wanted to let her know that I wanted to see her again, but that I would be out of the country a few days and would call her when I returned.

I dialed the number that Ed had given me and she answered on the second ring.

"Hello," her voice a bit apprehensive.

"Joanna, hi, this is Mike Parsons. We met for dinner last week with the group. I know this is kind of short notice, but I have to leave the country to help a friend with a legal dealing in Brazil. I should be back in a few days and was wondering if I might be able to take you to dinner when I get back. Certainly, that would depend on your schedule."

"I think I would like that. I did talk to Ed and I am sorry that I gave you a bad first impression," she said. "I was just thinking that maybe if it was just us and not around such a big group, we would have a little time to talk and get to know each other. Maybe we could sort of start over?" Joanna asked with a hopeful tone.

"Sure, that would be great. How about when I return, I give you a call and you can be thinking of a place you like and I will think of a place I like and we can pick one of those?"

"That sounds really good. Have a safe trip and I will be looking forward to your call when you get back," she replied.

"I will be looking forward to it too."

Hanging up the phone I couldn't help but remember that first time Ed put us together. She was seated across from me and her face and her smile were so clear and so fresh. Here conversations with everyone except me, had me wanting to butt in and to have her notice me and talk to me. But it seemed like I was watching from afar and that in my mind I knew that this person was going to be someone that was so different for me. Someone that just might, if things go well, bring this guy Mike Parsons out of the depths of despair. Maybe I was over-thinking this thing. But there was something about Joanna Presley that I couldn't put away. There was something in her face and her smile that just defined sincerity and truth. Something was there that made me feel that I was redeemable. Yes, it was right to call her, but maybe we should just save a date to run away together and get away from all this crazy stuff. But, look, you're jumping the gun again and getting way ahead of yourself. Take it slow, just take it slow...

I woke up Wednesday morning to a blaring alarm. I shut it off and knew I had to shower and get ready for the trip. I was packed and ready to go and stumbled to the bathroom and checked the stubble on my aging face. *Not old yet but you are getting there Mikey. I called myself Mikey? I hate that name. It is a bit of the reminder of HER, yeah HER. Why hasn't the thought of the two faces of Allison Branch left me? One, the face of an angel that was so soft and warm and gentle. The other, the angry, demonic face of the one that swore to end my life. I can see them both, still see them side by side...*

I shook my head and then again saw the stubbled face of an aging Mike Parsons in the mirror. After a shower I got dressed and called my brother, James. We had not talked for a couple of weeks. My brother had always kept in touch but lately we were having trouble finding the time for each other. Families do that sometimes. The business of immediate families sometimes doesn't intersect with what is happening in life at the time.

"James, hey this is Mike. How are things going?" I asked.

"Hey Mike, just getting ready to go to work. Things are good here. Kids are off school today and Monica is taking them to the hockey rink as the boy has practice and Janie wants to go skate with a couple of friends. How's it going for you?"

"Well, I got involved with Andy over time and we were talking about a case he is on, and how it was intersecting into another case. I know you heard about Branch's escape and he feels that somehow, they are connected. It's kind of complicated. I really want to talk about it, but I am leaving this morning on a trip and wanted to call you before I left."

"Look, you don't need to get involved in the police matters again. I know you like Andy and all, and so do I, but you need to stay away from that police business. I don't want to be going to hospitals anymore or chasing you around the countryside."

"Yeah, I know, but, hey, I will be back in a few days and I'd like to share with you what is going on in my world right now. I think I am getting better and there is a woman I am going to ask out when I get back."

"Oh, yeah?" he said. "Well, good for you brother. Where is she from?"

"She teaches at the university with me. I see her at

meetings but never really noticed her before but Ed is the one that sort of set us up for the first time. It was awkward, as is usual for me, but I asked her to dinner when I get back. There were just a lot of people around last time, and maybe a little more intimate setting will help us get to know each other better."

"Maybe so, brother. But keep it slow, you have been through a lot, make sure you just take your time with it," he said just like fatherly advice from my little brother that James liked to give.

"I will, but listen, I'll call you when I get back."

I really didn't tell James what I was doing or where I was going. I knew he would try to talk me out of it and somehow, I wished that would happen. I wasn't really sure how much I wanted to go to Brazil with Andy. But, the curiosity was killing me and I was wondering all the time, what was going on in the mind of Allison Branch? Would we find her and would we even recognize her? Would we be too late and miss her? This is a stab in the dark, but it is too late and the minds of two people that work similarly on the gut feel, Andy Marx and I, were on the same trail. We weren't going to be happy until the conclusion of this crazy, dangerous affair was put to rest. Yes, it was like turning the crank on the box hearing the nice little music that played, only to have that crazy clown jump out of the box staring at you with that crazy face! Surprise!!

CHAPTER 18

Revenge- the primitive, destructive and mostly violent response to anger, injury, and humiliation.

C arrianne and Allison had a long conversation by the pool. They had decided to return to their rooms. Carrianne had learned many things about Allison, now known as Lynnette Huber, in her new identity bought and paid for by the cartel. Allison Branch had now disappeared in Lynnette Huber's mind. Carrianne had learned that Lynnette Huber was a simple Midwesterner, who found out early in life that she was without the attention she needed so much. Being raised by her mother, Lynnette had been devoid of the father she so desperately needed and the discipline that could have served her much better. The new goal for Lynnette Huber was to transform the shame and humiliation that had haunted her young adult life into pride that she had righted all the wrongs. As Lynette told Carrianne about her prior life,

105

she knew in her heart that her losses were permanent and no matter how hard she tried, no revenge could ever take the place of those losses.

Carrianne knew that remorse for something could not be coerced. Allison Branch, aka Lynnette Huber, would only try to defend the honor of her person. Lynnette obtained the mantel of victim long before she would seek her revenge. She was the victim of the incredibly shallow Mike Parsons. She was the victim of her always perfect partner, Andy Marx. She was victim to the loss of her friend, Breanne Jackson. She was the victim of her father never being there. Her rage was from her painful adolescence and lack of nurturing, and these factors turned her into a hunter, one who will now forever be entrenched in her pursuit of the only thing that is left to ease her pain. It was her intention to kill before, but now it was becoming all-encompassing. Carrianne knew these things, because she had also known the same humiliation but for different reasons. She knew that all Lynnette had to do is ask, and she would certainly play on her team.

They got back to their rooms and Carrianne told Lynnette that she would wait up for Julio. Lynnette Huber closed her door and walked into her room to change.

Tomorrow would be the day, she thought. I can finally see what the good doctor had done. She dropped her towel and took off her suit. She stopped to stare at her own perfect lines of her fit body. The body she had so willingly given to Mike Parsons. The one who had so totally refused her, but yet the one that she cared for so much. He just was that one guy, that one who could make me feel that I was special. Why can't anyone see or recognize the conscious dreaming that was taking place in me? The boiling mentality, the rage that is already starting to build up inside me? What I wished for was almost what it was, I was almost there, but the wrongs HAD to be turned into rights, didn't they? He had to pay for his rejection of me, when all he needed to do was love me. Just love me...

She walked into the shower and carefully cleaned up without getting any of the bandages wet. The water felt warm and safe and she stood in for several minutes still thinking...*and then there is Marx, the cool, sophisticated, ex-partner that I tried to kill. He thought he was better, he always did. His confidence should never have been used to stomp on my pride. He did it on purpose and I hate him too. He will also pay the price. He won't know me, he won't see me, he will never even know what hit him. He still doesn't realize who he is dealing with! Mr. Smart Guy, Mr. Head of the Class, is going to pay for all the mistakes he never knew he was making with me. I was better, I was meant to be first, not second. He will get his in the end. He should have died before but this time, he doesn't get a fair game. He is getting a rigged game. One where I hold all the cards and he cannot win! Not this time, not this time...*

She turned off the shower and toweled off. She was tired and ready for sleep. She lay down on the bed and began to feel sleepy. She quickly dozed off and was sent into a deep sleep...

Carrianne heard the door handle turn and in walked Julio from his amazing night out and right behind him was their best friend, Andres. She shut the door behind him and lit into Julio. "You are the most stupid person I think I know. You can't just let your libido control what you do, especially in this situation. Now, we have issues and you just screwed up!"

"What?" Julio gestured with his palms face up. "I

just go out for a few hours and it's like I stole from you or something."

Andres responded by backhanding Julio in the face. "You are young and very stupid. You just have been seen out by many people who can probably identify you. Then you hook up with this American, that also can put the finger on you. You must be out of your mind!"

"But Andres..."

"No buts here. We have problems. I had to kill a man who was tracking your sorry ass. Had to get rid of the body. Then you hook up with this girl. She needs to be disposed of as well. Can't you see what kind of position you have put us in?" Andres said as his nostrils were flaring, showing his intense anger. It was something anyone didn't want to provoke in him. "Get your things together and we are leaving tonight. I will pull the car in to the lot. You let the girls go out first. I'm going to wake up Branch, and then then go get the car. Damn, you're going to get us killed someday, Julio."

Julio looked down and would not look Andres in the eye. He was tough but certainly no match for Andres. He looked at Carrianne who shot him a look of disapproval.

"Okay, I 'm sorry. But the girl, don't hurt her."

And with that, Julio dropped his head. He knew what was in store for the tourista.

Marx and I landed in Brazil at the Santo Dumont Airport. From there we would take our rental car to the main area we would search. But where to start? Marx knew a bit as he had planned with his buddy Brian where to start. We headed to our hotel and began to unpack the few things we had brought with us.

After unloading our things, we headed into town. We began to check the bars, but as one would guess, we were having no luck with the locals. We had a picture of Branch, Jake, and Carrianne, but nothing else to actually go on. We had spent three hours checking with barkeeps, waitresses or anyone else that would talk at all. Most people had heard or seen nothing of the people we showed them. We finally got lucky at a place called Largo do Guimaraes. We showed one waitress a picture of Jake.

"Oh yes, he was here last night. Danced with a girl, an American girl. Very pretty. He left with her around I'd say 10:00 pm," the young waitress said.

Marx pulled out Carrianne's picture. "Was it this one?" he asked.

"No," she said. "She had much lighter skin and light hair. Not as dark as the one in your picture."

"I see," Andy said. "Do you know by any chance where they may have gone?"

"No, but the man, he said he was staying at the Hotel Santa Teresa."

"Okay, thanks. You've been a big help."

Andy left a tip and we headed to the hotel. It was a lucky break that would put us on the trail of Jake and Carrianne Benson and possibly Branch. I didn't think we would get this lucky, but we got in the car and headed to the hotel. I looked at Andy and for the first time since I knew him, I could see the worry and the lines in a young face that never seemed to tire.

"You okay, Andy?" I asked thinking that he would just brush it off.

"No, I'm not," he said. "These cases are getting to me. I have a lot on my plate and I have this gruesome feeling that something bad happened to Brian. I don't know if we find them or not, but I wish we had more help. Too many questions and I am feeling we bit off more than we can chew here."

"What do we need to do?"

"Look, Mike, you have the gun I gave you. The holster and gun, strap it on and don't pull it on anyone until I tell you. We go into the hotel, ask the front desk if they have seen these people. If we have to go their room and break in, we ask for local help," Andy said with a grim look that gave me the goosebumps. *Hey, I'm a college teacher not a trained cop here.*

We pulled up at the Santa Teresa about 4 PM. Andy parked the car and we went up the front steps and into the lobby. Andy calmly walked up to the front desk and showed his badge.

"I'm an American looking for these people," he said as he showed the pictures of Jake and Carrianne. "Did they happen to stay here?"

The male desk clerk looked at the pictures of the two and replied," Yes, these two did stay here."

"How about this one?" he asked as he pulled out the picture of Branch. "Was this person with them?"

"I did not see this one," the clerk said. "They did have another woman with them, but she had bandages on her face and wore a scarf. I could not say it was this person or not."

"Are they here right now?" Andy asked as the look on his face seemed to intensify.

"I'm afraid they checked out early this morning."

I looked at Andy and could tell he was thinking fast. He was on to something and he was now in mode to follow quickly. He asked the clerk if there were cameras on the front desk. The clerk said there was and he would check with his boss to see if we could look at them. He returned shortly and took us to the back room where the manager let us view the tape of the night before.

We sat waiting for the footage to come up. It was just showing several people checking in at high speed until Andy barked out;

"There, those three. I think that is who we are looking for," Andy said as he stood up to be closer to the monitor. "That third lady, you said she had bandages?"

"Yes," the clerk replied. "She and that girl in the picture did go to the pool together last night. The guy, he came in late. He had left earlier in the evening by himself."

"Wait, pause it right there. That big guy walking past them with bags, who is he?"

"I don't know sir, but they were only checked in with three names, it was as I have it, Jake Benson, Carrianne Martinez, and let's see, hmmm, Ms. Anna Jones. There is no fourth person."

"Can you print me out a still shot of the big guy. It is hard to see his face, but at least it is something to go on."

"Yes sir, I can do that"

"Thank you, you have been very helpful."

Andy and I left the hotel and went quickly to the car. He quickly made two calls, one to the local police and one to the home precinct. He told the local police of his missing friend, Brian, and that he would come by there to make the report. He would let them know he is headed back to the states following a case and that he had a friend that was missing.

"Alright, Mike, we're headed to the police station to make the missing report on Brian. I think we have what we are looking for, but they are way ahead of us. We just missed them and we can't stay long if we hope to catch up. They could possibly be back in the states already. It's going to take us a while but I filled them in at the precinct of what may be going on and to check the Florida airports and all the local airports as well."

"When I saw Branch or Jones or whoever she is, I just knew, it had to be her. We are not going to recognize her. I'm really worried for you, for me and for Katy. Whoever these people are, they are playing to win, they don't play to lose."

"I get it, for sure. But listen, this has to end. For us, for me and you, and everyone else involved, you hold an important key to nabbing her again. For all I know about her, I probably know less than you. There is a strong feeling of something there, something she won't let go. She will show herself, but where and when will be a difficult thing to predict. She won't stay hidden forever. You can't trust anyone."

With that we went to the police station to file a missing person report and it took Andy longer than he wanted it to. We went to airport and tried to get the next flight out, all the while knowing that they were getting time on us. It was valuable time that would be hard to make up, even if Andy had notified all the stateside authorities of what was going on. They could be about anywhere...

It took us three hours to catch a flight, and it was again, just a hunch that Allison Branch would show up in the states. But why would they use that name in the states, or would they. She was smart and the people she worked for were no dummies. This would certainly be another chapter in my life that I had no idea of how it would turn out. I had to ask myself on the plane back, *how in the world does my life put me in these crazy positions? No one can draw this up. It is just too crazy and with that I fell asleep and drifted off to another one of my nightmares...and of course SHE was in it.*

CHAPTER 19

Allison Branch was back in the states. She was riding with Andres in his 18-wheeler headed back to his farm in Wisconsin. Today they would stop somewhere along the way so that she could finally take the bandages off and inspect her new identity.

They had talked little. John Middleton was a quiet man and Allison was lost in her own thoughts. It was only the two of them as Carrianne and Jake had stayed behind in Brazil so that they could leave for the states on another day. Middleton had given Jake the strict orders that his new friend Clarice was to be eliminated. Jake did not like this. He had killed before but it was other men and he never had to snuff out a woman, especially one that had earned his heart strings.

Allison's mind drifted back to the bar, the Sidecar, where she was having a drink with one Mike Parsons.

"Mike, do you believe in destiny? she asked. "You

know, like when you meet a guy and you really like him...a lot? You just know that meeting was just meant to be. Do you believe in that or not?"

"Well, I never do when I meet a guy."

"You know what I mean, Mike. Do you believe?"

"Well, that depends. Sometimes I do, but there always seems to be a black cloud that follows me around. It tends to rain on my destiny, at least it has before."

Ha ha ha. You have no idea how much the damn black cloud is about to rain on you! He was such a smart ass how could I have wanted him like that? He has no idea that the depths of my revenge has no bottom. How much I hate him has no ceiling. To him it was all luck. To me it was destiny. He has no idea how bad his luck is going to get. All he had to do was pick me, not reject me. How could he? My hunt for all of them will come to a close and I will no longer be a victim, but the winner! Katy, Marx, and that man, that man that I couldn't get out of my head...Parsons!

Tears were starting to well up in her eyes. Andres saw this as she was staring straight ahead through the windshield of the truck.

"You okay?" he asked.

She didn't answer.

"Allison, hey, are you alright?"

"Oh, sorry, yeah sure, I'm okay. I was just thinking that maybe we should stop and get some rest. I really am anxious to see what is underneath the bandages."

"Sure thing, we'll stop at the next fuel stop and then find rooms. I'll let you have some privacy to inspect your new face," he said knowing that he needed to keep his distance from her. She could never overpower him. Yet, he didn't trust her. She was smart and sneaky. There was something about her that could lure you in and then like a shadow she would just be there sometime to slit your throat. John Middleton feared no man, but he feared this woman. He studied her eyes and then just had to look away. What is it in those eyes? Something bad, something dangerous lived in there and he knew to keep his focus when he was around her...but those eyes, they hold you...

Allison went to her room and Andres to his. They were back in the states now. She quickly went to the mirror and suddenly froze. It was time to take off the bandages and see the good doctor's handiwork. She slowly peeled away the bandages that were in their last stages of protection. As it is true with most people who have had facial plastic surgery, the initial shock would come with the new face viewed for the first time. As the bandages peeled away, she could see the skin as it was smooth and no scars to see so far. She finally got to the bottom layer and very soon she would have it all revealed. She turned away from the mirror to peel off the last of it and was ready to slowly turn and face her new identity.

In the mirror, her reflection made her freeze. What she saw was stunning indeed. Her reflection was looking back at her, and even though it was someone she did not know, it was someone whom she was instantly attracted to. Her new face was beautiful, maybe even more so than what God had given her. A smile slowly began to creep onto her face. The shock she had prepared for never came. The good doctor could not have done better for her personal ego! Although the chin, cheeks and jaw lines of her face were different and gave her the new identity, there was something there that she so desperately wanted to keep. And Glory Hallelujah! There they were, the weapons she had used all her life, those eyes. Those eyes that hold you...

We hit the ground and I awoke from the dream. We were now in Miami and would catch the connecting flight back to Wisconsin. We needed a home base to start this over. We couldn't get on the trail until we re-capped all the events that had happened and to get a line on some things. We were headed back to home base and for some strange reason, I was feeling we were heading in the right direction. I felt deep in my gut that she would find us before we found her.

Carrianne was back in Brazil with Jake. They had gone to visit her mother in the slums. After the visit, Jake had known that Andres might have taken care of Ms. Clarice. They too knew, that they must leave as well. Carrianne had thought often of her new friend, Allison Branch. She was taken with the idea of helping her. Carrianne liked her and there was something about being a partner to her in this idea of revenge that was appealing to her. She put it in the back of her mind for now. As Andres had told her, she must be the one to hold things together for her and Jake. Jake had slipped up more than once lately and Andres trusted her more than Jake. She would be the stronger one, she would control his impulses and get him back on track. Tomorrow they would be back in the states but they would have to be careful as Andres would come for them and all the airports had their picture. Back in Wisconsin, the risks were going to be much higher. Andres would protect them and let them stay with him. He had promised their mother to take care of them. He had always kept that promise.

Carrianne thought to herself that she would love to tag along with Allison, to be her partner and learn the ways of the police as she would need those skills. It intrigued her, but who would watch her crazy brother to make sure that he didn't mess up and get himself killed with his impulsiveness? So many things going through her head and so many possibilities. Andres would be back soon and then her life would soon be back in focus. They would be back in America by the end of the week.

They met their contact that Andres had arranged and were going to be transported to their pickup spot airfield where they originally landed on the trip here. Their job was done and they had protected Allison Branch and made her a new identity. They would be rewarded well and financially, Carrianne would be very well set. But in this cartel, the getting in was easy but the getting out was near impossible. She longed for a new and different life, but how? Maybe her new best friend Allison could help her, give her a plan. Allison was crafty and Carrianne liked that. Liked it so much that maybe Allison was her new hero? But Jake...what about Jake?

_____

We landed finally and our trip was over. We had so much to do, so much to go over, but we were both exhausted. Andy was looking worse to me. His eyes had become puffy from worry and lack of sleep.

"Hey Andy, what do we do next?" I asked.

"I don't know about you partner, but we can't wait too long but I'm trashed. I need to start tomorrow."

"Yeah, that's right. But you know, I've had this thought that she won't be able to contain herself. That she won't be disciplined enough to let us hunt her. I think she will be on the hunt quickly," I said.

"You may be right, partner, but in working with her I can tell you this much, she has a way of getting places that many times I thought were not possible. She might be the sneakiest cop I ever worked with."

"What time do we start tomorrow?"

"Don't you have a job?"

"Yes, but I took a month off. It may be one of the craziest months of my life, but I am ready to get on this and maybe we can see her apprehended."

"Okay, partner, get some sleep and get to my office by 6:00 am. Don't be late we have a lot to do."

"Got it."

He called me partner. Am I a partner now with smart-ass Andy, which I regretted calling him that earlier. Being his partner actually is an honor and I can't let this guy down. He was a part in saving my life as well as my brother James. Now I am driving home to my condo and although I need rest, I don't know if I can sleep. Where is she? What is she doing? Is she plotting my murder? Marx's murder? Is she going to hurt Katy? Where is Oscar Stephenson? Who is that big guy in the surveillance video? With my mind spinning, I had one last thought. Am I getting better? Or am I headed for another setback? Surely my mind had better thoughts and I was better to people. Was I coming around heading in the right direction or would I fall once again to my own needs and desires? What is holding me back, what is keeping me from committing to a peaceful existence like other people I respected and admired? Too many questions and not enough answers.

I turned the key to my condo and stepped inside.

CHAPTER 20

I awoke the next morning and had that first cup of coffee. Taking this sabbatical was a new thing to me. I was used to working most days and these days off, well, they really wouldn't be days off. Today I was meeting with Marx and there was a lot to go over. I went to shave and I couldn't help thinking, as I stared in the mirror, of all the circumstances that had affected my life in such a strange way. Part of me wanted to just back out and stop all this detective stuff. I didn't know if this was right for me. I hadn't straightened out Mike Parsons yet, much less try to figure out everyone else.

The one thing that still eats away at me is Branch. I just couldn't let go of wanting to know what drove her, what made her into what she was. It was strange that she could haunt me in a couple of ways. She could appear in a thought, reminding me of how I fell hard for her. The hair, the face and the smoothness of her skin were so vivid in my senses. But so was the anger, the kidnapping and the violence she seemed so incapable of committing.

I got in the car and drove and during the drive I listened to a local news station. A man came on and started the story of the missing escapee from the state prison. The former detective, Allison Branch, and the hunt for her that now seemed mysterious as she had left no trail. A chill came across my back thinking of where and how I would meet up with her again. I would not know her, I wouldn't recognize her, but I was certain that when she did appear in my life again, it would not be for fun and games. The bad thing was, if Marx was right, I would never see it coming.

I pulled into Marx's place and shut off the engine. I locked the car and headed up the steps to his home. I rang the bell and he answered, looking like hell, he handed me a cup of coffee and we went to the kitchen table. Spread out across the table were photos and documents in neat separate piles. He had some connecting photos taped to a white board on an easel. This looked like a guy that didn't get much sleep last night due to the work he was doing at home.

"Looks like you've been at it pretty hard, my friend," I said still gazing at all the photos.

"I haven't gotten much sleep," he replied. "I have been trying to make our discussion this morning easier by getting some of this organized. We need to really recap this and see if there is something that we missed."

Okay, then," I said taking a sip of the strong coffee he had made. "No reason to slow down now, let's get to the story."

I looked hard at the white board with pictures and began to be the educator and organized person that I was and on my legal pad wrote Branch on one side and Stephenson on the other.

"Branch is one investigation, Stephenson is another investigation," I said taking another sip of coffee. "Let's separate the other characters to each side. Then we have us and how we connect to both sides"

"Good idea," Andy said as he took the pictures and taped them to the right and left side of the white board.

"First, let's take Branch," I said and wrote her name on the left side of my paper and circled it. I made some arrows coming off the circle. "Who in this case is connected to her?"

"Well," Marx began, "you have the three of us, Katy, you and me. We are the victims in the original case. Then you have Breanne, who is dead, my new partner Mo, who is dead, my friend Brian who is missing, and the prison guard, Henry Hannah, who is missing."

I wrote their names and circled each with arrows pointing to Branch. I left Brian off that list and put his name connected to us. Marx arranged the pictures to match my graph.

"Next, there is Jake Benson and Carrianne Martinez who seem to be in the middle and connected to Stephenson in some way. But how?" I was looking at this and it didn't make sense to connect them to Branch. But something was telling me to leave them in the middle and they were a 'maybe' to draw arrows to Branch.

"Look, stopping there, I think there is some connection. I think you and I are seeing this. Hold onto that thought as we go through this a bit more," Andy said as his eyes were showing more intense study and thought.

"Now, the story is, as I see it, Branch has escaped, changed her identity, we think, and was helped by Jake and Carrianne. We see some big man helping them check in, so we know they are involved with him. The question is, where are they?" I said looking more at my paper and back to the pictures. "The big guy looks to be the one in charge of taking care of all of them. I think he's a carrier and taking them back and forth."

"My hunch is that there is something about this big guy that is starting to click. But who does he work for and what is his purpose?" asked Andy.

"It's the drugs, it has to be the drugs. But why help her escape, she was just a worker for them, just distributing and collecting. She was a cop on the inside that knew people and had connections to make the drug trade go. The kids are helping the big man, too. I just have that gut feeling. We need some background on Jake and Carrianne and this big guy, we have to find him."

I drew the arrows from Jake and Carrianne to Branch, too, and now we had the top level of our graph done. I also wrote "big guy" under Jake and Carrianne.

"Okay look, that takes care of Branch's side, but what about Stephenson?" I asked. "That is the side that is hard for me to get."

"Yeah, that is the hard part, but let's guess at that. You followed Andrea Stephenson Raines around and she did meet with a guy. That makes her a person of interest here. She's involved in some way, but as of yet, we are not sure how," Andy said.

I drew her name in under Stephenson, and put a few question marks between her and Jake and Carrianne. I was not sure but my thoughts were beginning to dovetail with Andy's. What we were starting to see was a cartel, somehow being run by the big guy and recruiting these kids, as well as Branch, to do all the work here in the states.

"We need more info from Brazil about which

cartels are producing the most trade here and who the Feds are following," Andy said.

We stared at our graph and then back up at the pictures. We have a few theories that are starting to make sense. These people would be hard to flush out. Getting Branch to surface would be near impossible. It seems crazy that all these people were involved in the same group. It seems maybe, at times, we were barking up the wrong tree. And yet, it could make sense.

An hour had already gone by and were still looking at the pictures silently. Neither one of us spoke but our eyes were moving from one photo, to the next. We were making theories in our heads. Silently, we played out each scenario and I had a feeling that we were starting to get somewhere. The key was where to begin and how in the world were we going to protect ourselves from this monster big man, and his invisible partner, Allison Branch, or whatever her new name would be? She was the most feared, the most dangerous, and the hardest to find, because when and if we see her, we will have no idea of who she is.

"I'm for the first time encouraged. I feel like we have some targets here. The easiest ones could be Jake and Carrianne as well as Andrea Raines. The one thing that is still out there is, where is Stephenson? Who is Oscar Stephenson and how does he fit in with all these characters, or does he? Is he even alive?" Andy asked.

"My guess is that he is. But I am not putting money on that at this point. For your sake, it would be better if he is connected to the case. But if not, you still have two separate cases," I replied.

"True, but if your gut is thinking like my gut, then this guy is involved in some way. I just don't know how. I have got to talk to Margaret and I know you didn't want me to, but she may know of a connection between Jerry and Oscar here that may lead us in the right direction," he said as he looked at me with a very serious look.

I really cared for my ex-mother-in-law as she had been through a lot. But I knew he was right.

"I could do it for you and that way, maybe we keep her out of the limelight and at the same time get the information we need?" I asked.

"Sure, I'm okay with that, but also we need to follow this Andrea woman a bit more. You go see Margaret and just ask off offhandedly if she knew this Oscar Stephenson. I can put another man on Andrea Stephenson Raines. Somewhere down the line she will connect a dot or two for us."

"Okay," I said as I looked once more at our graphs and pictures. "I'll head to Margaret's and I'll meet back with you."

"I need to go to the station and clock in and get back to you this afternoon. Let's meet about 3:00 back here." Andy said.

"Okay, gotcha. Thanks for the coffee. I'm beginning to like this work."

"Don't like it too much. I think we are headed for some rough stuff," Andy stated. "I think you need to be careful and be safe and don't forget your piece. Carry that gun with you all the time. You never know when she is going to show up."

"Yeah, see you later, Marx."

"Be careful, I mean it," he said.

"Sure," I replied as I headed for my car. It was cold and I started the engine and let it warm up a bit.

Yeah, be careful, Mike. Carry that piece with you all the time. You never know when she is going to show up, her or the big goon or anyone else that has it in for us. Katy, Marx and me are the three who could all be the possible targets of a drug cartel or one of the craziest people to ever walk the face of the earth, Allison Branch...

CHAPTER 21

I headed for Margaret's house and the idea had crossed my mind that Jerry knew Oscar Stephenson. I just didn't have an idea if it was business or drug related. This craziness of people who were in business and high-ranking positions involving themselves in the drug trade wasn't unimaginable. I just couldn't understand why they put themselves in the high-risk group when they already had some money and prestige? The only answer is greed. Greed and selfishness did funny things to people and why would I not know that better than most people. If I just stopped and looked back on my life, I could easily define the moments where I disregarded the feelings of others for my own gain. I am sure it wasn't money for me, but it was having the independence from moral obligation and the mentality of doing whatever I wanted without responsibility. To corrupt myself just for the sake of having no moral responsibility left me *thinking just what it was that I believed and what was inside me. What was I made of and where did my life begin to go wrong? When did that start to happen?*

I pulled into the driveway at Margaret's house. I had last seen her about a month ago. We had talked briefly over the phone a few times, as I always liked to check on her from time to time. She had lost a lot and her mental state was not always the best. Her doctors had kept her on medication for anxiety and depression.

I knocked on the door and waited. She opened the door and smiled a faint and whimsical smile that may have been from a brief flashback of better days when Sheila and I came here together.

"Hello, Mike," she said as she let me in to the house. "Please come on in to the living room and sit down. Can I get you something to drink?"

"Thanks Margaret, coffee's fine," I said trying to think in my mind how to start this line of questioning.

"What brings you over here today? It's been about a month or so since I've seen you."

"Yes, sorry I haven't checked in more. Are you doing well?"

"I'm pretty good. The days get depressing at times, but I am getting better all the time."

"That's good," I replied. "I've been busy and have been on a short sabbatical lately. I hesitated to come over to share with you what I am doing. But, I feel like I could always be honest with you and that you deserve to know this. I am working with Detective Marx on the Branch case. As I am sure you know, she has escaped and that we are trying to track her down. I didn't want to bring back the memories, but if it wasn't me doing this, it would have been Marx or another cop. I told Marx that I would rather do this and he allowed me to question you about something."

"Well, okay I suppose," she said as she looked somewhat puzzled as to how she could be of help.

"Marx asked me about a guy that Jerry may have known. His name was Oscar Stephenson and he disappeared about three years ago. Did you know Mr. Stephenson or do you know if Jerry knew him?"

Margaret's expression froze for just a second. The look was one of trying to recall or remember.

"Yes," she started. "Jerry had some friends at the club he played golf with. He did mention a guy named Oscar and said he was a bad golfer, but funny guy. Jerry said he had money, and liked to throw it around buying drinks for the club members at the bar. Jerry said that he wasn't married and didn't have a lot of family. So, we never got involved with him. I wouldn't know the guy if I saw him."

"I see," I replied. "Did he ever mention any business dealings with him?"

"No. Jerry never shared his business interest with me, as you know, he pretty much kept all his business dealings private. Does Detective Marx think he has something to do with Jerry and the drug trade?"

"It may be possible. I don't know how, but I have a funny feeling that Marx may be right," I said feeling that I was making Margaret uncomfortable. She had been through a lot already, but I had to press on.

"I think that there may be a connection, and that it may also connect to Branch. We don't know if Stephenson and Jerry were in this together, or if Stephenson was a victim of possibly knowing too much. But, we do have a few theories."

Margaret sat silent for a moment or two. I tried to formulate a couple of more questions, but I was feeling bad that I was making her once again familiar with her late husband's failings. I just had to ask a few more, but I was getting reluctant.

"Margaret, did Jerry ever speak of wanting to do business with Oscar and his company?"

"He rarely talked of business until things were going bad. I tried to ask him, but he never wanted to open up. But there was a phone call once that he took in his room as I felt he didn't want me to hear. I walked down the hall and the door to his room was slightly open. He was saying things to a person, I think her name was Andrea, yes, it was Andrea. Telling her that since both businesses were failing, it would be a good idea to attempt to join forces. I just assumed that he might discuss a merger."

Oh boy, here we go. That's the connection and the merger wasn't for their real business. I couldn't tell her the facts here, but it was looking more and more like the drug trade had sucked them both in. How do I ask this last question?

"Margaret, my last question may set you back a bit, but please understand I am trying to help Detective Marx. Do you think that Jerry had a mistress?" I asked immediately hating myself.

The look on her face when I asked was all I needed to see for an answer....

"Look," she began. "I had that thought when he was talking to this Andrea lady. He had left the house several nights, with no excuse and had come home drunk. He stayed late at work, no phone calls or anything to let me know. He got home at 12 or 1:00 am and that name kept coming to mind. I could never get the strength or will to confront him about it. The weakling that I am, I just let it go and was hoping it wasn't true. But, my heart was telling me something else."

Her eyes began to moisten with tears. I don't think there was a time when I felt worse. It just seemed like all I could do was make people cry. I just wanted to go home and take a shower and get rid of this feeling. It felt like Sheila's death all over again. I needed a drink and a scotch would be perfect. But I had to be better about that.

"If it wasn't me, it would be a stranger asking you these things and I thought it would be better for me to do it. I feel just terrible about this."

"It's not your fault. I know what you have to do. I try not to live it over and over in my head. When we lost Sheila, we just fell apart and there was nothing I could do to stop the snowball effect on our marriage. It was rolling too fast downhill," she said immediately bringing back to mind all the awkward feelings I had when my ex-wife committed suicide.

I felt so bad for this lady. I was feeling all the things once again that seemed to block me from getting better: the low self-worth, the awkwardness, and the inability to help anyone, much less myself. I knew it was time to leave but I had to let this woman know, that I would help, that I would see this through and that my visit would be followed with my promise to be here for her. She deserved that much from me.

"Margaret, please, anytime you need something call me. I'll be here for you. But in the meantime, please understand who we are dealing with here and be careful. Marx and I will get this solved, but if you hear anything or feel unsafe at any time, please give me a call."

"Yes, I will," she said, still trying to dry new tears. "Mike, I do understand what you have to do, but I want you to be careful too."

"I will, be safe and I will call soon."

With that, I walked out of the living room and to door and left Margaret. This was one day that I found myself once again hating myself. I was feeling, well...awkward.

CHAPTER 22

I dialed Marx, anxious to give him my new-found information on Andrea Stephenson Raines. I told him that Margaret thought that she was having some sort of affair with my ex-father-in-law. I gave him time to digest this information and then he spoke.

"Look, this Andrea must be followed and we have to question her. I'll send a guy to bring her in for questioning. She's important here and it's our first big break so far. Thanks, Mike."

"At least I am earning my keep in the case. But please, let's stay off Margaret for now. She has been through a lot here," I said.

"Sure...sure, we can leave her alone for now. But we need to put the full court press on Raines. She knows something and we are going to find out what happened to her brother," Marx replied. "I'll call you back after talking to her."

"You bet, I'll stay put until you call."

I hung up and thought about Andrea. What does

she know and who is the guy I saw her with? The two questions that need to be answered are still hanging in the wind. The guy was at least 55 or so, dark hair and graying at the temples. Perfect age for Andrea to date, but was it a date or was it business? I couldn't tell. If anyone can get to the bottom of this, Marx will. I keep seeing Raines as a key figure, but with Jerry, I just couldn't wrap my head around it. My ex father-in-law, involved in the drug trade, mixed up with who knows what kind of people, including my ex-lover Branch. It makes me feel Oscar Stephenson is in on this too, and that he is not really missing. But maybe he is dead and Branch is running the show now. There is also that giant hit man out there somewhere. What about those two kids? Where do they fit in? They are helping her somehow, but they would be crazy to come back here and show themselves. Damn her, why does she have to stay in my life?

I snapped out of my thought process and remembered I promised to call Joanna. I dialed her number.

"Hello," the sweet voice on the other end answered. Immediately I felt my head spin slightly as her voice had such a warm hint.

"Hello, Joanna. I was wondering what you had going for tomorrow? I was hoping for dinner and maybe a couple of drinks. I am free tomorrow if you happen to be free also," I said almost expecting to be turned down.

"Well, I have play practice until 4:30 but I can get home and be ready later," she said almost teasing a bit.

"Great! Can I pick you up around 6:45?"

"Sure, I'll be ready then."

"Okay, then it's a date."

I hung up and immediately began to think about her and why it is that she interests me so much. Was it her hair, her face, her body, or her intellect? Maybe it was none of those things but maybe all of those things, all wrapped up in one? Or was it something different?

Joanna's warmth was genuine. It was real and sophisticated. She had something for me, something that was good and kind. I could not put my finger on it, but it was there. I had been so many places in my life in so many different scenarios with women. They could never hold me and I could never hold them. Most of them just came and went like silent messengers telling me all that was wrong with me. This one was different, I knew it and tried to deny it. Wasn't every relationship I ever had just destined for doom, destined to be just one more in a line of failure? Well, it is just one date you know, don't get too excited. But, I just knew deep down inside, that she was something quite special...

Allison Branch had no bandages today. She was traveling the last ten miles to John Middleton's farm, where a new ride awaited her. Andres had arranged a new car for Allison to take. At this point, he was instructing her on what to do next. If she cleared the farm alright, she was to head to Milwaukee and then look for a job. No one would seem to know her and her new face and she possessed some wigs of blonde, red and streaked colors to change into when needed. But for now, she was the classy brunette with a new face. She just couldn't wait to get back in the hunt. She was excited and now renewed in her new-found identity. Oh, the games she could play now! Her list was quite long and for the several people she wanted to find, one sat at the top of her list, Mr. Michael

Parsons.

The 18-wheeler pulled into the long driveway of the farmer John Middleton. His helpers opened the large doors to the warehouse and he drove the truck inside. Inside were two more grain trucks and a nice, shiny, black Lexus waiting. Allison got out of the truck and one of the workers helped her down. Andres got out and walked around to the other side to talk to Allison before she left.

"From now on you are Ms. Lynnette Huber. You stay out of sight for a while. You are no longer Anna Jones. You have two trac phones to use and I only have one number for you to call and you already have that one. Keep the calls limited and don't address me by my American name. These people here all work for me and they are loyal, but don't talk to them, only me. I don't suspect you will be back here any time soon but remember, I am here to help you. You get in jam, you call me. We can't screw up as the Boss wouldn't like it. The Boss doesn't play by any rules. One more thing...we need you in this operation, you can get us inside where we need to be, you know where the cops hunt. Your information is valuable. You hunt, that is your business, you screw up and it becomes the Boss's business. Don't forget that and... be careful," Andres said handing her a packet of papers that would cover her identity and the ability to look for a job.

"Oh, I will. I'll be very careful. You know you can count on me. I'm good. I'm very, very good," she said sending him the quickest of winks.

John Middleton wished he had looked away. He was not a sucker for many things. He had navigated the roughest neighborhoods in Rio and had run a full-fledged drug operation for his Boss. The Boss had told him once to "never let your eyes go to a place where you don't know how to come back." John Middleton was a sucker for one thing and one thing only...those eyes.

With that, Lynette Huber was on her way to Milwaukee. She already had a place rented for her in advance and she was looking forward to flooring the Lexus' gas pedal on the open highway. She always did like speed. As she drove away, she couldn't help but think she wanted to do well for Andres. He had taken care of her, so it was on her not to mess things up. But in the meantime, she had some hunting plans to make. Soon the farm was out of sight and the open road was beckoning. Lynette Huber was free, finally free, never again in her mind to be Allison Branch. Well, never again except for one last time...

I had just hung up and my thoughts turned once again to Andrea Raines, the mysterious Andrea Raines. I never knew how much people could change in their lives. What caused this, what life event was that serious that people get desperate and evil to make everything in their world seem right? Bad parents, bad romances, what motivates the bad guys to be bad? Everyone has choices in their life. We have free will to make those choices. But what goes wrong in a mind that moves them towards destruction. What went wrong with me? A question I couldn't answer for now, but for the most part the answer only lies deep within me. Before my life is over, I intend to revisit those choices in my life and figure it all out. I just needed something or someone to make that happen for me. I still don't know what it is...or who.

Joanna set her phone down and contemplated her new date for tomorrow. Mike Parsons was a good looking, handsome man that to her was a bit mysterious. She told herself to be slow on this and not to dive in too quickly. Yet, her anticipation of their date tomorrow brought the intense feeling of something that had always escaped her in her younger years. She knew that her heart was capable of loving someone, but could she feel loved in return? She had always felt she was kind and caring. She had a good feeling for people and understood that her past relationships with men had not hit her level of expectation. She had debated with herself often about how much of that was her expectations being too high and how she had managed to say all the wrong things at the wrong time. She had never been willing to settle for just anyone and the prospects for remaining single for the rest of her life were becoming quite real. Even so, she had promised herself that she would never again settle for someone that treated her as poorly as Ted Fairfield had before.

Ted Fairfield was Joanna's ex-husband. The marriage may have been doomed from the start. The fact that Ted traveled a lot contributed to it's failure. He had worked in the film industry and had traveled around the country and met a lot of rich and pretty females at parties. He was gone so often that Joanna began to feel that she wasn't married at all. When Ted was home, it was one argument after another, leaving her more alone when he was there than when he was gone. They decided to divorce ten years ago, and Joanna began to branch out on her expertise in theater. She ended up in the same university as Mike and had, by chance, thanks to her friend Ed Weston, met Mike Parsons.

Joanna realized that she could not show in any way that she was anxious to be with him, but she could not just push him away either. It had been a while since she had dated and she was very much looking forward to this date, but just had to stay in control. It's a fine line to where you seem too anxious and then could also be too distant. She liked Mike Parsons. She wasn't going to fight it but she had to be at her best because she did not want this one to get away.

I sat up for just a while longer to catch the news and thought of my date for tomorrow. For some strange reason I couldn't get Joanna Presley Fairfield out of my mind. I was looking forward to our date and had totally left the restaurant choice up to her. She had so many good qualities, I almost was talking myself out of the date knowing I would once again be unworthy of someone of that caliber. But, just as quickly, I talked myself into a more confident approach. I was having good thoughts about tomorrow night when the local newscaster was running a report on HER;

"In the case of the escape of Allison Branch, a former local police detective, authorities say they have no leads. The spectacular escape and police investigation has turned into a dead end. They believe that she may have left the country or is assuming a new identity. As you recall Branch was the perpetrator of a heinous kidnapping of Mike Parsons and a friend Katy O'Brien, two Milwaukee area citizens as well as the shooting of an area detective, Andy Marx. She was serving a long sentence for her crimes at Oxford. She had gained her freedom in a daring move, escaping from the transfer guards with the assistance of armed accomplices on their way to the local hospital. There has been little trail except for the burned vehicle that left no evidence behind..."

From there I could no longer hear the voice of the reporter as I fixated on the picture on the screen. There she was, once again, and I had tried so hard to block that out of my mind. That image of the woman that had so captivated me, then almost killed me. Once again, the fear and concern washed over me. Where was she? Was she out of the country? Was she in the country? Was she standing outside my condo? I knew that she could be anywhere. I stared at the television photo once more and caught what everyone else gets a glimpse of, those eyes, the ones that hold you, frozen for just a short enough time to deceive you. Once again, I feared for Katy, for Marx, for Margaret, and most intimately feared once again that I could re-live the nightmare that I had put to rest for some time. It was now very fresh in my mind. The beatings, the drugging, the escape, the chase, the shooting, and the blood all came racing back like a runaway freight train. My head was dizzy with the thought of the gun pointed at Katy and me. The loud pop and the blood flying made my senses feel what I felt at that time.

I dropped down on the sofa, and sat frozen, impervious to the television screen or the words of the reporter. This just had to end. I had to call Marx to get a handle on all of this. Without letting myself get too much further into the nightmare, I dialed his number. He answered on the second ring.

"Hey, Mike, what's going on?"

"Look, remember I told you Margaret thought Jerry was having an affair with Andrea. It connects Jerry and Stephenson to the drug trade. If he is still alive, that is," I said with urgency in my voice.

"You could be right and for now, I am assuming he is still alive and in on all this," Marx said. "I think the guy had partnered with Jerry and they were going to make a big fortune in a merger. I think Stephenson is in first, with Jerry coming on later in desperation."

I pondered this for a moment and thought back to the bar and seeing Raines with that man. "We just have to find the guy that Raines was with and he may be someone that leads us to them. I have a feeling that he is the main man running this whole deal."

"Mike, you may be right. But, let's not go there first. We may have to get out and find those two kids. I have a feeling that if we get one, we can get the other to turn. They are not going to show face here, but we have to get leads off the APB we put out. I guess you saw the news item on TV. I was the one who put it with all the pictures. We have people to investigate but with the pictures out, we may get a good tip."

"Yeah, I saw the piece. To tell you the truth it froze me in my tracks. I was actually sweating. Damn, I don't know what she looks like, or where she is. She could be outside right now, for all I know."

"Yeah, this is a tough one, but if we get together and solve this thing, maybe your life can get back to normal. Here is one more thing for you to digest. Raines is gone. My tail man lost her trail and can't pick it up again. She is an accomplice to something here, but just what we don't know yet. Either that or she is suffering the same consequence as her brother."

"Well, my bet is that she's in on this and so is he. I think they are both still alive."

"Look, I have some things to tie up in allocation of staff tomorrow. Maybe we can meet the next day and move this thing along. I think it's time for the hunt," Marx said with a bit of energy in his voice.

I breathed a bit of a sigh of relief. I felt better that I had talked to Andy and that we would begin to go after some people. Also, I was a bit relieved that I could keep my date with Joanna. It was something that I was looking forward to.

CHAPTER 23

Am I chasing my dreams, or running from my nightmares? Or, am I somewhere in between trying to do both? Maybe my dreams and my nightmares are one in the same, confusing me.

I always have trouble falling asleep. Ever since the ordeal, my fear of sleep lies in the oncoming nightmares that still exist. When I wake up, I just sit up on the edge of my bed, take deep breaths and wipe the sweat from my face, go to the bathroom and splash cold water on it and look in the mirror. In the mirror I see a better me taking myself into the new day, seeing a better dream to chase in the future. The little guy on my left shoulder tells me I can't, because these nightmares will always be there. The little guy on the right says that I should forget that guy on the left, he doesn't control me. You have to be positive. I look at him and try to brush the little guy off my shoulder, but he bends and bounces back upright with his feet firmly planted on my shoulder. He laughs and says I can't beat him. Splash... give it time. The guy on the left laughs, a cruel and hideous laugh, that tells me I'm stuck with him. Splash more water on my face, and then both little men are gone. A new day. Time to leave my nightmare behind and walk into my dream...or vice versa.

It is what happens almost every day and most times I can shake it off. But tonight, it was a little harder to fall asleep. So many things on my mind. The case, Joanna, the newscast, and all the characters involved. Who is that big guy? Where are Jake and Carrianne? Who killed Mo? Andrea Stephenson Raines and Oscar Stephenson are involved, but how? Who's that man with Andrea? Then HER, yes HER, where is she and what does she even look like? Is she blonde, brunette or redhead? Will I know her face? But rest assured, buddy boy, she's planning to come for you. You know it, Marx knows it, everyone knows it...just rest, breathe and sleep, sleep...

There has to be some point in falling asleep you go from reality to fantasy. But they are one in the same in dreams. Who's to say that it's not really reality? But I was there, somewhere in that place, and reality was taking place.

I was being led into a place, someplace I did not know by a woman and a man. There were others with me, but I did not recognize them. We walked slowly through a dark and crowded hallway. The walk was awkward because we couldn't use our hands for balance. They were secured behind our backs. The woman and the man did not speak, but only poked us and prodded us with something, guns I think, yes, guns. We were pushed into an open room. There were no windows, no light, no furniture, just a door. I can't see who these people were that were captive with me. It was too dark and I couldn't see their faces. But I heard Eric Clapton's *Sunshine of Your Love* coming from somewhere.

It's getting near dawn, when lights close their tired eyes.

I'll soon be with you my love, to give you my dawn surprise.

I'll be with you darling soon, I'll be with when the stars start falling.

I've been waiting so long,

The door slammed and the music continued. The man with me was cursing and the woman was crying. The music was getting louder as Clapton hammered out the chords on the electric guitar. The guitar solo now piercing in volume was ringing in my head. Bam! the door loudly opens and our captors enter.

"Get up!! Let's move. Time's up and the games start," bellowed the booming voice of the man...

I sat up straight in my bed. Wednesday morning had arrived. Sitting on my bed, I wiped the sweat off my face and was breathing heavily. I trudged to the bathroom, tired and dizzy, trying to shake off the latest nightmare. I bent over the sink and splashed cold water on my face and looked into the mirror. *Hello there, little men. One on each shoulder telling me what to do and what to think. Guess it's time to leave my nightmare and chase my dream again. Or vice versa....*

Lynette Huber awoke from her best sleep she had known for weeks in her new place in Milwaukee. Carrianne had gotten there before her to set up house. She laid there thinking of her plans and what she needed to do. Andres had instructed to lay low for a few days, but she wasn't one to sit still for long. Andres had a couple of shipments coming soon and she would do her part to make sure that they got to the suppliers of junkies in need. She was well versed in the routine and understood how not be detected by cops. That job was easy. But the job she really wanted to do took planning and she needed an accomplice like Breanne used to be. Breanne was tough-minded, like her, and always had the needed intensity to finish a plan. She couldn't use Carrianne, as she thought of her as too soft. But Carrianne could do other things, but she wouldn't go on the hunt with her. No, she needed someone with grit, determination and loyalty to her. She just couldn't see Carrianne as loyal to her like she was to Andres.

Carrianne had been loyal to Andres for bringing her and Jake to America. He got them out of the slums and made sure they had everything they could not have as children. Andres was their keeper for sure. They would die for him. Lynette knew that they would not be so quick to die for her. Not like Breanne was.

Andres had made sure that her old contacts knew about her new life and would still protect her in her dealings. She just had a different face, but she was still Branch to Andres, and he still feared her dangerous personality. Yet, he had given her so much room to do what she needed to do. Andres certainly had done a lot for Branch.

Carrianne poked her head around the corner of the door checking on her new friend Lynette.

"Hey," she said as she walked into the room. "Would you like me to get you a cup of coffee? I made some earlier."

"Sure," Lynette said getting out of bed and walking to the window. "I can get dressed and go out to the living room for it. I was thinking before you came in, that maybe you would like to go for a ride today. The weather looks right. It's just a bit cold but the roads look good today."

"I'd really like that, but I'm not sure if Andres would like that," Carrianne said with a doubtful look.

"I know that he wanted us to stay low, but I'll go get a few things for us this morning that will help hide you when you are out and then we can go," Lynette replied.

"Well, I guess it wouldn't hurt."

"Sure girl, just out for a little ride. We won't be out long. Andres won't know. There is a new shipment coming in soon, so he's probably busy with that. Let's go have that cup of coffee."

"Okay," Carrianne replied and started to leave the room.

"Hey, Carrianne," Lynette said.

Carrianne turned to look and saw that Lynette was standing by the mirror. Brushing through her hair with her fingers, Lynette turned to look at Carrianne.

"Carrianne, honestly, how do you think I look now? Really be honest here, how do I look?"

"Well," she said carefully choosing her word. "Stunning, yes stunning is the right word."

Lynette smiled as she looked at Carrianne. "Thank you, dear, thank you."

At that particular moment Carrianne wanted to look away. *Lynette was stunning. Her makeover had gone well. She was pretty before, but now, that doctor did a number. She was gorgeous. It wasn't her tight and fit body, or even her face which was done perfectly to make her face fuller with fillers. But her eyes, there was just something about those eyes, they were stunning. They held Carrianne frozen for just a second. Just a short time telling Carrianne that she just had to like this woman, even though Carrianne knew she was dangerous. Lynette Huber was a beautiful woman now, but on the inside, Allison Branch still resided there. That point worried Carrianne. Allison Branch was dangerous, that much she knew. But those eyes, those eyes so riveting and so captivating, there was something in there that showed hurt and anger. That's what was lurking inside the new Lynette Huber. Inside of her, no matter how much change was made, there was evil, pure, unadulterated evil. She could lie all she wanted to about anything and everything. But the eyes, oh those eyes, could not lie.*

They went and drank coffee together and Carrianne asked here questions about her life as a cop. Lynette answered most of them and the conversation was light, nothing too serious. For the next half hour, they talked about many things and laughed some. They were getting along just fine.

"Well, it's time for me to go shopping for a bit. I will be back shortly."

Lynette moved to her bathroom to shower and Carrianne used the other. They finished and both came out dressed casually for the day.

"Keep the doors locked and be watchful. Be careful, and don't answer the door if anyone comes. I won't be long. When I get back, we'll go out for a little ride."

"That would be nice," Carrianne replied. "I'm excited!"

"I'll see you later. Be back in about an hour."

With that Lynnette Huber was back in society and free from steel bars and was no longer a prisoner. She was free and she would make the best of her new freedom. That is before she would risk it all once more so she could finish them all off. She had a shopping list, alright. She had it in her head and when she got something in her head, it was hard for her to let go. It was something that had always scared her mother...

CHAPTER 24

Lynnette thought of herself as just 'little ole Lynnette.' She no longer had in her head that she was Allison Branch. "Allison who?" she mouthed out loud as her car flew down the open road highway like a heat- seeking missile. I like this new person, she thought to herself as she often looked up to see the new face behind a slick pair of sunglasses. It is going to be easy to be her, certainly not to be confused with her former police detective image.

This girl behind the wheel would become much more fun and wilder than Allison ever thought of being. Each day was going to be a new adventure, she told herself. They almost stopped her once, but she survived as she always had. Now, there would be no more wasted time, sitting around waiting for the right things to happen. From now on, Lynnette Huber would make everything happen. She had it all. She had the brains, the guts, and the strongest will serving her. She thought as she drove on, hitting the exit to the nearest shopping center, of all the things that had gotten in her way and the people that had tried to put her away. The people that she had on her list were to be dealt with and they would pay a heavy price.

Lynnette pulled into the parking area and snapped back to reality. She locked the car and headed into the store. She walked down the aisle looking into the faces of complete strangers. She saw no recognition of her by them. Of course, she was actually someone different and, how could they?

She found what she was looking for in clothing. She picked up two hooded sweatshirts, black and fleece, and ventured over to find two black baseball caps. Next, she picked up a couple pair of sunglasses, large frame with reflective lenses. She headed to the checkout and on the way stopped and added a 12 pack of beer. On her way out, she was feeling like someone was watching her. She had no reason to think it, but she felt that somehow, eyes were on her. She shook it off and put the bags in the car and left the parking lot and back to the open road.

Her first venture out alone had gone well. She didn't think Andres would want her venturing out so soon, but she had to get out and have some fun. Carrianne couldn't just sit there, cooped up in that place. She would need to get out, too. Huber hit the gas and sped onto the freeway headed home to pick up Carrianne. They had to dress up in the new things she had bought and they were going out scouting. There is always the scouting and planning before the hunt. It was the way she had always done it. But this time would be better, she would not miss a thing. Every detail planned to the highest degree. She hit the gas harder and she was flying, the adrenaline was flowing and her thoughts were almost allowing her to enter another world. She let off the gas and slowed her thoughts down. She had to not get picked up for even speeding. She could not mess things up. She eased off the accelerator and got back down to speed limit. *Good girl, that's right, slow down before you find trouble you aren't looking for today. Everything in due time, don't rush, relax...*

I was starting to get excited about the evening. I had not thought of dating much since Branch. I had almost given up. But something was different about Joanna. I don't think I had ever run across a woman quite like her before. I went to the store and picked out some clothes that were casual yet dressy. I wanted to make a good impression on Joanna. I found a pair of slacks and plaid shirt that I could wear with a suit jacket. I had everything and headed back home.

When I got home, my phone rang and it was Marx.

"Hey Mike, just got off the phone with my guy who went to pick up Andrea Stephenson Raines for questioning. He says she's not there. Car is still in the driveway but, nobody home. I think I'm going to send out an APB on her, we have to have her. No doubt, she is key to this case and she must be found. We know that she is missing. I hate to get the FBI involved, but I'm afraid I might have to. Any chance you can come by tonight?"

"Oh man, look, I have a date tonight with a lady I teach with," I responded. "I just can't break this one. Any way it could be tomorrow that we meet?"

"Yeah, I suppose, but tomorrow has to be it. We have to make some headway before it gets too messy. If we can't find Raines in the next 48 hours, we will have to file a missing person report on her and investigate another disappearance."

"Okay, tomorrow it is. What time?"

"Meet me at nine or so. Come by my place and we will make plans to move forward, we have to find some of these people. We are starting to feel some heat downtown and in the press."

"Okay," I said and I hung up.

Lynnette came through the door and handed Carrianne her packages and the 12 pack of beer. Carrianne opened the bags and pulled out the hooded sweatshirts.

"All black?" Carrianne asked thinking that the color was quite odd.

"Sure, it's kind of cold out and that will absorb the sun's heat. Also, it is much harder to be recognized in black," she said knowing from past experience, of course. "These are what Breanne and I wore when we terrorized ole Mikey back then. I thought it would be fun to wear them again."

"Well, I'm not so sure we should be going out. I'm also not sure about wearing the sweatshirts too. I am afraid that you are heading into something here that will just get you into trouble again. I don't want to have Andres thinking it was okay by me and that I got you going on this thing again. I am worried what Andres would say if he knew we were not staying out of sight," Carrianne replied.

"What are you going to do Carrianne, stay here inside and vegetate?" Lynnette asked eyeing her young friend. "C'mon, where is your sense of adventure?"

"I...I don't know," she stammered. She knew Andres well and she feared him yet trusted him. "He has made some sacrifices for me and Jake. I hate to let him down."

Lynnette stopped and her face turned into a slow smile and her eyes became fixed on her new friend,

Carrianne. It made Carrianne want to look away, but like so many, she just couldn't. Those eyes had a way that froze you to where you could not say no. Of course, Carrianne could not.

"Okay, but let's not stay out all day. I really don't want Andres finding out we did this. I am supposed to keep watch on this place. I owe him a lot."

"Okay, okay, but let's take a ride," Lynnette said still rocking that crazy smile, "even if just for a short time. There's a few places I have to show you."

"Okay, but just for a while."

They got dressed and put on the hooded sweatshirts and ball caps and sunglasses. They headed out and it was about noon. The air was cool and brisk and the top on the car was up. Lynnette was driving the speed limit and heading to the Milwaukee area. She would be on a little tour this morning, showing Carrianne her old stomping grounds that would become her hunting grounds, if all went well.

They got to her old apartment and Lynnette pointed it out for Carrianne.

"That's where I used to live. It was nice and was convenient for me to get to work," she said with just a glint of sadness in her voice. "My life was different then, started out thinking I would be a good cop and find a nice guy. But something inside me kept me on the dark side. Something called to me that was competitive and daring. The money from the drug trade was hard to resist and keeping that from my partner was tough duty. Money began to drive me, but I still felt empty," she said as they sat still in the car on the street. "Like I told you, I almost found that guy, the one I wanted. Not once but twice. It just didn't happen, he didn't pick me."

Lynnette drove on, heading towards Mike's condos. She told Carrianne they were going by there. She talked of her work as a cop and how she felt torn between the good and the bad in life. They pulled into Mike's parking lot and sat far away from his unit. She began to speak:

"Why don't you give up this drug life, Carrianne?" she asked. "You are young and have so much life ahead. Why don't you just have Andres take you back to Brazil and meet a nice, rich Brazilian?"

"I won't go back there. There is too much violence and we are too well known in the trade. My only chance at a different life is here, in America," Carrianne said as he looked away from Lynnette, out her window. "Jake, he is such an immature boy. He needs me to watch over him. I told mama when we left, I would take care of him. He is quite the impulsive one. But we are in this with Andres because he helped us. I don't think there is any way we can say we are out without paying the ultimate price. As much as the Boss has cared for us, the Boss would not let us just leave."

They both took a sip of a can of beer that they had opened while sitting in the lot. Carrianne was staring forward and finished her first beer. Lynnette had done the same and they each got another one out of the box.

"What is it with this guy Mike Parsons, the one you are trailing right now? Why are we back here, just watching his place? Do you still love him?"

"To tell you the truth, he was exactly what I wanted. He was cool, kind of strange and awkward, yet always attentive. He was handsome, and intelligent. He had a good career going but he and his wife were on the outs. Seemed like marriage wasn't his thing and he ran around a lot. I was going to fix him, and in my mind, I thought I could. I was shameless in throwing myself at him, but he ignored me. He just wouldn't pick me when I needed him. He left me stranded in a bar for some bimbo. I was his solution and he just left me hanging," her voice beginning to escalate.

"Easy, easy there, Lynnette, maybe we should be leaving now before you do something really crazy," Carrianne said. "We can stay away from any trouble."

"Wait!" she whispered. "There he is."

Carrianne saw the man get out of the car and walk to his unit. She looked over at the frozen face of Lynnette, fixed on the image of Mike Parsons. "Hey...HEY!"

Lynnette whirled in her seat to face Carrianne but caught herself. She was about to grab the door handle and open it.

"No, not yet," Carrianne implored. "You can't do that. You are letting your anger get to you. Wait until he gets inside and let's leave."

Lynnette was breathing hard. Carrianne knew what Andres would think of this and it wouldn't be good. "Look, let's leave. You are just upset and you need to go back and relax," she said.

"He didn't pick me, he didn't pick me...", Lynnette was mumbling over and over.

"Lynnette, don't mess this up. You have time to think this through. Right now, your mind is making mistakes," Carrianne was pleading.

Lynnette seemed to snap out of her trance at these words. She started the car and they drove peacefully out of the parking lot. As she got near the condo unit, she stopped and stared up at his second-floor place. Was she trying to get one more glimpse of him? Or was she just about to stop and go finish him off?

"Lynnette, please..."

"Okay, you're right. Let's go."

Lynnette pulled the car into the street and drove away. She was silently admonishing herself as she let old Allison Branch back in her head. She was supposed to be Lynnette Huber and she just kept wanting to eliminate Allison Branch. But the past would not let her go this easy. This would be much harder than she ever thought. She turned to Carrianne and at the stop sign said, "Thanks." Lynnette had one more place to go and she would then be okay with going home. She just had to see it once more...

CHAPTER 25

It had gotten to be about 4:30 in the afternoon and I was anticipating my date with Miss Joanna Presley. With reservations made, clothes picked out and a good attitude, I was promising myself that this would be much more fun than our previous luncheon with the faculty. All I had left to do was shave and shower and I would pick her up at 6:00.

I was contemplating somethings about the case as I sat there when my phone rang again. It was James and he had been with his kids all day in the city. It had been a while since we talked and I needed to plan something to do together.

"Hey, brother, good to hear from you," I said as I moved to my window to look outside. "I was thinking about you and hoping we could plan something together."

"Sounds good. Monica and I just got back from taking the kids to the new science center downtown. They had a blast."

"That's great," I replied, "I was wondering when we could plan something together. Maybe go to a Brewers game or something when they break spring training."

"Hey, that sounds great. Maybe we can do some early fishing also out at the lake place. Just you and me and the fish."

"Let's look at early March and see if we can catch some of those walleye on the troll," I said missing the days we used to fish together as younger men. I glanced at the calendar on the kitchen wall and looked at a date in March. "How about the 17th of March and we'll celebrate St. Patrick's Day while we are at it. I can find some Jameson that can help us light up the weekend."

"Sounds good," James replied. "I'll check with Monica and see that we don't have something planned, but I think that weekend is going to work."

"Great, that will be fun," I said. "I am going out on a date tonight with a lady that teaches theater at the university. Ed introduced me to her, and I have to say she is very intriguing. You know the struggles I have had, but this date just feels different. It's like, no pressure, just enjoy. I don't think I ever had a date like that before."

"Look, be careful though," he cautioned. "I know it has been a while but be sure what you are doing before you get headlong into this one. You deserve a good one, but you also have that history of getting in too deep too fast and that makes you run away. Take it slow, buddy, and just let it take its course."

"Yeah, I know. I have a tendency to rush and it leaves me feeling anxious and nervous. Then I make some mistakes. But I do feel that this one is different.

"We are going out to dinner," James said. "Take care brother, and I am looking forward to our lake trip."

"Alright, see you later."

I hung up the phone and looking out the kitchen window, I saw a car stopped at the exit of my parking lot. What I saw, I thought, was two women in a car, with hoodies and ball caps on. I rubbed my eyes thinking I was seeing things, but when I opened them up again, I saw nothing. The car was gone. I grabbed the kitchen table chair and stood there for a moment, wondering if I really saw what I thought that I saw.

Okay, look, that car wasn't two girls with hoodies and ball caps. You know it wasn't, so don't make this up in your mind. But, you did see it right? Okay, I'm feeling a bit dizzy, the mental turning into the physical. My therapist told me that. She told me I could have episodes of the mental turning into physical difficulties due to the intensity of my experience. Not tonight, not now. I had to shake this thing off. Forget about it, it was your imagination. It's Branch, isn't it. I'm thinking it is her, but who is she with? No, it was just my imagination. I am going to shave and jump in the shower and shake this off. There was no car, no women, no hoodies, none of that. Now get going and let it go. I am just seeing things.

But actually, I wasn't...

Lynnette and Carrianne drove out of town, heading to the place that Lynnette just had to see. Carrianne had no idea where they were going, but she was extremely nervous.

"Do you really need to go somewhere else? I was thinking that maybe we should be getting back," Carrianne said with a hopeful look.

"Relax girl, everything is going to be just fine," Lynnette replied. "There is this nice quiet spot I want to show you."

The drove for twenty more minutes, mostly in

silence, until they reached the gate of Mike Parson's lake place. Lynnette got out and opened the gate. They drove up to the house and Lynnette got out and slowly turned to survey the house, the lot, the lake and the dock areas.

"C'mon, get out and check this place out," Lynnette said.

Carrianne got out of the car and asked, "Where are we?"

"This where it all happened," she started as she walked up around the house and yard area. "Here is where we kept poor Mikey and his friend Katy in a locked storm shelter. We had them tied up and kept them drugged. Me and Breanne and ole Jerry had the plan to kill them both. We gave Jerry the shot at it and that brother of Mike's shot Jerry. Ruined everything and from there on we were cooked. We got inside and were ready to finish off my partner, Marx, and he shot her, shot Breanne and me. Breanne didn't make it, but I did."

Tears were starting to run down Lynnette's face. Carrianne was feeling chills and knowing that this woman was just crazy.

"Look, let's go back. This is just upsetting you. Andres will be checking on us and you don't want him mad at you, trust me."

"I'll get them back you know. Andres wants me to. Breanne wants me to. I want to. Those are people that need to pay for what they did. Especially HIM, he didn't pick me!"

"Let's go, really, let's get back," Carrianne pleaded.

With that, they both got back in the car and left. They drove in silence for about fifty miles until at last they were in the parking lot of Lynnette's new place. Lynnette parked the car and they went inside. Carrianne breathed a sigh of relief as they turned the key to their place and walked in. Her relief was short lived...

CHAPTER 26

Inside they found exactly what Carrianne had feared. Andres Montoya was sitting in the living room and stood up as they entered the hallway. Carrianne's heart sank and she knew this would be an explosion. Andres was angry, she could tell. He thrust his arms upward and his voice boomed as he spoke even though he was trying to be quiet.

"Just what in the hell do you think you are doing? I told you to stay out of sight for a while, especially you, Carrianne. Your picture is out there with the cops and the FBI!"

"I'm sorry, Andres," Carrianne said carefully choosing her words. "We just wanted to take a ride and get some air." Carrianne looked at him, hoping his anger would not escalate.

"You have to be kidding," he started. "We are trying to get this operation in order and the heat has to die down. You two should know better. What are you trying to do here? The Feds and locals are all over your escape, Branch. You will never become another person without letting go of this past. You need to give this time, you need to settle down and get in a different mode or you are going to get us all arrested or much worse, killed."

Andres was very angry and he began to pace like someone that was ready to completely blow their top. He stopped and looked directly at Lynnette and began to chastise her.

"How selfish do you want to be? I watched over this kid and her brother for many years. I did so for their mother. You, without any care or consideration, are likely to expose her to the authorities. You might be the most selfish person I ever met. Yes, we need you and you need the organization, but you keep this shit up and you will find yourself in the bottom of the ocean getting fed to some sharks. You better shape up and shape up quick, or you are going to be no one, not Branch, not Huber, not anybody!! Just dead!"

Lynnette looked down for a few seconds and hung her head. She looked to Carrianne to say something in her defense, but Carrianne was silent and not looking at either one. Andres moved closer to Lynnette and looked her in the eyes, oh yes, those eyes, and he was silent. Her face turned a rosy hue and she had a silly grin on her face.

"Surely, Andres, you know that I am all in with the organization. I wouldn't want to hurt this girl. She has become a good friend. And you, I want to do good for YOU," she said as her eyes turned an ice blue color. "We just needed to get out and I didn't think you would mind us taking a little drive."

As he looked at those eyes he stuttered, "Well uh, well...you...you know what I am saying. Stay out of sight for now. If you can't do that, there is a price to pay," he said as his voice trailed off.

Carrianne was truly worried watching this exchange. She saw power that she was truly afraid of. Not his power, but hers, was what was quite confusing. She had seen Andres deal with the most fearsome humans, and never once had she seen him cow down to anyone. Not until now. Andres had always protected her and kept in the safest harbors in her life. But was this going to be different? She was now more afraid of Lynnette Huber than ever. If she could cast this kind of spell on Andres, her life around Huber would be filled with fear and danger.

"Just a short ride and I am sorry, Andres," she began. "It won't happen again. I know you have protected Carrianne and I get that. I won't let anyone harm her."

"Good, just keep it that way and I am asking you for the last time, and I mean the last time, stay hidden and inactive for a while longer. I will let you know when you can get out. Just let it simmer for a few more days before you do anything else. You got that?"

"Okay, I get it, Andres," she responded looking away from him to me and back to him again. "I'll be good. You won't have to worry about me. I know how to take care of myself and I will take care of Carrianne, I promise."

"Carrianne, you stay inside and stay out of sight. I am going to look for a place for you and Jake, but I will have you moving out to my farm shortly before we move you again. Don't mess this up. We have come too far to screw things up. The Boss is already upset that you have been out and trust me, as I have told you before, you don't mess with the Boss," Andres said reaching out and touching Carrianne on her arm.

"I will, you can trust me, Andres," Carrianne said with a sideways glance at Lynnette.

"Alright, don't make me come back here again

because you have some foolish desire to venture out near trouble," Andres said as he walked past Huber. "I just have a few more things to tie up before we start getting things back on track. You both need to shut it down for a few more days. Don't disappoint me."

Andres shot his last, hard glance at Huber as he walked towards the door. Her eyes followed him but he did not look at her directly. He knew better and kept telling himself how much trouble this detective is. *We need her, she is important to the operation. She knows how to protect our dealers. But she is deadly to any man, or any woman for that matter. There is something in her that is not matched by anyone we have working for us. She can be controlling, intimidating and downright dangerous. All because of those eyes. Do NOT look at her as you walk out. I have to think about something and decide. Do we keep her as an asset or do we kill her? It will come to that at some point.*

He turned the door knob and left, looking all around the parking lot first before walking on. He put the key in the ignition and started out of the lot. *She's trouble and I don't know how to read her. I know she is dangerous, very dangerous. You have to decide, Andres. You're going to have to decide.* He drove on and headed out to John Middleton Farms. He had much to do.

I rang the doorbell at Joanna's place and she answered all dressed up and looked stunning.

"Well, hello," she said. "Would you like to come in?"

"Sure, thanks," I said. "You look absolutely marvelous."

"Thank you, Mike, you look handsome yourself."

I sat in the chair and she sat on the sofa. Her eyes were bright and shiny, they were eyes that had no secrets, no fears, just eyes that seemed to be happy at the moment. She had on a skirt and top with a very smart jacket. Her hair was done straight with just enough curl to be effective. She had an air about her that was open and honest.

"How are things going with your case?" she asked.

"Pretty good, I think. Marx is looking into so many things it is complicated but I think he has a few leads to go on. I know I will have lots to do when I get back from leave. My students will not miss me though and I think they are glad another teacher has them for a while."

"I'm sure they miss you," she said. "I am excited to try this new place. I've heard a lot of good things about it."

"Me too," I answered. "Hey let's get going. They have this great enclosed area with a good view to have a couple of cocktails before dinner. We can carry on this conversation there. Are you ready?"

"Yes, let me get my coat," she replied.

I helped here with her coat and we left as she locked the door behind her. We walked to the car and I opened the door for her and then got in. We drove away and headed to the restaurant.

We got there about a half hour before our reservation so we went to the enclosed area to have a drink. Of course, mine was scotch and she ordered a white wine. We got a table for two near the window and sat down to have our drinks. The waitress delivered them to us and we both toasted the evening.

"So, tell me, what do you do for fun?" she asked.

"Well, I fish a lot and love to golf when the weather is nice. I have a lake place that I go to when I want to get away. I love drinking coffee on the front porch there. It gives me time to think and get perspective on things when they get hectic," I started. "How about you?"

"I like to go to plays, musicals mostly. I love the outdoors, too, and love long walks on warm summer mornings. I like a good ballgame every now and then as my dad had Packers tickets for several years. I learned how to freeze my butt off in Green Bay," she said as she looked directly at me for the first time in our conversation. "You were a pretty good ballplayer back in your day, according to Ed, right?"

"Ed lies," I replied, trying to be humble. "Yes, I played a lot of ball back in the day. Something that I really loved. Hey, maybe we can take in a play together sometime. Or maybe go to a Brewers game? Sort of like sharing our hobbies?"

"Well, we will see, won't we?" she said smiling enough to make me think this is a good sign!

After a bit of small talk, we were led to our table, and the waitress took our order. I had been thinking of how I felt about Joanna and was starting to see things in her that were good, logical, and something in her mannerisms making me feel like I am looking for things that are better inside of a person than maybe looking on the outside. I was sure that she was a good human being. The question would be, is it someone I am going to fall for or is this just a date that will be over and we won't see each other again? Who knows, right?

We ate and talked about other things we liked like our favorite movies, television shows and some about our childhoods. I think our parents must have come from the same generation and the same backgrounds. We were raised a lot in the same way and some of our values seemed to be matching. It was rare for me to have a date like this. Most of the women I dated were of the pick-up variety and I rarely saw them again. This was starting to feel like something, yet to me, it was so plain and simple compared to the complications of taking someone home and then trying to avoid them after. It was the side of me that was bad, the side that was something I had to fix if I wanted to find happiness. But it was difficult because I had gotten so used to being alone that I stopped trying to find what it was I was actually needing.

We left and drove back to her house. I walked her to the door and told her what a wonderful time I had and that I would like to have her out to my lake place for our next date, if she was inclined to come along. She said she would. Wow! I am actually starting to treat women as I should have years ago. But why this one? There is something there, something so different and unique that I can't put my finger on it, but most assuredly, it is there. I hugged her with no intention of being anything less than a gentleman here, but she raised up and kissed me on the cheek. Her lips were soft and warm on my face and she had no idea of how she made me feel with something so simple as that kiss.

"What about next weekend? Could you be up for a little lake time next Saturday? Too cold for the fun boating stuff, but the front porch has a great view and the drinks, well, they are awesome, plus I am a decent cook. Living alone has taught me how. Not really a hobby but a necessity."

"I'd love to," she answered looking up at me. "What time should I be ready?"

"About 9:00 am," I said. "That will give us a full day away from all the rat race and hustle. You will like it, I hope."

"Sounds really good. Good night, Mr. Parsons. I

really enjoyed the evening. I am really looking forward to next Saturday," she said with a smile that I had not seen before, one that instantly hooked me on her. It was the moment I would look back on later as the one that made me know I felt something for Joanna.

"I'll call you next week and we can plan," I said and leaned down and kissed her on her cheek. In my mind, it was almost like junior high school, but it was something that put me in a proper place and frame of mind that was going to change my life. At the time, I had no idea. But things were going to change for me. And, of course, they just had to.

----▲----

I got home and walked into my place feeling like the ground beneath me had made a seismic shift. I had learned something. I had come to know for maybe the first time, what it is like to want to actually know someone. I had gone a while in this life not knowing it. But, it was something good, I did know that.

It was 10:30 and I put on a t-shirt and pair of shorts as I always did even in the dead of winter. My phone rang and I walked over to the counter to answer it. I could see it was Marx.

"Hey Marx, what's up?" I asked hoping to have time to sit and think about Joanna for a few.

"Hi, Mike, I was wondering if you had a few minutes. I have something that might be of interest to us in this case. I was wondering if you could come over for a bit?"

"Well, yeah, I think I can do that. Let me get dressed and give about twenty minutes and I will be there."

"Okay, great. I will see you then."

I hung up and dressed quickly. I should be thinking of this as an interruption but I had come to think of these times as new and exciting. The adrenaline was starting to flow and I started to understand what it was Marx had tried to tell me once. He called it "hunter's high" and it was starting to hit me. Looks like we had some hunting to do. I grabbed my keys and coat and headed to the cold parking lot. I looked around as I am always paranoid that I will get slugged in the back of the head. I watched shadows, movement, or anything as I always had. I kept my head on a swivel now. I made it to my car and found that I was once again breathing heavy. It was because of this paranoia, this pretense that every move I made was followed. I started the car and began to move out of the lot slowly. I stopped at the exit onto the road and thought of the hoodies and ball caps that I had seen or not seen. Should I tell Marx, or is it just my imagination? I turned on the street and headed to Marx's place.

I will decide before I get there, whether to tell Marx or not. I just can't be sure of what I saw as it happened or didn't happen so quickly. What is it about the human mind that makes you question what you have seen. Marx had told me that witness accounts were sometimes questionable based on what their mind was seeing through their eyes. Once again, I am starting to question myself and my state of mind. I think until I decide I saw it for real, I will just keep it to myself. But, I still had the hunter's high and was ready to get back into the case. I was wondering what information Marx had and I know in my mind, I want this one over. We had to find her and get her back in jail. We had to...

CHAPTER 27

I pulled up at Marx's place at about 11:00 pm. I went to the door and he let me in and offered me a beer. After a couple of scotches, I declined, didn't want to drive loaded. He had us sit at his kitchen table where his notes were strewn about the table.

"I got a call from the Feds in Brazil and it seems that my old buddy was found, at least his remains were. The report said he was strangled and the body dumped into the ocean. It was badly chewed up. The coroner thinks that whoever did this to him was a very strong person, which to my mind leads us back to the big guy we saw at the hotel. I'm pretty torn up about this, we were good friends."

"Oh, man, I'm sorry, Marx, this is bad. You going to be okay?" I asked.

"I have to go by tomorrow and see his mom. We did a lot of things together in high school. I owe it to him. It seems I have to do this stuff too much and the pressure is starting to build up. I have got to nail this thing down and soon before anyone else gets hurt."

"Look, it's not your fault, you know," I replied trying to sooth what I knew was bugging him. "You're a good cop and if anyone will get this done it will be you."

"Thanks, but let's think a minute. We need to decide if they are here or down in Brazil. Stephenson and his sister are missing or are they down there? There is some connection between those two and the big guy we are looking for and it is just a hunch. Nothing from any interviews or evidence tells me that, but I feel it."

I thought about that for a moment. Thinking back to my conversation with Margaret, there was a connection. That connection was Andrea Stephenson Raines, who thought had had an affair with my late ex-father-in-law, Jerry. Stephenson and Jerry had to know each other as Margaret said they had golf outings. But one of those people are dead and two of them are missing.

"Andy, I think the Stephensons are both alive, just my guess but since we knew that Branch was in with the drug deals, I think so are Andrea and Oscar Stephenson. I would put my money on them being out of the country and not missing. Of course, that is my hunch, not based on anything concrete that we know."

"I'm thinking you are right on this," Marx replied. "But it puts us in a dilemma. Who is more dangerous to us right now?" he asked.

"In my mind, it is Branch," I said. "She's hidden and more than likely has changed her identity. This makes it bad for both of us. The invisible force. She will be hard to flush out. The two kids, Jake and Carrianne, I bet are in with the big guy and are covered for now. We can hope to see them somewhere, but is it here in the states or in South

America?"

"Look, you and I are taking care of ourselves, but what about your friend, Katy?" he asked. *Oh shit, how could I forget about Katy? She needs to be under some sort of protection. But maybe I could have Marx speak to her and let her know to be on the watch.*

"Marx, maybe you could speak to Katy. I can give you her number and her address. I just can't right now and you know why."

"I could do that. But we also need to decide where we are going to focus. Is it here in the states or do we go to Brazil?" Marx asked.

"That's complicated but as confusing as this case is one thing is for sure, it is hard to trust any woman that crosses my path or just walks by me on the street. Anybody can be her. You should be very worried about that too, Marx."

"My hunch is to stay here until we have a more solid idea that they are in Brazil. The big guy might be down there, Jake and Carrianne may be down there, Oscar and Andrea may be down there, but I am betting the big guy and Branch are somewhere near here. She is more in control of this situation than we can possibly know. I worked with her for so long. She had you, then it was the prison guard, Hannah, now it's the big guy. She has roped him in and he is all in with her. She's a bulldog and her anger is real and her background is tough. To her, there is nothing more important than the win and to be first. Her ego won't let her get very far from the prey. You can bet that in the next few days, you may not see her or know her if you're in a bar or walking down the street, but she for sure knows who you are. It's my guess she is going to test the waters shortly."

And now my life is screwed up again. Joanna

came to mind immediately. How am I going to tell her all of this without looking like some sort of bad guy? Will we even have the time to have that lake date next weekend? The thought of Branch watching me or just passing me in the street gave me the cold chill, as if I could see that angry face and feel her pulsating anger that was like an electrical charge...

"Hey! Mike...you okay?" Marx interrupted my flash dream and it startled me back to the moment.

"Yeah...um yeah, I'm okay."

"I understand the danger that you are in and have been in. Most of that is my fault and if you want to get out and just protect yourself, that's okay," he said with a sincere look of concern.

"No, no I am in on this one hundred percent," I replied. "I'm with you, just let me know what you want me to do."

"Listen, I'm going to go see Katy tomorrow and give her the warning and let her know I'll be checking on her. I will call you tomorrow and make plans to try and flush these people out in the open. And, oh yeah, I almost forgot. The FBI got a call from a guy who owns a place in Santa Teresa. His name is Charles Vinson. He said his daughter went out with a guy that matched the description of someone we are looking for. That someone is Jake Benson. Her name is Clarice Vinson. I need to make contact with that family and make sure she knows she is in danger as well."

"Well, I feel that the living nightmare is back in focus. Jake and Carrianne in Brazil, Branch somewhere in the states, a big guy helping her, and two missing siblings. Sounds like it's enough to keep us busy for years," I said.

"Well, let's hope it doesn't take that long," Marx said with the look of determination I had seen before.

I headed for the door and turned to Marx and said, "Hey, do see Katy soon. I care about that kid."

"First thing on my list tomorrow."

"Good, thanks."

I left and got into my car and turned on the ignition. The soft tune playing on the radio brought up the face of Joanna as I drove back to my place. I really needed to keep this Saturday date. I felt as though something good was happening in my life. I didn't want that to fall apart. But I also felt that something very bad was just around the corner. And, I was right...

CHAPTER 28

Allison Branch was having trouble sleeping. She lay on her back with her steel blue eyes staring at the ceiling. She was once again in a state of conscious dreaming. She couldn't understand how others could not recognize it. She could stay in the darkest of places where her mental illness would continue to ferment, unseen by anyone else.

Revenge is a primitive, destructive and usually violent response to anger, injury, or humiliation. Her rage from adolescence and lack of nurturing had provided the perfect backdrop of her becoming a victim. The role of victim must be obtained before she could seek her revenge. She was the victim of her abusive father, of Andy Marx, and, of course, that Mike Parsons who did not choose her.

Her father was not there to show her the affection that she so craved and needed at the time. He was absent, as he had left when she was very young, so no male role model to call dad while her few friends around her all had their daddies. She slowly gravitated away from those friends and hung out with other girls like her that had no fathers. She could only recall him from pictures and she kept several of him her mother gave her. In her thoughts, she knew she would find him someday and she would get even.

As for Marx, he had killed one of the few people in her life she had truly loved, outside of her mother. Breanne was special, and Marx had taken that away. *He always, ALWAYS, thought he was a better cop than me. He was so damn cocky. He killed Breanne and for that he would pay. But he also killed me by trying to have me put away. He thought he was so smart. He thought he shamed me, but no, I will turn that shame into pride and I will not be stopped. I don't know how it ends, but Marx will see his demise. I will be sure to make that happen.*

And then there is Mikey. Oh, poor Mikey. He could have had me, I was the cure for whatever was ailing that man. He knew it, too. I had him, and I couldn't finish him. Thanks to that stupid brother of his. I'll do away with that guy too. That will be the one that hurts Mikey. That will be the knife to the heart that will ruin the rest of his life. I still can't believe he didn't pick me. I was right there! Right there in the bar and he picked that bimbo. His day will come and not without some torture and humiliation. The same humiliation I have felt for years.

Then there is the silly little barmaid, Katy. She thought she had Parsons. She had nothing over me and all she did was get in the way. If only his brother had not shot Jerry, this would all have gone my way. Katy and Parsons would both be dead, and Breanne and I would be far away together, just like we had planned.

All three of them will be in play. All three of them

are the prey in this game. They will all have the ending I so desperately want and need for them to have. Yes, they all need to be gone. And you too, daddy, and yes daddy, you too...

Allison turned to look at the clock. It was 3:00 am and she had fought sleep so hard. She turned over on her side and tears fell from her steel blue eyes, dropping silently on her pillow. Tomorrow, she would go out into the world and be Lynnette Huber. She would have a job, be out socially and hunt for her prey. She had a plan and for that plan she needed help. Most hunters need bait or decoys to lure the prey closer. Lynnette knew she had changed her name, but on the inside, she would never change. She was still Allison Branch and she was going to be the winner.

In her dreams, she had made the plan over and over. At 3:20 am sleep took over for Lynnette Huber, and she dreamt one last time of how it was going to play out. The perfect plan, the perfect hunt was going to happen. When Lynnette Huber awakens the next morning, day one of her wicked and evil plan would begin. It could not possibly fail. After all, she dreamed of it over and over while behind bars while sleeping on the musty bunk in her cell. Or was she consciously dreaming it and no one was really recognizing it? Not even herself....

Carrianne had not slept well that night either. The drug trade had been good to her and Jake, but his woman, this Branch, Huber or whoever she was, well, she was just downright scary. She picked up her phone and dialed Jake. Jake answered on the third ring.

"Jake, this is Carrianne. We have to talk," she said in a low whisper.

"Hey, what's up?' he asked sounding a bit weary.

"It's Branch. I think she's bat shit crazy. Today she went close to Mike Parsons again. She bought us hoodies, caps to wear and sunglasses. Like we were stalking the guy. I don't like it, it's not a good idea, with us having to lay low and such."

"Boy I bet Andres wouldn't like that," Jake said.

"He was there when we got back. How he knew we had gone, I had no idea. You know he is like a ghost and that he appears out of nowhere all the time," she said blinking to see in the dark. "I worry about her and keep my door locked at night. I want to tell Andres that I can't stay with her, but I can't let him down. He was very angry that we went out."

"Do you want me to come over tomorrow?" he asked. "I know we are supposed to stay hidden but I can be there if she is bugging you that much."

"Why don't you, just to let her know I have some protection. I know we have Andres, but I want her to know that you can show up too."

"Okay, I'll be over tomorrow about nine. Don't go out anywhere until I get there. I have a few disguises for us to use when we do get out. We can't go out without these. The players in the hood know I am wearing these because I call them and tell them what I have on. It's a risk but it is the only way I can deal with our pictures being all over the news."

"Okay, thanks, brother. I know I can count on you. We always had each other, even back home," she said relieving some of her own fears.

"Okay I have to go. Andres doesn't want us on the phones too long. I will be there in the morning."

"Thanks, Jake, you're the best."

"No problem, see you tomorrow."

Carrianne hung up and somehow felt a little better after talking to Jake. But this Branch, what in the world made her like this? Carrianne thought her to be quite unwound and a bit off, but she enjoyed the conversations they had had about men, sex and falling in love, something Carrianne had so desperately wanted to experience.

She rolled over and felt better, knowing that her rock would be there tomorrow morning to calm some of her fears. Carrianne wanted a real relationship and she was growing weary of this business. There was so much mystery and suspense, so much danger. She would never find a man and settle down. Andres just had to let me get out, maybe return to Brazil and live a real life. She could have a real life and have children, something her biological clock told her was necessary. She could love and be loved, the one thing in life she desperately craved. Sleep took her around 4:00 am.

CHAPTER 29

Miss Lynnette Huber woke up the next morning and looked into the mirror. She was really liking what she saw. The doctor had done an amazing job, even making her appear younger. Today she needed to get out and look for work, but she really didn't want to do anything except be a cop again and control the drug traffic as she had always done. But that was in the past and she had to seek out some type of employment, helping her establish this new identity.

She found a few opportunities she saw on line and would make a few calls this morning. But first she had to shower and dress up if she was to make an impression. She paused to look in the mirror once more, just to be sure that her new instant, manufactured beauty had not left. Sure enough, with those steel blue eyes, blonde hair, and great body, they were going to have to pick her, right? She laughed a bit under her breath, knowing that she could not possibly be found out and that in the not so distant future, she would have the revenge she desperately sought.

"Hey, Lynnette, you up yet?" Carrianne asked from outside her door.

"Yes, I'm awake," she replied. "I'm going to go out and look for a job today so I'm going to shower. Is there anything good to eat for breakfast?"

"I'll see what I can fix up for us. Andres left a lot of groceries for us as he wanted us to stay inside," she replied.

Lynnette undressed and headed for the shower. The warm water felt good on her back and shoulders that were tight from the tension she went through last night when she couldn't sleep. She felt relaxed for once and began to wash herself and then her hair. She finished and put a towel around her and then wrapped her hair in a separate towel. The towel did not cover her completely and her ample breasts were in view. She went on into the kitchen to see if she could help Carrianne with breakfast. She picked up the two plates and put them on the kitchen table and set some silverware by them. Coffee was brewing and Carrianne turned to speak.

"Thanks for setting the table. I would have done it."

"It's okay, really, I was never much of a homemaker," Lynnette said. "My mom actually said I was hopeless. But, setting a table, well anybody can do that."

Just then there was a knock on the front door. Carrianne went to look through the peep hole and was relieved it was Jake.

"Hey, sis, something smells good," he said as he walked through the front room to the kitchen. "Oh my, and something looks pretty good too," he added as he watched Lynnette move in the kitchen in nothing but her towel.

"Well, thank you, Jake," she returned not blushing at all. "I wore this outfit just for you."

"You can close your mouth now," Carrianne interrupted.

"He just likes what he sees, don't you, Jake?" Lynnette said in a sultry voice.

"Oh, stop, Lynnette, he's just a flirt. Breakfast is almost ready, so let's eat," Carrianne said, glad that the little exchange between those two was over.

They sat down to eat and talked some about their new place and how they would have to stay hidden for a while. Jake was worried, especially about what Carrianne had said in her call last night. He was getting the vibes that Carrianne also felt about her. Not to trust her, and not to get to close to her. She was truly dangerous...in many ways, yes in many ways....

"Well, you did great with breakfast, young lady. I will help with the dishes and, Jake, maybe you would like to help me? Lynnette asked.

"I think he just needs to watch TV, Lynnette, I'll help you," Carrianne said.

Jake went into to the front room and turned on the TV. The girls finished the dishes. Lynnette walked seductively past Jake, whose eyes followed her every step. Carrianne rolled her eyes watching Jake. When Lynnette reached her room, she turned and said, "Hey I'd like to sit and talk with you more, Jake, but I need to get ready. My loss," she said following up with one of her best smiles.

Jake didn't say a word. He just kept staring until the door was shut behind her.

"I told you," Carrianne started in a low voice so as not to be heard. "She's crazy, she flirts with men and women. I think she is getting a bit unhinged here. Jake, don't fall for that stuff. You know she is trouble."

"Yeah, I know, but there is something more sinister than what she says or does. I just can't put my finger on it," he said. "She has some sort of control over you, some sort of voodoo. No, wait, I know, it's her eyes. It's those steel blue eyes. They just don't let you go, when she has them locked on you."

Lynnette closed the door and began to speak to herself; *See, you still have it. You have the sultry, the sexy way with men. The way that helps you lure them into a trap. That boy out there is no challenge. But Mike Parsons, I trapped him before and I can do it again. I just need a little bit of help, maybe Carrianne, maybe Andres, or maybe both of them. But it's in my plan. Take a couple of weeks, check things out, get a job, get settled and then start setting the trap. It won't be easy, but it will all be avenged. Every last one of them will pay. Then it's back to Brazil and a life that I had always wanted...*

Carrianne and Jake were interrupted by breaking news on TV.

"Milwaukee police, have a few clues as to the disappearance of local business man Oscar Stephenson three years ago. Detective Andy Marx is with us today and Mr. Marx, what do we know about the cold case disappearance of Mr. Stephenson."

"Our unit has a few new clues about this case. We want to keep some of them to ourselves. If you should see either one of these people, please call our department with any information you may have. They are originally from Brazil, but we do have two photos we would like to show the public. These two are Jake Benson and Carrianne Martinez. Their real names are Julio and Maria Santos. They posed as boyfriend and girlfriend but are actually brother and sister. I was going to bring them in for questioning in the Oscar Stephenson case, but they disappeared and have been involved in drug trafficking. This second photo is of a woman named Andrea Stephenson Raines. She is the sister of Oscar Stephenson, and is either missing or in danger, possibly with her brother. Any information at all would be very helpful to the case. We are investigating in Brazil as well, but it is hard to coordinate that effort from the states."

"Thank you, Detective Marx. Any news yet on the escape from prison of Allison Branch?"

"Nothing yet, we feel she may have changed here appearance so a photo does us no good right now," Marx said staring into the camera.

"Yes, true, my old picture would do no good. In fact, I am much prettier now, right Jake?"

Carrianne jumped at her voice. It scared her as Lynnette had quietly entered the room sneaking in behind them.

"Well, uh, yes Lynnette, you are very pretty," Jake responded. "But as you can see we need to stay out of sight. I'm leaving these disguises with Carrianne and don't take her out without letting her put one on. Different glasses and different wigs, different make up. Please make sure we don't get noticed. Our lives depend on it."

"Sure, Jake, sure. I won't let anything happen to her, I was a cop remember?"

With that Lynnette left and went job hunting as Andres had requested. In the not too distant future, she would go people hunting. That prospect filled her with a sense of pride and great anticipation. She felt warm all over. She got into her car and took the two pills from her purse and popped them in her mouth. She needed to be under control and these pills helped her to remain calm. Her mother had tried to get her counseling and medication when she was young. She would not do it and now being illegally medicated, she was able to keep her emotions under control.

That Marx will get his too. Yep, I've changed, Marx. Not you, not Parsons, not that dumb little Katy, none of you, will ever know who I am. You won't find me, not until it's much too late to do anything about it. Much too late. Thanks meds, at least I am not crying.

CHAPTER 30

A ndy was driving towards Katy's house thinking of how Branch could and would show up. It would be nearly impossible to detect her. The only thing I have to check on will be fingerprints, but by the time it comes to that it may be too late. Marx knew every hangout that she liked and knew her as well as anyone. But how and when? He knew she would be hard to catch and hard to find. Then, there is the big man and his connection to Jake and Carrianne. That has to be figured out. If he found them, then he could put a lot of pressure on them.

His car pulled up in front of Katy's and it stopped his train of thought. He would check up with the Feds and see what they had after he talked to Katy. He got out of department vehicle and headed for the door and knocked while he rang the bell. Katy answered and was surprised to see Marx at her door. After a quick moment to gather herself, she let him in.

"Come in, please," she said. "I'm sorry for my

hesitation there, I was just surprised to see you."

"I understand. I just wanted to drop by for a moment and let you know some things that are going on," he said as he was noticing her dark hair and dark complexion. Her features were quite striking.

"Well, I did see the news feature last night. That woman scares me, bad."

"She can scare a lot of people. Here is what we have so far. We know that she may have changed her appearance. It's why I wanted to let you know to be very careful and trust no one. You won't be able to recognize her. The only thing I have to go on is fingerprints, and her eyes. Of course, you know her eyes, too, but she could wear contacts so that may not be possible either. Everyone that comes into your bar could be a suspect. I don't know if you can be careful enough. I just want you to be sure to contact me if you see anything at all suspicious. Here's my number."

Marx looked at Katy and again was surprised at how nice she looked. He actually had not noticed before. He shook it off and began again.

"Mike is helping out and has given me some insight into her. I think I have a line on what I need to investigate and places I need to be," he said.

"Well, yes," she said and had frozen just at the mention of Mike's name. She had been doing better and getting over him, but just to hear his name brought back a flood of emotional feelings once again. "I hope he helps you. He's a smart guy."

"Well, I have to get back but remember she is working with several others and I have brought you some pictures to look at that may help you. These pictures are some of the suspects we think may be working with her. The big guy is really dangerous. Couldn't get his face but if you see a large man be very cautious. He's not your average punk. He is probably extremely dangerous," he said as Katy thumbed through the photographs.

"Wait, these two, the young couple, I have seen them before in the bar. They are boyfriend and girlfriend, I believe. They sat at the bar together one night, but funny, they weren't very intimate for a couple. He flirted a bit with me and that kind of put me off thinking that he was hurting her feelings."

"Is there anything else, anything at all you can remember that will help? Distinguishing marks, anything else?" Andy asked.

"The girl, she said something like...something about Johnny wouldn't like that. It seemed so crazy, but yes...she said Johnny wouldn't like that."

"Okay, good," Marx said as he wrote some things down in his notebook and then closed it. "That's helpful. "I've got to get back and get some word out on what you told me. Be safe, keep your doors locked and I will call someone to occasionally check up on you. Be watchful and call me if you need me."

"Okay," she said as she walked Marx back to the door. "I'll do my best." But she didn't sound convincing.

Marx headed out the door and Katy thought to herself as she shut the door...*the guy is really handsome. He is nice, too. But am I over Mike? I have to be, don't I? Life has to go on. Maybe this is the day I get over it. Thanks to Andy Marx. You are just confused. When will this life ever get normal again? You're feeling a twinge of something, something you have consciously avoided for some time now. Something you have no control over. Don't try to hide it, you felt something for that guy, didn't you? Be careful, yes, be careful...*

▲

Marx got back and called his buddies at the FBI. He told them he had a name only John or Johnny, but it was a name and Marx had a hunch it was the name of the big guy. John could be millions of people across the country or it could be someone right under their nose. But John was a start. It would be a while before John's name would be used against Andres, and in one of the strangest ways...

Lynnette walked into one of her interviews with the university. They were looking for a secretary for the theater department. Lynnette was about to meet Joanna Presley, the department head and several other department members to do a face to face interview. She walked into the meeting with a lot of confidence as she did in most of her endeavors. She had a seat at the table and met each department person one at a time. They asked her some simple questions and she answered noting all of her capabilities with technology, writing and communications. She was very, very good. She knew she had nailed the interview when she left. Joanna had told her they would make their decision and call her and they all rose and shook hands politely. Lynnette left knowing she had the job and left the number of her trac phone to be disposed of later. She would then get a new one and be employed. Lynnette Huber, secretary of the theater department. It had a nice ring to it. She left in her car and went back home. There would be no need to interview for the rest. She knew she would get hired. She would get hired because the assistant department head was an easy mark for those eyes. She held him on a few of her answers and she swore she made him blush once. In her mind, she would be at work tomorrow.

She dropped by the old neighborhood of the one and only Mike Parsons on the way home. *Yes, should I play with his mind a bit? Sure, why not, as she parked in his lot and waited. Just to see if she could get in a glimpse of her prey once more is thrilling isn't it? Oh, wait here he comes now. Well, hello, Mikey. Do you believe in destiny, Mike? Or are you just so damn stupid, you can't see what is right in front of you. Sitting in the car watching you is the one you could have had! You could have picked me, you know. But, no, you couldn't see destiny right in front of you!* Tears rolled down her cheeks as he walked into his unit and disappeared. She took out two more pills before she did something just a bit too soon. She lay her head back on the head rest. The song "Black Irish" by The Devil Makes Three came on her radio,

"If I could only do all the things I want to, while that spirit is rushing in my veins"

"I want to feel that blood rushing my veins, I don't want this night to turn into day"

She was lost in her mainline dream about how and when she would end this nightmare. How she would feel her blood rushing through her veins, just once more, the feeling that she could not stop no matter how many pills she took. They were only a temporary fix. She knew her mind took her on these strange and long nightmares. She thought for just a moment, just one short moment, just take me now, and relieve me. Make it go away, but she opened her tear-filled eyes and it was still there flashing before her. All the things he wanted to do with the spirit rushing through her veins...she drove away.

When she got home, Lynnette was composed again. She had regained, for a moment anyway, her composure that she seemed to lose more often. Her phone rang and she answered.

"Hello," this is Lynnette Huber.

"Yes, Lynnette, this is Joanna Presley here at the university. I just wanted to call and congratulate you on getting the position with us here. Welcome to our team."

"Oh, I am thrilled," she said in her best attempt to be excited. "When do I start?"

"Tomorrow, if you can," Joanna said. "I understand if you need more time."

"No. Oh, no, tomorrow is fine with me." Lynnette said. "What time do I start?"

"We start in the office at nine. We would like you to be there by 8 to answer phones and schedule appointments and such. I will see you tomorrow and we can go over where everything is located and give you a tour of the University."

"Ok, thank you so much. I'll see you in the morning." She said as she hung up. *Geez woman, I was a cop there. I know all about that university. But I just have to act like I just don't know anything about it. I'll be there though and get set up for the hunt. I think it's going to be perfect for finding my prey close by. Yes, Professor Parsons, that will make me pretty close to you and you aren't going to know a thing. I'll probably just walk by you a few times just for fun, but you won't notice. I wonder if you will believe in destiny now?...*

I wasn't thinking straight before going to bed. I had too many things going on inside of me. It was just one more time that I couldn't find relief from the past I was trying to escape. Tonight was "beat myself up night". Yes, all the way back to Sheila's suicide and through the whole crazy ordeal with Allison Branch. You know how guys are supposed to "man up" and not talk about what really hits them hard. I was thinking I was sliding back, sliding fast, feeling my skin turn cold and slick against a hard-blowing wind. I froze in my chair, I froze and could not move. Yet, if I close my eyes, there it is, the old nightmare, being captive, being tortured beyond what I thought I could endure. I keep waking up, beaten, bruised and bloody. I see Jerry's head exploding and Katy and I being rescued. The courtroom, dimly lit and she walks in, I see nothing, nothing at all except for steel blue eyes...*Move damn it, move. You have to move, I know I am awake so get up, get out of that chair! Steel blue eyes locked on me, got ya, got ya, I got ya!!*

Finally, I moved, finally I got up, sweat pouring from my forehead, dripping off my nose. Not a trickle, but a river flowing. *Stop this, stop right now...*

I got up and splashed water on my face, shaking my head into reality once more. Standing in the kitchen, I thought I saw car lights through the curtains. *Go ahead, look, it's okay.* I reached out for the curtain to pull it to the side and see who was out there. My hand froze for just a few seconds and then I pulled the drapes to see. No one is there, no one. *See, for nothing, your fear is for nothing.* I walked away from the window slowly questioning myself and my wellness once more. *But I know, man up, nothing is wrong with you. You just can't let a dream control you, you are okay. Don't think or talk about it and it will go away, right?*

I sat back down and wondered to myself how in the world I was going to be any good for someone else when I couldn't be good for myself. This thing, this mental health thing, it's real, it happens, and my mental health was being manipulated. By HER, once again, by HER.

I called Joanna and we talked for a while. She was

feeling like my life preserver. She was the only thing that somehow kept reality in sight. The conversation ended with a new date agreed upon and that I would come by to see her on my way to my car after leaving my office. I promised I would come by and we could decide if the date was my place or hers and who would cook. I hung up and felt a little more at peace. I went to lay down and thought that the one thing I was the most content about was Joanna Presley. There were so many things about her that made me feel different. It was a genuine feeling, a real feeling. The way she looked, the way she smelled, and the way she smiled. I was feeling like, finally, I had come to a place where I felt something about a woman, that was all about the right things to feel.

Andres Montoya was having thoughts that took him back. He wondered to himself why he ended up where he was at this point in his life. He grew up very poor in the heart of a place he hardly recognized anymore. He remembered his parents who taught him work and responsibility as a young boy. He was always bigger than most of the other boys he worked with. So, naturally he always did the most work, the heavy lifting and always protected his friends. Protection was a thing he was very good at as he learned to fight at a very young age. He was taught by some very rough characters and he had a thirst for it. Being poor made him realize he needed a way out and he thought that possibly if he was tough enough, he could get out of this life. He had few friends, as most were scared of him. The ugly scar across his forehead reminded him of the many battles he had with those who wanted to try him out. But he always won, yet he thought back on whether it was really important or not. He wasn't a bully, but he mainly would fight for what was right.

His life became really different when he was approached by Miguel Santos. Miguel was a top dog in the local drug culture and was becoming the leader of the newest cartel in the Complexo. Miguel needed a strongman who would be his protector. There was no one in the Complexo more qualified than Andres. Andres had the right make up and personality for the job and he became the enforcer and lead lieutenant for the cartel.

Miguel sent him to clean up an issue with a rival gang when he was eighteen. He knew it would be a tough task, but he was prepared. It was the first time he would use a garrote on someone and it wouldn't be the last. He took his prey from behind in the dark alley, choking the life out of the thirty-year-old rival. It was fast and his strength made it a quick kill. From that day, it got easier to kill and take care of the cartel's business.

Miguel and Andres became friends, but Andres kept him at arms-length. He knew his violent temper and he did not want to cross Miguel. Still, Miguel treated him like a brother, always inviting him to his home for meals and drinks. Andres drank very little, as he always considered it a weakness and an impediment to his daily operations. He could not let down his guard during the day and especially at night.

When Andres was twenty-two, Miguel's wife, Angelina, gave birth to twins. They were named Julio and Maria Santos. Andres had always felt a special connection to those children. He needed to protect them and he would do just that. He had his reasons, and he would forever stand by it. They would be his obligation.

Andres lay awake considering everything that they had planned to this point. He had usually thought of all the angles, all the possibilities, but he had forgotten just one thing that all of the sudden hit him. That woman, the woman Julio was with had slipped his mind. His mind that was so sharp, so detailed had forgotten this one thing and he jumped out of bed. *That girl, her name? The one Julio was with that night in Santa Teresa? She was probably back in the states. She has probably seen the news, and she had to be eliminated before it's too late...*

Clarice was just getting back to Chicago from her trip to Santa Teresa and was watching the news. There, before her eyes, was the picture of her most recent love interest, Jake Benson, also, a picture of his sister, Carrianne was next to his. They did look a lot alike she thought. She froze for a short time, wondering what it is she needed to do? *He is handsome, right? Maybe I don't need to do anything...he was kind of exciting. But, my friend, they know what he looks like and I can't trust them not to tell...* Just then her phone rang. She looked at the ID and it was unknown.

"Hello?" she answered.

"Hi, it's Jake. I've been wanting to call you, but I have been busy," he said.

"Well...hi," she stammered and was confused. She was glad to hear from him, but now, she was struggling, knowing that her friends had seen this, too. She had been enamored with Jake Benson and had waited for this call. But now, knowing something bad had happened, she was conflicted on what to do. "It's... good to hear from you," she stammered. Trying to find some sort of diversion back to practical thinking. Trying to tell herself that she had chosen the wrong guy to hang out with. "I was hoping that you would call."

"What's wrong, you seem to be upset?" he asked.

"I'm...just surprised to hear from you I guess," she was stammering and was aware of her nervousness. She wanted to hang up on him, and yet, she couldn't help from feeling she needed to help him. He didn't do anything wrong, he was just a witness right? But her instinct was telling her she had slept with the wrong guy.

Jake was picking up on her nervousness. Andres nodded to him as he continued to track the call.

"I thought maybe we could meet somewhere for a drink. Do you have any suggestions? I'd be glad to fly in to see you," he said.

"Well...I...uh...I have to work this week, so I don't really know..."

"You seem so nervous, like, is something wrong" he asked.

"Oh no, nothing, I just got back and had not expected to hear from you so soon,"

She knows, Andres thought as he listened in, still tracking the call. Just a few more seconds and he would have it. Keep talking he thought.

"I understand", Jake said. "We had such a good time, I just wanted to see you again. If you don't want to, I understand.

"Well, I have to go, I need to work tomorrow and I have to get there by eight."

"Okay, but can I call you tomorrow, I'd really like that?" Jake said.

"Please do, I will be more rested tomorrow."

"Take care, I will call tomorrow," he said as he hung up.

Jake knew the drill as Andres said he had tracked the address. He knew what was about to happen and he regretted involving this innocent girl with the dark hair, wide eyes and beautiful smile. But it was too late for regret, as Clarice was about to have a bad accident.

Jake drove Andres to the airport and he boarded quickly as he had to be there before morning. He had to track someone and there was no time to fool around. Andres needed to clear up this one loose end. The one loose end he had so carelessly forgotten. Jake's mistake, and he had to clean it up. He couldn't send Jake. He knew it because Jake was too soft. Women can be a man's downfall he thought, and there had been one time when it was his, too. He quickly put it out of his mind and boarded his flight, headed to a town he knew well. The ticket was easy to get as he had connections and his mind was focused on something that had become second nature to him. Andres was off to take care of some pressing business. He had promised and he was obligated for a very good reason.

CHAPTER 31

C larice Bergman had to go see her dad. She was too frightened and had to tell him about Jake. There wasn't much time and she had to let her dad know that the guy on the tv was her date in Santa Teresa that night. She dressed quickly and headed for the front door. She stopped to lock the door and began to walk down the sidewalk to her parked car. Suddenly, from the nearby bushes a large figure quickly wrapped the garrote around her neck, pulling hard and lifting her off the ground. She struggled and gasped for air that would not come. Quickly her breathing ceased and she was no longer of this world. Jake's girlfriend was dead and would never be able to tell her father who Jake was. The body would be disposed of and, in short order, Andres would be back at the airport and headed back to his farm.

A news flash from a Chicago TV station carried the news of young Clarice Bergman missing from her home. Her father was pleading on camera for any information that may lead to finding her. One of her friends immediately picked up the phone and called Clarice's father to let him know there was a man in Santa Teresa that may know something about this, or even be a suspect. They called the police and gave them all the information. Jake Benson's information was on TV again, the hunt for him and Carrianne was going national.

Andy Marx immediately called the Miami police and knew that those two kids were involved and the big guy too. Andy was now on point. He wanted to get started right away and he would go to Chicago if necessary, to interview those two girls and the father. This was the first clue and the first chance he had to follow something. He called me at midnight and said he was getting on a plane and heading to Miami. He would call me later and fill me in. We both thought the same thing as we knew Branch was somehow in with these people and the big guy had a big role. He had to be in the air somewhere. Andy was going to check all the local airports along with the local police.

But as always Andres Montoya had it all figured out. He rented a truck and was traveling by land. He would catch a flight somewhere else. It was starting to get complicated and he thought of eliminating some of the baggage he was carrying around. But he promised their mother to take care of them. And besides, he just couldn't. What about HER? What about Branch? It would be easier, but he had become attached to those eyes and he couldn't do that either. But the BOSS, he's not going to like any of this and the body of the girl won't be found and neither would that friend of Marx's. He just needed for the kids to move until he could get them back out of the country. They would be too big of a risk in the states. He needed for them to survive and maybe the time had come to take them home. Their pictures were all over the news, not his face but his large body, the kids' faces were there, they had to stay out of sight. He had to think and think hard. The Boss doesn't like screw-ups. Think...

The next morning was cold and gray. Typical for this time of year up north. I was starting to feel depressed about what was going on, but also a bit apprehensive about Branch. I knew she was out there hiding and waiting to find the right time. But where? I had to get dressed and today I was heading to see Joanna at her office. I was anxious to hear from Andy, too. I was curious as to what our next step was going to be. I hurried and dressed and headed to my car. I suddenly stopped and remembered I had forgotten to set the security system, something that got me in trouble before. I went back to the door and set the code and closed the door. Getting forgetful these days; old age must be setting in.

I drove to the university library and went through the old articles I could find on Branch, the violence, the trial, trying to find something that would give me a lead in my thinking. I read about Branch and her time of service in the department, about Breanne, Jerry and all the characters involved, and yes, the hero, Andy Marx, who had saved that clumsy, awkward Mike Parsons. The pictures of Allison Branch in the papers showed the anger, the frustration. The circles under her eyes at trial belied her beauty. I had never looked at her like this before. She presented something different to me. In some strange way I felt sorry for her. How could someone so pretty all of sudden become so ugly? I tried to make myself hate her but I couldn't. Something was like the counselor in me for a moment, someone who I was sure could help her. I knew she was sick and that she was out there somewhere planning my demise. But she was pretty to me once, was she not? I read a few more pieces about her sentencing and her escape.

I wondered who it was that picked her up when Henry Hannah had so royally screwed up. Where was poor Henry? There had been no clues on the guy. I printed off a few pages of the escape and put them in my folder. It was nearing time to go see Joanna and I didn't want to be late. I started to feel better and let go of Allison Branch once more as I had to do several times before. I looked down at my feet and scolded myself for those feelings, shook my head and slowly trudged through the library to the front door.

I am pretty good at torturing myself. I had done it many times in my life, always coming to the ultimate conclusion that most things were my fault. Nothing wrong with taking responsibility, but I over did it. It was my worst fault. Had I grown up feeling differently, I may have had an easier life. But I took way too much on as being my fault and not enough times could I just let something go as being just a part of life. I felt like I needed to have control over everything and when I didn't, it was because I had a weakness, or so I thought. Life would have been so much easier not carrying fifty-pound weights in my life's backpack every day. It made my shoulders slump forward. It dropped my head a little and caused me sometimes to not look people in the eye. I didn't believe in myself all the time.

I shook off my temporary negativity and headed across campus. *Time to gain some confidence if you are going to see Ms. Joanna. Time to take the weights out of your backpack and walk a little more swiftly. Just breath, try to forget, and look forward. What's done is done and Branch chose her own fate. It's really not your fault.*

I moved on walking a bit better with my shoulders much straighter. Today, is a new day and many of the things I was thinking recently were in my past. I was looking forward to seeing Joanna. For some reason, she took some of that weight off me. She made me feel whole and new again. I can't say that for many, but still it is just the beginning. But I trusted her, a lot.

I walked into the office and waited out front. Joanna showed up with the smile that I had come to know as so good for me. It made me smile back. She was dressed really business smart but showing enough leg to gain my interest. She was beautiful and that smile always made me feel like I was "home."

"It's great to see you," I began. "You look very nice today."

"Well, thank you, Mr. Parsons. You look pretty handsome yourself," she replied.

"I thought you were hiring a new girl for the front?" I asked.

"We did she is in the back, doing some filing right now. I'll introduce you to her later," she said.

"Okay, well, I'd like to go to lunch if you have some time. Maybe down to Mac's. They got a great lunch menu and they are pretty quick." I said.

"Okay, let me get my coat," Joanna said. "I'll be just a second," and she disappeared back to her office.

In a few seconds she came back and my lunch date and I were off. From the back of the room, the new girl, Lynette Huber appeared, but after we had walked out the door. She had heard the conversation from the back and waited until they left to come back out to the front. *Well, well, Mike. I guess you picked my boss and not me again. You haven't even seen me yet. I am actually much prettier than before. If you saw me, you would change your mind. You really wouldn't even recognize me. How much fun would this be? Really, Mike, the game has just begun. This will be the most fun I've ever had! Just when you think you have it made, I will truly put you in your final sleep. I did love you, always did. But I think the time is getting near and that demon is flowing through my veins. I don't think I can stop it from happening. This time though, I will get away and you won't, you'll be dead.* A small tear rolled down Lynnette Huber's pretty cheek.

CHAPTER 32

Katy was getting ready for work. The thought of Andy Marx had stayed with her most of last night. Although he was handsome and someone that she could easily be interested in, Katy was deeper in her thoughts about love. What she felt she needed at this point in her life was a man that could make her stronger. Someone that would allow her to grow and feel the value of her own life. She wanted to be significant, yet she wanted the independence that a strong man could give her. She didn't need the jealous type who was going to stalk her every move. She needed the freedom, but yet still liked to feel as though she could get close when her heart required some rebuilding. It was not her intent to use anyone, but to be helped while becoming a much stronger and independent woman. It was something that she realized that Mike could not give her. She wanted that, but he wasn't capable because he was having his own troubles fixing himself.

It was only a thought at the moment, but the thought was intriguing. She stopped and stared at herself in the mirror. She had always been pretty, always had a youthful look to her, but she saw that she was aging a bit and her face had become somewhat lined with worry and fear. She had feared that she would never find the right guy. She also feared that she may run into Ms. Allison Branch again. She had armed herself, she had locked all her doors and windows. Even so, her fear was real and tangible and it almost choked her at times. Studying herself in the mirror, she looked deeper into her own face and wanted a new Katy to appear. She wanted to see herself as forever young and invincible.

The longer she stared into the mirror, an image was starting to appear over her shoulder. She squinted to see it more clearly. Suddenly, there it was, the face that she had dreaded for so long now, Allison Branch, smiling at her over her shoulder. The smile was hideous and so real, every nerve ending in her body tingled as she thought quickly about what she should do. She grabbed the scissors and spun quickly and raised the scissors above her head to attack. But then, her hand slowly dropped to her side and she lay the scissors back on the bathroom sink. There was no one there. Her fears once again had created the image that she saw. She walked around her house, looking in all the closets and rooms. She re-checked her entrance door to make sure it was still locked.

Exhausted, Katy flopped down on her bed. She picked up her phone and pushed the contacts button. The names Mike and Andy were there side by side. The longer she stared at them she was so tempted to push Mike's number. Her thumb moved to it, hovered over it, but in the end, she chose neither and scrolled down to her counselor's number. She made an appointment for the next day and then she finished getting ready for work. Today, she made a choice for her, and that was to be stronger and to get through this on her own. She would call Marx later. But for now, she had to exorcise the demons that haunted her. She had to do this on her own. From this day forward, Katy vowed to be stronger, vowed to get better, and vowed not to need Mike Parsons again. But she would, and somehow, deep inside, she knew it...

My lunch with Joanna was at Mac's which was a quiet little bar and grill that was tucked into a shopping mall. The seating was about half-full and our seats were cozy in the corner of the place. A young waitress came by and delivered two menus and water and said she would return and asked if we would like a drink. We both declined, although I would have had one if not for the fact I had been trying to cut back. She left us alone and Joanna took a sip of her water. On the TV behind her a local news station was carrying a story on a disappearance of a young woman in Miami. On the screen were two young ladies, friends of the missing girl. Pictures flashed on the screen, and there they were, Jake and Carrianne, in all their glory, once again in the news. The reporter asked questions and the story of Jake, leaving with their friend Clarice in Santa Teresa came to light.

"Please excuse me, I have to make a call," I said and left the table for the restroom. I immediately called Andy.

"Hey Marx, what is going on? Just saw the news piece. Do you have any information? What do you think is happening? That Santa Teresa story connects with us," I said.

"I've been checking airports, wondering if Jake

Benson or the big guy have been around," Andy said his voice sounding tired. "There's not much, but I have to feel that those two kids are involved and with all the heat on them, they may be easier to spot with their pictures all over the news. The big man is a key and he is hitting all these witnesses hard. We just have to locate where they are. I am thinking we need to look here in Miami area, but maybe you can keep your eye out there that even remotely gives us a clue about them until I get back. Let me know if you see anything that points in their direction. The local cops here will be doing some investigating, checking out car rental places, but I may head back tomorrow."

"Got ya," I said staring at Joanna from a distance, knowing I needed to get back to her. "I'll keep my eyes peeled, but if you want my opinion, and I'm not saying this because I have a big ego, I'm guessing they are near here. I believe she wants to kill me and I think she is not going to wait long to do it."

"You need to be careful, Mike. These people are dangerous, especially the big man. He's crafty and good and has money and access allowing him to move around the country pretty quickly. I'll be back tomorrow and we'll get together then."

"You be careful, too. I'll try to do some things this afternoon before you get back. I'll do some snooping or maybe we'll just get a lucky break. But, I'll talk to you tomorrow."

"Alright, see you then," Andy said and hung up.

I went back out to our table and the waitress soon came to take our order. We had a quick lunch but the conversation started to move on to other things more related to Joanna and me.

"I didn't get to meet the new girl," I said. "How is she working out?"

"Well, it's only the first day, but she seems nice. She

doesn't seem to need a lot of direction and she is a self-starter, so that is good."

"Well, that's good. Maybe I can meet her when we go back," I said.

"Sure, if you like," Joanna said. "But, she's pretty and I don't know if I really want you to meet her. She may try to steal you away when she finds out you're on staff here."

"Well, you need a good hire. Maybe she will work out for you. Not to change the subject or anything, but how is your play coming along? I know you haven't started rehearsing yet, but I am excited for you to get your casting complete."

"I'm having trouble finding a girl to play the main character's sister. It's an important role but being a campus/community play, my main characters are usually my students. The one I was planning on has had an emergency back home and had to leave school. Maybe I can find someone in the community to do the role. But I am still looking."

I stared at her eyes and saw her interest and fire about her play. It made me interested. "So how long before you decide, you know you only have a week?" I asked.

"Well, I am having auditions tonight. Maybe someone will show up and be good," she said. Maybe you could come by and watch?"

"I may be able to do that," I responded. "I have to do one thing for Andy, but what I really was hoping for was a quiet evening after play practice. Maybe you could come by my place for a drink?"

"I think I would really like to do that, Mr. Parsons," Joanna said with the clear and clean smile I had always found sexy and refreshing. It made my pulse go just a bit faster.

"So, with that, we have a second date on the same

day?" I asked.

"I believe we do," she said with a killer wink, that made me jump ahead to about nine hours later.

"Great, let's pay the bill and get out of here. I can go back and meet your new girl and then I can take care of business and get my slate clear to concentrate on the prettiest girl at the university!" I said, looking into her eyes that showed approval and possibly anticipation. "Ready?"

"Thanks for lunch, it is always fun to be with you," she said getting up from the table.

She walked with a grace and style that not many really have. Her walk was fluid, confident and with a small swagger in her step. I called it elegance and it only belongs to a small number of women. I could feel my confidence grow every minute I spent with her. She was easy to talk to and easy to be around. I was finding my attachment was driven by the simple thought of her and a smile that came to my face. She's repairing me somehow. I can't totally put my finger on it, but it's there. Something is there and it feels good all over. She may not know it yet, but I am becoming quite attached to her.

Our drive was quick as Mac's was not that far off campus. We pulled into the visitor's space and my phone rang. It was Marx.

"Hi, Andy, what's up?" I asked.

"Look, I have a tip came in from the department that I want you to check out for me," Andy said.

I looked at Joanna and tried to hide a bit of this conversation as I really didn't want her involved.

"Sure," I said and continued, "can I call you back in just a few minutes?"

"Sure." And I hung up

"I'd love to come in and meet the new girl, but I have a few things to get done that had to do with that call. Get those off my plate, and we can have some nice, quiet time together this evening. How's that?"

"I'd love that. I understand. But, do call later and we can get things arranged. You know, I am a time person."

"Will do. And, thanks for going to lunch. I really enjoyed our time together."

With that she left my car and walked her gracious walk up the steps and into the building. I was looking forward to tonight's get-together. I had to make sure, that it went well. I was becoming very interested in the lady.

Joanna walked back into her office and found Lynnette at her front desk on the phone. She waved and walked on back to her office. Joanna was struggling with trying to find someone to play the part of the lead actress's sister in her play. The role wasn't extremely challenging, but she needed someone to fill in for the original young lady. She walked to the door and called Lynnette back to her office.

"Lynnette, I know this is a crazy question for someone who just came to work for her first day, but have you ever acted before?" Joanna asked.

"Well, I did a few things in high school but never something in a community play," Lynnette lied. *Well, of course, I have acted a lot in my life. I am pretty damn good at it, too, you fool. I am good enough to fool you, Marx, and that stupid new boyfriend of yours, too. Actually, I am the best actress you could find, you just don't know it yet.*

"I just have a short time and rehearsal is just for one more week. The role is not too extensive and the lines aren't overwhelming, yet the part is very important. I was hoping that maybe you could help me out?"

"I could give it a try," Lynnette said. "When is the next practice?"

"Well, tonight. I know it is short notice, but I can give you a script and you can look it over and it sure would be a favor if you could help us out," Joanna said looking hopefully at Lynnette.

"Well, if you really think I can do it...I uh, well sure, okay, I'll do it."

"Great!" Joanna said smiling at Lynnette. "Practice is in the theatre auditorium at 7:00. I really can't tell you how happy I am that you said yes. You are very pretty and fit the role really well."

Well, of course you are, you silly woman. You couldn't possibly find someone so quickly on this short notice. I will do it only because it will get me closer to hurting that new boyfriend of yours. Even though I have nothing against you, it may just work out that you are collateral damage, but hey, get involved with Mike Parsons and that is what you get. If you only knew, if you only knew...

Lynnette snapped back quickly and told Joanna she would be there tonight for practice and thanked her for the opportunity. It was another opportunity that Lynnette seemed to be lucking into lately. She had been lucky lately, yes. But her luck in her life was overall pretty bad. Lynnette was on one of her good streaks now. Her life was going to get better.

She walked back to her desk and in her purse, she got one of her pills and took it with a swig of bottled water. She would finish her day and head home and study a few lines. She was going to steal the show. She just knew that she would...

I called Andy back and was curious to what the tip was. Come to find out, he had a tip on the big guy and his whereabouts. He had a call from someone at a rental car business that had rented a car to a big guy. It was a just a hunch by the man working the rental counter, but seeing the pictures on TV, he thought the big man was somebody that may have been of interest to the police.

"Mike, I'm going to see what I can find. If I get something, I may want you to check it out. This one will take a lot of caution on your part. Don't go on this tip until I get back to you. I want to run some of the info. I'll call you back."

"Okay, Andy. Let me know what you find. If this is the guy we are looking for, he is dangerous and I know you are aware of that. Just make sure that you have help if you go after him," I said.

Andy hung up. I sat there in my car thinking of what to do next. I was really looking forward to my night with Joanna. She had somehow worked her way into my heart. It wasn't pre-meditated, it wasn't forced. Casually, without a plan or a purpose, she had started to weave her way into my soul. Something wasn't final about it, but I could see that picture of us together in my mind. Her pretty smile, walking up behind me on the dock and putting her arms around me, making me smile in return.

It's a great picture. One that I just couldn't formulate in my mind for my whole life, until now. There she is, smiling that smile and looking into the camera, me smiling too. It's what I feel could be us. I wondered how real it was. Was it like the two little men on my shoulder that appeared sometimes? They fall off and then bounce right back up. Is it a mirage, or is it really what my mind wants, what my soul so desperately needs?

I snapped back out of my thoughts and started the car and drove back to my place. I had something to do for Andy and I wanted to be able to clear my deck for tonight. I was going to be with Joanna and that was the highest priority on my list.

I got back to my place around one. I entered my unit and looked around, as always, making sure someone wasn't going to crush the back of my head. Things were fine and no people hiding in my closets. My phone rang and I answered, "hello?" ...

———▲———

Carrianne was worried. She knew what had happened. She saw it on the news and it was just a matter of time before Jake knew his new girlfriend was dead. The heat was going to get more intense and they would have to continue to hide and play the games Andres wanted them to. She began to feel like a prisoner in her own skin. Once again, she felt that her life had been nothing but fear, danger and doing people favors. She never had imagined such a life. She had only thought of marrying a handsome man, having children, a normal kind of life. In her mind, she had been grateful to Andres, but now, she was starting to resent all the things she had done and all the things she was and didn't want to be.

Just then, Jake came in the door, dressed hideously in a skimmer hat, with a fake beard and sunglasses. Carrianne wanted to laugh but knew by his face that he knew.

"She's dead. Andres did it and you know it, too," Jake said through clenched teeth.

"Yes, I am afraid that is true," she answered wishing that things were different. "This is what we get, Jake. This is all we are going to get, ever!"

He slumped down on the sofa, putting his palm to his forehead. He was growing weary of what they had to do. He also had no life, just like his sister. Things had gotten to a point of reckoning and he really didn't know how to handle it all.

"Andres has been there for us. It would be hard to run from him now. We owe him everything, Carrianne. We can't quit him now. He needs our help."

"Jake, I know that, but when are we ever going to have a life, we need to break this chain. We can't do this forever. I want my own life and I know I just couldn't say it to Andres. We try to run and we could easily be dead," she said.

"Right, but do you think he would really kill us if we ran?" Jake asked.

"I don't really know, but he scares me and I don't know if we could get away with running."

They stared at each other in silence for several minutes. Neither one of them could speak as they knew how dire their situation was becoming. People made choices sometimes, that really were made out of desperation. It was like reaching for something that was just barely out of your reach. It seemed close, but your hand was just inches away from touching what it was that you wanted. This is how they were feeling and they were becoming desperate. So much so, they were willing to get the stepladder to finally reach what they were trying to get. Then they could reach it, but at what consequence? Would they drop it, break it or even fall off the ladder and kill themselves? Yes, desperation was a funny thing and the decisions made when surrounded by it, certainly put you in survival mode.

As brother and sister, they had acted out many charades, many scenarios and they had survived. They could leave well enough alone, or they could make the desperate decision. They were close and they knew what each other was thinking. Jake was just about to open his mouth to speak, and SHE walked in.

"Hello, kids," Lynnette said. "Why all the doom and gloom?"

"No problems, Jake just got here we were trying to coordinate our disguises a bit and make some plans," Carrianne said.

"Hi, Jakey," she cooed. "Guess you didn't know you were looking at a famous actress, did you?"

"What do you mean?" Jake asked.

"My new boss is the theatre department head at the college and she asked me to take a part for a young girl that had an emergency. Here's my script. I have practice tonight and you know, it's kind of exciting."

"Well, really it's exciting because you are getting close to hunting," Jake said under his breath.

"I heard that, Jakey, and yes, that's right. But also, I like a challenge."

Carrianne shook her head and looked to Jake as if to ask 'Are you convinced now, it has to be time to run' but she said nothing. Jake knew what she was thinking.

"Well, I've got to change, do a little script study and then get ready to go," Lynnette said as she walked slowly past Jake. She took off her blouse and turned to Jake as she walked towards her room. "You think I will be good, Jake?" she asked. "At acting, I mean?" she asked, smiling as she walked away. She shut the door and left them.

Andres was making his way back. Back to his farm and under the name of John Middleton. He would make it back, but for how much longer?

These kids, they are starting to make too many mistakes. I can't cover for them forever. I have done this for so long. Often, I think 'when will be the last time' to kill and for how much longer can I keep this up. I could take the kids, I could run, but people like the Boss, they find you. No matter what, they find you. There are a few things that the Boss can never know.

Andres picked up the phone and called his place. His farmhand answered and Andres gave them instructions to leave. They would be gone in thirty minutes. Andres was headed home to an empty farm. He knew someone would be by to check and look. He had a few things to cover up. He would expect company but when they came, he would be gone, long gone. If not for Jake's carelessness, he wouldn't be in this situation. But he promised their mother, to take care of them. Otherwise, he would have probably taken care of Jake already. Damn kids. Nothing but a heartache...

CHAPTER 33

Jake and Carrianne looked at each other, both knowing what the other was thinking. They both knew they were tiring quickly of watching over this Allison, Lynnette, crazy woman that she was. They were also worried about Andres. They knew that Jake had screwed up, seeing that woman in Brazil. When you screwed up with Andres, usually you had to pay. Jake leaned closer to Carrianne and whispered to her.

"You know, he killed her. You know he did. I know he did. It was one girl I really liked, really felt close to. Yeah, I've been around but she was special," Jake said as his voice trailed off.

"I know Jake, but you know how Andres is. He never lets anyone get close. He stays at arms distance from everyone, even me and you at times," she said.

"I have to ask you, although I don't want to," Jake said as he licked his dry lips. "Do you think there is a point when he turns on us? You know, do you still trust him? He seems to trust HER more," he said pointing to the closed door in the bedroom.

"I know what you are saying, Jake. But I still think he feels obligated to mother and to us. So, yeah, I still trust him. I just don't know how he feels about Branch," Carrianne pondered. "He acts way different around her than he does anyone else. Sometimes I think he has a thing for her, but then I also think he is too smart for that."

"Yeah, maybe. Funny, I have never seen him get close to a woman," Jake said. "He has had his chances, plenty of hookers in this business. He could have had anyone he wanted."

"He's sort of like that crazy uncle. You can't help but like him, but he is so quiet and so strange. No sense of humor there at all. But you always seem to know where his heart is," she said.

"The heat is really turning up. Should we run, should we go back to Brazil and tell Andres we are done?" Jake asked.

Carrianne thought for just a moment. This idea was tempting, but the idea of running from Andres was just foolish. You can't do anything without letting him know. "He always finds us, he's always there when we think he has no idea of what we are up to. But you do know how I feel. I wish for a different life, a different opportunity. Sometimes, the only way I think I would get there is to run, but I just can't do it. Don't ask me why."

"More than that, you know who our stepdad is. The guy that married mom is just that, we aren't that close to him. Andres feels more like our dad than him. But Andres told mom he would watch over us, and I believe he is going to do just that. So, for me, I am not going to run. But you need to help me with Branch. There are some things I like about her, but I never feel safe around her. If I ever ran, she would be the reason," Carrianne said, still talking quite low.

Just then, Lynnette came out of her room in here jeans and bra, no shirt. She did this for Jake, but she also wondered if she wasn't doing it for Carrianne.

"Hey, kids. What's up? Lynnette asked.

"Don't you think you should maybe put a shirt on?" Carrianne asked.

"Why, it's kind of hot in here, isn't it, Jake?" Lynnette said. "Besides, I am just about ready to leave and I am trying to feel my part in the play. My part needs to be the sexy, sultry sister. I am sexy and sultry, aren't I?" she asked walking so much closer to Jake. She then turned to look at Carrianne. "Aren't I dear?" she asked her, giving her a look that was more than teasing.

Carrianne swallowed hard and looked at Jake, who smiled ever so slightly. He knew what Branch was up to. Carrianne knew also.

"Well, you sure do, never more convincing. The director must be very smart," Carrianne added.

Lynnette's mouth turned quickly from a teasing smile, to a faraway look. Carrianne knew she had said the wrong thing but couldn't figure out what had turned her so fast from tease to furrowed brow and pensive stare. The look was so wrong for this conversation. It didn't fit.

"Yes, I suppose she is," she said turning abruptly and walking away to her room.

In just a few more minutes she had her script, her coat and car keys, ready to go to practice. Jake was kind of relieved when he was being honest with himself. She could be fun, but like Carrianne said, she was spooky.

"I'll be back later," she said. "Don't wait up for me."

With that, she was out the door. Jake stood up and

was getting ready to leave her. Carrianne was worried and he could tell. He sat next to her on the couch.

"I know," he said. "She's a hard one, but Andres wants us to protect her. We just can't be visible. We have to trust that she will do what she is supposed to do and not go off the rails. Are you making sure she has her meds?"

"Yeah, I ask her and I check that she has them when she leaves. Why do you think she changed so much when I mentioned the director? You saw it too, right?" Carrianne asked Jake.

"I did see that. Something about the director. Something, maybe, we need to ask her about. But, now quite yet," Jake said. "Wait for just a bit. I may say something to Andres."

"You are staying the night, right?" she asked hopefully.

"Yeah, I'll sleep on the couch. I know you have some fears about this woman. But don't leave her alone with me. I have fears about her, too. We have a lot to think about, a lot!"

CHAPTER 34

"There's two angels sitting on my shoulders, all they ever do is disagree. One sits on the side of rhyme and reason, the other on the reckless side of me." The SteelDrivers

Andy called back and had his tip. A man had rented a vehicle and it was under the name of John Middleton. When Andy ran the name and he found that he lived not far away from the Milwaukee area. Andy wanted me to check it out. Timing could be right as he could be getting back to the place as the time line would be just about right. Andy gave me the address.

"Do you think you can take a camera out there and get a photo of the guy when he gets back to his place, that is if he does get back. It's a long shot, but if you could that would be great. I'm going to hop on a plane here and be back in Milwaukee about 9:00. Let me know what you find out and if you do get a picture, send it to my phone. Be careful and if you see anything half-way dangerous, call me. I'll call you later." Marx hung up the phone.

Okay, having the address, I had time to do this before play practice and my night with Joanna. Hoping I could get a photo before dark, I made my way out to the address he gave me. I was at a juncture where the road went left and turned to gravel. The air was fresh out here and the cold was sharp today. I rolled slowly down the gravel road trying to notice things as I went and keeping my eye out for John Middleton.

I was assuming that Andy had the photo of this guy as he said he had a driver's license ID. My picture would be for verification I was sure. I was being careful and finally reached the place and just drove by slowly, looking for any sign of John Middleton. The house on the property was nice and well kept, but there didn't seem to be any sign of anyone there. I drove on down to the next intersection and turned around. I sat there for minute and tried to decide how far away I could be and still get a good shot. I was planning where to sit and how I could actually stay hidden. I thought there was a vacant barn across the road maybe two-hundred yards from the house. Maybe I could park my car somewhere else and walk to that barn and hide inside. But it was so damn cold, I forgot about that for a few seconds.

I thought just a minute about why I had ended up here and why I had I would enjoy pretending to be a cop. *I was an attorney and law professor, not a cop. I knew that, but it was HER. That was the reason I had ended up here on this gravel road, trying to take a picture of possibly the most dangerous man I had never met. Her attempt to kill Katy, Marx and me had put me in this predicament. Her escape, and what that entailed, had put me in a new state, one I had never imagined, until now. I remembered so much about her. Her smell, the way her lips tasted and the passion that I felt. It had disgusted me, yet still hung with me, even when I tried to wipe that slate clean. What was her destiny question all about? Was it always about tricking me? Was it something she really felt? I was starting to admonish myself for feeling this way. Why? Why am I feeling sorry for her? This thinking must stop, and it has to stop now. I've started down this road to solve this and help Andy, keep Katy safe and to prove to myself that I can do things for all the right reasons. It was about redemption, right? Sure, it is, it's all about that, but as much as I didn't want to admit it, I didn't want to kill her, I wanted to help her. Being that conflicted, there they were again. Those two conflicting angels, one that was sitting on the side of rhyme and reason and the other on my reckless side. It was certainly reckless to think that I could possibly help her. To survive and not be killed, maybe I would be faced with killing her were thoughts in my head. Could I do it? I tried to imagine the scenario and asked myself once again, 'Can you do it?'*

Just then a rap on my window startled me and made me jump. My skin crawled and felt like a thousand needles were pricking at both of my arms. My breath increased and I felt my heart pounding in my chest. I could feel the blood rushing to my face. I rolled my window down, not wanting to be suspicious.

"Hey, neighbor. Are you lost or do you need help? I saw you from my place back there just sitting there and thought maybe I could give you a hand," he said as he spit tobacco juice on the ground.

"Well, really I am fine. I just stopped to take a call and was just getting ready to leave. But thanks, anyway," I responded feeling uneasy about the tobacco spitting farmer.

"Well, alright then," he said as he started to walk away. He turned back and said something I couldn't make out and waved. I waved back and started my car. *Damn it, Mike. You have got to watch all the time! If that was HER, you would be dead. I should call Marx and tell him what this guy looked like. There he goes, he is heading back to where he said he lived. I just don't trust the tobacco spitter.*

I started my car and began to drive back past the house but I had decided that this was going to be past my abilities and was worried. I made the turn past the house and was heading back towards the paved road. I looked up in my rearview mirror and saw the tobacco-spitter's truck going the other way at the intersection. *Something's not right here. My intuition was my best attribute and I wanted to trust it. But I also didn't want to blow it for Marx. He was probably harmless, but just something there I didn't trust. I'm calling Marx...*

Play practice had started and no Mike Parsons. This disappointed Joanna somewhat but she quickly got into doing her job at which she was very good. She loved directing plays. She loved letting actors get into the roles, to feel their character. She knew how to get the most effort from the actors.

It was five minutes into the script that Joanna saw a bit of talent in her new hire, Lynnette Huber. She was so confident in her approach. She read from the script with feeling when it was her turn to speak. Her passion for the part was perfect and Joanna was very pleased.

At the break she had complimented Lynnette and had a brief conversation with her. She was so lucky to have found someone who fit that part so well.

"You are doing an amazing job, Lynette," Joanna said smiling at her new hire.

"Thanks, I always wanted to do this kind of thing," Lynette said as she was thinking to herself that it was easy because I had done this most of my life. "I guess, I am lucky for a chance. It's something I can scratch off the bucket list."

"You're doing great, but remember memorization is good, but for me, if you forget a line for some reason, it's okay, I am confident you can ad lib. It's okay, we're not giving out Oscars or Toni's anyway."

"Well, let's get back to it. Do your best to memorize, but a little ad lib is good!" Joanna exclaimed.

Lynnette hopped back on the stage and was thinking to herself. *Sure, I love doing this. I am doing it in real life and you really don't know who I am, do you? If you only knew who I really was, you would not have hired me. You wouldn't have asked me to be in this play. But I am a good actress. Actually, better than I had ever imagined. But my whole life has been a play. I just had to act out all the scenes, the good ones, the bad ones and the ugly ones. I had all of them and to portray me was always my greatest challenge. But damn, I did it well...*

CHAPTER 35

The drama department theater was only four years old. It was built in a 1940's style that suited Joanna just fine. She had always felt the most comfortable and in charge in this setting. Ever since she began directing plays, she had found something that thrilled her. It became her passion. Inside these walls and sitting in the front row of this new building, Joanna was the master of her own universe. She directed with passion and truly felt connected to her actors. They were more than just the moving pieces in her productions. They were her kids. She pushed and prodded them, coddled them, and truly cared for them. After each play, she invited her cast to her home and cooked and entertained for an all-day Saturday affair.

Joanna was that person. Truly good to her inner core. She was not pretentious or fake. What you see with her is what you get. Her simple approach to things always left her hurt, when the shady and scheming types came out and tried to hurt her. She had the patience of Job, the heart of gold, and the genuine personality that made her very real.

Watching scene three in act two had been a struggle thus far. The kids just weren't meshing with her new actress, Lynnette Huber. It seemed that just when they almost had it, she broke off into an ad lib that confused the other players. Joanna was hard to frustrate, but she was increasingly becoming agitated with having to say cut and called for a break.

"Okay, guys, let's take a rest," she said showing her frustration for the first time in the evening. "We have to bring this scene together shortly or we won't be able to get ready in time. I don't want to just accept a mediocre take on this scene. It's an important one."

Just then, the lead actor came over to talk. He was a tall, good looking student actor who had great potential. He was seemingly anxious as he walked over.

"Ms. Presley, we are struggling here and I think you can see it," he said looking over the top of her head and not making eye contact. He shuffled from side and finally said it. "It's the new girl, she's ad-libbing the crucial line and I think It's best if we stuck to it. She's not getting along at all with our lead actress. It's almost as if she wants to steal the show and take over. If she would just do her lines, we would be fine. She is also older than many of us and we just don't seem to fit."

"Okay, Brent, look, I'll talk to her. I think you're right and if this scene doesn't get fixed, we will struggle big time," Joanna said. "She is new in my office and she is good looking and fit this part so well. I just thought I would give it a try since the other girl quit. For some reason, I feel kind of sorry for her, but we just can't sabotage the great efforts of everyone else for just one person."

"Thanks, Ms. Presley, but don't say I said anything. I'm not usually feeling this way but the way her eyes looked at me one time, it was kind of scary. Not trying to be too judgmental here, but I don't think she's the type I want to make mad."

"Okay, sure," Joanna said. Just then she saw Mike walk in and smiled. He was handsome walking down the aisle. Her attention was taken away from the problems of the play momentarily. Her heart jumped to a new pace and beat and she had to catch herself for just a moment.

"Well, hello there, handsome!" she said.

"Hello, beautiful," I returned. "How's practice going? Looks like you are on break or something here."

"Well, we hit a little rough spot with our new player." Joanna said, wincing just a little. "She's also the new girl I hired for the office. She is older than our students but was a good cast for the older sister of the lead. Our lead male, Brent, said they are struggling with her ad-libbing and I am afraid that may have been my fault. I need to talk to her before we start again."

"Oh, I see. Which one is she by the way?" I asked.

"She's the one sitting over by the couch that no one is talking to," Joanna replied feeling sorry for Lynnette. "I really need to talk to her before we start again and get her going or we will never get ready."

"Sure, go ahead," I said as I looked at the woman. "Yeah, I'll be here to cheer you on when you get back."

Joanna went over to the stage and called her over. She seemed pretty, and even though Joanna said she was older, she didn't look much different than the kids on stage. Her hair was brunette and she had a fit body. She was leaning over the stage and her face was concentrating on what Joanna was telling her. She seemed to nod and approve and she finally smiled and headed back to her place, while she mumbled something to herself.

Joanna returned and was seemingly ready as she shouted," Okay, everyone, places and let's get this scene right. We have a lot to get covered in the next hour. We can't be here all night."

The actors plunged into the scene as Joanna yelled, "and action." The players jumped into the scene that seemed to go remarkably well. I could tell Joanna was pleased and the look on her new actresses' face was telling me her remarks had hit home, that she had pushed the right button. I thought the new girl looked very pretty and it was hard to take my eyes from her, not just because of her beauty, but the way she moved around. She seemed confident, almost cocky. Kind of odd for someone coming into the play brand new. But I let it go, and actually, was enjoying my first preview of Joanna's production. I thought of her talent for a moment and was amazed at how intense she was at directing. She was fun to watch in her craft. Studying her for a moment, she seemed like a sweet cure for me. *I couldn't believe that I was worthy of such a person. If only she could see herself as I was seeing her through my eyes, she would know that she was having this heavy impact on my soul, which by the way, was a soul that was very much in need. I just had to get it right this time, didn't I?*

The practice moved on and it was going on nine. My thoughts had jumped back for a moment to the country road outside of town. The rap on the window and then the pick-up truck following me as if to escort me away from the area. Something was weird there and I had to call Andy and let him know what was going on. But I would do it now, so it didn't interfere with my evening that I had planned for Joanna and me. I walked back up the theatre aisle and called Andy.

"Hey, Parsons, what's up?" he asked.

"Look, when I went to scout the area, I got lost in some thoughts when a rap on my window scared me. The guy at the window just asked if I needed help, which I said no to and told him I was just making a call. He said he lived up the road," I said wishing I wouldn't had said I was scared.

"I'll check that out tomorrow. Give me a description of the guy and the truck and I'll send someone out there tomorrow," Marx said seeming to be in a hurry.

"The guy was probably about mid 40's, stubbled face and dark hair. Thin, but hardened. The truck was red and old. Flatbed type with a hay fork on the back," I said.

"Okay got it. Tomorrow we need to talk, I think there is something happening close to us, we are just not seeing it," Marx said almost anxiously.

"Alright, we'll talk tomorrow," I said and hung up.

Okay tomorrow is another day, but for now, all I am thinking of is my evening plans with Joanna. I am convinced that something is circling around us, Marx and me. We will take care of it tomorrow, but for now, practice is over and this new love interest of mine is getting my total attention.

—▲—

We drove separate vehicles to my place and we parked next to each other. We both got out and walked close together to the condo. I was thinking to myself to make sure that I had cleaned up everything and that my bachelor place was presentable. It was the one thing my father had always said and I still think to myself as well; "A place for everything and everything in its place." It is one of the things he taught me that I still used to this day.

We entered and I shut the alarm system off. I asked her into the living area where she took a seat on my couch and I went to the kitchen to get us a drink. I asked her from the kitchen what she would like, I told her I had most of what people drank. She said she just wanted a glass of red wine and I poured me a Chivas and water. I came back to the room and handed her the glass of wine and she thanked me and smiled a very alluring smile. I smiled back and sat on the couch beside her. I took a sip and set the glass own on the coaster sitting on the coffee table.

"I have to say that your play is really starting to take shape," I said starting the conversation. I hope you get the new girl in line before the opening curtain."

"I guess I should be worried, but somehow she shows more confidence than the younger players. For some reason I think she will do okay," Joanna said looking hopeful.

"Well, of course, she will. Nothing to worry about," I said trying to reassure her.

"Do you really think it will be okay from what you saw?" She asked.

"Certainly, it can't fail with you as director, can it?" I questioned.

"Well, you're just being nice in saying that, Mr. Parsons."

"No, seriously, it looks like it is coming together and I know you have the skill. I am not patronizing you."

"Thank you, sir," she said as she looked kind of quizzically at me. "You know, I am a bit curious about the new girl though. She works hard as far as I can see, and it only has been a day. But there is one thing I am not sure of, something that makes me pause. Don't ask me, to put my finger on it, just a gut feeling. It's probably nothing."

"Probably. Just be happy you found someone who wants to work hard. That seems to be a quality that is hard to find these days," I said.

The conversation switched to the university and our jobs and she asked a bit about how it was going on the investigation. I was evasive about Branch, which was probably a good thing. No use going back there with Joanna right now. Maybe sometime later, but not now.

For the first time, I was starting to fall for someone for what I saw in their face, the honesty, sincerity, her true intelligence. She had a sense of humor and she could make me laugh. I started to feel something inside of me that wasn't just a come and go type of feeling. It was the kind of feeling that could grow if it was attended to. I had thought it before with her, but I was almost assured of it now. Something was hitting me and I know it was something that I couldn't have possibly ever known before. It was new, it was different, and it had the "right" feel to it.

We took a few more sips and the conversations were turning to both of our pasts. It seemed to be that moment that she said if she was ever going further with this, that she had to know me, really know me. This would be my exam and if I passed it, I may be capable of loving someone again. But, I had to pass, if not, I think this woman would walk away. She had that much character on the inside, and with her face, she showed the same concern that she too must pass the test. It was if we both knew the next questions that would be asked. We could both feel it and maybe that was it. We both had that feel for each other, and maybe that was what felt so different. I didn't with Sheila, Katy or Branch. It was as if I knew that she "got" me and that I "got" her. But, most certainly, this conversation needed to be had. She started to speak.

"I hate to ask you the kind of things I am going to ask, but I guess I have to know."

"I understand and I will do my best to be as open as I can with you," I returned, knowing that it was that time.

"What was it like, you know, well, your first marriage to Sheila?"

"Tough question. We married young, but we just couldn't connect. We had no children and I guess we grew apart. I think we were both unfulfilled in the relationship. She sought out another lifestyle after we divorced and I think she must have felt very conflicted at the time. To tell you honestly, I strayed, and I wasn't faithful. No excuse except that we just couldn't connect. Everything with us sexually was awkward and I couldn't love like I thought it was supposed to be. Maybe I expected too much. I had this conversation with myself a lot before. I still come up with the same answers, that it was me, that I didn't try hard enough or I didn't think she did either. I became emotionally unattached and I just couldn't ever fall back in love with her again. What about you?"

"Well, with me, my ex was abusive. I couldn't live that way. Day after day I lived in fear and I couldn't trust him. It is even hard right now, even with someone I feel a lot for, like you, to trust in a relationship. I badly want to, but my past, your past, they are hard things for us both to overcome," she said tearing up just a little. "I know what I feel, for you that is, and I want to trust it. There really isn't anything that should make me feel that way, but your honesty is what I want, and I think I am getting that."

"You know I have longed for a day that I could find within me the redemption that I seek. I was thinking that I would have to do this myself. I was pretty convinced that I would have a hard time changing myself. When Ed put us together, I was not thinking about having someone ever again. He must have thought otherwise. Now, I see that it is possible for me, that I can find something in my life that I haven't been able to feel before, and it is you that has brought me closer to it," I said wondering if I jumped too far ahead. "With Branch, there was something with my expectations of what I thought I liked in women. She put me in a trance that damn near got me killed. She was pretty, she was fascinating, but she is and was very dangerous. I was just too shallow to see what was going on. My ego kept driving me."

"I hate to say this," she said as she leaned in closer to me. "But, Mike, you are bringing something out in me that is very good, too. I thought I would always be trapped in this shell of me, never to venture out in the relationship world again. I light up when you come anywhere near me. I just feel so different than before. You bring out something in me. It's something that at my age you tend to give up on."

God, I wanted to kiss her. So bad. I studied her eyes for a brief moment. Then I saw it, the sparkle and light, the shine that only a person that is truly genuine has. Those eyes could see right into my soul. The eyes that shone with truth that made me know from this very day, this very minute, I would never fool her ever, I wouldn't even try. I knew that she could see right through me. She could look all the way into the bottom of my heart, a heart I wanted saved, a heart I wanted redeemed.

I kissed her and at that moment I could feel my

heart begin to melt on the spot. She had me, right then and there, she had me. It wasn't the kiss that took me in, but it was that sparkle, that shine in the eyes that saw my heart and soul. She was everything that I missed in life, she was the one, I knew, that could redeem this crazy, tortured soul.

The night moved from the living room couch to the master bedroom. We made love in a most passionate and feeling way. To extend this and to play it for as long as possible was what my heart was wanting now. I wanted this to last forever, and it did long into the night...

———▲———

The person in the car, watching from the parking lot, started their car. It was time to go. There would be another time, but once again, she was feeling victimized. Once more, life had unveiled another of it's ugly punishments. *Not only do I work for this person, she has the man I wanted inside his place doing who knows what. The one who didn't pick me! Don't worry you two, the hunt is already on and you are both going to have to pay. No one ever understands me, they have no idea what I can do. They are clueless, unfeeling human beings.* She put the car in gear as the people inside were wrapped up in one another. Tears once again fell out of those silvery, steel blue eyes. As she drove away she thought, *they have no damn idea...*

CHAPTER 36

Awakening the next morning, I felt her warm body snuggling up against mine. Her body warmth gave me a certain security that made me feel I was covered or blanketed with a new hope, a new sense that I didn't have to be lonely any more. It was hope, it wasn't a done deal. But it was hope. Her legs stretched and she ran her smooth feet up and down my leg. I put my arm around her shoulder and stroked her hair lightly with my fingers. It just felt different, just being with her in this early morning light had given me a sense of renewed energy and a readiness to face the day. I slipped out of bed and went to the kitchen to make a couple of cups of coffee.

I looked at the clock and it was 5:00 am. Joanna had also gotten out of bed and snuck up behind me.

"Good morning, handsome," she said lightly touching my cheek with her open palm. "I had an amazing time last night. I really wasn't planning to spend the night, you know. But, I'm so glad I did."

"So am I," I said as I looked down at her wondering if this was real or if it was just a dream. "I got a feeling this may be the best cup of coffee I have ever had with anyone."

We sat in the kitchen both half dressed, and as we talked, her smile and her face were so very stamped into my mind. Our discussion was light, and time had gone by so quickly I hardly noticed that it was 6:00 am. She also looked up at the clock.

"Oh, Mike, I do have to get going. Sorry to say, but I have to get to work. Please call me later when you get a chance. I had a wonderful time, I want to do this again, very soon."

"Oh, I will and we will do this again, very, very soon," I replied.

She walked her confident and almost swaggering walk back to get her clothes. She came back dressed and ready to leave, and I met her at the front door. We kissed that one more time before she went. Holding her in my arms, I felt that I almost couldn't let her go. I want to have this feeling many more times with Joanna. I needed times when I would watch her leave and wish for the time to fly by so she could be back again.

My phone rang at 7:00. I had already gotten showered and dressed. It was Marx. I was expecting his call, but in some ways after being with Joanna last night, I wanted to back out of this whole arrangement. But something kept me going and I am sure it was that whole past episode. The part of me that wanted HER back in prison. I had those conflicting feelings about HER being in prison but also in treatment. I wondered if someone had treated her condition earlier, how she might have turned out.

"Hello, Andy, how are you this morning?" I asked.

"Good. I've got this feeling that where you were yesterday holds an important piece. I think we are drawing a bead on the big guy and this John Middleton's place is where the key to solving this is. Just my feeling. What do you think?"

"It could be. I think the guy that stopped me was following me and watching me. I could be wrong. Have your guys never found the truck? Maybe he didn't live around there but was working for the guy. What time do you want to go out?"

"I'll pick you up at your place around 8:00 am. It will take us about an hour to get out there. I'm taking a long lens camera and maybe we can get photos. Not sure I want to do a raid yet until we have more information or evidence. I'm working off that gut feeling right now," Marx said.

"Okay, see you then." I hung up and finished getting my coat and made sure my phone was charged. I waited for Marx.

———▲———

Lynnette Huber was driving to work. She had taken her medication this morning, so she was more in control of herself than she was last night. She really had tried thinking to herself that she had done well, not to break in and cause a scene right there. She gripped the steering wheel tighter but made herself breathe slower. Her grip began to ease on the wheel as her breathing became much slower and measured. She arrived at the parking lot and sat for just a minute since she was early. This having to work for a while just to make some deals for the drug boys was already boring and she hadn't done it for a week yet. But she was the restless sort who had always wanted things to happen now, right now. She grabbed her purse and decided she would behave, today was not the day. *She needed to know more about Miss Joanna. She needed to find out her habits. She needed to know what she liked and didn't like, where she went, who she talked to. She already knew all she needed to know about Mikey, she had that one down to a science. But, Joanna, she would take care of her, too. Just like many of the unsuspecting others, she always had a plan for them. How to take care of business. But her business was unfinished with these two. Then there was Marx. Lynnette had a plan for him too. It was all in the hunt, the hunt she had designed in prison. So many days she made the mark on the wall, counting the days incarcerated. With each mark, one more day went by and she became closer to making her hunt begin. She had already known, when making those marks, that she would get out, she was too good to keep in that hell hole behind bars. Her boy had helped here out of there and from that day forward, she knew she would have Henry Hannah killed. The others would follow, yes, they would follow. They were the prey and she was the hunter. Yes, in and out of these dreams. So crazy isn't it? I am not really sure what is real and what I dreamt...*she snapped out of it, but it was harder every day to come back to reality. She took another pill even though it was dangerous to not follow the prescription. But she had to keep it together, just for a while longer. Staying to the plan was the key. Don't get distracted. She got out of her car and began to walk toward work. She jumped when she heard a voice near her.

"Good morning, Lynnette," the voice said.

Startled, Lynnette gasped and then caught herself. It was her boss, Miss Joanna. She recovered.

"Well, I was in a thoughtful moment and you sort of startled me," Lynnette said. "But good morning to you, too. Did you have a good evening after play practice?" she asked already knowing the answer to that.

"Well, yes, I did in fact," Joanna said. "And you?"

"Just fine, really," Lynette said. *Not fine, really. I know what you did. If only you knew I could have killed you easily last night. You wouldn't be so cheery this morning! Yep JUST FINE!*

Lynnette smiled back at Joanna and hid every thought and every intention from her. *She would have fun with this one. Torturing this woman would be a pleasure.*

They went inside the door and to the office. The work day had begun and Lynnette Huber would make it another day, she told herself. She wasn't ready yet. Besides she had a play to do. It would be one of her better performances, but not her best. Her best was yet to come, playing the hunter on safari. Her best performance was about to become the stuff Academy Awards are made of. The funny thing was, the hunt was all natural. No acting necessary. It would be the acting that got the unsuspecting prey ready for the hunt. They won't know, they won't see.

Lynnette sat at her desk and organized her work load. She got up and went back to Joanna's office. She had some things she wanted to find out. Things she needed to know. She took a deep breath and knocked on the boss's door.

"Come in, Lynnette," Joanna said...

My ride got to the condo at 8:00 sharp. Mr. 'On Time' Marx was there to pick me up. I took a deep breath and headed out my door. Ever since I started helping Marx on this case, I felt that every time I stepped out of my door, it could be my last. I couldn't feel that way forever. But it was my fear. I felt HER around every corner, every dark place, everywhere I went and walked, I expected the unexpected.

I got in Marx's car and we headed out of town. It was the first time we had time to discuss where we were in the case. We had an hour to talk and he filled it up with information.

"Here's what I have so far," Marx said as he drove at a good clip. "Going back to the beginning, we have an escapee out there somewhere. We feel that she had gone to Brazil for plastic surgery. We don't have an ID on her yet. My partner, Mo, is dead, my friend, Brian, is dead. They know we are on their trail and they are responsible for those deaths. They are erasing people, but the big guy is doing this, he is the one we need. This tip on John Middleton maybe being the big guy, it's all I have to go on."

"Do you think this last girl missing is his work, too?" I asked.

"I am thinking that. Seems like he rented a vehicle near the area that the missing girl is from. I figure he's coming back here, if it is him. I just have to have evidence of seeing him being at this farm that we can help us get a warrant for a raid, "Marx added.

"You know, with HER, you know Branch, on the loose we could end up in some sort of trap game. Every day I walk out of the house, I can still see her around every corner. The problem is, I knew what she looked like. I don't know what she looks like now," I offered.

"She's certainly the X factor here. She could come out of nowhere, but we find the big guy, we are that much closer to finding Branch. But I have an idea of how we can draw the big guy out if we don't see him here," Andy said. "We won't use it until we have to, but if we do that, we are in it for the chase and it could be a dangerous and desperate move."

We got closer to our destination and Andy was telling me how we were going to approach the surveillance. We could leave the car and hope no one else comes by like last night. We would try to walk on the property and get close enough to shoot the house with the long lens and see if we saw anything through the windows. The barn was a place of interest and Andy was not against trying to slip inside of it and see what we could find. The plan was getting a bit scarier at the moment and I didn't know If I was into storage buildings that much anymore. The last storage building on my own property became my own personal prison. I had a huge phobia about it and was against going in there. But for now, I was playing along.

We got out of the car like Andy said and on foot we walked into the woods at the side of the road. I kept looking back over my shoulder for the truck to come by and see our car tipping someone off. But it never came and soon, we were deep into the woods and I couldn't see the car anymore. The house would be on the other side of the clearing that we could see up ahead. We walked a little further and thought we had just about gone far enough for surveillance purposes. Andy got out the camera and hooked up the strap and placed it around his neck.

"We need to get a little closer," Andy said looking through the lens. "I don't think we can get the shots we want until I get about a hundred yards closer."

He motioned me to follow and we began to walk up closer to a large tree. Our pace slowed as we were getting closer to an opening and we might be seen. I took my next steps slower and tried to make as little noise as possible. I noticed the ground was still hard due to the winter's cold. Each step felt like I was on a concrete sidewalk. The next step though alarmed me, it was soft. The ground shouldn't be that way, right? I stopped dead in my tracks. Funny so did Marx. We looked at each other as if we knew something was wrong, our gut feelings telling us we are onto something bad here.

"Are you thinking what I am?" he asked.

"Yeah, I'm thinking dead bodies under me," I said.

"Me, too, leave a marker. I am getting photos of that house really quick. Then we'll go back and radio in, we have to know what's under here. It may ruin catching Middleton anywhere near here and I am sure it will tip him off. But it may just be a soft spot with nothing in it. I have an idea, but let me get the pictures first, just mark it."

Marx walked ahead and I found a branch and stuck it in the soft earth. I found another stick to lean on it that would make it unique. Marx then hustled back having the photos he wanted.

"No sign of anyone moving around near the house. I think your boy in the truck may have been in on this and tipped off the big man. He's not coming here, but we have to know what's in here. I have a tire tool in the trunk, I'm going to get it and we'll dig down in the soft spot and see if we get anything. If we find something, we need to turn it in and get people out here, if we find nothing, then we can still work on the surveillance," Marx noted.

With that, Marx headed to the car...

CHAPTER 37

Marx walked quickly back to the car and I could see that he was now out of sight. I began to claw at the soft ground, not wanting to consciously hit anything. I feared what may be underneath and I would just let Marx handle it or whoever he called could dig into this area. I was most certain we would find something here, and whatever it was, it wouldn't be a pretty sight.

The longer I stood there, the more I was getting paranoid. I was expecting the guy in the truck to arrive out of nowhere and give me just another crushing blow to the back of the head. I looked all around me in a circle. No truck man here. I had to tell myself that I was just overwhelmed by past events and had to slow my thinking down. I had nothing to fear and Marx would have the calvary here shortly. I started to breathe faster and was getting a headache behind my eyes. Time was a slow drip like water out of a leaky faucet; drip, drip, drip...my body started to feel rusted and weak as every joint started to ache. I was becoming frozen in time and space, I could not see through the thick fog that seemed to surround me.

Stop! You've got to stop. C'mon, man, you've got to fight. Where is Marx? What's taking him so long? Maybe it's just only been minutes, sure, just a short time. He'll be back soon. C'mon, Mike, focus. There is no fog, there wasn't any fog when we came here. You created it in your mind. It's not real. If I didn't know better, I was feeling like I was sleeping and this was only a dream. But I knew I was awake, just tensing up. I couldn't move.

"Hey! Hey, Parsons, HEY!" Marx shook me and I quickly caught myself. I saw Marx, but I couldn't speak.

"You okay?" he asked.

"Uh yeah, sorry," I said in a voice obviously shaken from my dream on my feet. "I just got lost in the past. I have to quit this. Maybe I need help?"

"Maybe you should talk to someone. We can talk about that later, but for now, I've got some help coming and we need to find out what is under your feet," Marx was saying as parts of reality began to register with me again.

The air was clear again. There was no fog. My imagination was running wild with me. I wanted to walk away and walk all the way back to town. I wasn't cut out for this, but I stood there with Marx and waited. The cavalry arrived and I could hear Marx talking to hem quietly describing where we were. Two or three vehicles had shown up. The place would soon be crawling and John Middleton's farm would soon be crawling with cops. The dig would start soon...

John Middleton had called Jake and Carrianne and

let them know that his place was now off limits and that they would all soon need to take a trip and get out of town. They wouldn't be coming back here, ever. Explaining all this to the Boss was going to be the most difficult thing he would have to do. The Boss is going to be upset.

Andres was going to pick them up, and they would be heading to Miami. It would be time to separate themselves from Allison Branch. Andres had not figured on doing this. He contemplated how to do this. It should be easy, but two things made it hard for him to make a plan, the kids and HER, Allison Branch. They were causing him the most problems, but he really cared for those people more than he wanted to admit. The hardness of the man who grew up in the toughest place in the world was weakening. Was he tired of this work, was he tired of his responsibility, was he just tired? He didn't really think he had any way out. But, was he starting to think of leaving the Boss? No one left the Boss, no one...

The CSI asked Andy questions about checking the warrant he had to surveil the property. They too would have to wait for their own warrant. Sitting around and waiting was the worst part for the CSI. They were never eager to get the work done as most of their finds were grisly scenes.

Brandon Styles was a field guy with CSI. He was leading the group of four that were going to be assigned to this spot. There wasn't a lot of interviewing or anything like that. Their business was to find and collect evidence. Andy did help them define the outer perimeter of the crime scene and they taped off the area for the outer perimeter and set up the staging area where media would be around soon enough. That would be hard for Marx and I would be a subject of many questions. Marx was preparing me for what lay ahead and the questions I would face.

CSI would take our pictures as no one was left unsuspected at a crime scene. Everyone could be a suspect and the pictures and video were two of the most important things done by the CSI. Brandon Styles had asked Marx if anything at all had been moved as they came out of the wooded area. They would soon go in when they search warrant arrived. But before the media arrived, the place had to be secured.

"This is a rather large area to secure, Andy," Styles said as he asked Andy a couple of questions. "Who's your friend here?" he asked.

"This is a department approved consultant, Mike Parsons. He's helping me with some profiling as he is a former witness on another kidnapping," Marx said as he didn't want to divulge too much until he had to.

"Okay, step over here a minute and let me get your picture and his. Then we can get back to what you have seen so we know what we have for a scene," Styles said.

He took our picture and then he resumed his conversation with Marx. I stepped to the side but could heard what they were talking about. Styles was probably around forty or so with dark hair that was graying at the temples. He had brown eyes and a heavy stubble probably from working long hours and not shaving as much as he would like. He was about 6-2 and was in good shape. He seemed sharp and competent. He was all business and not about small talk. He was like a race horse, in the starting gate, chomping at the bit to hear the bell and shoot out of the gate. The good ones were like that. On the inside,

Styles had seen a lot and probably had seen more than his share of scenes he would never forget. It was the one thing that most likely gave him the all business appearance.

"Andy, what have we got? Styles asked.

"I was surveilling the property, trying to get photos of the house and surrounding area. We came across a very soft spot in the ground. I feel like we have a shallow grave, and I didn't want to disturb the area any more that we already did and knew that you would want to do the dig yourself," Andy said.

"Yes, thanks for that. The less disturbed, the more evidence we can preserve," Styles said.

"I tried to look around the scene and see if I missed anything in a tree or bush. I didn't seem to see anything like that, but a second look by you and your guys could discover more."

"As soon as the warrant arrives, we will want to do a grid search and crisscross the area. I don't want to disturb exterior evidence on the way in by rushing to the dig. We'll head that way, but if the dig scene is where you are telling me, we won't want to miss anything on the way in. Recovering the bodies is paramount, but we have to be careful not to destroy evidence."

The complicated work of CSI was about to begin, but I had a funny feeling of what and who was in that shallow grave. I just didn't want to say anything until I was told to. Marx was in charge of what I said. My mind was working extremely fast. I was thinking I already knew.

———▲———

Joanna had Lynnette into her office and asked her to take a seat and have a coffee together. Office space at the university was small for most professors. Joanna had very few pictures in her office and the furnishings were very plain. Her desk was solid oak and was clean and there was very little clutter. She was organized and a very neat person.

Lynnette sat across from Joanna, crossing her legs and sitting up straight, she thanked Joanna for the coffee and smiled as she was handed her cup. Joanna poured her own and then sat down in her leather chair.

Joanna's purpose was clear in her own mind. She just wanted to get to know Lynnette a little better since they would be working together. Joanna would ask plenty of questions, as she was a curious person by nature.

"Well, how do you like being here so far?" Joanna asked.

"Pretty good. I'm starting to find everything here in the office and have an easy drive to work," Lynnette replied. "I think I am going to like it here."

"Great, I am glad. I was just wondering a little about how you feel about the work and also happy that you are going to be in the play as well," she said as she sipped her coffee. "You have done well so far. I have been impressed with your ability."

"I have had a little practice as I was in a few plays in school back east. It wasn't much, but every time I watched a movie, I thought, heck, I could do that," Lynnette said to Joanna with confidence.

"You told me you weren't married before. I was wondering if you had any family?" Joanna asked. "Not that I want to be terribly nosy, but I just want to get to know you better."

"Well, my mom died when I was twelve," Lynette lied. "I never knew my dad. I lived with an aunt, but she has since passed away." The best liar and actress in the world was starting to play the part of Lynnette Huber. Poor Lynnette, no family, no one to care for her. Almost right, but her mother was still alive and her father that left her, probably was too. The aunt was never a real person, but she didn't want to put her mom into this. She had suffered enough. She was going to be careful what she told Joanna.

"Well, I am sorry, but you know if you do need something, I will be glad to help in any way I can," Joanna said in a sincere manner. "Life had not been always good to me either. If you ever want to vent, I will be here. I know I am your boss, but I want you to feel comfortable here and enjoy the job."

"I understand. I'm kind of a private person, but if I need some attention, I will let you know," Lynnette said while thinking to herself; *I've never needed anyone before, just your new boyfriend. But you won't have him for long. Right across from me is the woman who slept with him last night. I'll be hunting soon, dear, and you and he will both wish you had never met each other and I will be your worst nightmare come true.* "Thanks for having me in for a quick coffee. Maybe we can do that whenever you like and I will catch you up on my boring life."

"I would be glad to. Can't wait for practice Friday. I am so happy you decided to help us out in the play. I couldn't have cancelled this play with so many foundation backers sponsoring. That would have been a nightmare. With the play coming up Saturday, I think we are getting much closer to being ready. I just feel really good about how the practice is going,' Joanna said getting up from her desk. "You just might have saved the day, dear," she said with a smile.

"Well, I hope I have helped out. I better get started on my work. I have some mailings to get out for you and some public relations statements on the play you were needing me to do. Like I said before, thanks again,' Lynnette as she smiled that smile of hers back at Joanna. Joanna found it a bit odd, almost eerie, that it held her attention for so long. But she passed it off as nothing but a nice smile, warm, friendly and caring.

Lynnette walked back out to her workspace and opened her computer. *Joanna's nice enough, but she is collateral damage. She should have stayed out of it, but she just had to have Mikey, didn't she? She shouldn't have messed with him. I just have to add her to the list of the hunted. It was her own fault, not mine.* Joanna walked past and Lynnette smiled and was thinking to herself, *yep, as much as she is a likeable person, she's just a part of ending all that haunts me. If she happens to be in the wrong place at the wrong time, that is not my fault. If she can stay out of the way, she could be spared...*just then Lynnette's trac phone rang and a familiar voice was on the other end...

The search warrant had arrived and the CSI were about to go in. Marx and I would be witnesses and I would wait in the staging area. Marx would go in and help re-locate the potential grave. Officer Styles was the lead and Marx was the key detective. Styles was careful to note to the other CSI, as well as Marx, that they should be sure to note what they saw, heard or smelled. This could all lead to the evidence that they should not miss. They would certainly take video and pictures on the way in. They began the grid walk towards the place we came from and they stopped several times along the way. This would be a slow process.

I began to wonder about who was in there and what it all meant. I was sure that Branch was connected to this, somehow, some way. Those thoughts once again came to the forefront of my mind. The moments I was in love, the moments I was taken by her and lured into her trap and the days of captivity by someone as evil as she was. Being drugged in that storm shelter, dark, dingy with dried blood all over me. Katy, Marx and I would be forever affected by that bloody scene day after day. What it did to the lives of three of us.

I also thought of Sheila, and her father, Jerry, that had both died. Her mother, Margaret, who had survived them both only to be getting worse by the day. Jerry shot in the head by my brother, James, who had saved both Katy and me. James and his family had gone through a lot for me, and I was grateful yet sad that he had to do that. Why had everything I had touched been hurt, physically and emotionally? Worse yet others died because of me. I was at the center of it all. Now, I began to feel that shame once again. It was the feeling that even in my search for my own redemption, I had hurt and affected so many people and the game of self-blame and loathing began to take center stage. I was in that old game once again; it was me to blame for the scenes of blood and destruction of lives that were trying to rebuild themselves from the scrap heap.

All of a sudden, I was withdrawing once again. Starting to pull deep within myself, I was back in a place I thought I was escaping and the two angels sitting on my shoulders started talking to me again. One on the side of rhyme and reason and the other on the reckless side of me. The sensible angel was saying," *Look, it's not your fault, it was truly coincidence and you didn't know about HER! How could you have known?" The other angel, the reckless one, jumped right in and noted, "Ah look at you trying to rationalize all that we have done? We have been through a lot together, buddy boy, and you know you made those choices based on all of the fun things we did in the past. You remember, right? Did we really care? We were filling our ego, you and me. It was just a game you know, nothing to be so hard on yourself about. It was just libido, just the sex, you just liked being rewarded for your best lines, your best efforts to try to have all that attention you needed. You loved the response you got from those women, especially HER...*

"Hey, Parsons! Hey!" The voice of the cop brought me back to reality. "Marx is on the phone and wants to talk to you." He handed me the phone and like waking up in the morning, I was groggy at first.

Yeah, it's Mike," I said trying to focus.

"We've got something here, appears to be a couple of dead bodies in the soft area," Marx said with urgency in his voice. "We won't be going anywhere for a while."

"Okay, but just between you and me, I know it has got to be the prison guard, Henry Hannah. The big guy helped Branch escape, I think you know that, too. You know, also, that this John Middleton is the big guy. It makes sense," I said in a low voice. "My gut is also telling me Branch and those two kids are not that far away."

"Look, this is going to take some time to process," Marx said in a voice that almost sounded stressed. "Styles said he will call and get you processed and released to go. I'll send a car to get you. I'm going to be here for a while, but I'll call you later tonight. This scene is going to take a few days to process and the lab even longer. We won't have any answers and they may be running right now. Be careful. Call you later."

My official police car ride came for me. I had been here before with Katy. In the back of a police car at the gruesome scene at the lake, Katy and I had sat silent and broken all the way to the station. This one sort of felt the same. I sat in silence the whole way just giving the cop directions for dropping me off at my place. My world around me was starting to get dark again. Just when I thought things were working out for me, they were now only at a new beginning. A new beginning of terror and days and nights that would once again affect me and those around me. Everything was a blur around me. I just wanted to go home. Curiously I wanted to talk to Katy. She knew how I felt, but I didn't need that. I needed Joanna. Somehow, I knew if I called her, she could help me.

The officer dropped me off at my condo and I thanked him. I went inside and shut the alarm off to get in. I was sweating profusely, which I had not noticed until I got inside. Just the thought of what may be around each and every corner was making me once again, weak and very awkward. I sat in my recliner and started to dial Joanna's number. I stopped and hung up. I called Katy. It may have been a mistake but, I just had to warn her. I had to let her know...

CHAPTER 38

I dread the events of the future, not in themselves, but in their results. I shudder at the thought of any, even the most trivial, incident, which may operate upon this intolerable agitation of soul. I have, indeed, no abhorrence of danger, except in its absolute effect—in terror. In this unnerved—in this pitiable condition—I feel that I must inevitably abandon life and reason together, in my struggles with the grim phantasm, FEAR. ~Edgar A. Poe, The Fall of the House of Usher, 1839

"Let me call you back," Lynnette whispered into the phone. "I can't talk right here. Just give me a few minutes and I will call you back."

Lynnette hung up and went immediately to ask Joanna if she could run some PR flyers over to the administration office. Joanna said it would be fine and she would see her back here when she returned.

She had a few other things about the play and post party arrangements that she wanted to discuss with her. Lynnette grabbed her handbag and coat and headed out of the door.

When she exited the building, she didn't even put her coat on and the chill of the Wisconsin air hit her. She shivered and then dialed her phone.

"Okay I got away and can talk now," Lynnette said into the phone.

"We have trouble. The cops are crawling all over my place. They may have found those bodies we had buried in the woods. I can't go back there and we are all going to have to split up. You will have to be on your own for a while," Andres said.

Lynnette bit her lip. She knew this may take her away from her hunt, the one she could not have avoided if she had tried. Damn!

"You have to lay low for a bit, you can't, I mean you just can't go after these people right now, the time is all wrong. I am heading back to Brazil and Jake and Carrianne are headed for Miami where we will meet up in a week or two to take them back also. It won't be safe here for some time. You should be okay there as long as you stay under control."

Lynnette could tell that Andres was serious and that this would mean putting her plans on hold.

"Okay, look, I am going to do this play thing then I will quit my job, and head that direction," Lynnette said, hoping that Andres still had that crush on her. Enough of a crush to take her with him at some point. Once she was done here, she could live in Rio. No problem. "Stay in touch, I really want us to be together. We can have a good life in Rio, Andres. Just you and me."

Andres replied, "Yes, we can, but maybe we can do it sooner than later. I know how I feel about you. I'm just not sure if you may need me or not. You know I will help you, if you can wait."

Lynnette Huber didn't like to wait for things. She wanted them now. Right now. But she relented, knowing that what she had to do took some patience and timing would indeed be everything.

"Alright, dear, but you know where I will be. I think I will change apartments though. I will take care to clean this one out completely and leave nothing behind. Send me the cleaner to take care of leaving no trace evidence. I don't think anyone could put me with those two kids right now. I will be pretty much invisible when I move," she said, knowing that for her, this would certainly be the best place to hunt from and she knew exactly where her new home would be. "I will call in two more days. Hugs, baby."

Andres had emptied his place of workers and anything of consequence and had his plan to get away. A sketch drawing would be up soon and the Feds would surely get involved. Andres knew what he had to do next and he was on his way to do it. Then to Miami and then on to Rio. The Boss would not allow a misstep. He had to be perfect. *"Damn, that woman. It's those eyes. I have been with many women, some very beautiful, he thought. But those eyes, so easy to fall in love with. Demon eyes, yes, demon eyes..."*

Lynnette was headed to the administration office to drop off the papers. She had a plan. She had seen the apartment she wanted was for rent the other day. The one with the view. The exact view she had needed. The perfect home base from which she could work. Her game would begin soon, but she needed to get this place. This would be necessary. She usually got what she wanted. She was smart, tough and clever. There was not much she couldn't have, except for one thing. That man, that one that didn't choose her. Why? Why not her? Why?" ...

———▲———

"Katy, this is Mike," I said with a hint of fear in my voice. "I had to call you, to let you know what is happening. You know I have been working with Marx on this case and today, well. We found a soft spot in the woods on our surveillance trip today. The cops are out at the place and they are most likely going to find bodies. I just want you to be prepared before it hits the news. I think Branch is involved and something tells me she is close to us. Be careful."

"Oh, no, not this again," Katy said, trying to remain calm about the one thing that causes her great panic. "She really needs to be caught, but I fear even going outside my door. She's evil and that face, and those eyes, I think she's out for us and she is not going to stop until she kills us."

"Look, you just need to be extra careful," I said. "We just can't go through this again. I may have to, but you need to stay as far away from this as possible."

"Where's Marx?" Katy asked.

"He's still out at the scene. He's going to call me if he has news," I said not wanting to involve Katy any more than necessary. "I am afraid of what happens next. We know her, and she is off the charts crazy. The worst part is that you won't know her. You have to suspect everyone and I mean everyone, strangers, anyone walking down the street. Keep your gun on you. This is crazy, I know, but in the end, she will be caught. I trust Marx and he's a good cop."

"Mike, you be careful too. I mean, you know, watch out for yourself, okay?" *Why can't I get you out of my head? I need to emotionally leave you and I just can't. It has been so long, so, so, long. I thought I was getting past you. Just hearing your voice brought me back to a time when I watched you walk out my door to never see you again. I cried. I cried big tears. I missed you when you took the first slow step as you turned away from my door and down the sidewalk of my place. I still do...*

"Katy, hey Katy, are you still there?" I asked trying to break the long pause and silence.

"Oh yes, sorry, Mike, I just got lost there for a minute. Thanks for calling, and I have to get ready for work. I will be careful and you do the same. Let me know what you hear," she said, almost in a sullen voice.

"I will," I said and hung up the phone. *Katy was not over this and I was not sure she would ever get over this. This Branch thing has gotten way out of control and she just has to be found. I had to end this for her, for me, for Marx. Where is she? She's near, I feel it all over my soul. It's almost like I can feel her eyes on me...*

Lynnette Huber was in the apartment complex office and she didn't take long to pack things after Andres had called. She had brought just a small number of things with her to move in and she was ready to pay the first and last months rent and sign the lease. The manager was a young woman in her early thirties that was very nice to Lynnette. They exchanged pleasantries and she handed the keys to Lynnette after she signed all the paperwork. She left the office and went to get her things to unload. Just a few doors down from her target, this would be the place where her hunt will begin. The game she was going to play would be so gratifying. She would have it her way and the new girlfriend, her boss, would also be right there with him. She would be sorry for ever getting involved with that man.

Lynnette liked being Lynnette. No one, and she knew no one, would ever see this coming. Lynnette Huber's life wasn't too bad actually. There were times in this new life, she thought maybe she could just step away and find rejuvenation. But, every time she thought that, she just couldn't drop the hunt. The plan had gone to form except for the fact that Marx and Mikey had found something in the woods that Andres needed to hide. *Damn them, we had to move on this soon. They couldn't get too suspicious of me. I have to be incognito. But it wouldn't be much longer before she would act. The play was tomorrow night and after my great performance, I will begin my hunt. No more Lynnette Huber after Friday. Allison Branch will be back. Mikey's worst nightmare will once again surface. Sorry, boss, you can't have him either.*

Lynnette turned the key and let herself in to her new home. She would be comfortable here for a few days. It was small, only a one bedroom. But she wouldn't be here long. It was a place to stay until the hunt. Just for one more night. The furniture was not elegant, but comfortable. The room was done in steel blue colors. Ironic as it matched those eyes. The ones she had used so skillfully to lure her prey. The bedroom was small and she laid her things on the bed, covered with a patterned comforter that went with the blue. She sat on the bed and put the few things she had in the closet and in one drawer. She carefully placed the needles and drugs in the drawer. The tools of the beginning of the hunt. The tools were handy once before, they would be so again.

With everything put in its place, she went to the window to check her view. She could see across the way and it was the perfect spot. With her eyes on his front door, she waited. *Well, there he is. Mikey boy, where are you going? I could just accidently bump into him on his way out, you know, kind of start up a little conversation about the play? Ask him in, seduce him, make him love me like he should have?* But she turned away and went to get a drink of her water. She took out a pill and quickly swallowed it with the water and a hot, steamy tear ran down her cheek. Then she smiled, she had resisted, she had kept her composure. He made her feel so different. She wanted him and then she also wanted to kill him. She knew this and knew it well. "Boss, you just can't have him, you just won't. I won't let you!" she exclaimed as a second hot tear ran down the opposite cheek. Tears drove her and motivated her to do the unthinkable things that people who struggle could sometimes be driven to do. They always did for Allison Branch...always.

Lynnette had one more call to make. He picked up on the second ring. She told him the arrangements were made and that everything was set for tomorrow. He assured her that everything was a go from his end and that arrangements had been made and the Boss wasn't happy. That tomorrow was the latest that they could stay. The conversation was not long but the exact plan had been hatched. They needed to leave before the heat got intense, and it was going to get intense.

CHAPTER 39

Life asked Death, why do people love me, but hate you?
Death responded, because you are a beautiful lie and I am a painful truth.

Marx was at the dig. He seemed to know what was about to take place. The grave area was shallow and the smell began to permeate as the CSI men dug deeper. Decomposed bodies were a terrible smell and it was a smell Marx had known before. Shortly, one of the men had hit something and the dig was done now by hand to not disturb evidence. Photos were flashing and video taken as the dirt was being slowly moved away from the ground area.

"I got something," the CSI agent said. "I have a body, I think. No, more than one!"

The blood rushed to Marx's head, as it always did, turning his stomach to a sight that he had seen before but never accepted. It was the sight of decomposing human remains. It was certainly no better with time or experience. It was always a revolting sight, and all you could do was stare and be still, not being able to turn your eyes away.

Men began to slowly collect evidence and this would take more than a day to collect. Trace evidence, impressions, footprints, weapons would all be searched for and documented. The bodies would have to be observed for bunched clothing. Were they dragged? Is there blood spatter? Shot, stabbed or other methods of death. Two bodies, and a long couple of days ahead for Marx.

The death he saw here, reminded him of his near-death experience at the hands of Allison Branch. He got lost for a few seconds in the nightmare, the dream where he was slowly bleeding to death from wounds inflicted by his partner and her friend Breanne. As he stood here, watching this horrific scene, he started to feel his soul slowly bleeding out of him. He had not before been hit with this thought so hard. He wondered to himself how he could keep doing this work and why he just didn't go to law school...

He quickly caught himself and made a call to the department. He told the chief what was happening and that soon the media would be buzzing about like flies on honey. He hung up and thought that he had better stay with this until they could no longer work at it. It would take days. He dialed his phone.

"Hey, Mike, this is Marx," he said into the phone. "We have two bodies it appears. The CSI is taking evidence and the media will be all over this shortly. Are you thinking what I am thinking?"

"If you are thinking of Branch, yes, I think her friend the prison guard, Henry Hannah, is one of the bodies, but who is the other one?" I asked.

"No idea, but the connection to Branch and the big man, John Middleton, is clear to me. Got to get this to the FBI and they have to get in on this," Marx, said sounding like he needed a friend more than anything right now.

"I think it's Branch and the big man that have to be found quickly. But, they both have to have someone telling them what to do. Right now, we have a couple of fugitives, and a couple of young accomplices who are also at large. We would be better off if we got lucky and found one or both of them and get them to turn on those two and whoever controls them," I said with a hint of guessing in my voice.

I wanted to object to my thoughts of going to help Marx because I didn't want to cut my night short with Joanna. But, it was too late, he already hung up. I was on my way to take her out for dinner and drinks and this thing we had was going well. I would soon be there to pick her up for our dinner that I hoped would relax her before the big play. For some reason, I could feel my soul changing each and every day. Joanna was giving me something that I could never grasp before. My anxiousness to be with her, to listen to her talk, watch her smile and actually feel her presence by my side was filling me up with something good. I just wish I hadn't said yes to this thing I was helping Marx with, but my loyalty to making his world right again, was something I was committed to. I would make the best of it.

I was thinking so deeply that I missed her street and had to turn around and go back. Finally, I turned on her street and the feeling of anticipation of seeing her face was giving me the feeling that I have longed for most of my life. I parked in her drive and headed up the steps and headed up to the door. I checked to make sure I was dressed right as it was always something weird about me. I always thought my clothes and dressing right could help my average appearance. Low self-esteem, I guess. But it was there and I wanted her to be happy to be seen with me. Shallow, of course, but there was a lot of things I wanted Joanna to feel about me and I hope I wasn't trying too hard. I knocked on the door and she answered quickly. It wasn't the look I expected.

"Mike, come in quick, you have to see this," she said and pulled me into her house by the arm. We went to the living room and watched the breaking news on Channel 7. The video of the crime scene where I had been showed only the taped off area and news helicopters were flying above the scene, trying to get a view of what was happening in the wooded area. The trees had not bloomed yet as spring was not here and the video was able to pick up crime scene investigators kneeling down. They cut to the FBI spokesperson, a guy named Paul Chrisler. His partner, a female, Jenna Holmes, remained off to his side. He didn't give away much about the scene, only that two bodies had been found and they would be investigating. But pictures were posted of the supposed fugitives who were being sought in possible connection with the case. I stared at the one of the big man, and of Jake Benson and Carrianne Martinez. It was the first picture I had seen of the man named John Middleton, an alias for the much sought-after man, Andres Montoya, in connection with drug running in the country of Brazil. The sketch of Montoya was done by an FBI artist and the informant, who gave the detailed information about John Middleton, wanted to remain anonymous. The informant was someone close to Montoya and they were adamant about not using their name. I stood and stared when the picture of Branch was flashed on the screen. There she was, for me and Joanna to see. This night was not going to be what I expected. The moment HER face hit the screen all the thoughts of a wonderful night had turned to ashes. I wanted this night to be without thought of the past, just a wonderful night out, sharing some of ourselves with each other. This was more than the daily routine problems we see every day. It was something much, much more that haunts Katy, Marx and me. It was just something way too hard to put aside and enjoy the evening, but I had to try.

Joanna was beginning to know me and what my facial expressions were saying. I was numb and couldn't take my eyes off the screen.

"We don't have to go out, you know," she said in a sincere and caring voice. "We can just stay here if you want, have a few drinks and turn off the television and put on some good music."

"I appreciate that, but I'm not letting that craziness stand in my way of having a life and all the good in it. That includes you, my dear," I said as a I held her shoulders and moved closer to kiss her on her cheek. "We are still going out and having a night that you deserve. I know you are nervous about the play and all that goes with it. You gave them the night off and practiced earlier. So, you need to relax, and I am your relaxation guy."

"I'm serious," she said looking up at me with her eyes locked on mine. "We can do this anytime, and I know what you feel about all this. We can stay here, really."

"I won't have it, you deserve the night out. Shut that off and we will be headed to your favorite place to eat and have some drinks. Besides, I want to show you how to relax before your big play debut tomorrow night. I promise, we will have fun."

"Okay, let's go. I will make you relax, too. You can count on me. We may even dance one or two with the live band that plays there," she said.

"I'm not very good at dancing but I'll try," I said, almost dreading seeing myself awkwardly fumbling around on the dance floor. Every guy's nightmare is to be an awkward dancer and if I ever took videos of my dancing, I would probably never do it again. Damn, I'm awkward, really awkward at times. "But for you, I will try."

"It doesn't matter, we will do the slow ones, because I just want to be able to hold you and sway you. Who knows, it just might be my way to seduce you," she said with that playful grin of hers.

"I'm in, gorgeous," I said. "This will be fun, but you can say anything about my dancing when we get home, but just don't laugh while we're out on the floor. I apologize in advance."

"Let's get going," she said with her arms wrapped around me. She looked up at me and we kissed. My world was getting better by the minute and this phenomenal person, this wonderful woman, was making it that way.

We got her coat and headed out the door. I promised myself no interruptions or changing our plans, not even if Marx called. This was that one special night, I was feeling her so close, so *within* me, that I was not letting go. I could no longer hold back. It was a time I knew something right at the moment that it happened. It was the exact moment I fell in love with Joanna. I wanted to tell her, but I couldn't find those special words. Awkwardly, as usual, I could not express what I was thinking. I just wanted my profession of love to her to be perfect and the words to ring in her ears and in her mind for a long, long time. But, as I usually did, I held on to those words as I was never in my life sure of what to say but I always was sure of what I was thinking. Joanna is special, very special...

Lynnette Huber was eating out alone tonight. She had gone over all her plans and was sure that she had just this one more night and one more day before she would once again, be on the run. Everything will have been completed and her revenge exacted in just the way she had it pictured. It would be satisfying, more so than possibly anything else she had done in her life. The hunt begins tomorrow and she knew that she had been patient, but circumstances now dictated she move faster. No meds today or tomorrow as she had to get that spirit within her moving once again. She needed to be unleashed, unhinged, and it was the perfect mind set for her to begin a journey that would include her favorite things, like kidnapping, torture and perhaps murder. Her mother would not approve of this and she thought back to those early days when as a child she could not understand what was happening at home. She wondered when it was exactly that she first felt like killing. She could not pin point it exactly but she knew what had happened... she recalled it so clearly and vividly in her mind.

It was a Saturday, I think, maybe a Friday. I can't remember for sure. But it was about 9:00 PM. My father had come home is his usual state, smelling of cigarette smoke and whiskey. My mother had cried earlier, tears that made me ask her what was wrong. She gave me a hug and said, "never mind dear, I am fine, I am just having a bad moment." But now, here he was, the drunken dad, yelling at my mother when she questioned him on where he had been. She was scolding him for never being here to take care of us. Never wanting to be with his family. He yelled. She yelled. They said things that I could not understand. He slapped her hard in the face, knocking her to her knees. I ran to her, yes, I remember running to her, trying to defend her. I was so little, there was nothing I could do, but my instinct was to stop this. He PUSHED me down, a little girl, pushed me down, I cried and ran to my room, knowing there was nothing I could do I thrust myself on the bed, buried my face in the pillow and cried, big, heavy floods of tears that seemed to never stop. There was no way to tell when the yelling stopped, but it did stop and I heard the door slam. That time he pushed me down and hit my mother was the last time I saw my father. I remember his face but I haven't seen him in years, so many years. And there will be a day when I do, just one more time. And it will be the last...

Lynnette snapped back to reality as the waitress asked if she needed another drink. Lynnette wanted one, just to erase what she was just thinking so she ordered another wine, even against her own judgement as she needed something to calm her down. Going back in time did not help her anxiety issues and she didn't need to have a panic attack in a public place. She nodded yes and smiled at the young woman, trying to reset her mind. She took a deep breath and returned her soul to some sense of civility for the moment.

The waitress arrived with her drink and the instrumental band was playing a slower number, *Sway*, and she thought of her relationship with Mike Parsons. She remembered how she had tried for maybe one last time, to see if she could have him instead of kill him. It was a choice she struggled with, as she had also struggled with her own sexuality. She wanted to not feel conflicted but she imagined herself dancing just one more time with him, but then thoughts of Breanne dying from the shootout brought back the darker side of her mind. She loved Breanne, not Parsons. She had convinced herself of this. But, as she stared out at the dance floor and the three couples slowly dancing to *Sway*, she could see a fourth couple, just a light gray image of the two dancing around the others that she saw in technicolor. The gray couple moved much more gracefully, swirling in and out of the technicolor dancers. The gray couple were translucent and as they moved around the other couples, she could see through them right to the technicolor couples. She was trying to make out faces of the couple, the translucent gliders that were so good together. The female dancer was much better than the male. She guided him around and made the couple seem to dance as one person. He was handsome, she thought, someone she would have picked out to dance with to a slow number. He was the kind of man that she could hold close, the kind of man she could seduce. Lynnette placed herself in the woman's place and her mind was so lost now, that she became the woman drawing him into her. She moved even more gracefully now as she didn't realize that Lynnette was such a good dancer.

Yes, that is me, dancing with the handsome, taller man that she had to look up at to see into his eyes. She knew him from somewhere, his gray face now coming into focus. I'm feeling almost sick and woozy because I know this man.

Lynnette squinted and tried hard to make out the faces. She knew her face, but who was this man? Her breathing became heavier and she felt as though she may soon pass out.

I am dancing with him, with Mike Parsons! It is me, right? Why am I dancing with him? I want to kill him. This is my imagination, I am dreaming on my feet again. My meds... need one... no you can't. Why didn't you pick me? We could have danced this way forever. I could have made you happy. Her mind began to slow down and the technicolor couples were finishing their dance. The translucent couple kissed, and Lynnette then saw them in color, just like the others. They were walking towards her. *Me walking towards myself? No, not me, but who, who is with Mike?* They were closer now and they spoke. The voice was that of her boss, Joanna.

"Hi, Lynnette," Joanna said as Lynnette tried to gather herself and escape this bad dream that was now based in reality.

"Oh, uh, hi," Lynnette said stuttering to get the words out of her mouth. She felt as though she had just awoken from a deep sleep. "Excuse me for being so sluggish, but I am on my second drink and the lines of the play were going through my head."

"You are working too hard dear," Joanna said. "Lynnette, this is my friend, Mike Parsons. Mike, this is my new administrative assistant, Lynnette Huber."

"My pleasure," I said as she was holding my hand much longer than she should have. "I saw you act the other night and it looks like you have some talent."

"Well, thank you," Lynette said, smiling more than politely. "I am just glad to get an opportunity to do something I have always wanted to try. Why don't you two join me and have a drink with me?" *God, he doesn't know, does he? Surely, he cannot recognize me.*

"Mike, do you mind?" Joanna asked.

"No, that's fine with me," I said still staring at the new employee of Joanna's.

They both sat at her table. The girls had wine and I had a scotch, my favorite. The conversation centered on the play and mostly was between Joanna and her new employee. I really tried to be attentive but found myself drifting away from it.

It could be anyone, it could be a person just walking down the street. Where was she? She had to be found or Joanna, myself, Marx, Katy would all be in jeopardy. Fugitives out there, a blood thirsty killer or two and a missing business owner from

CHAPTER 40

Sometimes the obvious is so close, that you look right past the answer.

We talked for just a bit longer as I studied Joanna's new employee. She was very pretty. She really didn't remind me of anyone that I knew. She was tall and long legged, nice curves and an easy to like face. Her eyes were the only thing that set the rest of her apart. Not remarkable necessarily, but somehow her eyes did not blend with the rest of her. Her facial skin was remarkably smooth and looked tender to me. She seemed to wear too much make up for her clear-toned skin.

Joanna gave me a look as she chatted on that maybe it was time to go back to our table. I was ready fifteen minutes ago. We said our goodbyes and Lynnette said she hoped I was going to the play tomorrow and that it was going to be a huge success. I told her I would be going and looked forward to her performance. Whether I was or not didn't matter. It was the polite thing to say.

Joanna and I got up and went to our table to finish our meal. I don't know why the conversation we had was getting by my brain. I was able to hear enough and respond but my mind was thinking of Lynette Huber. *Nothing remarkable...eyes don't match the rest of her. She is pretty and seems young, but is she? Age can be deceiving. Something is off and it gave me a red flag. I was trusting Marx and his warning that it could be anyone. Someone walking down the street right by you.*

"Are you okay?" Joanna asked. "You seem a bit far away like an actor who forgot their lines, trying to remember."

"Oh sorry, this case has been a funny one and I didn't really want to share it with you. My intention was for us to go out and have a good time. I guess that the bodies found in the woods has got me going," I returned.

"Should I be worried?" she wondered out loud.

"Look, you and me, we are going to be okay," I said being careful not to bring her into my thoughts on the case too much. "I have been waiting for Marx to call back and I hope he can wait until we have completed our date."

"Well," she said tipping her glass towards mine. "Drink up. Maybe we can sneak out of here and find a nice quiet place. Maybe yours, maybe mine?"

"I'm in," I said and smiled at her. "Here's to you. I see trouble, the good kind."

"I sure could be trouble," she said and blinked her beautiful eyes.

I got the check and we left the place walking by where Lynette Huber had sat, but she was already gone and I had not noticed. I shrugged it off and walked my dear Joanna to the car. With the gentleman's touch, I opened the door and watched her gracefully get into the car. She moved with style and never seemed to be awkward, very much unlike myself, who felt every move that I made was clumsy. Did I deserve someone like this? I only knew that for the whole way home, she lay her head on my shoulder and kissed my neck a few times. My blood was beginning to boil and my thoughts of Lynnette Huber and Allison Branch were slowly leaving my mind. It was a good feeling putting Branch out of my mind, but it would be a mistake.

The weather was cool and brisk, but not too cold to enjoy walking her to my place. We talked a little and having my arm around her made me feel I could protect her from the cool wind that blew slightly into our faces. I wanted to tell her she shouldn't have been involved with me and this case was too dangerous. But I felt so much closer to redemption, that I just knew she would be a big reason for it. She had become close. She became implanted in my thoughts daily. It was something not in my daily routine for much of my life. Before, I had been too selfish. I wondered about her every day and how her day was going. Certainly, something new for this guy.

We finished walking to my door and we went inside. We made love, in probably the most meaningful ways to us both, in the way that makes you know that you are committed. We totally gave ourselves to each other. It was lovemaking that made us feel a part of each other, making us whole. We became a pair that night, a couple, a committed couple to the well-being of each other. I really don't understand the chemistry that makes something like that happen. You just feel it when it does. You know that it's right. We slept for a moment, tangled together in our arms and legs, breathing some sort of slow and easy breath of life into each other. We needed each other. We needed us...

Lynnette Huber watched them go into his place. Mikey boy and his new girlfriend. They won't last long, she would see to that. She was on the phone. Andres assured her that things were on track. He had the kids moving in the right direction and they would catch up to them later. The kids had who they needed and we get Mike and his girlfriend. The Chemist will take care of the rest.

"You and I have our jobs to do. We get our two and the kids have the other. You will be able to end those who you have grudges against before we go back to Brazil. The Boss will have people meet us in Miami. The Boss has a safe house for us where we can go undetected. We make sure we get these two here and get as far away from my farm as possible," Andres said beginning to worry they would run out of time.

"One more day is all I need. The plan is perfect and it will be easy to complete. Since you are still in town, just come over later and you can stay all day tomorrow. The truck and car will both be in position by then. I'll get them in here, don't worry about that."

With that, Lynnette hung up the phone and stared at the door wondering why he picks these other women over her. *Such a fool. Such a fool, she thought as a small line of tears ran down each cheek. She had taken no meds, and she would not take any more. She had that spirit that was beginning to rush through her veins. Just not tonight, not tonight. I had a play to do first...she smiled.*

CHAPTER 41

Marx called at 1 am and woke us both. The rings startled Joanna awake. I jumped up to answer.

"Hey, Parsons, Marx here. We need to talk. There's a lot going on. I've got some evidence that the big guy, John Middleton may still be around and that Branch is, too. I got an eye out for Jake and Carrianne on the street. I need to come by and we can put this together. We need to have a plan by tomorrow before something bad happens," Marx said his words flying over me and I couldn't catch up.

"Yeah, uh, sure. Let me take Joanna home first, give me until 2:00 am. I should be back by then. See you shortly," I said and hung up the phone.

"Joanna, I am afraid I am going to have to take you home. You have a big day tomorrow anyway, but I've got to talk to Marx. There is a lot happening and he wants to catch me up and make plans. I'm really sorry, but it's important. These people have to be caught."

We both dressed quickly and I grabbed a quick coffee for us both from the kitchen as she finished. The ride home seemed gloomy but I just had to tell her for her protection I would go inside with her and check the rooms before I leave. We will check every room and lock all your doors. She seemed to understand but I am sure she questioned what was involved here. We went inside and checked every room, one by one, closets, behind doors. The works. Making sure everything was locked, I went on to the front door and got ready to depart for home.

We stood looking at each other for what seemed to be quite a long time. I saw the fear in her eyes as she leaned into my chest and I put my arms around her, rubbing her back gently.

"It's going to be okay," I said. "This will be over soon and I promise, we'll go somewhere exciting when we get these people in jail."

"Look, you don't have to come to the play tomorrow. I know you have so many other things on your plate," Joanna said, looking sad.

"I wouldn't miss it, really," I replied not sure if I could keep that promise or not. But I was sure going to try.

We kissed and I hugged her tightly. This was the woman I would not fail. Not if I could help it. I looked at her one last time and told her to talk to no one, keep her doors locked and that I would see her at the play tomorrow. I pushed her hair back from her eyes and kissed her once more.

"I had a wonderful time," I said softly. "You make me feel like I have purpose and my life has meaning. I could regret many things in my life, but you, my dear, are the best thing that has ever happened to me."

I kissed her one last time on the cheek and then turned to leave.

"Mike, you're the best thing that has happened to me, too. I think I'm in love with you."

"I'm in love with you, too," I said, wanting to go right back in. But, I had to get back because Marx may beat me home.

"Remember, doors locked," I reminded her.

She just smiled and nodded her head. I'll never forget that look. She closed the door and I headed home.

On my way home to meet Marx, I thought of Joanna and her safety, for the most part. I did wonder though what it was that Marx had in store for me. The evening had become more like early morning on some of the nights I used to have, being out way later that I should have been and drunk, driving home. I didn't miss those days I told myself. I think I was finally getting somewhere with my life and I had turned a corner. This time I was sober, and my thoughts were mostly good ones, good ones about Joanna that flooded my consciousness.

I got home much sooner than I thought. The time had gone by very fast, without much traffic. I got to my parking lot on time and hoped that I was getting there before Marx. I parked the car and headed to my place, awaiting all the good things Marx was about to tell me. I had the strange feeling that I was about to learn about what I would be chasing for the next week. It would be a lot of information. More than I wanted to hear, but it would be clear, that the dangers we were about to encounter would be coming from many sides...

CHAPTER 42

I got into the door maybe five minutes before Marx knocked on it. I opened the door and despite the early time and the morning fog, I could truly say I was glad to see him. We had become friends and looking at his face, tired and worn, I became concerned.

"Come in, Andy," I said almost dragging him inside. He had looked like he had a long day and needed a seat and a hot coffee.

"Good to see you, Mike," Marx said. "I really had a long day but I thought I would review everything and then we can both talk about what you think the story is and how we attack this. I have my own ideas and it gets complicated. But, here it goes, strictly between us, you can't share this with anyone, not even the new girlfriend."

"Okay, I got it," I said and when he told me that, I thought about maybe having to miss the play that Joanna had worked so hard on.

"Here's what we have. I'm going to break it down into four themes. One will be what we have from the woods, two, what we have about the two kids, three about the big guy and four about Branch. Let's start with the woods. They belong to a guy by the name of John Middleton with the FBI finding he has an alias, Andres Montoya. The guy came from one of the poorest slums in Rio de Janiero. He has been serving as a heavy enforcer for a drug cartel run by an American living in Brazil. They call the American the "Boss" and they say he is ruthless. Of the two bodies found on his property, only one has been positively identified as that of one Henry Hannah, the prison guard. You and I have both suspected this since the beginning, but through dental records, that's who the one is, the other body, has yet to be identified, but had been at the site much longer. CSI is still working on that one." Marx drew in a quick breath and looked at me like, this was only the beginning.

"Andy, how did Hannah die?" I asked.

"He was shot," Andy said and drew a long sip of his coffee. "There were several bullet holes in his clothing. We think that Montoya's thugs did him in and brought him to the farm for his official burial. We know this is in connection with Branch, because we feel that he helped her get her new identity, when she had escaped, and the escape was arranged by Montoya's group. The Boss wanted her out of prison for a reason, which we are not sure, except that she was good for the drug trade around here, helping the dealers be undetected. So, we know, that Branch and Montoya are connected. Not so much romantically, but as two blood thirsty villains with the same desire to eliminate people that have gotten in their way, Montoya, doing his for the Boss and Branch doing hers for revenge. He's definitely going to be helping her."

"Okay, so far I have this picture of the murderous big guy, Montoya, and his connection to a drug boss, just known as the Boss. I have in my mind, knowing Branch, this other picture of those crazy eyes luring Montoya to do whatever it is that she wants him to do. He doesn't seem like the kind of person I want to confront in any way. He's much more dangerous and he will defend her to the end. He has been taught to always respect his duties, but there is something about her that makes him wish he could be with her. But he knows the he just doesn't stack up and he's more based in reality than I was. Her eyes made me do things I didn't think I would do for anyone. It was just her way. She was so manipulative." I stopped and looked at Marx wondering what he was thinking about her and how he saw her. He seemed to be recalling something. I then paused to sip my coffee. I let it go and didn't ask.

"Now for the two kids, Jake and Carrianne. They have the connection to Montoya as they both came from the same slum as Montoya. Their real names are Julio and Maria Santos. They are really brother and sister and they have worked the drug trade here for the Boss for a few years now. They worked the same area Branch helped to grow in the Milwaukee slums according to one of my informants. It was where Branch came up with all the cash we think," Marx said barely stopping to breathe. He seemed to be more on a mission than telling a story. It was like he was connecting all the dots in his head and was so far ahead of me, that he almost found it annoying that he had to "catch me up" on the latest. "Those two may be easier to grab than Montoya, but you can bet he won't let them get out of his reach. You can also bet on the fact that they will run soon and the invisible Branch will show up soon. So again, Mike, you have to really be careful. I have two FBI agents working on Jake and Carrianne and they have a couple of leads on their path. You can bet they are the first to run. The agents are two of the best and they will do good work here. I am confident they can catch up to the kids and maybe make them flip on the other two."

"Okay, you've covered, the wooded area grave, you've covered Montoya, and the two kids. Now the obvious question, what about Branch?" I asked.

"Well, that is the scariest of them all," Marx replied. "We don't know where she is, or when she could strike, if she even decides to do that or run with the rest of them. We just know we are dealing with a real danger with her being invisible. What even puts you, me, Katy, and I hate to say this, but your new friend, Joanna, in greater danger, is the idea that she may be very close, closer than we know."

"I have had the same feeling. I don't think she will show herself until you least expect it. She has a unique and satanic way of thinking up the wildest schemes and to appear when you think you are in the clear," I said stopping cold and thinking of Joanna and thinking I needed to call her, now! But I calmed down and started again. "Through my whole relationship with Branch, I felt for her, felt sorry for her after she exploded during the scene at my lake home. I know I was looking at that wrong and I surely won't make that mistake again. I even had the feeling that she is even watching me at times. She had some kind of obsession and she wasn't going to end it until she kills me, or worse, kill any and all of us. She has appeared in dreams I have had. I wake up in a cold sweat and try to deny it, but it won't go away."

"I know what you're thinking," Marx said, almost with sympathy. "Ever since she shot me and I thought she had killed me, I too have dreamt of ways that she would finish me off some day."

"Alright so what is the plan, who is doing what?" I asked. "I am not sure where I belong here, and you know I want to help."

"I hate to say this but keep your piece on you all the time. Just be aware. When I hear from the FBI agents, we may be traveling to catch those on the run. If we can just get lucky and catch those two kids we may have something to work with. We do know that if he sends the kids ahead, Montoya can't cover them and Branch at the same time. Our moves will be made in accordance to what the FBI gives us. Until we move on them, carry on and call me when you see anything suspicious."

Just then, Marx's phone rang.

"Marx here." It was the CSI at the department.

"Andy, we have the ID on the second body. It's Andrea Stephenson Raines."

"Oh shit, that ties into my cold case and maybe this one," Marx said anxiously into the phone. "Her brother is missing and she is dead. This complicates things a lot. Thanks for the heads up, Styles. I'll be in touch."

Andy turned to me with a look of almost desperation. "These people, they may be my match. They're slick and are always ahead of any predictive reasoning I can provide. Andrea Raines is the second body and we have trouble now. Trying to decide where Oscar Stephenson fits in to this plot is tough. Is he dead or alive?"

He turned and looked at me and said, "We're going to get this done you know. We'll find her, we'll find them all."

I think I believed him and said goodbye. I watched

him walk away and started to shut the door, but I stopped and looked at a room across the courtyard. I could have sworn I saw a curtain move, but I couldn't be sure. I took it that I was just tired and needed sleep. I shut the door and went on to my bedroom to lie down. My eyes were dry without the sleep I too had desperately needed. This case was connecting better, but it also confused me. I thought of Andrea Raines and how she was now just another casualty in this mess. People losing their lives over some drug boss seemed so senseless. But, money and danger talk to people in such strange ways. I was feeling much sleepier but I could start to see images of HER. Branch seemed to be hovering above me, watching me. I knew she had to be close. I felt her. I fell into a deeper sleep and the dream began...

I was in a room. It was hot and sweltering, and sweat was running off my nose, dripping onto my soaked t-shirt. I saw us there, all of us, Katy, me, and no, please no, not Joanna. People yelling at us, as we could not move. Once again, I could only try to slur my words out. They were thick and not coherent at all. Katy was crying, Joanna was near lifeless. None of us could move. I ached and I was bleeding, I thought I should be dead. Is this my second try at survival? Maybe I would not be successful this time. Maybe we were all three going to die. So thirsty, so tired...the girls' hair was soaked and matted to their faces. What was the temperature in here? I had never been in a place so hot...

Just then, my phone rang and I jumped out of bed, sweat pouring off my face. It was my friend Nick from the restaurant and bar that Katy worked. He sounded frantic.

"Mike, this is Nick," he blurted out. "Katy didn't make it to work and didn't call. I called her and got no answer. I went by her house and her car was there so I knocked on the door and got no answer. I panicked and called the cops, but she is missing, nowhere to be found.

"Okay, Nick, be calm. I will call Marx and let him know. I know a few things but I am not table to tell you, but Marx and I are on it. I'll call you if we get any leads, but for now, my mind tells me she's been taken."

I hung up and called Marx to let him know. We both had the same feeling. She was rounding people up. The hunt was on. He reminded me to be careful and carry my gun at all times. I called Joanna next, it was four-thirty and I hated to wake her, but as much as I hated to say it to her, it was time to worry...

CHAPTER 43

K aty sat bound and gagged in the back of a cleaning company van that had been arranged for by Andres for Jake and Carrianne to drive. She had begun to feel nauseous as the shot she had been given by Carrianne had begun to take effect. Katy was numb and she had the idea that she had once again been kidnapped. The haze, she fought to see through, would not allow her to see her captors. The picture was just too fuzzy. The language they spoke was something she could not make out, but she was sure it wasn't English, or was it? Katy began to fade in and out and could barely now see the two figures through the metal screen that was between them. In five more seconds, Katy was out and she would be for some time.

Jake and Carrianne were well-disguised. Jake had a deep, full black beard and glasses. He wore a ball cap with the cleaning company logo on it and a shirt to match. Carrianne had a blonde wig and also a company uniform. Her new blonde hair was tucked up inside the ball cap, which almost gave her a boyish look. They had done so many things for Andres, many of them very risky. But this idea was the riskiest and they both were nervous once again. They tried to calm each other as they had so many other times. They were resourceful and they were clever. They had learned so much from Andres, but this kidnapping thing was far out of their element. They just could not make mistakes at this point.

"We have to get through the night and into Alabama by the afternoon," Jake said in Portuguese to Carrianne. "Andres said that by the next day we have to be at the meeting spot. South Florida is a place where we can easily blend in and the address is in an area where we can easily hide. One of the cartel's soldiers will be there to help us store this one. The main thing is to keep her alive, but not functioning very well. The shots will help but until we get there, we have to be very careful when and where we stop. We don't want to be very visible at all."

"Jake, this is far more than I have ever done," Carrianne said. "I just don't know if we are in over our head on this thing. I would do anything for Andres and so would you. But would you do anything for HER? She was fine when she just managed drug drops and protected deals as a cop, but now, I think she's gone off her rocker. It seems like Andres is dead set on helping this woman, but why? He had always been independent and only bowed down to the Boss. She has some kind of hold on him, but what?"

"Look Carrianne, we just can't question Andres. He has always known what he is doing and he has always kept us from harm," Jake said as he monitored the cruise control, checking to make sure he was staying within the posted speed limits. "But you know her eyes, Carrianne. You have seen them just like me. She makes men do things with her eyes that they do not want to do."

"Women, too," Carrianne replied quickly, almost too quickly. "Women, too...

At this point, the old slum was the final destination. By then, this one in the back would be certainly dead and gone. Then Carrianne could get out of this business, find her a man and have the children she always wanted to have. This was definitely her last go around, and she was going to have a normal life, whatever that was. She had never known normal before...yes, a normal life. But, no one leaves the cartel. No one gets away. They know too much. She was fearful that if she left the country, she would never find the life she was seeking. She had many thoughts going through her head and many of them she wasn't sharing with Jake.

Joanna was wide awake. She had trouble sleeping because she knew that at this point in Mike's work with Andy Marx, she knew Mike was in danger. Most assuredly, she too may also be in danger. She had been supportive of Mike's work with Andy, but now she desperately wanted to ask him to get out of this. She was scared for him and also for herself. She was scared for them. The play was tonight and she had to complete this. She could not cancel. She was banking on the new girl, Lynnette, to save the play by being good at her part and she had been good during rehearsal. But something about all of this was beginning to make her feel like bad luck was right around the corner. She had been so lucky lately, being able to hire an efficient new assistant who, also, by the way, was filling in for an actor pulling out of the play at the last minute. She had found a new man she was falling for. Yet, she felt he was in trouble, or was he trouble? Which one was it?

She continued getting her coffee and was getting ready for work. One more day and maybe the police can get to the bottom of all this. *Bodies in the woods, a crazy woman on the loose, possibly one that could even target me. I'm not sure if I am the kind of person that wants to live with this tension. I see him change. He is getting tired and he is starting to fill himself with all the old memories. I can see it in his face. He is changing some right before my eyes. So many things l like about him, but is this what I need? I just can't leave him to do this by himself and I do love him, I know I do. At this point in your life, can I just go all in for this guy? I just hope he can come tonight, I do feel I'm all in for him. I want to share things with him, like this play. He just seems like he truly is interested in everything I say, and that is so unusual to find a man like that who listens. I just hope he can make it and this thing he is working on ends soon. I worry for him. I worry for us.*

Joanna finished getting ready for work. She grabbed her things and made sure all the doors were locked before going to the garage. She opened her garage door with the wall button and the door began to rise. She thought she saw something move quickly, a shadow or something? But then she just blew it off as something in her mind. She was just too edgy this morning. She closed the garage door with the car button and headed on to work. The weather seemed nice today and she was going to be happy, by god. Today would be a long day with the play and all, but she really didn't know how long of a day it would be. She drove on and she really had no idea how long she would be gone from home, she really had no idea...

Joanna's assistant, Lynnette Huber, was herself taking a nice, warm shower. The water ran all over her, soothing her nerve endings on her skin. She had always had nerve sensitivity and the lightest touches could calm her nerve endings which always seemed to be on edge like needles pricking up through her skin. But, this shower was a therapy of sorts. One that would do what the meds she was no longer taking could. Calm her, just for now, just until it is time.

You know, I just have to do this acting thing. Just this one time, I have to show how good I am at all things, especially for HIM, Mr. Mike Parsons. He just has to see the talent I have, the things he missed, I could have been his. I would have made him happy. He was just too blind to see it. I found my refuge, sometimes in other women. Women were easier for me to understand. Men never did do me right. But HIM, he had my interest, and it was him and only him, the only man I could have ever been with who rejected me, didn't pick me.

The needle like sensation on her skin began to be much more intense. She turned the water up hotter and let the hot, steaming water calm her once more.

Easy now, be easy, let your mind be silent. You have to quit thinking of HIM. But you know Allison, it is the others that will pay, too. It's that stupid Katy, my dumb ass ex-partner Marx, my new boss that is hitting on Mike, and, of course, HIM. All of them, they all helped kill my Breanne. They are all going to pay. All of them.

The warm water and the tears were now flowing down her cheeks as one. Both were hot and both seemed to converge into one hot river of water running down her new, pretty face. Lynnette caught herself and reminded herself she only needed to be this Lynnette chick for one more day. One more day that she had to hold her composure. She could do this, she had to do this, and she would make sure that her plan all came together. Before work, she would make one last call to finalize the details.

She shut off the hot steamy water and began to gently towel off her nerve sensitive skin and the needles began to recede. The towel felt good all over and she was beginning to calm down. Yes, "Allison's Hunt" as she referred to it over and over in her mind was about to happen. The event she had escaped for. She could kill them all, she wouldn't mind going to jail again. But if it was possible to pull it off and still be free, even better yet. She finished toweling off and stood before her full-length mirror in her bedroom. *Look at me, I am pretty, what man wouldn't want me? Talented and pretty, right? Yes, yes, you are Allison Branch. Pretty and smart. Pretty and evil. You are evil, yes, yes, you are!* Then she smiled the crooked smile that she had always used and those eyes, oh yes, those eyes gleamed with great anticipation of this hunt, the one she dreamed up while in prison. *Well, it is here now and you are ready!! Let's go hunting!*

Marx was one step behind and he was feeling the pinch of not getting anywhere. These two cases were now becoming one. He was driven to solve them both. He didn't know how much longer he could keep this torrid pace and not lose his mind. He had always been strong and had an uncanny ability to persevere. His constitution was extremely solid and his intelligence had always kept him in the game. Even so, these last two weeks had made him question his own ability to keep doing this work. Retirement began to sound good, or maybe even a good desk job. But he knew it wasn't him. These events had the makings of another showdown and he was going to be there at the end. He just had no idea although he had several scenarios in his mind. It was his strength to determine just how and where things would come to a head. But this case, well, he knew he had to step up his game. He was a step behind. Period. He parked his car in his lot and would get to the phone calls right away, this day would be a day when events would turn his way. It had to be...

———▲———

I called Andy and said I wanted to meet him. I had things rolling in my mind and this day was going to be a busy one. I had to try and make the play for Joanna. But I had something pressing in this case that needed to be discussed. There were a couple of things that worried me and I had to get those out to Marx. This was going to be a very long day and I had a lot of work to do. These two things had been on my mind ever since I woke up.

Next, I called Joanna and wished her good luck with the promise I would be in the audience for the play. I didn't know if I could keep that promise or not, but I had every intention of doing so. I had fallen for her, it was evident. I had begun to think of her in everything I did. I thought of our more quiet and peaceful times together that I wish were the norm and not the exception. There were many things I loved about her, but the true peace she gave me was what I had loved the most.

Then one last time, I thought of HER. She was out there and was Katy in grave danger? How much danger were we all about to experience? She had a calling card and it was her eyes, those eyes that hold you, that allowed you to be hypnotized. It was one of the two things I was going to tell Marx this morning. The other was something he had never thought about, as of yet. It would help us, I thought. Those two things could be key, but then again, I am not a cop. But there are two things I feel right now and one is that all these characters are tied in closely and that someone's pair of eyes were watching me. Watching me right now.

I got in the car and headed out of the parking lot and my feeling was right. Someone actually was watching me, only I didn't know it...

CHAPTER 44

Lynnette Huber was on her way to work, leaving from her new apartment complex, HIS apartment complex, which was also now hers. She was sure he didn't see her, and she pulled out just shortly after Parsons had done so. Today was going to be an exciting day. For today, she would be an actress. She would be best on stage, of course. She had experience in real life, which made her the best. She could appear to be just about anything she needed to be.

When her dad left her and her mother, she had begun her acting career. Whether it had been at school, with friends, even with her mother, she always could be what she wanted to be for that particular time. It was a gift, the need to be the best, not just one of many, that many people seeking to be professional actors wish they had possessed. She had this in spades. She had strived all her life to be the best at anything and everything. Of course, no one can possibly do that. But that wasn't important, it was actually believing she could that was.

The plans had sped up because of the bodies found in John Middleton's wooded area. She wasn't sure if she liked that or not. She knew as a cop that criminals tended to make mistakes when they rushed. But Andres called her to let her know if she needed his help the heat would soon be on his trail. So, it was today or maybe never, and she thought, even though they were beginning to rush, she had all things planned perfectly. She just needed to act in this play and be convincing in just one more act when it was over. Of course, she believed that she could do this. She thought she could do anything. For Andres to trust her and get the hunt carried out, she had to do it.

She arrived at work on time, but she just couldn't recall the drive. She drove it by instinct more than actually remembering the route. Her day dreaming had now become more intense. She needed to control that today. There had to be no tipping anyone off. It has to be just another day, sticking to the routine. Until the play was over, then all the dreams and reality would mix into one beautiful and cleverly planned hunt. Showtime. She walked on to her office.

I walked into the Department Offices at 8:00 am sharp. I told the desk captain I wanted to see Marx. I gave her my name and said I had an appointment. She motioned me to wait in one of the benches until she could get him to come out front. Marx appeared just minutes after she had called back. He looked like shit. He had been up all night, it was obvious. The circles under his eyes had gotten darker. He had not shaved in days and he looked worn and creased in the face.

He looked over at the desk captain, and said, "It's okay, he has clearance."

"Hey, Marx, you're not looking so good today," I offered. "You haven't been getting much sleep, have you?"

"Hey, you don't look so hot either," he said as we walked back towards his desk. "You are not going to win a beauty contest today my friend. So, let's just get this crap over with. We have needed a break and I think I might just get one."

We arrived at his desk. It was extremely cluttered for Andy. He was always so neat and organized. It certainly appeared that he had been thrown off his game. Something was off with the Andy Marx I had known. Soon, I would know why.

"Have a seat, Mike," he said and asked if I wanted coffee. I took him up on it as I was as much sleep deprived as he was.

Marx didn't wait long to get into the facts of where we were on the case.

"Look, Mike, we have Katy gone, and you and I both know what we are assuming. We both believe Branch is somehow involved. We just don't know how yet. The big man is a fugitive of justice as is Jake and Carrianne Martinez. On the list is you, me and possibly your girlfriend. I think they are around and we are just not seeing it. They have to rush and when they do, they will make some mistakes. What I'm not sure about, is where does Stephenson and his dead sister figure in on this?"

"That one is funny and hard to figure. There are couple of things that worry me. One is that all these characters are tied in closely and, also, that someone's eyes are watching me. I worry for Katy. I don't know if she can get through another one," I said. "Do you have any information on her at all?"

"We deferred that one to the two best FBI agents we could get, Paul Chrisler and Jenna Holmes. They are the best at tracking and using the several informants they have in the drug world to find people. If anyone can do it, they can. They are on the road as they already have one tip that they may be headed south, possibly Florida. Florida State Police have been notified, but we are not sure what they will be travelling in. My assumption that it will be a rental vehicle. They are checking all outlets here in the Milwaukee area. I think I am heading that way tomorrow afternoon to be near the area they are predicting to be their destination. Right now, the web is pretty large so we haven't narrowed it down and they couldn't possibly be there yet."

"Do you think I could go?" I asked, probably wondering why I wasn't going to leave it to him and the police.

"I think you can choose to do what you want, but we can't ride together. You could drive your own car and we can communicate by phone to stay together," he said sipping his coffee more frequently. I could see in him that he was also ready to go on the hunt and that he was getting all his ducks in a row before taking off. Marx knew he needed me to possibly get to them, but he didn't want to risk it for me. He was the kind that always followed protocol.

"Yeah, I do want to go," I said looking straight ahead at all the busy cops. "In some ways we are together in this, you know, emotionally and all. It wouldn't be right if I stayed back here. Even though my training is nil, I still feel like I can help."

"Good, then we will plan on leaving in the morning, let's say 6:00 am. I should have more tracking info as we get closer in the chase."

"I just need to see this play of Joanna's tonight and then I'll go home and pack and get ready to go," I said not so sure of what I was actually committing to but I was sure it was going to be dangerous. SHE had to be back in jail, SHE was evil and SHE had to be stopped! This bunch was so capable of so much mayhem and destruction. It was all around us, yet so far away and invisible. I couldn't imagine the next time I would come face to face with HER, but I was almost sure it would be sooner rather than later.

"Okay, then let's meet at the station here at 5:30 am and if I hear more about Katy, I'll give you a heads up," Marx said with a look of determination. "We're going to get them all, you know. Every last one of them."

He did say we, right? Like, him, me, the both of us? He did say we, I heard it.

"Okay, I'll be there. This thing just has to have a good ending. Maybe life is about to turn out better for the both of us," I said, not so sure that it really would.

"See you tomorrow," Marx said as we shook hands and I left the department. It was the last place I would feel safe for quite some time. When I walked out of the glass doors into the Wisconsin sunshine, I felt the cool wind hit my face. It was almost like a warning. *You can still take it back. You could hide back here with Joanna and then be safe and your life would be just fine, just like you have always done. Sometimes, you have to care more for the lives of others to find your own mission and who you are. No, not turning back. This time, it's paying it forward to help someone else. This would be over and my redemption that much closer. I felt I was nearly there but I had to finish this one thing. It had to be done. I would break it to Joanna after the play. Right now, I need to look at photos. The ones I had at home. They put me in the game and let my instincts take over. I had to study them, the characters in this real-life play that had very high stakes. I had to feel these characters.*

I didn't know how long I was sitting in my car. But I realized I needed to start it and get going. My daydreaming was increasing as the days went by. I started the car and headed home to my apartment.

"The Chemist" is an assassin. He is a man for hire, and he only had recently contracted with one group only. It was the group that paid him the most money, of course. He built his bombs for occasions just like this. He was one of the highest paid soldiers in the cartel. The "Boss" had been using him for the last three years. He was trained in making IED's, while he served in special forces military. He was only twenty-eight years old, and he had become quite wealthy in a short time. He had planted devices in cars, trucks, and remotely detonated them.

His bombs were pieced together with parts of radios, cell phones, egg timers and watches. He was very resourceful as he had learned his trade in Iraq. He had driven this truck for miles now and was very careful to keep the detonator dead until he was ready to park it. He had many miles to go before he was at the right place. The parking of the truck would be according to the plan of one Andres Montoya.

He was trained to be the best. He knew he was the best. These jobs had been easy for him. He had special talents and he had been compensated well for his expertise. He would not mess this up. He traveled along in his truck, heading to Miami-Dade County. His destination already picked, he was on his way to the next job. The placement of the truck would be key. He knew exactly where to go...

Joanna and Lynnette were sharing conversation about the play. They both were excited for different reasons. One of then excited for all the right reasons. The other, not so much. But excited just the same. Lynnette had drawn Joanna in, just like so many others before her. She was the best actress, of course. This day was going to be no different. She would win the Oscar with tonight's performance. The after party would be awesome, just the three of them. It was a party she had been looking forward to all week.

Today was her last day of work, but there was no going away party. Lynnette was the only one that knew it was her last day. Joanna had no idea.

Lynnette just kept smiling and nodding, pretending excitement at the prospect of being in the play. Or was she pretending? There was a fine line with who she could become at different times and who she really was. She took the part of each character and then brought out the best parts of her where it mattered. In Allison Branch, Lynnette Huber, or whoever else she needed to be for this play, it didn't matter. She could play them all! She believed it every step of the way.

"I'm very excited for the play to happen tonight," Joanna said smiling at Lynnette. "I have looked forward to this for a year. I am also excited that you said yes to the part so late in the process. You have really taken to the part so well."

"Thanks, I am excited, too!" Lynnette said with a smile that maybe a ten-year-old would use. She was almost giddy. "I have looked forward to it all week. I just hope I remember all the lines and don't let you down. You have been so nice to me."

"You will do just fine. I am thinking you were made for this acting thing," Joanna said, patting her on the arm as she was getting up from her chair. The touch made Lynnette uncomfortable as her mother used to touch her just like that when she would console her. *Don't get weak, not now. This one just happens to be collateral damage. She's just in the way, and the guy that didn't pick you is sleeping with her. DON'T BE WEAK!*

"Thank you, I won't let you down, I promise," Lynnette said with a smile, a smile that made Joanna slightly uncomfortable. It made Joanna feel something strange, like she was being manipulated by a young child. It wasn't the smiling teeth or the mouth that formed the smile on her face. It was the smiling eyes. They froze Joanna for just a second and she felt fixed on her assistant.

"Well, let's get some work done and then we can all get to the pre-play meeting with all actors at 4:00 pm. We're going to have a great time," Joanna said still staring at those eyes. It was something she had not noticed before. It was almost as if with her eyes, she was bringing you to her own world.

Lynnette then got up and went to her own desk to begin to get some of the work done. Joanna broke her gaze from Lynnette and picked up the phone to make some arrangements with the workers at the auditorium to set up for the play. All the while she was talking and making these arrangements, she could not release the vision in her head of those steel blue eyes and what effect they had on her.

The play was just nine hours away...

CHAPTER 45

Sometimes, the best tip is the smallest piece of evidence found and also maybe the most ironic. Styles from CSI had called Andy Marx. For the first time, Marx felt like he had something to go on that would help find these people. If he knew who the person on the card was, he could get Chrisler and Holmes of the FBI on it and question them. Styles was reading the information on the card. Marx told him to pass it on to Chrisler and Holmes as he wrote it down himself. Maybe, just maybe, he had something here. It was just a business card, of a female named Anastasia, found in a shirt pocket of Andres Montoya found at his farm. No last name was on the card, but there was a number and the business name, *The Pleasure House*. The location was Miami, South Beach.

Marx felt like he had seen the first light after traveling a dark tunnel for weeks. All the while, he had crawled along on hands and knees through this dark tunnel, finding nothing along the way but more miles of dark tunnel. As small as this break seemed, it was just a brief light that gave Marx hope. Hope that even the smallest piece of evidence would produce what they needed. Anastasia and *The Pleasure House* needed to be found and Marx certainly needed a break.

Chrisler and Holmes immediately got their people on *The Pleasure House's* location and were sending two agents to the location. They would soon have Anastasia in an interrogation room, firing questions about why that card was in the farm house of one John Middleton from Wisconsin. They would get their answers. They would let Styles and Marx know when they had made contact.

It was 3:00 pm and I stopped by the flower shop to grab some roses for my favorite play director. She had called earlier and said she had a meeting with cast members at 4:00 pm and we agreed that we would be able to meet at the play. I had asked her to my place for a little private celebration for her. It would include a nice bottle of champagne, a box of chocolate strawberries, and a lot of quiet time together before I headed off to who knows where tomorrow. I balked at letting her know I would be leaving with Marx and figured I could break this to her later tonight.

I recalled something in our conversation as I was checking out with her flowers. Joanna had said that she had a nice conversation with Lynnette, her new assistant and cast member. She had the strangest feeling she was taking care of a child. She felt as though the new girl was looking to her for help. It wasn't in her voice or her smile or even her words, but it was in her eyes. This thought bothered me somewhat, but I passed it off as the way that women could communicate better than men. They could truly understand each other because they listened better. No, couldn't be, could it? But it was HER eyes, hmm, I don't know. I quickly put it aside as I was looking forward to my evening with Joanna.

Most of my life I had trusted my instincts, my gut feelings and my observations. Part of me thought that I should look into this Lynnette Huber person, maybe tell Marx about how I felt. But I wanted to trust Joanna and her thinking. It was a part of me that I was working on, trusting the thoughts and ideas of others and not always having to be right because I "felt" a certain way. I put it aside one last time and headed out of the flower shop with something for the woman I now trusted and believed in. I would have my one more good night before heading out tomorrow. I pushed those thoughts aside and told myself I was trusting Joanna on this one. My common sense and trust in Joanna took over and I quit thinking of Lynnette Huber and just thought the young lady was needing a mentor and she had picked Joanna. Joanna never having had a child may have looked at this as an opportunity to help someone that could be like a child to her. It was Joanna's good heart and my not trusting my gut, that would lead to risking the lives of others and to one more nightmare in my life that I was emotionally not prepared to handle.

I sat in my car with the two little guys on my shoulders, arguing on what was best. The sky was grey today and had becoming darker as the day wore on toward late afternoon. The little guy on the left was saying that I was foolish to try and trust someone else over my own feelings. It was my large ego guy over there. The guy on the right was telling me to let it go. It was time to step out in faith. She had been good to you, Mike, don't screw it up by not trusting her. I brushed them both off my shoulders and started my car. I had to go home and get ready for the play. I think I'm going with the guy on my right shoulder, my ego and selfishness needed to disappear before I could find what I was looking for...just trust.

I drove home to my complex and pulled into the driveway about 4:30. The sun was low in the sky and my feelings were going along with the darkening sky. As I walked towards my door, my feelings were sinking somewhat like the sun in the sky behind the clouds heading toward dusk. The glow of what I had felt earlier was giving me pause. Just like the sun hiding behind the clouds, I felt something sinking in my head. It was pressing against my brain and causing me to have that ominous feeling of bad karma once more. I turned the handle to the door and opened it slowly. I peeked behind it, walked into the foyer carefully, turning on the lights one by one and checking the doors and closets in all the rooms. I began to sweat as I placed the flowers in the fridge to keep them cool for a moment. As I turned back, I was sure I saw a flash of a figure go past my living room window. I went to the door and peered out through the peep hole to see if someone was out there. I could not see anything.

Out of my view, to the right, was a large figure who had moved quickly out of my sight. The figure was not expecting me home so early and he was nearly caught but managed to hide in the alcove down the walkway. The man wished he could just kill this guy and get it over with. He had tired somewhat of the charade that Allison Branch had made him play. He needed to be gone. He needed to be back in Brazil. But he had promised her, that he would save the prey for her. She was crazy for sure, but she had been a valuable asset. His breathing had slowed and he moved away from Parson's door and walked the long way around back to

Lynnette's unit. He let himself in and just hoped he hadn't been spotted. He was taking big risks for her. Yes, his only weakness, and the one that would bring him down, was women.

I shut the door and walked away after locking it. *I just had to get over the shadows and imaginary people. This thing has played with my mind for so long that it is always standing in my way when I think I am almost home to the promised land. Something inside of me was still missing. The peace and understanding that comes with trust. But who is it? What is it that I am supposed to trust? Always feeling I could take care of any problem I encountered, I never needed anyone else's help. Tough, strong and self-reliant, I could manage. I always had before now. I was in some sort of danger and had been for some time now. I wonder where my life is heading. I question my luck, which has always been poor. But SHE had said once, "do you believe in destiny?" I said I didn't, but I was starting to feel she knew more than me, that she accepted what happened to her as destiny and not fought it. I didn't believe in destiny, did I? Maybe I should have.*

I was sitting at the kitchen table wiping the sweat from my forehead. I had to get ready and shower, but I couldn't shake this feeling no matter how hard I was trying. It was now five-thirty. I had to get ready.

The pre-play cast meeting was going well. Each actor had received their last set of instructions from the director, Joanna. She had made sure the last instructions and wardrobes were ready and nothing was missing. She had paid attention to detail and her mindset was intense when she got to this stage. She had counted each staff member and reviewed the set movements with the crew. It was almost time and she was very excited for her new man, Mike Parsons, to be in the audience. She had peeked a few times through the curtains to see if by chance he had come early, but he had not yet arrived. She so much wanted to impress him with her ability. She had thought that this new man would be the one. He had made her feel alive again and she had begun to feel hope. They could talk and discuss things they both liked and she had never had that before. She felt brand new and she smiled just a brief smile to herself that the thought of him could raise her spirits so much...

"How do you think I look in this first set outfit?" Lynnette asked interrupting Joanna's thoughts.

"You look great, dear," Joanna replied holding her hand.

"Thanks for having the confidence in me," Lynnette replied squeezing Joanna's hand back. She felt the warmth in it, the genuineness in her touch and she almost felt a tinge of regret that the selfish Mike Parsons had gotten involved with her. She dropped her hand as if to say she couldn't be that close to someone she would soon destroy. "I won't let you down."

Her eyes met Joanna's and at that very moment Joanna suspected something strange was going on with her. Nothing she could put her finger on. She sensed a bit of nervousness in Lynnette and had decided to pass it off as a bit of jitters about the play.

"Good luck, Lynnette. I know you will be a hit," Joanna said as she turned to check on the two lead characters.

"Thank you," she called after Joanna as she walked away. *You have no idea just how big a hit I am going to be. I had to act my whole life. Your silly little play is a no brainer. Yes, you will see the true to life Lynnette Huber who really is Allison Branch. You've*

seen her on television, and she scared you to death.
Yeah, that's really me. The one on television. But,
dear Joanna, you really don't know me. It's not my
face you see, it's young Lynnette Huber that you have
grown attached to. I know you think you are
stepping in to take care of me. The girl with no mom,
lost here in Wisconsin and nobody to lean on. I have
plenty of friends, all just as evil as me. I have enemies
too, and you're not really one of them. I do really
think I could like you. But you see, I can't. It would
ruin my plan, my hunt...

"Okay, places everyone," Joanna called out as the
play was about to begin. She had pulled the curtain
back slightly to find Mike. There he was sitting in the
first row with the special ticket she had gotten for
him. She smiled and then went to center stage with
microphone in hand. She stepped through the
curtains in front of everyone. She had worked so hard
on this and she was hoping for a huge success.

"I just want to say welcome to the Events Center for
tonight's play. I want to thank our generous donors
and the administration of the college for helping to
make this event happen. The actors have worked very
hard in preparation for this presentation. I'm
confident they will do their very best to make this a
memorable evening," she said as she looked directly at
her new love Mike Parsons and smiled. He smiled that
great smile back at her and her heart was now full.
"Thank you for coming and enjoy the play." She
disappeared through the slit in the curtains and
walked off to the side to begin her work. The curtains
opened to Act One, Scene One. It was showtime!

Lynnette Huber stepped onto the stage for that one
and only time in her life, that she could possibly hear
the cheers and applause. Something she had somehow
missed throughout her life. *Adoration, that was it,*

adoration! She would steal it from the two leads, yes, it will be me that they just love. Love, that was it, love, that had been missing from life. It was what I wanted most but could never seem to have. My heart is beginning to separate from my brain, the way it always had. They are opposites of each other. Just play the part, girl, play the part well with your heart and then with your brain, figure out the rest. The hunt. The one you have waited so long behind those bars to create and now tonight, act out. Damn girl, you are good. Very, very good...

CHAPTER 46

"Law enforcement has always had informants and people they've had to deal with, who walk a certain line. They're choosing between the lesser of two evils. They befriend one person to gain access to another person, who is a bigger fish."

Chrisler and Holmes were on their way to South Florida and on the trail of Anastasia, aka Anjanelle Strickland. She checked out as an informant to the drug dealers as well as the cops. She had been paid well by both sides and she had tip-toed the red line between the two. She grew up street smart in Atlanta and had made her way to South Florida through the only means she knew, prostitution and drugs. Both profitable enterprises to be sure, but also if you could walk the thin red line, there was income to be made as an informant. She had learned early how to work both sides but it was dangerous and the only thing that kept her in it was the money, which she had used to send to her three other siblings that took care of their mother, sick with cancer.

Anastasia had no idea the FBI was coming for her. She was working tonight and she had arranged a date with a popular local entertainer. It would be a private date in a private place. He was married and did not need the publicity. She looked into the mirror in her private room at *The Pleasure House*. The mirror lighting showed some stress on her face as her mother's condition had gotten worse and required more intensive chemotherapy. Anastasia was pretty and her caramel skin accentuated her beautiful smile. She had high cheekbones and her eyes, worn with worry, had needed the most work tonight. She put on the make up a little heavy but her eyes were what made her so desirable and they couldn't let her down on this big pay day. Her eyes sparkled with contradictory looks of seduction and sadness. It was a quality that had always served her well in the profession. She dressed slowly, taking care to accent her every curve to her liking. She was ready to go out. One more time selling herself for the cash she so desperately needed. She wondered if there really was any other way. It was all that she had known. She never experienced the other side of life, grow up, go to school, get a job and raise a family. She actually never thought it to be possible. Her life was exciting and very dangerous indeed. She had taken risks for more money and had played the games needed to survive. She was getting older for her profession at thirty-three, and although she was still very beautiful, she was getting tired and didn't know how much longer she could go on. But for now, she had to keep going. She had no choice.

She was finished getting herself ready, looking stunning in her tight, form fitted and short dress that revealed more than what was comfortable for most women. She looked into the mirror one more time and headed outside for her private ride to her destination. Once outside *The Pleasure House,* a man and woman approached her and flashed their FBI badges at her and asked her to step over to their vehicle. She did so without resistance. She had been here before with other cops, but not FBI. This bothered her as she knew this was no ordinary occurrence and she immediately thought of her mother. They drove away to a hotel room that was small and inexpensive. She would be questioned for the next two hours...

The play was going well according to Joanna's observations. Lynnette had been more than good. She was great! It was intermission and the applause like music to her ears swelled to a crescendo. She took a quick peak to see if Mike was still there. He was standing by his chair, talking to an administrator from the college that he knew. She was hoping that he was enjoying the play and she began to feel the anticipation of being with him later. It was nearing time for the last half of the play.

"Places everyone," Joanna called out. "Let's really give them your best in part two. I'm really proud of you all."

The actors were in place and the curtain parted. Part Two was well under way and Joanna was very pleased. They had a hit so far. As long as everyone finished in style, this would be her best production yet. She was beginning to feel accomplished and her life was coming together nicely. She stopped to pray and give thanks for her newly found life. *It just couldn't get any better could it?* No, but it could get worse, much worse and it could come crashing down in a hurry...

The play had concluded and the curtain call for the cast was greeted with a thunderous round of cheers. Taking her bow, more profoundly than most, was the replacement actress who had so little time to prepare, Lynnette Huber. She had stolen the show with her ability to portray the jilted lover and she had been so convincing. I noticed that she smiled a large and proud smile but something else seemed funny as she bent low to take her bow and held hands with the other cast member. She had tears rolling down both cheeks as she seemed to look directly at me, like she knew me and was pleading for something. I shook it off as nothing and just someone happy that she pulled something off that she didn't think was possible.

The curtain came down and I walked near the stage to wait for my favorite director to return. I held the flowers in my hand that I had brought with me. She appeared shortly and she had never looked better.

"Great job!" I exclaimed handing her the flowers.

"Oh my," Joanna replied. "You surely didn't have to do this, That is so nice of you." Her face had a glow to it that only someone who had worked hard and earned the praise of all those around her could show. I was so happy for her and we seemed, at this point, so together and on the same page. When you want something for someone else as bad as you have ever wanted something for yourself, then you truly have become connected to that other soul. I smiled at her as friends and colleagues came to praise her work. I was able to stand back and truly be happy for someone else and I let her soak it up. I took a few steps back and looked around, taking in this scene. In the background and just to the right, I saw Lynnette Huber, walking off the stage and she looked back over her shoulder. I was sure she looked at *me,* causing me to freeze for one moment and it became imprinted on my mind. It was not a happy look and I just figured that someone had said something to her to upset her. My thoughts quickly returned to my new love, Joanna.

"What a great night," I said. "How about you and I get out of here and to my place? Then, we can cap off your awesome production with a wonderful night together. I have some nice surprises for you."

"Oh, that would be wonderful," she said with a mischievous smile. "There is no one else I would rather spend my time with."

I reached out and hugged her and we went backstage to get her things. We were exiting the back door and she said goodbye to cast members and hugged a few on the way out. But I didn't see her assistant who had played her part so well. I didn't know why I expected for her to be one she hugged on the way out, but I thought that might happen. We went out the door and to our cars.

"I'm going by the house to drop my car off. Could you pick me up there and then, for the rest of the night, I'm yours," Joanna said with a gleam and smile that meant tonight would be the best ever.

"Sure thing," I said and helped her with her things and opened her car door for her. "I'll follow you and pick you up there."

I closed her door and I headed off to get my car as she waited in hers for me to follow. We both drove off the lot heading to her house. Of course, thinking of Joanna I hadn't noticed the car that was following at a safe distance. In that car, Lynnette Huber was making sure that the plan was carried out and there weren't any changes in logistics. It was important they ended up at Mike's place. The hunt couldn't start without them being there.

I parked the car and waited for Joanna to come out

of her house. She carried a leather overnight bag with her and got into the front seat of my vehicle. I had a feeling that this night would be one I remembered for a long time.

"Let's go, professor," she said in a voice so smooth, it made me want to drive 100 mph to my home. "We have nothing but time."

We cruised along and headed to my house. We talked about the play and I complimented her once more. She was very humble about it. She admitted she was really glad it was over. We were in our world and it was a good world. We seemed to get lost in each other so often these days. We were so lost, we didn't even see the red sports car go by us as I turned down the street that led to my condo. The sports car had made it ahead of us and a female figure got out and headed to her unit. We arrived a few minutes later and from the window of her unit, Lynnette Huber was watching Joanna and I walk down the sidewalk in front of my unit.

Lynnette's cheeks flushed with heat, the kind that a jealous person feels when she felt she was being jilted for another. *Look at her, feeling so safe with her head leaning into his chest and his arm around her! That should have been me. Why not me? Why?*

"Stop," the deep and low voice said from behind her. "You have one more part to play and you have to remain calm to get this done. I am here for you and this will be easy. You just have to get them over here. Stay with the plan and no variations, you have to get them through this door. Once they walk through it, we take care of the rest. It will just take seconds, but you know what to do. I have the place to go and then you can do with them what you please."

Andres looked into the steel blue eyes of Allison Branch. He could not help but feel for her, that she could be so wrapped up in this guy. He felt a little rush of blood to his face, too. He didn't like Parsons, Marx and the rest of the people that Branch despised, but he would do anything for this woman, and maybe, just maybe, he would have time together with her. But Andres knew that if he ever had a chance, two things had to happen. One, he had to make sure Parsons was dead and two, he had to allow Branch her hunt, her fantasy. He had to make sure he could make it all happen. He had taken care of so many details, and he was set. Now, he had to come through for Branch.

Anastasia, aka Anjanelle Strickland, was being questioned and the FBI knew a lot about her, not only from the local police but others who would snitch on her in a heartbeat. She made enemies in this business. She was feeling vulnerable and exposed.

Chrisler and Holmes were good at good cop, bad cop. They had done this routine many, many times. The vulnerable Anastasia sat before them on the edge of a bed and they pulled up two chairs facing her. Holmes was playing bad cop today and she started right in on Anastasia.

"We know what you do and we also know you know some of the bad folks we're looking for. So, for starters, let's not play games here," she said staring hard at Anastasia. Anastasia was not blinking but she already knew that she was going to try and not tell this FBI bitch anything.

"I don't believe I know any of the people you are talking about," Anastasia replied. "Don't think I understand what you're talking about."

"Look," Chrisler said. "I think you know a guy named John Middleton. He's wanted for murder and on the run. I think you know where he is going. Why don't you just come across and tell us and make things easy for yourself."

"I know lots of "Johns", Anastasia replied. "They're just clients. Lots of them, they come and go. They visit and they are gone. I have lots of high-end clients, and they pay well."

Holmes broke in again. "I know your mother's got cancer and being an informant in this situation would pay very well. More than you get working the street. Now, you'd turn on him before you turn on your mother and your siblings, right? We can make it so you never get to work again and you lose any chance of helping her out. Your choice," Holmes said as she moved in closer to Anastasia.

"Hey, easy, Holmes," Chrisler said using the good cop tactic once more turning to Anastasia. "We really need your help. This guy has already killed several people and to keep you safe and your ability to help your mother intact, we need your cooperation."

They knew too much and Anastasia was in a tough spot, but she knew her choices and she really had none. Her mother had been her reason for working this profession. She had to be able to continue to help her. She had no choice.

"Look, he's just another client," Anastasia offered. "I've seen him a few times in the past year. Whenever he comes through this way, he stays with his friend near Coral Way, a rougher neighborhood in Miami-Dade. There is an alley beside the house with a "grow house" on the back side. The side and front parking area is large enough to hold four to five cars."

Holmes leaned forward and put on her smirky face. "You better be right, dear. We will have people headed that way to stake it out. If all this is a bad lead, your mom is going to suffer. You don't want that, do you?"

"No, no, I don't," she replied, looking down and biting her lower lip. All things considered, she was going to protect her mother's treatment. No one else could rise above her mother.

They got the remaining information they needed and told her to be assured that she would be rewarded nicely and her mother's treatment would be able to advance. They finished and checked out. They got back to the city and she immediately made the call to her date for the evening, who was still willing. They let her off in front of *The Pleasure House.* Her ride to her date had waited and she got in without looking back at them.

"You know, I kind of feel sorry for her," Chrisler said. "She's had a tough life."

"She chose it, Chrisler, she chose it."

"I guess you're right," he said. "Pretty girl that's going to age fast without ever knowing what raising a family is."

"C'mon, Chrisler, she's an informant for hire. I wouldn't trust her as far as I could throw her," Holmes said in a matter of fact way.

"Yeah, but there is always her mom. That will keep the information we have gotten tonight most likely accurate and we just need her to make one phone call when it is all in place. I don't think she will do anything to hurt her mother," he replied.

"I hope you're right. There's a lot of life at stake here, maybe more than we know."

Jenna Holmes was pretty smart. She had enjoyed working with Paul Chrisler over the years. He was tall, good looking, and always played the good cop with female villains. He was good looking enough to convey the thought that he may even care about them. But he was just a bit too easy in situations like this. He had a good heart basically and grew up with lots of values. Jenna Holmes did not and her street-smart demeanor had served her well in law enforcement. If anyone could be the skeptic, it was Jenna. They drove to make the call to Marx about what they knew and made plans to get over to Coral Way with a surveillance team. The next 24 hours were going to be very intense, thanks to the help of a hooker that was about to take down her "John", Mr. Middleton aka Andres Montoya for some cash that she needed. It seemed like a simple world to Jenna. It was much more complicated for Chrisler. But they both had been successful together, and they combined their skills successfully for many years. Somehow, this one case felt different to both of them. And, of course, it would be the most unique one they had ever worked...Anastasia was a small fish, there were bigger fish to fry.

CHAPTER 47

Joanna and I had sat down to our first glass of champagne and I was about to grab a strawberry and feed it to her, when we heard a knock on the door. Having no idea who it might be at this late hour, Joanna went to the door. She opened it and a voice from the other side sounded so familiar to me. It threw up a red flag immediately in my mind that something just wasn't quite right. You know, it was my gut feeling. I got up from the couch to see who it was but by the time I got there, Joanna had closed the door and said it was Lynnette Huber asking us to come over for one celebratory drink. I hesitated and wanted to tell her something, but she seemed ready to accept the invitation.

"Mike, it won't be long. Just for one drink," she said.

"Okay, but I was just settling in for a very nice comfortable evening with you. But I will go, but let's only stay for one. I want you all to myself tonight," I whispered with a slight hint of playfulness in my voice.

"Deal," Joanna said softly into my ear as we both went out the door and followed the walk to the unit across from me.

"I had no idea she lived here," I said as we walked. "I never saw her around."

"Neither did I," Joanna said. "She never talks much about her personal life."

We walked on and things were starting to feel somewhat jumbled in my mind. *That voice, I know that voice. I have heard it before but where? I began to feel queasy and I knew for some reason I felt this was a bad idea. Something funny about this Lynnette Huber. Even Joanna had mentioned it. Something about HER eyes...it could be anyone. Just someone walking down the street...*

Joanna had knocked on the door. Lynette opened it and invited us in with a smile and we walked inside. In a heartbeat a needle was stuck in side of my neck and I couldn't struggle. *It could be anyone.* Two very large hands grabbed my shoulders and I was sinking to the floor. I saw Lynnette Huber putting the needle into Joanna, too, as I dropped to my knees. My vision was still clear, but I was unable to speak or move. I saw it then and there as Lynnette looked right at me. *It could be anyone, anyone that passes by you, Marx* had warned me. Joanna said something about her eyes, I saw them there, I realized that the voice that went with those steel blues eyes was that of not Lynnette Huber, but a stone-cold killer named Allison Branch. This was it, she was ready for revenge and we had been had. I was about to pass out and the vision was getting more unclear, but my mind had told me that this person with the new face and the voice I realized was hers, much too late, was going to kill us. The final thing I saw was a smile that I had seen before and steel blue eyes filled with hate staring right at me. Like the boxer that was hit squarely on the chin with that right cross, it was time to say "goodnight". Out cold...

Marx had waited long enough. Mike Parsons was really late so he decided to go to his place and roust him out of bed. He had to get going. Chrisler and Holmes gave him information he needed and he and Mike needed to get to the airport quickly. He hurried to Mike's condo and saw his car and hurried to his door and knocked hard on it. No answer. He knocked again, still no answer. He took out his cell and dialed the number. He got a no service recording. Marx quickly ran over to the office and woke the manager. He flashed his detective's badge and said he need to see if Mike Parsons was okay and he needed to get access to the condo to check on him. The attendant quickly got the spare key and went with Marx to the condo. They opened it and a strange scene with open champagne and a small bowl of strawberries sat on the coffee table. But no trace of people anywhere. Marx was slow to open the bedroom door but he did knock first. No answer. He slowly turned the knob again. He swung the door open and again, nothing.

"There's no one here. Something's happened to him," Marx said to the attendant. "I have to make a call, excuse me."

Marx dialed the office. He reported Parsons as missing and said that they needed a few men here and CSI to process this scene. He needed photos, he needed fingerprints and the names of everyone that lived in this condominium complex. Soon Mike Parson's face would be all over the television news. Marx also needed to catch a flight, but now he was going alone. He called CSI's Brandon Styles to let him know if he found evidence and to keep him posted. Styles was good and if anybody could come up with something, it was Styles. Marx left as soon as he got someone there to take over the scene and headed for the airport. He called Styles back on the way and told him to check on Parson's girlfriend, Joanna Presley.

"She teaches in the theater department at the college. I need to find her too, she may have an idea of what happened here. I have a bad feeling you may not find her either. Call me if you hear from her," Marx said into his phone.

"You got it, Marx," Styles replied. "I'll buzz you when I get the info."

Marx pulled his car over for just a second. His eyes were fuzzy from lack of sleep and he was needing to take a few deep breaths. He was running on fumes now and maybe, he could sleep on the flight. He pulled back onto the highway and headed for the airport. *He had to find out what happened to Katy, who killed Andrea Raines and Henry Hannah. Where is Parsons? I have got to find some answers. This nightmare doesn't ever seem to end. I'll find her, I'll track her down. Prison will be too good for her. Track her down and end her. But would it be the end? How many more Branches would he have to hunt down? There were many more, more than he or anyone else could count. I need a vacation...*

Brandon Styles called Marx. He answered, "Marx here."

"Andy, I sent a couple of men to check on the girlfriend. She's gone, too," he said.

"Damn," Marx said. "Even though it's becoming more complicated, I am seeing it better. Keep me posted."

CHAPTER 48

"Here I am, on the road again, Here I am, up on the stage
Here I go, playing the star again, Here I go, turn the page."
-Bob Seeger, "Turn the Page"

Mike and Joanna were both tied up, out cold and headed south in a moving van with Andres Montoya at the wheel and Allison Branch in the passenger seat. Branch was thinking of how to end the hunt. Andres was trying to figure out how he and Branch would end up together, but first he had to deliver for her. He had to get them all in the right place and let Marx come after them. The Chemist could take care of the rest.

Branch was used to scheming, planning and carrying out horrendous events. She had learned from the best in the cartel. Now, she had conquered the acting profession. She was brilliant and the echoes of the applause still rang in her ears. *Yes, they loved you. Of course, they did! I was great. I can be anything. I was so damn talented and Parsons could never see it. Marx knew it and he fought hard every day since police academy to stay ahead of me.* She smiled to herself as she saw the whole story begin to come into focus. *The ending was near for many of them and the beginning of something new and exciting for her. They would get there in the morning and drive all night and the games could then begin.* She was excited to perform in the play, but this real-life stage was where she really shined, mainly because she was so damn evil. Yes, the song, 'Turn the Page' by Bob Seeger was playing in her head. Here she was, back on the stage again, Allison Branch, leaving Lynnette Huber behind, and becoming the star once again. God, she loved this...it was her sickness.

Chrisler and Holmes had made contact with Andy Marx to give him the information he would need to possibly get to the right place if all the information was correct. He had no idea of what he was heading into, but, at long last, there was something tangible to sink his teeth into. Chrisler and Holmes were good at what they did and if anyone could turn something up, it would have been them. Marx was thankful for the information, but now he had to fly to Florida and not with Mike Parsons in tow. Andy almost felt like going to the lake house again, but surely, they wouldn't do the same thing twice. So, he put that out of his mind quickly and called for his airline tickets. He checked in with Brandon Styles one more time to see if he had anything from the scene. Styles said he picked up something from a new rental across from Parson's place. It was rented by a woman named Lynnette Huber and she was working at the college for Mike's girlfriend, Joanna Presley.

Holy shit! I think Huber is Branch. So close to him that he didn't see it.

"Look," Marx said quickly. "Do you have any photo ID of this person who rented the place?"

"Just a driver's license, but the picture is small," Styles responded.

"Make a copy for me and I'll be right there to pick it up. I am heading to the airport soon to catch a flight to Florida. Got some information that they may be headed there. Keep it quiet, as no one else is supposed to know that," shot back at him. "I'll be there in 15 minutes. By the way, try and get the video from the play. I think the Huber girl was in it"

"Got it," Styles said and then hung up. He directed that a copy be made in the condo association office for him to get for Marx. He held a piece of paper and looked at it. It only had one word on it. The word DESTINY was traced over and over in pencil until it almost tore the paper. He wondered what it meant, but he would also give that to Marx when he came by.

I awoke to a blurred vision that made me very claustrophobic. I was in some kind of corner with a wall only three feet away and I wanted to take my hands and rub my eyes to clear them so I could see better. They were behind my back and not moving. Through the darkness there was another image slumped in the opposite corner from me. I felt we were moving or riding maybe in a vehicle, but our space was cramped and I couldn't get up and move around. It was cold in here, and I feared I was back in the storm shelter at my lake. I was captive again. Oh no! That wasn't Katy with me, it was Joanna. I remember now, what happened before blacking out. That new girl Lynnette Huber invited us for a drink.

We were kidnapped I thought. Just like before. But it was Branch, not Huber. Huber was Branch. Not again, please not again. I could do this, but not Joanna, not her.

It could be anyone, Marx said it could be someone just passing you on the street. You may not see it and it may be hard to pick her out, but I just now realized what I had missed. It was so easy, that it made me feel so incredibly inept. Of course, you missed her eyes. But you really didn't miss them. You thought you knew, you saw them at the table at the restaurant. You looked right at them, but you just had to deny it. You saw it on the stage during the play and after when you were leaving. You just didn't want to believe it. You couldn't believe lightning strikes twice in the same spot. So foolish. So very foolish.

Just then the two angels that sat on my shoulders appeared to me again. I had thought that they left me for good, but here they were back again for another debate with themselves and my soul. In my groggy state, I looked at the good one, who opened the conversation.

"You should have learned your lesson and understood that the only thing for you to do was to stay away from relationships. You failed her again just like all the others. You let your ego get in the way. You could have protected her, but you dragged her into another one of your crazy ideas. That you could be a cop or something like that. Wow, I thought I had you convinced."

"Oh, come on, really?" the bad one countered. "Mike and I have never had a conscience. We just do, we don't think. Life is what it is, my friend. It's not his fault as he and I both operate with a recklessness that is cool and daring."

"Well, your super cool attitude and daring has gotten more people in trouble. You are not helping him. If he ever has a chance to get his life back, you need to go away Mr. Reckless!" good guy yelled back. "Quit getting these innocent people caught up in your crazy ego."

"It's just life, things happen," said little reckless guy. "I know Mike better than you. He likes me to hang around more than you anyway. So why don't you just go away?"

Just then an abrupt stop of the moving vehicle or whatever we were in shook the two little guys off my shoulder and they were gone. A door in the wall opened and I saw no light but just a dark image come through the door. I tried to get to my feet but I was slugged hard with the back of a huge hand and I tasted blood in my teeth. The next thing I felt was a needle and slowly, I began to melt back into a floating state watching from above as he gave Joanna another shot, too. I tried to open my mouth and yell, but no words came out. Sleepy, I was going out again. I called for the two little men in my mind to get me out of this, but they never showed up to save me. It was just me and Joanna, drugged in the back of some vehicle on our way to who knows where to encounter who knows what. Say good night, Mikey, say good night. *Good Night..."*

Marx jumped out of his vehicle and ran to Styles. He grabbed the photo and he looked at it carefully.

"Here is something else," Styles added. "I found it in a drawer in the bedroom dresser. Not sure what it means, but you may know."

Marx immediately knew what it was and who had made it. This was Branch. Mike had told him the story many times that Branch had asked him if he believed in destiny. "It's Branch," Marx said. "It was her that changed her face and took Mike and his girlfriend. I have information on where they are heading. I have to make my plane so I have to go, but, hey, Styles, thanks. You always do great work."

"No problem and hey, Marx, be careful. These people are very dangerous." Styles looked at Marx and raised his eyebrows. "Especially her."

"Yeah...especially her," Marx replied. He then hurried to his car and headed for the airport. He was headed to Florida on a mission to stop this hideous group of people once and for all. He was tired, worn and mentally cracking, but he wasn't going to quit. He had to have this person eliminated. His thoughts were getting far away from police protocol. Bring them in alive, get them to trial and let justice be served. *Not this time. I'm thinking just kill her and get this over with. She's a menace and if she lives, she has one more opportunity. She doesn't need one more. It's her or it's me. Once more, a clever duel with his ex-partner, and this would be over. If I have to, I will end her miserable life. Then the thought changed to "I will end her miserable life, soon."*

CHAPTER 49

The Chemist was nearing the state line of Florida and his mind was starting to go back to his military days. He remembered that one night at 3:00 am when the enlisted men were rousted up by the Sergeant and their gear was thrown all over the room. It was a late-night training stint and the men were tired. The Chemist, recalled how he had looked at the officer and how the officer responded to his look with asking him to come outside with him. The officer struck him several times in places that would not leave bruises. He came back to the barracks with a limp, terribly sore, more so than he had ever been. He wanted to kill that man, right there and then. But he had a promotion coming, and he wasn't going to jeopardize it. But, in his mind that always thought three steps ahead, he would get this guy. Justice would be served. He hated bullies and because of his small stature, bullies seemed to have picked him out in crowds to be their whipping boy.

He did get the promotion after learning how to make bombs. He was one of the better students in that training and had become the best over time. The officer that abused him knew really well how good he was at his job and stayed clear of him after he became a specialist. He knew he could blow up the old Sergeant about any time he wanted to. He just hoped for his sake to avoid him, because if the Sergeant got close, he would make it happen. It was a thought he had every single day and would the rest of the days of his life. Someday...that 3:00 am tantrum would be repaid.

Marx was tired and slept during most of the beginning of his flight, but lately, these quick and brief moments of sleep came and went. He never slept more than two hours at a time for the past two weeks. He was still a relatively young man, but the job was aging him quickly. He woke up and ran his open hand against his two-day stubble. He needed a shave and shower and would get one when he got to Florida. But first, he had to meet Chrisler and Holmes before going to the hotel and make the web to catch these people. He felt as though he was closer, much closer than he had ever been in this case. But, two things still bothered him. One was the fact that he just wasn't sure what the big man, Andres Montoya, was capable of and how this ending would play out. Two, where in the hell was Oscar Stephenson and more than that, who was Oscar Stephenson? Marx thought for sure that his sister's death would have brought him out if he was still alive. But in his mind, Marx had a gut feeling that Stephenson was alive and that he, too, was involved with these people. Maybe Stephenson had more to do with his sister's death than anyone knew. It was just a hunch, but Marx had been very good at playing hunches. He was smart and he knew criminals well. He had that knack for being ahead of them but this case had him spinning in circles. Now, he was starting to see things that his old detective mind used to see that made him the top dog in the department. He was getting his Mojo back and he was ready to act on his hunches. Marx had new life. He was focused and on point. He was ready to play.

Marx's plane landed and he was wide awake. He gathered his thoughts one more time and got focused for his meeting with Chrisler and Holmes. They were already at the airport waiting for him and together they went to a nearby hotel where he would be briefed. They would get their plans for moving in on what could be a violent scene in trying to take down this group and get the people who were missing back, if all their hunches were right. If they missed their guess on this one, there were many lives at stake and a killer that was insane was on the loose. They had to be right.

Carrianne Martinez told her brother to pull the van over at the rest area to check on their hostage. She went around to the back of the van and opened the double doors and stepped into the back of the van. She closed the doors behind her and Jake stood guard outside. Katy was awake now and although she seemed to be weary from the last shot, they had hit the Florida line and there was just about enough time for one last shot. Carrianne had debated long and hard about this latest kidnap event. She had thought of turning them all in and maybe getting a deal with the Feds. She was tired of all the violence and things she had to do. They always seemed to be hiding or be on the run. She loved her brother, but she was also afraid for him. For Jake, there was no turning back.

She could not see him leaving the cartel. For herself, she had envisioned something different for her life as she was beginning to age. The thought of having children of her own was so strong now and she was getting to the age in her life where this was a serious matter. Carrianne needed children to complete her, and she needed to love and be loved. She was getting to a desperate time, and she had to pick between staying in this dangerous life or finding a new one. Her decision would come soon enough.

She gave Katy one last shot that would hold her over until they reached their destination. Katy's terrified eyes saw the needle coming. She was crying as if to say, "please, let me go" and Carrianne not only saw that but she felt it. Carrianne was feeling herself becoming weaker and wondered what kind of life this Katy was having and how she had been kidnapped twice in her life. The terrified look on Katy's face was almost enough to allow Carrianne to cut her loose, but she knew Jake would never allow this to happen.

She jammed the needle into Katy's arm and watched her eyes roll back in her head again. Soon Katy would be out and they would deliver their captive. Carrianne dropped her head and she was so conflicted. She needed out, and she needed a new life. But for now, she had to carry this out. There was no way to cut and run now. She got out of the back of the van and closed the double doors and returned to her seat in the front.

"Everything alright?" Jake asked.

"Yeah, I gave her one more shot and I think it will last long enough to get us there," Carrianne answered.

"Well, we need to get gas one more time," Jake said. "We'll stop at one of the larger stations we see and that way, we will be less noticeable. I will feel a lot better when we get this trip finished. Once we get to

Andres and Branch gets what she wants, we can go back to Brazil and lay low."

"Jake, you know she's crazy, right?" Carrianne questioned. "You need to let her go do her own thing when this is over. You know what she has in mind, and when that is done, you need to keep your distance from her. She is dangerous and would kill you in cold blood in your sleep if you gave her the chance. She will use you and throw you away just as quickly as her eyes had you suckered you in."

"I'm a big boy, Carrianne," he said taking a deep breath. "I can take care of myself. I know what she is and I will be careful." If only Jake could possibly know what was in store for him, he would have never believed what he just said. But just like Andres, Henry Hannah, Jerry and Mr. Mike Parsons, Jake would never see it coming. She was that good. She was convincing, and she just had that way of making any man do whatever it was that she needed. She could make any man feel that she really cared for them. Jake Benson would be no different. He just didn't know it yet.

Andres had just gotten off the phone with Jake and things were progressing as planned. Maybe things were going too well. He had learned over the years that this was when you had to be the most careful. When things seemed to be going too well, that was when you let your guard down and forgot something or missed something you should have seen. He knew and he was being careful.

Branch sat in the passenger side and thought back on her life. All of this was not her fault, of course. She had been the victim of a bad father, a weak mother, a greedy partner and a lover she could not have. But, she was going to fix all that, except for her weak mother whom she loved despite her weakness in handling her as a daughter. It was more her father's fault anyway. He should have stayed and been proud of his daughter and loved her mother. But no, he had to be cruel and leave her and her mother to fend for themselves. *But, we did it without you anyway. We really didn't need you. We were fine by ourselves. But your selfishness would be taken care of soon. Just like I am about to take care of the others. You will be the last one to go to the depths of the ocean and I will be glad to watch you sink miserably into the deep.*

"Hey, hey, Allison," Andres said startling Branch. "You okay?"

"Yes, I'm fine," she said smiling back her smile that draws you to her. "I was just thinking about some things. How much further to go?"

"We have about five more hours," he said. "I just got off the phone with Jake. He said their trip is on target for us to get there nearly the same time."

"Oh yes, Jake," she said with a wistful look. "He's a good man, actually. Where do you think he gets those good looks?"

"Of course, you know where he gets them," he said.

"Of course," she said knowingly. She always knew a lot. She made it her business to know more than everyone else thought she did. She knew exactly where Jake got his looks...*oh this crazy thing would be so much fun.*

CHAPTER 50

It was no accident that the two delivery trucks had arrived at nearly the same time, delivering the prey for Allison Branch. The neighborhood was to be surveilled this morning, but they had beaten them there and had no idea they would be on them soon. The team would not be set up for a few more hours. Under the disguise of a cleaning company and a moving truck, they had gone virtually unnoticed.

Marx, along with Chrisler and Holmes, would be heading to a command post area to get instructions and intel from the other surveillance cops. The surveillance van was also a company van equipped with various technology for communications and video.

They arrived at approximately 9:00 am in the van and they did so on foot, parking their car a few blocks away. They stepped inside the van and began to communicate with surveillance. No one had seen anything yet and the sun had been up a couple of hours. They waited and Marx knew that soon a confrontation would take place. It would be her or him he thought, and he knew already what he was going to do.

Chrisler looked at Marx and said, "I think we are going to have one shot here. We haven't seen anything so I figured that they have beaten us here. We know which house, so I think we are going to have to try and negotiate this thing somehow. Our information told us that they would be here sometime this morning. We just didn't know what time."

"Damn, I was hoping that we would have beaten them here, but I think you are right," Marx said. "With live hostages, every minute is life and death. Let's hope we can move in and save them from their nightmare."

Andres and Branch had made it to the house around 3:00 am. Their two hostages were moved from the truck in the dark of early morning to the storage and grow house in the back. Mike and Joanna were put on the floor bound and gagged. Although it was dark, Mike could see the fear in Joanna's eyes as she had come to consciousness. Her look was pleading with him to get her out of this, but Mike knew all too well what would happen next.

The door of the grow house closed and a bright light came on. I very much expected to see the figures in hoodies and ball caps, but to my shock and surprise I could make out the figures of a very large man and that of one Lynnette Huber, aka Allison Branch. She looked like the same Lynnette Huber I had seen on stage last night, but something was different. It was her eyes. They had changed from a nice and soft, steel blue, to a fierce and menacing gray. I had never seen that in Allison Branch before. I knew the spirit of evil was running through her veins now and she was in a mode that would push her over the edge into who knows what.

Joanna's eyes were groggy and the fear in her was quite evident as she recognized her captor. Her eyes pleaded with Huber, but there was no sympathy in the gray eyes of Allison Branch. As she walked closer to Joanna, I cringed as I knew what may happen next. I looked around the room with the concrete floor and tables with marijuana plants growing. In the corner I noticed boxes stacked with what I assumed was more drugs or opioids ready to be delivered to the pushers. My senses dulled as I almost passed out again. I was dehydrated and sweating. My head was pounding.

"So, yes Ms. Joanna, it is me, you know, the person on television you had feared the most. I am Allison Branch as you have by now figured out," she said moving in even closer to Joanna. "I'm so sorry that you trusted me and now find out that your new man's ex-girlfriend is here to tell you all about him."

Joanna looked at me with despair. We were gagged and there was nothing we could say. Tears had begun to move down Joanna's cheeks from the fear and terror she now felt as Branch was leaning close near her face. I tried to get up, but the large figure who I knew must be the man that helped her escape, backhanded me in the face, causing blood to flow from my mouth. I was angry but helpless. My body wanted to save Joanna and my mind almost flipped out on me knowing that there was nothing I could do but watch.

"Yes, my new face is even better than my old one. You hiring me was all that I needed to get close to Mikey boy. Once I was in, the rest of the plan was easy. I really kind of liked you. You treated me well, but you see, you just happen to be in the wrong place at the wrong time. You have become collateral damage, professor," she said pacing back in forth in front of Joanna. Allison turned towards Joanna and delivered a blow to her jaw. I cringed and couldn't move or help. This was another nightmare that maybe both of us would not survive.

Just then, the door opened and another hostage was thrown into the room. There was my friend Katy, bound and gagged just like us. She looked like hell, three kinds of it actually. She was put down between Joanna and me. Looking up, I saw the young Jake Benson, smiling and seeming proud of his delivery of new prey. He looked towards Branch, seeming to ask for her approval. She smiled a crooked smile at Jake that appeared to be enough to make Jake feel appreciated. Katy's eyes traveled back and forth between me and Joanna. Tears flowing down Joanna's cheeks and blood flowing from my mouth, my mind was saying, *"welcome back to our personal nightmare dear Katy."* Once again, here in captivity with my new love, and my favorite bartender, who I once almost considered to be my new love and the one person I feared most, that evil Allison Branch. I craved a shot, one that would put me out for good. I needed to punch my last dance card and check out forever. Whatever I had done, it seemed like everything I touched turned to ashes. Poor Katy and Joanna, brought into something they never had a hand in. Only because of me they were here. I had to get us out of here. Our death was imminent if we gave in. We had to keep playing. I owed it to them.

"You three have a treat coming," Branch said as she began to pace back and forth. "It is my game, I call it my hunt, Allison's Hunt. Not a real hard game, easy in fact. All you have to do is survive, like animals in the wild. Only the wild is the streets here in Miami-Dade County. It's really a jungle out there, boys and girls, and if you are fast enough, strong enough and good enough, you can survive. There is also your hero, Andy Marx, who I am sure is trying to save you, but we have a surprise for him and all those who come looking for us. A big surprise. So really, you are all on your own. For now, I am leaving you to freshen up just a bit. I will be back soon and I will give you the rules of the game. Don't try anything you will regret. Your only chance is to survive the hunt. Try to get away and the nightmare will end in total darkness for all of you. Just play by the rules, my rules of course. It's your only chance."

Carrianne Martinez stood back and took it all in. She looked back and forth between her brother, whom she loved and this crazy woman Allison Branch, whom she had come to despise. There was not going to be a good ending to this if she stayed in the game. But there may not be a good ending if she got out of the game. She had come to the crossroads that she had thought about so often. It was soon going to be decision time and there would be no turning back, whatever she decided to do. Her heart was aching. She dropped her head and left the grow house and headed back inside with Branch. She had made her decision and there was no turning back...

Once back inside, Carrianne noticed at least four other cartel members milling about and planning. Andres had come back in and was giving directions. Andres' phone rang and he answered it. He had eyes all over the neighborhood and they were checking in all the time. Andres walked into the other room and the voice on the other end was finalizing a time schedule with him.

"You need to be here by 3:00 in the afternoon," Andres said. "I think they will probably be on to us soon. This is very risky but if we time it right, the diversion will get us out of here. Make sure it's three. I'll get the rest in order"

"I'll be here by 2:45, parked and ready to detonate," the Chemist said. "By 3:00, you will be out of here."

"Good, safe travels my friend and let me know if you see anything suspicious out there."

Carrianne moved from the hallway to the bathroom after listening to Andres' conversation. She pulled out her trac phone. She was going to make the call to save herself. The one that would get her out of this life in the cartel. She thought back to the times when she was a little girl in Brazil and how she and Julio would play in the slums together. She was happy then, but it was all too hard for her mother and raising them was hard for her. Tears began to fill her eyes as she thought of motherhood and what it could be like. She knew if she would ever have children, she would have to betray Julio and Andres, a dangerous move at best, to have that chance. She thought she could not convince Jake to turn and go with her. He seemed lost in all of this. He was also hypnotized by HER. She knew that this was something she was going to have to do on her own and Jake would be left behind. Her need was too strong and even Jake could not keep her from doing this now. She was ready and dialed the number.

"Milwaukee Department, how can we help you?" the voice on the other end asked.

"Could you please connect me to Detective Andy Marx?" Carrianne asked.

"One moment please," the voice responded. The phone range twice and Marx picked up.

"Detective Marx, how can I help you?" he asked.

"Okay, you know me, this is Carrianne Martinez. I know where your hostages are at the moment. I want to deal the information for immunity," she said quietly into the phone. Marx pointed to Chrisler to pick up the headphones and listen in.

"Okay look, how do I know you're not setting me up?" Marx questioned her. "We have a surveillance unit getting set up right now, and we know the neighborhood. I can get you what you want, but you have to do this all our way. I get you immunity and cash and you inform us where this is all going down. We have to take you into custody and here is what you will need to do."

Carrianne listened carefully to Marx's instructions and agreed to all that he said. It was risky and dangerous but worth her freedom if she didn't get killed in the process. He finished the plan and told her where they would meet. Marx would have to be in the right place to save Carrianne, but he had the idea and it would work as long as she could break free from the rest at the right moment.

"Listen, are the others okay?" he asked.

"Yes, so far, but soon Branch wants to hunt them. I really don't know her plan but I think she wants to kill them all and she has you in mind, too, Marx. She knows you will come after them."

"I figured that, do you know if there is any way you can get your trac phone to them. That would be helpful."

"I think so, but Andres watches very closely and Jake does, too. They will be watching so it will be hard but I will try."

"Get them cut loose and have them call me, I will tell them where to run. Here is my cell number to contact me. Let me know when you are about to give them the phone so I know to put people in place. This will work, Carrianne. But you have to be on time. If you are not where I asked you to be at the right time, there are no guarantees. I will do my best but we only have one shot at this, only one. If we mess it up, lots of people are going to die."

"I understand. I hear someone coming down the hall, I have to go. I have your instructions, I won't be late," she said looking down at the number she had written on a small piece of paper.

"Hey, Maria, I mean Carrianne, are you in there?" Andres asked.

"Yes, I will only be a second," she answered.

"We have some planning to do and we have to get this going. Time is too important. We'll be in the kitchen."

He walked away and as his steps became softer down the hall, she breathed a bit easier. *Yes, time will be important Andres, I'm sorry to say. I hate to leave you, but I have made up my mind. Yes, time, it's all about time. And mine is running out.*

Allison Branch was almost giddy. Right in front of her was her prey ready to be released for the hunt. She had planned it perfectly and she was not going to let anything stop her now. She walked from the grow house leaving them to be watched only by one man and entered the back door of the house. She went to the kitchen and joined Andres, Carrianne and Jake at the table. The four of them would now begin to plan the hunt and how it would be done. When she got there, she was in charge and there was no doubt about that.

"Okay, here is how I want it to go. Andres' boys bring the cleaning van back and I will load the three of them in the back. Andres will ride with me. We get out to the place and we will abandon the van and on foot we reach our destination. The three of them will be let out in the wooded area and they have twenty seconds to get lost in the woods and then I hunt them. The two women, Katy and Joanna, will be easy kills. Parsons will be different, as he is totally going to die a different death. Jake and Carrianne, you two will ride in the back and make sure nothing funny happens," she said, looking at Jake and making those eyes bring him to her. He would not say no. "When we are done, we get back to the van and head to the airfield and get on the plane to Brazil. It's all good, right?"

Carrianne was noticing Jake and how his eyes were lighting up to every word Branch spoke. He was in a trance it seemed. She loved her brother dearly, but she was not going to stop him now, he was buying stock in Allison Branch and there was no way he was going to get out of it. She would talk to him later, but for now she had two things to do.

"Okay, it all sounds good except what if they are out there surveilling us already," Andres said. "We don't know if they are watching us or not. Too dangerous to send out men right now, we have to stay put until it's time to go. We need the van to back up right to the grow house and get the people in quick and get it moving away from here. I'll get my men on task. This all has to do with time and we need to make the van disappear in two minutes and on its way. The plane will be fueled and ready for take off when we get there. Right now, we have two hours and that's all, to get ready. Jake, Carrianne, Branch and me will go back to Brazil to regroup. Everyone know your job?"

"Okay we're set," Branch said and shifted her gaze to all three of them, one at a time. She didn't want any defectors and everyone had to be all in, first Jake, then Carrianne and finally Andres. They all seemed ready and she was 99 percent sure they were in except the 1 percent that doubted Carrianne for some reason. It was her gut instinct and she just couldn't get her mind to trust Carrianne. But they had been together for so long, she had to at this point. But she would keep an eye on her. It was one o'clock.

"Alright everyone, go time is two hours at 3:00 PM," Andres said. "Don't be late and have them ready for transport by 2:30. Everyone is at the grow house by 2:45."

Allison walked away and went to the back room to load her weapons and what she needed for the hunt. She laid her hand guns out on the bed and loaded each one carefully. She had waited and planned for this for such a long time. Her thoughts began to drift as they usually did when she started to feel her anxiety.

There was no turning back now. There was only the hunt and it was the only thing consuming me. I think of my mistrust of Carrianne creeping in. I just can't trust her, can I? Why am I questioning myself and my judgement on this lack of trust? She just didn't look all in like the others. I've seen this before in informants who flipped on their partners in crime. It just seems to me like she's maybe done something already? But she was so good to me, and I have to trust her, she just wouldn't do this to us, not now. The other two, Katy and Joanna are easy to kill, but Parsons is different. I did love him, didn't I? Ha, love, what a crazy emotion. Something given to us to feel in the heart yet the opposite emotion, hate, stands so close by. It just blurs for me because of him. I love him, I hate him. I just have to kill him, because I will then be better. I will not be sick anymore. Sick with anger, jealousy, and self-hate. It will all be gone. Then I can go on with my life. HE is just in my way of happiness and all I can see right now is how he hurt me and didn't choose me. He had me right there. He could have had the best. But no, once again, passed over. By my own father, by Parsons, by the Department. There will be no passing over me after this. I will be the Queen of the Cartel. Just a few more things to do and then I sit on top of the mountain that was always so hard to climb...

Branch finished packing her arsenal on her person and she was now ready for hunting her prey. She looked down at the meds she also had placed on her bed. She had not taken any since before the play. She took them and threw them in the trash. She went to the mirror and studied her face, the beautiful new face that she was given. No lines or wrinkles in this face, just smooth and soft skin. The face had changed but the heart was still the same. She could become one thousand different people if she chose. Her heart would still be black with anger and violence. Her soft face had belied this inner feeling of desperation. She looked closer into her own steel blue eyes and was shocked with what she saw. They were black as coal. They matched her heart...

CHAPTER 51

"I don't think human beings learn anything without desperation. Desperation is a necessary ingredient to learning anything or creating anything. Period. If you aren't desperate at some point, you aren't interesting." - Jim Carrey

The three of us were desperate. One who loved me at the moment, one who used to love me and myself, who had always had trouble loving anyone. Three of us in our own ways, living in desperation and about to die in it. Katy and I understood this mode and why we felt this desperation at this moment. When we had been trapped in the storm shelter at my lake house, we had come to that point. We hoped for someone to save us, but at the end of our time in captivity, we had to make the plan ourselves. We had to do something, anything, or die. We did in desperation.

Joanna, on the other hand, had been captive to an

evil relationship. She had been bruised and battered by a man that wanted to possess her. She was desperate now and had no idea of what was going to happen next. But in many ways, she trusted Mike and she just had the feeling that somehow, they would survive like she had survived her earlier bad relationship.

We looked at each other, groggy from the drugs and thirsty from being gagged and bound. It was our eyes telling the story and the eyes all said something different. Joanna looked back and forth between Katy and myself seeming to sense our closeness and she had seen the look in Katy's eyes. I looked at Katy and then at Joanna, back and forth between them I saw my favorite bartender that I cared for as a friend and couldn't make myself love, and Joanna who I knew that I loved. It was a crazy triangle and we couldn't speak. We could only look and see in each one of us our own thoughts and could understand it even better than speech. We were trapped and in desperation we needed a plan.

Just then a figure appeared in the room and turned the knob to the door of the grow house. Once inside I saw the figure of Carrianne Martinez approach us. I knew we were in for more beatings but somehow, I felt relieved that at least it wasn't Branch and that big, violent thug, Andres Montoya. Carrianne got close to us and put a finger to her lips asking us to make no noise. She removed my gag, while keeping the finger to her lips.

"Don't speak, please," she whispered in her heavy Brazilian accent. "I have a plan, but I will say it to you, Mr. Parsons. When I am finished, we will cut each of you loose. Do not run, as they are still out there and they will shoot you. I have a phone for you to call Marx with and here it is. He will tell you the rest of the plan. They plan to come and get you about 2:45. You will be out of here by then and I am to go with you. I will cut your bands now. When I come and get you, we are running out of the back, Marx will tell you where you will be met by police. Jake is still on her side, I am turning them in. But HER, that Branch, she wants to kill you in the worst way. You just need to get out of here before she takes you."

She placed the phone in my hand. Then cut the zip ties from Katy and Joanna and took off their gags. They both gasped and wanted to talk and Carrianne once again put her finger to her lips to quiet them.

"Please do not speak, you heard my plan. Marx will have people for us to get to safety. Just call him and don't stop and don't look back when we run. If you go exactly where he tells you, you will be safe. I was only supposed to be giving you a shot, so I must leave now. I will be back around 2:30. Be ready, timing is everything," she whispered as she was leaving the grow house. She turned to lock the door and left.

Joanna looked at me with fear. "How can we trust her?" she asked. "How do you know she's really not leading us to death?"

"One way to find out," I answered. "I'm calling Marx. He will know if we can trust her."

I dialed the phone while Katy had the tears running down her cheeks that I had seen before. I wanted to comfort her, but Joanna, as her kind heart always told her, beat me to it. She embraced Katy and at that moment, Marx answered his phone...

Andres Montoya stood looking at his dream, this woman that had him enchanted. She had pulled him into this scene that was about to take place. He had longed for her. There was something magical about her. He knew her face as a colleague and member of the cartel. She had always been loyal and faithful to their cause. She had provided so many opportunities for them to operate without detection. He was going to protect her to his last day. He was just that way. When this was finished, he could take her away. Take her some place where she would be free from worry. He felt he had much to offer her in the way of protection and happiness that she had not known. He would heal her and make her well again. They would have plenty of money and he could take her to places she had never seen before.

Andres was still and lifeless, as he was mesmerized by her sheer beauty. She then noticed that he was standing in the hall looking at her. She smiled that smile that was unmistakably Allison Branch. His heart, so black and violent melted at that very moment. He didn't know it, but at that very moment, his downfall had been his American name he took, John. Yes, he was once the "John" of a prostitute named Anastasia, the one who had turned on him and now this one, Allison Branch, would lead him to a dangerous spot. His downfall would be women. His weakness for a man of great strength was about to bring him to his knees. He couldn't see it. He dreamed of wonderful new moments in his life, not his demise. He should have been much wiser, but he was living a fantasy in a pair of steel blues eyes that was holding him there in a trance.

"Andres! Andres, it is almost time," Jake said unlocking Montoya from his fixed gaze.

"Yes, Jake. It is, get the van ready and we will all synchronize our watches. Are you ready Allison?" he asked with an evil grin.

"Oh yes, I have waited a long time for this to happen. It's time to get rid of some people and get out of town," she said as she looked from Jake to Andres and back again. Two men that she held like glue, they both would do anything for her. She was lucky to have them both involved in this hunt with her. They would be sure to make this happen for her. She had brought them both to this point of loyalty over time. It was her scheme. She was so good at scheming. "Let's get Carrianne and get this thing going, it's only 2:30 but I can't wait any longer. What's fifteen minutes anyway."

"I'll get Carrianne," Jake said as he left to find her.

Carrianne had slipped out the back door and had told the guard to go back inside. She told him that she would watch them and Andres wanted to speak to him. She had to be quick and this would be risky but she went directly inside to the prisoners.

"It's time," she said hastily. "Quick, run to your right where Marx told you. He has someone waiting for you. Don't look back, go, go!...

CHAPTER 52

Fear is fake. Fear is our decision. We make fear. The danger is the real thing, though. The danger is the real thing, not fear.

Marx had positioned his people perfectly as he waited near the vehicles. He looked around and then to his watch. He knew they would coming to him soon if Carrianne had done everything he asked her to do. He told Mike where and when to run. He sat in the car anxiously awaiting a sighting. He knew that soon he would confront HER. He would know what to do. Marx had made up his mind that the only way to rid himself of the problems she had caused him was to end HER. His thoughts were intense on seeing the hostages running towards them, but his mind couldn't help but drift back to when she shot him at Parson's lake house. Once again, he felt it, the bullets hitting him, the blood running, hot and red flow that seemed to drain his soul. He was feeling himself die, and in a way, he was always feeling himself die, little by little, ever since it happened. He had so many pieces of himself taken by HER, that he knew much of it, he would never retrieve. He would never be all that he used to be. He would be more worn, like damaged goods. Day by day he felt the blood ooze from his soul, just like it ran from his body that day. This had to end. He had to stop his soul from bleeding to death.

Marx stepped out of the police vehicle and he should see them anytime and if he did not within the minute, he had to go get them. Just then he saw three heads running and turning the corner of the alley and they were in full sprint. He saw only three heads, all of them female. But where was Parsons? He began to worry.

"Get these three to safety when they reach us," Marx ordered. He could her them huffing and puffing and their faces were becoming more in focus. They were distraught and fearful. Katy had reached him first. She nearly fell as they were very near. Marx grabbed her and held her to keep her from falling. She cried and was sobbing uncontrollably.

"He, he, fell...he tripped. They may have gotten him...please, help him!"

"Hey, hey, slow down, what happened?" he asked.

Just then, Carrianne and Joanna arrived, helped by officers. Carrianne, who had seen this kind of danger before, was the calmest of the three.

"We left just when you told us, but they were coming for them earlier than they said," Carrianne said between quick and shallow breaths. "We all ran, but Parsons tripped and fell behind. I looked back and saw him jump the chain link fence and he was gone. Andres and Branch were chasing him. I heard a shot but they too had jumped the fence."

"I need you stay with these officers, I have to go," Marx said. He climbed into this car peeling out down the alley.

Carrianne, Joanna and Katy were put in a police van and received some medical attention. They were still scared, breathing hard and sweating in the Florida humidity. They had bruises and cuts to attend to. Joanna had become fearful that she had lost Mike, that once more her destiny was to be just unlucky to be in the wrong place at the wrong time.

Carrianne was then placed in a cruiser and taken to the police station to be held in protective custody. Joanna and Katy were then taken to the hospital to receive evaluation and further medical attention. Marx was on the chase to save Parsons.

Carrianne thought of her plight. She had no idea what happens to an informant and if she would have to serve time or not. She would soon be questioned by Chrisler and Holmes and in exchange for her testimony and help in the further investigation into the cartel, the Feds would make her a plea deal. She thought of witness protection and that she may just disappear under a new name in a new place. So much running through her mind as the car pulled away...she needed a lawyer.

The hunt had turned sour. Andres and Branch headed out when the guard came in. Carrianne had told him that Andres wanted to see him. Andres told the guard that he did not ask to see him.

"Stay here," Andres said as he motioned Branch to follow him to the grow house. They went out the side door of the house and saw them running. The three hostages were loose.

"Damn it, don't let them get away!" Allison yelled as they ran after them. She saw me trip and I knew she could draw her weapon and fire.

I jumped back to my feet. I was always at my clumsiest when it mattered more to be coordinated. I hopped the fence and ran through a yard. I heard a shot and it must have missed, I just kept running. I could hear his voice loud.

"Quick move around front to cut him off, I'll go the other way" the big man said.

"I'm going to kill you, Parsons!" she yelled as she ran after me.

They split and went separate ways, chasing me through back alleys that I was unfamiliar with. I was in a strange place, running through strange streets and alleys. The odds for my survival seemed to decrease with every step I ran. They were gaining on me, but my ears heard a police siren and I knew they were somewhere close. Maybe they could stop this before they put holes in me with a hail storm of bullets. Sweat was soaking my shirt and my mouth ached from the two missing teeth that the big man had dislodged from my gums.

Quick, come for me Marx. I thought of Joanna, Katy and the informant Carrianne and wondered if they had made it to safety. I thought of never again seeing Joanna's face. I thought of how much I loved her. It made me run faster, urging myself to survive. Where were they? I couldn't see them and now I was slowing down, confused on which way to run. I have to run to the sounds. The sounds of traffic, the sounds of the sirens. It was the only thing I could think. I had to run away from these alleys and side streets. Help me, Marx, no help me, God. Help me, please...

The Chemist had his vehicle locked and loaded. The explosives were in the truck and all he had to do was detonate. He had Jake on the phone and Jake was in his cleaning company van headed in the direction he was told to go. He would want to wait for the diversion, the one that would free Branch and Andres from capture and end this adventure in Florida. They would be on their way to Brazil and Allison Branch would then be his. He never knew Andres had the same idea. Jake was confident this would work. They would kill the hostages and he would have the woman he so desired. Jake was always confident. So confident, that he often made minor mistakes. He was reminded of this back in Brazil when Andres had sneaked up on him and reprimanded him. Yes, Jake would once again live to regret his weakness...his arrogance. The arrogance that made him forget little details.

Just then, Jake had heard the sirens and they were getting closer. He froze for just a second. This wasn't in the plan. He started to panic and told the Chemist to not detonate until he said. Jake was now unsure, he was in a high anxiety mode. Where were they? Where was Branch and Andres? Where were the captives? The sirens were getting louder. They made him panic on the inside. This plan is not working, he knew in his gut that something was not right.

The Chemist was sitting in his truck waiting for his command. He would put the truck in drive and jump from it, then detonate. He was waiting for the word...

I ran faster but I was tiring. I felt like I wasn't going to outlast them. They had gained on me and were getting nearly in range to shoot me. I had to speed up and finally the street was in view, not too much further. God help me, this was not going to end like I thought. I wasn't going to be the hero I thought I was going to be. They were good. Too good for me, they were going to beat me. I just hoped that Joanna and

Katy were safe.

"Go! Now!" Jake's voice screamed into his phone. It had to be now, Jake had to be right. The Chemist put the car in gear and started it for the target drive. It was all in motion and there was no turning back and Jake had done his best. He had missed that one little detail though, he didn't know which street they would be running down. The Chemist leaped from the car and rolled to the side. He held the detonator and he was ready. Three, two, one, now, he thought and he pressed the button. Jake passed the truck and turned to look...

CHAPTER 53

I was running fast. I could not let them catch me as it would be most assuredly fatal. This craziness was about to finally consume me and take my life. I had endured kidnapping, brutal beatings, drugging and addiction. I had endured my own wickedness that could have killed me at any time. I had endured my ex-wife's suicide and the pain that followed. Now, I was facing the one thing I had feared every day.

Their pace was quickening and I was losing ground to them. I could almost hear their footsteps and heavy breathing. My lungs were about to explode. In a strange city where I didn't know anyone or any place to go, I was going to meet my end. I prayed to God that HE had to know I was trying and I was getting better. I was just starting to find me, the guy I was really wanting to be and I was starting to live my life again. *Please do not let me die this way, I pleaded with Him. I really want to live, I want to know what life is about, to care and to love like I have learned to do again. Please, oh please, not like this.*

For the second time in my life, I began to see flashes of my life flying by in my mind. I saw Sheila and her bloated face in the casket. I saw Jerry with his head exploding on my boat on the lake. I saw Katy and me, kidnapped and suffering in the storm shelter. I saw Andy Marx, a friend and good cop, fighting for his life in a pool of blood, and of course, I saw HER.

Yes, HER again! That one with the silvery, blue steel eyes that hold you. I would never win this game. It was hers to win and she just wasn't going to lose. Driven by her anger over many, many years, SHE had the upper hand once again. Of all the times I thought of how she would have her revenge, this way never came to my mind. Yes, I thought it would be silent, in my sleep or maybe cyanide in my drink. But not like this. Then I made a grave mistake. I was tired and spent and I could not run any longer. I just stopped and turned around, prepared to fight.

Then I saw them, those eyes. Those angry eyes that held you...

Andres went first and she was behind him and what I saw then would be forever etched into all my bad dreams. A delivery truck hurtling down the street hit the large man, he could not escape it. My eyes widened as I saw her nearing the street as well. In slow motion I saw the gun she raised at me, ready to shoot. But the boom was tremendous and the fire leaped from the vehicle that at the same time hit the big man and exploded. I had never seen such a flash in my life. I was blinded and hit the ground. I lay there, trying to gain my senses and looked up from the ground. I was looking to see if anyone survived. I saw the big man's body engulfed in flames and a woman running, holding her face, she got into a car, a van? It was smoky, foggy and for me to see clearly. It was a van, wasn't it? I wasn't sure. It sped away quickly. It had missed me by five seconds. The woman's hair, it was smoldering? Was I dreaming?

"Hey, Parsons...hey!!" a loud voice was yelling at me and shaking me, asking if I was okay. It was Marx. I had rolled to a sitting position, smoke and fire all around me, just like it had been all my life, but somehow, I had survived again.

I was groggy and said, "a van, I think it was a van...went that way" pointing to my right. Marx hit the radio and let them know, but the time had passed, more than we knew. He called next for the ambulance to come get me and take me for examination.

"The others?" I questioned. "Did they make it?"

"Yes, they are at the hospital," Marx responded. "I have you going to the same place. You need to be checked out. Joanna and Katy are fine, Carrianne is in custody, but we're not talking about her. She turned on them and that's how we knew where they were holed up."

I was thankful to hear the words that they were okay. Once again, I had endangered other people and they had once again been exposed to the demons and devils that seemed to dance all around my pitiful life. I could not wait to get there and see for myself that they were okay. They loaded me on the gurney and I was headed to a Miami hospital.

Marx sent me on my way and through the back window of the ambulance, I could see him jump back in his car and get on the radio. He was on the chase already. He was one tough cop. As the ambulance sped away, I saw his car get smaller and smaller. In my mind I was wishing I could be there with him, to speed off and get on the chase. Marx was on fire and I knew, just knew, what he was thinking. It was probably the same thing I thought. *If I find HER, I'm just going to kill her, there was nothing else...nothing else.* Marx's car disappeared.

The little men were sitting on my shoulders once more, one to my left ear and the other to my right. Once again, I would have to fight them both back into submission. I had been lost, found, lost again and the one time in my life that I felt I was going in the right direction, my life was going to become complicated again...always so complicated.

"Are you going to leave or stay?" the little evil figure on my left asked. "I say you leave. You've done enough damage here."

"No, you stay. You stay with her and make this all you want it to be. She's a good woman and you know she is the only reason you can even keep it together. Don't be a fool," the angel on my right said.

I shook my head and all of a sudden, they were gone. *Do I really argue with imaginary people? Am I going to be okay?"* I slept, or at least I thought I did. My mind was so cluttered and confused. I was conscious when they unloaded me at the hospital. I was wheeled into the emergency area. They placed me in a room and the began to check me out. It was once again a replay, a scene all too familiar. This is not a dream, it was my new reality...

Jake Benson had missed his target by five seconds. It was those five seconds that was the difference now and the Chemist was angry. Jake was speeding on in the van. The Chemist had arranged for a car from the cartel to be placed in the nearby parking garage. The van's tires screeched as they entered the parking garage. The three of them hopped out of the vehicle as Allison was in a bad way. Her hair had been singed and her face was badly burned. They were needing to get some distance between them and the cops before they could help Allison. She had not screamed, but she had laid in the back, moaning and groaning from the pain. They knew they had to make the plane, but Jake made a call to the airfield to get medical help from the cartel. They would know how to get a doctor to them at the airfield that could help Branch. She was in a lot of pain. Jake finished his call and sped along the highway. They were gaining on the distance they needed and soon they would be at the airfield, ready to board the small plane with a doctor to go with them. She was burned badly and she would need a lot of medical attention.

Back at the scene, flashing sirens and fire trucks were putting out the flaming truck, there was police, fire and ambulance, first responders, and bomb squads at the ready. Andres Montoya, had been pronounced deceased before he could ever have been loaded in an ambulance. His life of crime and destruction had come to a very ugly ending. He had taken a secret with him to the great beyond. One that no one knew except him and Julio and Maria Santos' mother, and, of course, Branch. His body burned beyond recognition and bloodied severely, his injuries had killed him near instantly. His secret went with him, at least for a while. He had kept his promise that he could to never tell the secret and to watch over them and to protect them from harm. He had done what he was asked to do. The big man had kept his word, except for telling one person...

———▲———

Marx was flying at each corner, still trailing them by at least two blocks. He saw the van in the distance turn and he sped up to make that same turn. He found the entrance of the parking garage in front of him but no van in sight. He guessed that they turned in here but he had two choices of either going into the garage or continue down the street. It was only a guess, but he had to pick. He chose the parking garage and sped through the first up ramp and the first floor. There it was in front of him down the first row of vehicles, the van he had been chasing. He radioed for assistance and left his car to slowly hide behind and move around other parked cars. He drew his service pistol and moved carefully. He was only two cars away now. He crept closer thinking he was about to confront HER for the last time. Absolutely, positively, the last time. Marx had already made up his mind, he had every reason to shoot her on sight and he would. He heard the sirens in the parking garage. *Damn, not now, I have to do this before there is a witness.* He moved all in one motion to the rear passenger side of the van, ready to shoot her on sight. But, he saw no movement, he yanked the door open, the seats were empty and the suspects were gone. Just an empty van was all he had. The assistance had arrived and Marx, dejectedly, walked away from the vehicle. Marx told the cops to secure the vehicle for evidence.

Damn it! I had them, had HER, I was right behind them. How could they have gotten away? He figured it had to be Jake, HER and Jake. The two of them had slipped him. They had to be somewhere near, on foot, unless another person had helped them. Maybe brought them a vehicle?

He got back in his car and sped off, trying to find them on foot. He would not be successful...

CHAPTER 54

*No matter how far wrong you have gone, you can
always turn around.*

Marx had to radio in that he had lost them. He
had never been more frustrated in his career.
He had missed the opportunity he had been
waiting for, to end her miserable and conflicted life.
He headed back to the hospital, wondering what
would be next. He knew he needed to call Chrisler and
Holmes and get the information to them that was
needed for them to pursue the matter further,
domestic and foreign. The bombing investigation
would continue before they could get any leads on it
and the investigation of the many crime scenes here
would take time. He didn't have the time as Branch
was getting away with it again. He had to talk to more
people. He needed to see Parsons, Katy and Joanna.
He needed information from them. But, more than
anyone else, he needed to see Carrianne Martinez, aka

Maria Santos. She knew things and he needed her information most.

He was sure that he would need to talk to her defense attorney as she would be charged with crimes. But to make a deal, she had to give them the information they needed. That information would have to lead to the arrest of others for crimes of a higher magnitude than her own. That meant that she had to come in on the cartel, giving full names, addresses, dealing locations, types and quantities of drugs dealt, where the drugs were stored, and customer and family names. If she did all that, she would make a plea deal and be placed under witness protection.

Marx knew that DEA would need to make foreign liaisons, as this now would become a bi-lateral investigation. It got more complicated from here as new law-making and intelligence gathering systems would have to be put in place. Marx was in for one long ordeal, but this ordeal wasn't ever going to be done until SHE was taken out. Period.

I was able to focus better as I woke up, still feeling traumatized from the chain of events. I knew I had made it to the hospital, and the nurse standing over me asked me if I needed anything. I told her no and she left the room.

It had been two of the longest years in my life. I had changed a lot in those two years. My soul needed to survive, but this was not only about the survival of my soul. It was about the reviving of my soul that had once seemed dead to me. No matter how far I had once traveled in the wrong direction, I needed to turn around. I needed to seek out my soul and raise it from the walking dead soul that at times it had become. My soul had hidden in dark shadows and in places that I never before thought it could go. Whatever I felt in my heart, if the heart is indeed a feeling organ of the body, could not be satisfied until once again I saw Joanna's face. I knew that she had been placed in front of me to be the one that could bring my soul back to the living once more. I had found through all of this, that there can be and needs to be that one person who makes you better than you thought you could ever be.

My door opened and Marx's face peeked around the door. "Hey, Parsons, feel like company?" he asked.

"Sure, come on in," I replied lifting my head off my bed.

"Someone's here to see you," he said moving aside and holding the door open.

She walked in and my heart sped up. I was never so glad to see anyone, and even though her face had been bruised and she wasn't quite like herself, she still looked beautiful to me. I never felt that I would talk like that in my mind. But there she was, walking towards me with the grace that I had always seen. She reached out to grab my hand and she leaned down to kiss me on the forehead. The squeeze of my hand re-affirmed to me she was still here with me, still connected, still that person that could make me infinitely better than I ever thought I could be. I don't know how I could possibly know that at this particular time, but I knew that I did. I didn't know if I even deserved her, but I know that she was here, placed here by chance, by luck, by the grace of God, to be the person to redeem Mike Parsons. These were the two matched souls that needed one another. The two people that absolutely by chance had made a second date when I thought the first would be the one and only, now faced each other. Our embrace lasted for a long time. In silence, our souls had once again connected into one, a strange phenomenon, that I refused to seek out any other time in my life. I didn't want anyone that close.

"I was so scared that you would be killed," she said tears beginning to form in her eyes as she held on tight to both of my hands. "I had looked back, and you were gone. I was worried that you had been caught or worse, shot. I had thought that I had lost you forever. My hopes and my dreams were coming apart piece by piece until just now."

"I'm fine and I am here. I thought I would never see you again," I said sitting up in my bed. She sat next to me and we faced each other, both bruised physically and mentally. I dreaded the thought that I had somehow once more affected someone else's life, just like Katy, James, and Sheila. We kissed and she hugged me deeply, strongly holding me as close as she could. It gave me notice that she was in this relationship all the way and that for us this was the moment that we knew there was no turning back. I knew what lie ahead, but for this moment, the therapy for us was each other.

Katy was just coming out of the examination area and was being wheeled to a room for recovery. She had been in this situation before and she had Mike to help her along the way. He had been there for her until that day when he said he just had to leave and walked away from her door. She knew the long road ahead, but this time there was no Mike there to help her along, to give her encouragement. She had missed him, even more than she wanted to admit. But she had resigned herself to thinking that if there ever was going to be another man in her life, it wouldn't be Mike, whom she had always held close to her heart. He had helped her survive, even before the first incident, and after that time as well. But he had walked away. Now was that time that she knew she had to give it up. For that one moment, in her mind, she knew that her dependency and addiction to Mike Parsons was over. She had to move on.

She was wheeled into her room and she stood just fine and then sat on the edge of her bed. Detective Marx was talking to someone outside and he then entered her room. Katy had seen him before, many times, but this time there was something different in his eyes as he quietly asked her a few questions and filled her in on the others and their conditions. For the first time since she had known Marx, he showed a vulnerability and softness that she had never seen in him before. Something that moved her as she sensed that he too was feeling something similar to what she was feeling. He had tried to be very professional with her at all times, but today his mind was different and he was falling into something quite different as he remembered what Parsons had told him once.

"Good looking guy like you shouldn't have trouble finding a girl," Parsons said.

"Guess that I am too picky," I said.

Yes, I had been too picky, but that was a good thing. But now, I am feeling this attraction to this woman. I never before felt this kind of weakness, or whatever this is before.

"Well, you made it through another one," he said to Katy, almost awkwardly, not really knowing how to end their conversation.

"Please, stay just a minute," she said looking at Marx in a way that many women had before, but never able to break him down.

"Sure, I can," Marx said. "Is there anything I can get you?" he asked.

"No, I'm fine," Katy replied. "What happened and

did you catch that crazy woman?"

"Well, no. There was an explosion that killed one of the cartel members, but she got away and we are trying to track her now. It will be up to the FBI and DEA to get involved now," Marx said. "You know, you will have to go through a series of questioning sessions with them and us. I know that you are not ready to do that right now, but we have to get started as soon as you feel you can. I'll be back, in about an hour after I talk to some of the others."

Marx rose to leave, but Katy reached out with her hand and touched his arm. "I'm sorry you didn't catch her, but I hope you do soon. I still think she wants to kill us all."

"We'll catch her and when we do, we will bring her to justice," Marx said as he was walking out of the room. He turned and looked at Katy with his sincere and deep set, dark eyes. "You take care of yourself and try to relax for a while, I'll be back soon," he said looking at her in a way few men had looked at Katy before. She had melted in that soft spot in her heart that had once melted for Mike in the same way. She had become instantly conflicted in her mind, but she knew that she wanted to see more of Andy Marx. She was hoping for his quick return. She really did need to move on...

CHAPTER 55

Allison Branch was in great pain. Her face and scalp had been badly burned in the explosion that had killed Andres. Her life was now in the hands of young kid, named Jake Benson, and another man they called "the Chemist." Jake was communicating to the cartel in Brazil, saying what they needed when they got there. The voice on the other end was calm yet irritated by the turn of events. It was the Boss, the biggest person in the organization and you didn't talk to this person unless it was urgent. Jake was given directions on what would be waiting for him at the private, hidden airport landing area in Brazil. Jake understood the directions while the pilot started the plane that would carry them back home to Brazil. The medic had done his best to help Allison Branch. Her face had been burned and he gave her a shot for the pain. She would once again need some surgery to fix her now hideous face.

The plane's wheels lifted off the runway and Jake

could feel the slightest bit of relative safety as they were headed out of the country. He handed his phone to the Chemist as the Boss wanted to give him instructions for his protection. While the Chemist talked, Jake moved closer to Allison and laid his hand gently on her arm. He had been lured by Allison, teased by her, and now he was hooked on her. He would do anything for her. He was feeling the same anger she felt towards Marx, Katy and Parsons. He had also understood that Parsons now had a special friend who could become a special target. He smiled to himself on the inside, knowing that someday soon, he would help her get her revenge on them all. He was in for all he was worth and he was in until the end.

The Boss had hung up the phone. The Boss had just lost a good friend in Andres Montoya and his plan to allow Allison her revenge had backfired. The boy's sister had turned on the cartel. That was a big problem too. He went to the liquor cabinet and fired down a quick shot of Jameson. He was debating what to tell Jake. He knew Jake and Carrianne's story, and they had never known. He only knew because Andres had told him in confidence. The Boss and Andres were close. They had been through much together. But the Boss's heart was heavy with not only with the loss of a childhood friend, but with holding on to the secret that had been held for so long. Jake would be back soon and the heat would be on them shortly. The Boss was a calculator, taking the risks that made the most sense and being correct in thinking most of the time. The situation now was much more than risky. It was very dangerous. It was time to think. What was known about Julio and Maria Santos was one thing, and what was known about Oscar Stephenson was certainly another...

Marx had telephoned Chrisler and Holmes to see when was the soonest they could interview Carrianne Martinez. She was being held and awaiting an attorney. They thought within the next two days she could be ready for questioning. Marx hung up and headed back to Parson's room.

"Looks like you two need some privacy here," Marx said as he walked in on Joanna and I and he started to wheel out of the room.

"No, stay, Marx," I said. "I know you must have a lot to do, but I am curious as to where this has left us," I said through a few missing teeth. They hurt and I needed to get them fixed soon. Right now, I wanted to talk to Marx. "What do you know about her, did she escape?" I asked.

"Look, I tried to track them down and we still have the Feds trying to find them. They left no trail after the parking garage. They had just vanished," Marx said looking out the window of my hospital room. Marx looked back and forth from me to Joanna and then asked if he could talk to me alone for just a few seconds. Joanna seemed to understand and I rang for the nurse to take Joanna back and I told Joanna I would see her soon.

The nurse appeared and I held Joanna's hand and kissed it. She smiled and touched my cheek and left with the nurse, leaving Marx and I there in my room. Marx closed the door. We sat in the chairs in the room facing each other. Marx began to tell the story of what he had and where it was going to lead. I was fascinated by the details the cartel had gone through to kill us and how they had the truck explode on the street. I was even more curious about Carrianne and what she would be able to do to lead us back to Branch.

Marx told me of Carrianne flipping on the cartel. She now going to face these charges, and, hopefully, get a deal in exchange for immunity. He told me of the chase and how they had planned this perfectly. The key would be getting Carrianne to get him the information he needed to get the Feds, DEA and foreign authorities to help.

"But, Carrianne is not to be talked about, not even to Joanna. Yes, she knows that Carrianne helped you escape, but nothing I tell you about Carriannne is to be talked about with anyone else," Marx said. "We are glad to have her on our side now. She will be a key witness. She will also need protection, so the less we say about her, the better. You know, that broke up the brother and sister act and now Jake is working with Branch. We know she had to have medical help and we also know that they had to fly to escape quickly. That could only mean a private airfield and the Feds will be looking hard to discover that location. Those airfields are tough to find. Until I get to question Carrianne, we don't know and they have time on their side."

"I understand," I said. "I'm just curious if she knows anything about Oscar Stephenson's whereabouts?" I thought aloud. "I just have this crazy feeling he's in with this cartel and for what reason I don't know. We do know Andrea Stephenson Raines is dead and they have no reason to hold on to Stephenson. He just hasn't surfaced yet, but I think he's in with the cartel. I think he's still alive."

"Interesting concept," Marx replied. "I would put him in the suspect category much more so than the kidnap victim at this point."

"Look, Marx, you and I both have to be thinking the

same thing. It's about Branch and you want to end this just as bad as I do. But I have to know, just between you and I, if I ever come face to face with her and you are not there, I think you know what I will probably do. I just want to ask that if I have to do it, or even if you have to do it, will we survive it instead of just bringing her to justice?"

Marx focused in on my eyes and tried to gauge something inside of me. I wondered what he was thinking and it occurred to me just what it was. I had never killed anyone. Marx had already done that. It was his nightmare that would always reoccur. It was the rough part of the job. He would always have trouble sleeping.

"I was wondering," he began. "Do you think you can kill someone?" he asked slowly. "Think about it for a second. Think of Branch, Andres, even me. We have done it and that made all three of us dangerous to others. We had pulled that trigger. You have not done that, could you pull the trigger?"

"Well," I started to say hesitantly, thinking deeply and talking slowly. "I uh, well..."

"You see," he said. "In that moment in time, when it's your life or hers, when you know that unless you do it, this will continue for someone else, you would have to pull that trigger. We have seen it before. She is evil, mentally ill, and willing to do whatever it takes to end your life, my life or anyone else that gets in her way. Personally, I hope you never get faced with it. But if you do, and it's just you and her and she locks those eyes on you, can you do it?"

I looked out the window for a long time, staying silent. I looked back to Marx and out the window again. I looked out the window and my gaze fixed and staring at the memory of her old face, and then her new face, and then back to her face that I feel in love with. "I, uh, I don't know," I said looking down at my feet. I looked up at Marx one more time and fixed my eyes on his. "I'm just going to say this, and I hope you never remember that I said it, but I want to, I want to hunt her down and I want to kill her. She has made my life miserable and my mental state will never be quite the same, unless I know she is dead. So, my answer is yes. I hope I get to do it before you do, because I feel that you feel the same way as I do. There is no bringing Allison to justice. There is only ending her miserable existence so that she never hurts anyone else again."

Marx just nodded. He understood without saying it. I was sure of it. Whoever got to her first was going to kill her. It was the unspoken deal, not necessarily a race, but a knowing that if you get there before I do, we both expected it to be done. Not spoken to each other just like that, but we thoroughly understood each other at this point. It was our unspoken deal. Our minds shook hands on it...

CHAPTER 56

Allison Branch was hurt. She had slipped in and out of consciousness several times. When she had come to, she had pain not only on her face and scalp, but in her heart. Her mind began to fire up and anger once again consumed her. Unable to complete her task, she had not killed that sorry bastard, Marx was still chasing her, Carrianne was a traitor, and the bartender and new girlfriend had survived. Jake was holding her as the doctor was working hard to take care of her wounds that would surely scar her once pretty face. He whispered to her softly that they were going to be safe and that he would make sure she got the best treatment. He wanted her to sleep and the shot she got once again put her in a state of nothingness.

Jake had earlier contacted the Boss by phone. They would meet them in the hidden South American airfield and take them to the place where she could heal. Somewhere new for her, but that Jake had seen many times. They would be at the Boss's place and soon she would heal. The Chemist would disappear for a while. He would be useful again. But Jake was nervous as the Boss had expected the mission to go off without a hitch. Jake was at fault. He had panicked and poorly timed the release of the exploding vehicle. It was Jake's instructions that messed it up. He had frozen and waited too long. The Boss would not be happy with him.

They would soon land and Jake would have a lot of explaining to do. But for the time being, he had someone to take care of. Someone he had fallen hard for would change his life and at the same time endanger it. Just as the many she had brought close to her, Jake Benson, would also now be in danger. He just had no idea of how much. His sister had turned on him. Carrrianne was now very dangerous.

Andy Marx walked into Carrianne Martinez's room as she was finished with her treatment and the officers guarding her door allowed him in. She would soon be taken to headquarters to be questioned by local police and the FBI. She had wondered if all this was going to be worth her freedom. How much danger she was in for turning informant she did not know, but her life was certainly in danger now. She would need help and possibly a witness protection program.

Leaving her mother and brother behind was something she struggled with back and forth. Her mother would not understand. She sat on her bed looking out of the room's window.

"Ms. Martinez, I'm here to make sure you have safe passage from here to police headquarters where you will be questioned. Your attorney is right outside if you need him present for any further instructions," Marx said.

"No, that will be okay. I trust you but I won't answer any questions about the investigation without any advice," she replied. "What happened to Jake?"

"He and the others, including Branch are still being pursued," Marx said. "I will go over that scenario with you when you are questioned."

"What about Andres?" she asked.

"He's dead," Marx replied. "He was hit by the moving truck and the explosion killed him instantly. I am sure that bomb was meant for a distraction, but, unfortunately, Jake's timing was off and it killed Andres."

Carrianne just nodded and knew that she would probably not see her brother again unless it would be in a court. It made her sad, but he had made his choice. She had tried to watch over him for many years. He was always the wilder, more impetuous one. She had to keep such close reign on him, even as a little boy. She was the caretaker until Andres had come along and now, he was dead and Jake only had her to watch him? It made her fearful for Jake, but he was now on his own. She was alone too. She was torn between her role as his sister and her responsibility to herself. She decided right there and then that she couldn't stop going the direction she was going. She needed to have a real life, a husband and children that she always dreamed of having. She had no time left, her time was now. Her mother would someday forgive her, and she may never be able to go back and see her, but she knew this was her only way to go forward. She had made up her mind.

Marx left the room and got instructions to the guards and made arrangements on the phone to have Carrianne taken to local headquarters under heavy protection. He had a lot to do and called FBI's Chrisler and Holmes to let them know where Carrianne would be and that he would meet them there.

_____▲_____

Allison Branch was now awake and laying in a bed. Around her was Jake, the Boss and a few other men. She knew she had survived and she knew she was hurt and hurt badly. But who were these other people? A nurse came over to doctor her face once more. She had bandages on her face and the nurse had to remove them. She was in agony and she moaned loudly as the nurse removed the bandages. She did not want to know and she did not want to see. She could not see well and her vision was blurry. She had no idea who the people were, outside of the Boss and Jake. Jake held on to her hand as she went through this painful process.

When the bandages were pulled off, Jake could not look away. He was frozen with a look of disbelief on his face, staring at her disfigured visage. Allison caught his look and asked for a mirror. The doctor came closer and advised her not now, that she needed to rest and have the treatments work for her before she started to look. He was honest with her and told her of the damage that had been done, but for her safety and well-being, he did not want her looking at it quite yet. She would not be ready for that sight.

Jake could not look away. The sight had made him step back. She was in bad shape. She needed rest, she needed treatment and she would need grafting and maybe surgery. He was ill, he had no intention of leaving her side until she was well. *Where was Carrianne? The traitor, she had turned on us all and she would pay. Even feeling that way, he wished that she was here. She always knew what to do, didn't she? She would help me, right? But she's not here, and you are on your own, Jake. Wake up, she's gone for good. She's not coming back. You screwed up, Jake, and the Boss will have you spinning in circles after we get Branch settled. The Boss was not happy about any of this. The Boss had always liked you but you may not even live through this at the end of the day. I've got a lot of explaining to do and I have to be quick with my thoughts. I have to make this right for her, for the Boss and for Andres and I especially have to keep my position. Damn it Carrianne, why? Why???*

CHAPTER 57

The fourth person in the room where Allison Branch lay in pain was Oscar Stephenson. He knew Allison from before, from another time. She didn't know that he was there, her vision was blurry and it was probably for the best. Oscar Stephenson, the man missing from Marx's cold case, was, indeed, Allison Branch's father. Although he had left her years ago, he had always tried to hide from her where he was and what he was doing. If only she knew that he was there, right there in that room, she probably would have killed him on the spot. She had no idea that they worked for the same people and the Boss had never known that he was her father. He was evil and she had long ago had given up the thought of ever seeing him again. If only she knew he was standing right there, but she could not see. He had changed his name years ago when he left and Oscar Branch became Oscar Stephenson. No one knew who he used to be, except for Allison and the thought of her waking to see him or recognize him sent a chill down his back. He would have to kill her because if she saw him, she may kill him first. He had an idea. He was going to be proactive.

Jake had left the room and remembered that Andres had given him an envelope in case something happened to him. Jake had retrieved the envelope from his back pack, and he stared at it a long time before opening it. Andres had given it to him when they were at the safe house. He sat in a chair on the patio. He finally opened it and read Andres' handwriting.

▲

Julio and Maria,

If you are reading this, I had to have been killed. I had told you both not to open this unless that had happened. It had been years that I had watched over you and Maria. Your mother had told me not to tell of the fact that I am father to you both. I am sorry to have never been able to tell you this fact. I loved you both and I wish that I could have let you know. The Boss was your father in name only. He had married your mom and he believes to this day that you are his children. We had an affair that lasted quite a long time and you were both conceived by your mother and me.

I am sorry to have to let you know this, but it is for the best. Find your sister and let her know this, too. Be careful of the Boss, he is a bad man. I did the work out of loyalty to his taking care of me when I was a boy. I grew up under him in this business and there was no way out of my position in the cartel. He is dangerous and will kill you if he finds this out. You can never tell him.

He also does not know that Oscar Stephenson is Branch's father. I am telling you this because I knew when he partnered in, that this was true. When you can, you need to kill him or he will probably try to kill Branch. Do that for me, your father, before he ends her life.

I loved you both very much. Andres.

Jake looked down as tears fell on the sheet of paper. He could not believe what he was reading. The only father he ever knew was his Boss and the fact that his real father was killed made him feel even more guilty for his failure with the Chemist. He heard footsteps and quickly put the letter into his pocket. He quickly wiped his tears away and felt the slow burn of anger rise in his face. He had to keep his composure, as standing in front of him now was the Boss...

Marx was getting ready to have an officer take Katy to the airport who would fly back with her. Marx had become Katy's guardian and helper. He needed to make sure she was okay. He was careful to give instructions to the cop and would check on her when he was able to get back to the Milwaukee area. He had some things that he would be involved in before he could return. He was remaining professional in his distance but his heart was telling him something different about Katy. He was quite taken by her actually and making sure she was safe was important to him.

"Be careful and I will check on you when I get home," Marx said facing Katy with the cop that would fly back with her nearby.

"I will and you be careful, too," she said as she felt herself smile just a little. It had been so long since she had smiled at all that it made her face feel funny.

"Yes, I will. I have a few things to get to here and I have no idea where this chase will take me, but I promise to come see you when I get back. It shouldn't be more than a week," he said smiling back ever so slightly. It was if they both were at arm's length, but on the inside so much more willing to be closer.

Marx shook her hand and held it much longer than he intended to. Much longer...

I left the hospital that day with Joanna. We were heading home and for all we knew it wasn't over. I had to contact James and I would after I got home. Sometimes I needed to get stability from James. He had been a rock for me over the years. I had always kept him close and our relationship as brothers had always been a close one. We had been through a lot together. I think a fishing trip would be needed soon.

But first, I had to see where Joanna and I were in our relationship. She had definitely changed me. We needed to sit down and see where we fit with each other. There was so much ground to cover about ourselves, but we had a good start that was brutally interrupted by life- changing events. She had come into my life at the best time and yet the worst time. All I knew was that I needed her and I had to know how much she needed me. I had put her in a dangerous situation, not purposely, but still I did. I had no idea what lie ahead and I feared for her safety as long as Branch was still alive. We had so much to talk about and much of it was perilous to our relationship.

I put my arm around her and she leaned her head into my shoulder as we walked to our cab that would take us to the airport. Marx had secured our tickets back to Milwaukee. We were going home. Home, that sounded good. Home could be a place for Joanna and me. But, so many questions, so many complications to overcome, I just had no idea what would become of us. I only know what I am hoping for. I just wanted to be away from Florida and back home. Home.

CHAPTER 58

We were quiet on the flight home. Being around others, we didn't want to say anything about what we had been through. We didn't need any extra attention in our lives right now. I held her hand and squeezed it often. I wanted to tell her so many things. Things about me, about us, about our future.

My teeth and jaw were still aching but the pain pills had helped. I would need to see a dentist soon. Somehow, that still seemed very far away as I was trying to process in my mind everything that had happened. Once again, I would have to face nightmares, therapy and moving forward somehow, some way. I was quietly grateful this woman was now sitting beside me holding my hand. I was lucky to have her by my side. I needed her now more than ever.

Her head rested on my shoulder and I began to feel sleepy. The pain pills had kicked in and my jaw and teeth appreciated it very much. My mind was slowing down and I just wanted to sleep. I nodded off and began to see foggy pictures in my mind. It couldn't come into focus and finally two little men appeared in front of me. It was the same two little men that stood often on my shoulders, one on the left, the other on the right.

The little guy on the right spoke first:

"You know what Marx said," he began. "He said In that moment in time, when it's your life or hers, when you know that unless you do it, this will continue for someone else, you would have to pull that trigger. We have seen it before. She is evil, mentally ill, and willing to do whatever it takes to end your life, my life or anyone else that gets in her way. Personally, I hope you never get faced with it. But if you do, and it's just you and her and she locks those eyes on you, can you do it?'

"Well, can you Mikey?" he asked.

The little man on the left cut in, "Of course you can't. You still are miserable. She was your desire, but you didn't pick her. You still feel sorry for her. She has that spell on you."

"But you can, Mike," the guy on the right said. "You have to. For you, Joanna, Marx, James and Katy. You have to be the one to do it. You know you will be faced with it. It's going to happen. SHE will make sure of it."

"No, you want to save her," the little man on the left shoulder said. "You're just weak. Think you can save everybody. You have so many problems. You know you won't get better, maybe you still want HER?"

"You don't want to save HER, you want to kill HER," the guy on the right said. "I'm telling you now, you will be faced with it. It will happen and the only way you live any kind of life from here on out, is to end HER. You heard me right. End HER!"

I woke up and the plane was landing. Sweat was on my forehead and Joanna was whispering my name.

"Mike...Mike wake up."

She put her hand gently on my face. She seemed to understand I was in a dream. I think she knew it was about HER. Her eyes scoured my face trying to tell me that she was there and that things would be okay.

We walked off the plane that day and it was near sunrise. The morning sun had come up, reminding me of another day that lay ahead. One of the many more days that lay ahead for Joanna and me, actually. I was thinking of which day would it be? That day when I had to ask myself once more, "Can you do it? Can you pull that trigger?"

CHAPTER 59

In most matters in love and affairs of the heart, love has so many different meanings. It's not simple. It is complicated and complex. One day you're angry, the next you are calm and docile. You feel all emotions one day and the next day you absolutely feel numb. I have been on this journey for so long. When does redemption come to those who seek it? How you begin the journey may not be exactly how you come back from it. It tears at your soul along the way, leaving emptiness and regret. Sometimes you see the light, the spark that drives you to the end of your journey for your redemption. Sometimes, you see only dark days ahead.

The journey makes you change, whether you want it to or not. It just does. You are born to be a certain person, but the journey changes you sometimes for the better and sometimes for the worst. Most people call them life events. Those life events can be productive or they can be destructive. The most important thing is how you handle both.

Redemption is a reclaiming process. One in which you weigh so many options and the danger of choosing the wrong one, puts you several lengths back in the race. You do change. Everyone does. Even when you don't want them to, events change you.

I had changed.

All I can think of now is that life events will keep happening. I fear what most of those events will be. I wonder if I am so far behind in the race for my redemption, that I may not come back for the win.

SHE is still out there. SHE will appear again, one last time. One time where it will be up to me to decide.

"Can I do it? Can I pull the trigger?"

Made in the USA
Middletown, DE
29 December 2022

18060082R00225